Praise for
FINLAY DONOVAN JUMPS THE GUN

"Fasten your seat belts . . . murder most madcap."
—*Kirkus Reviews*

"Finlay's strong narrative voice carries the reader . . .
This is good, fast fun." —*Publishers Weekly*

"Readers who love fast-paced, action-packed mysteries
should pick this up." —*Library Journal*

"A spiral staircase of imaginative twists and captivating characters, *Finlay Donovan Jumps the Gun* never disappoints. And Cosimano continues to burnish her bona fides as she runs the gamut from murder to mirth."
—*The Free Lance-Star*

"The girl power in this book is fierce and the comedy even fiercer. It's a don't-miss addition to the Finlay Donovan series!" —BookTrib

"This series is magical! I'm in awe of Elle Cosimano. Every book lover in the world should be reading Finlay Donovan."
—Christina Lauren, #1 *New York Times* bestselling author of *Something Wilder*

Praise for
FINLAY DONOVAN IS KILLING IT

"Part comedy of errors, part genuine thriller . . . Deftly balancing genre conventions with sly, tongue-in-cheek comments on motherhood and femininity, Cosimano crafts a deliciously twisted tale."   —*Booklist*

"Suspenseful, funny . . . More, please."
                                                —*Kirkus Reviews*

"If you love thrillers but wish the genre would lighten up a little, then you absolutely must read *Finlay Donovan Is Killing It*."
                    —POPSUGAR (Best New February Books)

"Part screwball comedy, part morality tale, the amusing *Finlay Donovan Is Killing It* is also a tale about parenting, bad divorces, reinventing oneself, rising above misery, and, well, becoming a hit woman. It's a solid, thoughtful, and funny yet poignant mystery that never once becomes a one-note story."
                                —*South Florida Sun Sentinel*

"Funny and smart, twisty and surprising—Finlay Donovan is a character to root for. This suspenseful romp made me laugh but also kept me on the edge of my seat with its many surprises. I can't wait for the next book!"
                    —Megan Miranda, *New York Times*
                    bestselling author of
                    The Last House Guest

ALSO BY ELLE COSIMANO

Finlay Donovan Is Killing It
Finlay Donovan Jumps the Gun

YOUNG ADULT NOVELS

Nearly Gone
Nearly Found
Holding Smoke
The Suffering Tree
Seasons of the Storm
Seasons of Chaos

FINLAY DONOVAN
KNOCKS 'EM DEAD

ELLE COSIMANO

St. Martin's Paperbacks

This is a work of fiction. All of the characters, organizations, and events portrayed in this novel are either products of the author's imagination or are used fictitiously.

Published in the United States by St. Martin's Paperbacks, an imprint of St. Martin's Publishing Group.

FINLAY DONOVAN KNOCKS 'EM DEAD

For information, address St. Martin's Publishing Group, 120 Broadway, New York, NY 10271.

www.stmartins.com

Library of Congress Catalog Card Number: 2021042267

ISBN: 978-1-250-89640-7

Our books may be purchased in bulk for promotional, educational, or business use. Please contact your local bookseller or the Macmillan Corporate and Premium Sales Department at 1-800-221-7945, ext. 5442, or by email at MacmillanSpecialMarkets@macmillan.com.

Printed in the United States of America

Minotaur hardcover edition published 2022
Minotaur trade paperback edition published 2023
St. Martin's Paperbacks edition / September 2023

10 9 8 7 6 5 4 3 2 1

For the 2002 June Bug Moms

CHAPTER 1

Christopher was dead. They'd found him bobbing on the water's surface, his eyes bulging and empty, just after dawn. While I couldn't honestly say I'd ever killed anyone before, this time, there was no denying I was one hundred percent responsible.

"It wasn't your fault." Vero gave my arm an encouraging squeeze through the sleeve of my long black sweater. I hadn't had anything else appropriate to wear; it's not like I'd woken up expecting to attend a funeral. And yet somehow, my children's young and ultra-hip nanny had managed to pull off a pair of formfitting slacks, a killer updo, and a designer blouse. She offered me a wan smile. "It's not like you meant to do it."

My daughter's hand was frail in mine, her body tucked close to my other side, her eyes red from crying.

"In your defense," Vero whispered, "the instructions were in very small print. And at your age—"

"I'm thirty-one."

"Exactly. No one would expect you to be able to read those tiny letters clearly. You just gave him too much. That's all."

"He looked hungry." The excuse sounded weak, even to me. But every time I'd stepped foot in my daughter's room, Christopher had looked up from his bowl with those round, pleading eyes.

"I know." Vero's glossy lips pursed as she patted my shoulder. "You did your best, Finn."

My daughter's goldfish drifted in the cloudy water, his bloated belly pointing at me like an accusatory finger. Christopher had been a gift to Delia from her father, though I was certain Steven had bought the fish just to spite me. To pile one more responsibility onto my overflowing plate, just so he could watch me fail and then rub it in my face as he challenged me for custody. Ever since he'd left me for our real estate agent and they'd gotten engaged, he was determined to demonstrate that I was incompetent. It had become a competition for him, one that only became worse after he and Theresa split. I'd been bent on keeping the damn fish alive, to prove to my ex I was capable of providing for our children—and their pet—on my meager writing income without him. That I could feed and care for Delia, Zach, *and* Christopher on my own. Or at least, with Vero's help.

Christopher had survived in my care for less than a month. And while Zach wasn't old enough to rat me out to their father, Delia couldn't keep a secret to save her life. There'd be no keeping the news of Christopher's death from Steven. He'd gloat about it to Guy, his sleazy divorce attorney, and probably bring it up in court. *Your Honor, I'd like to call your attention to the fish in the evidence bag marked Exhibit A. The deceased went belly-up after a mere three weeks in my ex-wife's care. Clearly, she's unfit to parent our children.*

If Steven had any clue about the *human* who'd died while in my care over the last month (or where Vero and I had disposed of the body), he'd probably have a coronary—a possibility Vero had gleefully considered until she'd calculated the narrow odds of the news actually killing him. A month ago, after a woman named Patricia Mickler had overheard me plotting a novel with my literary agent in a crowded sandwich shop, she'd offered to pay me fifty thousand dollars to murder her husband, a horrible man who happened to launder money for the Russian mob. How Harris had come to be drugged in my minivan had been an accident, and though I wasn't the one who'd actually murdered him, his wife had been certain I had. She'd passed on my name to her friend Irina, whose husband was an enforcer for said very scary mob. Irina's husband's death had also been an accident. Regardless, both women had expressed their gratitude by giving me copious amounts of cash. And a tip: that someone had posted an ad online, searching for a willing party to murder my ex-husband for money.

Vero held the green plastic net out in front of me. "Care to say a few words?"

Zach toddled toward the fishbowl on pudgy legs, the frilly ends of his diaper poking out from under his black shirt. His sticky fingers clamped around the edge of the dresser as he pulled himself onto his toes to see. He touched a finger to the glass, drool spooling from his chin. Delia's breath hitched, her upper lip shiny with snot as she looked up at me expectantly. I took the net from Vero. "What am I supposed to say?" I whispered.

She nudged me toward the bowl. "Just say something nice about him."

I held the net to my chest, struggling to find the words that would calm my grieving five-year-old, who'd been hysterical since she'd awoken and found her pet floating in his bowl like a Cheerio. I was a writer, for crying out loud. I strung words together for a living. This should've been easy. But every time I looked at Christopher, all I could picture was my ex-husband's face. Not because I wanted to kill Steven. I mean, I did, I guess.

Some days. Most days. Definitely whenever he opened
his mouth. But no matter how contentious our relationship had become since he'd left me for our real estate
agent, Steven loved our children, and they loved him.
And I would never do anything to hurt Delia or Zach.

Someone wanted Steven dead. And it wasn't me.

"What can I say about Christopher?" I glanced
back at Vero for inspiration. The corner of her mouth
twitched as she gestured for me to go on. "He was a good
fish. A loyal and steadfast friend to all of us, he . . ."

There was a forceful tug on my yoga pants. "Tell
them about his smile," Delia said, wiping her nose
on the sleeve of her black leotard. "And how he blew
the best bubbles." She crumpled into my side, burying
her face in the folds of my sweater. Zach's tiny forehead creased with concern. I was grateful he was too
young to really understand what was happening as I
echoed Delia's sentiments and dipped the net into the
water, scooping Christopher out.

She held my leg as we marched solemnly to the bathroom across the hall. Zach perched on Vero's hip behind us, marking the end of our procession. We stood
around the open lid of the toilet, paying our last respects
as Christopher fell into the commode with a soft *plink*.

Delia grabbed my arm as I reached for the handle.
"No, Mommy!"

"Sweetie, we have to. He can't stay in the potty forever."

"Why not?" she whimpered.

"Because . . ." I threw Vero a pleading look. This
chapter was definitely not in my copy of *What to Expect When You're Expecting*. I wanted my money back.

"Because," Vero supplied helpfully, "he's going to
start to stink—" I stepped hard on her foot.

"But I'll never see him again," Delia sobbed.

A bubble swelled from her nose and I wiped it on

my sleeve. "We'll always have his memories." And the dozens of photos she'd made me post on *#goldfishof instagram.*

"Maybe we could go to the pet store and get another one." The words were out of Vero's mouth before I could stop her. Delia erupted in a fit of keening wails. Zach's lower lip began to tremble.

"I don't want another fish!" Delia shrieked. "There are no other fish like Christopher!"

"You're absolutely right," I said, raising my voice as they both began to howl. "There will never be another fish like Christopher. We should honor his memory with a moment of silence."

Delia's mouth pinched shut. The bathroom fell quiet except for my children's shuddering sniffles. I lowered my head, jabbing Vero in the ribs with an elbow until she bowed her head, too. I waited a full minute before reaching for the lever. This time, Delia didn't try to stop me, and with a swirl of orange scales, Christopher was gone.

Vero gently ruffled the tear-soaked spikes of Delia's hair. "Come on, Dee. I'll make you some cookies."

"Not too many," I reminded her. My mother was preparing enough turkey and stuffing to feed an army, and she'd murder me if I spoiled the children's appetites before dinner.

Zach squealed as Vero scooped him up and carried him downstairs. Delia lingered, giving the toilet one last look before following them to the kitchen.

As I reached for the light switch, I paused. Turning back to the toilet, I flushed it again. Because I'm not the luckiest person in the world, and I know better than to assume the dead don't come back to haunt you.

CHAPTER 2

An hour later, Vero and I buckled Delia and Zach into their car seats. Vero wiped cookie crumb evidence from their cheeks as I hauled two small Rollaboards into the back of my minivan and slammed the hatch closed.

"What's the luggage for?" Vero asked.

"I got an email from Steven this morning. He's moved into his new place and he wants to take the kids for the weekend." He'd attached photos of the restored farmhouse he'd rented in Fauquier County, careful to point out that the children's bedrooms and toys were already unpacked, and the kitchen was stocked and ready for them. He'd cc'd his attorney, Guy, who had replied to both of us, congratulating Steven on finding such a "great place for the kids," which was clearly lawyer-speak for *you have no grounds to fight this*.

It had been easy to keep the kids away from Steven's farm since his ex-fiancée's arrest. After five bodies had been found buried there and Theresa Hall had been implicated in the ensuing investigation, Steven had called off their engagement. He'd moved out of her town house within hours and had been sleeping on the sofa in the sales trailer on his farm since. He and his attorney had both agreed it would be best for the children to suspend their overnight visits until he was back on his feet. But they didn't know what Vero and I knew. That someone had posted an ad on an online forum, offering a hundred thousand dollars to anyone willing to dispose of Steven Donovan. As far as Vero and I could tell, the forum was a virtual cesspool thinly disguised as a mom's support group—an anonymous gathering space for hundreds of disgruntled middle-aged women to bitch about things that bothered them, namely their husbands, bosses, and boyfriends. Apparently, for those with means, it was also a way of getting rid of them.

Vero looked aghast as she slid the van door closed, shutting the children inside. "You're not actually going to let them stay with him, are you?"

"Of course not. I called my parents and asked if the children could stay with them. Then I emailed Steven and told him the kids already had plans."

A wicked smile pulled at Vero's lips as we climbed into the van. Her voice dropped to a conspiratorial whisper and she wagged an eyebrow. "Three whole days without the kids? I can spend a few nights at my cousin's place if you want to invite Julian over to play house for the weekend."

My face warmed when I pictured Julian in my kitchen. Or my bedroom. I snuck a shameful glance in the rearview mirror, but Zach's head was already drooping against his car seat and Delia's red-rimmed eyes were drifting closed. "I don't have time to play house." As tempting as it was to spend a weekend alone with the sexy young law student I'd been seeing, I had far more important things to do. "I have to figure out who posted that job offer. I won't feel safe letting the kids spend the weekends with Steven until I'm sure nobody's trying to kill him." And if that wasn't enough, I had a pitch due to my agent by nine A.M. Monday morning.

I turned the key in the ignition, wincing when the engine protested with a sputter before groaning to life.

Vero made a disgusted sound. "We're going car shopping on Monday."

"The van's fine. Your cousin just fixed it."

"No. Ramón put a Band-Aid on it. Face it, the van is toast."

I threw my aging Dodge Caravan in gear, praying nothing shook loose and fell off—at least nothing important—as it rattled down the driveway. "I can't afford to buy a new car right now. Not with Steven and his attorney scrutinizing all my expenses."

"You could if you took that job on the forum. One hundred Gs would buy a pretty sweet car."

"We are not killing my ex-husband for money," I whispered, glancing back at my sleeping children.

"How much do you think we could get for his lawyer?" Vero suggested. I threw her a withering look. "Calm down. I'm kidding. But that transmission isn't going to last much longer. You'd better get busy writing that book Sylvia thinks you've been working on."

"I know. And I will." My literary agent, Sylvia Barr, had been hounding me for sample pages of a novel I had supposedly started a month ago and my editor was expecting before the end of the year. "I'll work on it this weekend. I'll be at the library anyway." Vero and I had been taking turns rotating among nearly a dozen branches of our local county library system, careful to delete our search history each time we used their computers to check that no one had accepted the job offer on the forum. A month had gone by without a bite, but that didn't change the fact that someone wanted to murder my children's father, and now that Steven had a place of his own, I had no reasonable excuse to keep the kids from him. I'd spend the entire weekend at the library if I had to. I'd scour that women's forum until I figured out who posted the ad—probably one of countless women Steven had either scorned or managed to piss off. Then I'd make an anonymous call, report the woman's intentions to the police, and hope like hell this was the end of it.

"I'll come help you," Vero offered as we merged onto the parkway.

"Silly for both of us to waste the weekend. Don't you have any hot dates?"

"Please. You're getting enough action for the both of us."

My eyes strayed from the parkway to look at her. Vero had always been the one to lecture me about getting dressed in real clothes and going out. But she'd been staying in more and more lately. With the exception of her classes at the local community college, she'd been content to spend her nights off with me and the kids, watching movies in our pajamas. "Maybe you'd get more action if you left the house once in a while."

She rolled her eyes.

"What about that guy, Todd, from macroeconomics?"

"*Micro*economics," she said, with an emphasis on *micro*. "If you're trying to get rid of me so you can get naked with your boyfriend, I'd rather spend the weekend watching football with my cousin."

The van swayed a little as I studied her between glances at the road, making the guy in the next lane lean on his horn. "I thought you said your family wasn't spending Thanksgiving together this year because your aunt is sick."

"She is. My mom's taking care of her." I knew Vero and her cousin were close—she'd been living on his couch before she'd moved in with us—but when it came to everything else about her family, Vero was unusually quiet. In the month she'd lived with us, her family had never called the house, and even though her mother and aunt both lived just over the bridge in Maryland, as far as I knew, Vero hadn't once gone to visit them.

"If Ramón is home, why aren't you having dinner with him?"

Vero's answering laugh was dry. "Ramón's idea of a home-cooked meal is mac and cheese out of the box. Besides, I'd rather spend the holiday with you." She turned toward the window. I couldn't shake the feeling there was something she wasn't telling me, but as we turned in to my parents' neighborhood, I opted to let it go. She would confide in me when she was ready. Families were weird sometimes. I should know.

My mom and dad still lived in the same house Georgia and I grew up in, a brick-faced two-story colonial in what had once been a quieter suburb in Burke. My mother swung open the front door as I pulled into their driveway. Her GRANDMAS FIX EVERYTHING apron was speckled with oil and dusted with flour. The mouthwatering smell of roast turkey and stuffing wafted from the house as I roused the children and ushered them inside. Five days each year, I was glad to live so close to my parents. The other three hundred and sixty? Maybe not so much.

My mother frowned at Delia's hair as she corralled her in the foyer for a hug. The short blond spikes had grown at least an inch since an incident involving duct tape and a pair of scissors, and Vero had combed them to the side before we left, pinning them in place with pink barrettes. "Look how much you've grown! It feels like I haven't seen you in months!"

"You saw the kids last week, Ma." Diaper bag over one arm and a pumpkin pie in the other, I plunked Zach into my mother's waiting hands. She wiped a smear of chocolate from his cheek, frowning at me as she kissed it. Nose wrinkling, she reached for the diaper bag.

"Sorry. I changed him just before we left, but we got stuck in traffic."

Georgia appeared in the foyer, an open beer already in hand. Our mother rolled her eyes skyward, giving it up to god. "What?" Georgia asked, the picture of innocence. "It's five o'clock."

"Maybe at the Vatican," Ma muttered. She brightened when Vero dragged the two Rollaboards over the threshold. "Vero, sweetheart, it's good to see you. So glad you could join us." Zach giggled as they exchanged an awkward hug around him.

"Wouldn't miss it."

"Leave the bags," my mother said, gesturing loosely to the base of the stairs as she closed the door.

"Hey, Vero. Happy Thanksgiv—*oomph*!" Georgia's breath rushed out in a grunt as Delia plowed into her, wrapping my sister's legs in a bone-crushing hug.

"Aunt Georgia, will you come to my school next week? It's Work Day."

"Work Day?"

"Career Day," I clarified, setting the pie on the hall table and stripping off my coat.

Delia jumped on her toes. "I told my friends you're a policeman and they want to see your gun."

Georgia ruffled Delia's hair, shaking loose a barrette. "I'll talk to your mom about it. Go find your pop. I think he's hoarding the cookies." Delia took off for the living room, where the sounds of a football game were blasting from the television. Georgia raised her beer to us in salute. Before the mouth of the bottle reached her lips, our mother thrust Zach against my sister's chest. Georgia's cop reflexes kicked in and she caught Zach with her free arm as he slid down her sweater.

"You can change Zach in the guest room," Mom said, dropping the diaper bag at Georgia's feet.

Georgia's eyes went wide.

Vero backed away, hands raised. "Don't look at me. It's my day off." She retreated to the living room, pressing a kiss to my father's cheek and plopping down beside him on the couch.

Georgia sniffed, her pursed lips making Zach giggle. "Take him, Finn. I'm not qualified to handle this one." She held him out to me. I was certain she'd be more comfortable dismantling a bomb.

I plucked her beer from her other hand instead, sliding the straps of the diaper bag over it until the bag dangled from her arm like a jacket on a coatrack. "Think of it as a tactical bag," I said with a reassuring pat.

Georgia eyed the diaper bag, my name a soft plea on her lips as I took a long swig of her beer and turned for the kitchen, following the buttery-sweet smell of candied sweet potatoes and stuffing. Sinking into a chair at the kitchen table, I closed my eyes and sipped, grateful for a few moments of peace.

Something heavy thunked down on the table in front of me. I opened one eye. The bowl of green beans was piled high, a tangle of pods and stems. "Work on these while I baste," my mother said, drawing on her kitchen mitts. I set down my beer with a sigh as she hauled a steaming turkey from the oven.

"How's your book coming?"

"Great," I lied.

My mother looked at me askance as her baster sucked juices from the bottom of the pan. "Have they paid you yet?"

"Only half. I get the rest when I finish." *If* I finished.

"Put that half in savings. Just in case."

"In case of what?"

"In case you need it for an attorney." She grunted as she hefted the turkey back into the oven. I knew better than to offer to help her. Mom liked to handle some things herself. Holiday dinners—cooking and feeding her family—was a job we would only pry from her cold dead fingers. The sole reason she was letting me prep the beans was because that was a job I couldn't screw up. "Is Steven's lawyer still pestering you?"

I snapped the head off a pod. "It's fine, Ma. I can handle it."

"I thought Steven had agreed to weekly visitation."

"He wants the kids every Friday afternoon through Monday morning now that he has a house."

My mother made a disgusted noise, dropping a cutting board on the table and slamming down a knife. Joint custody wasn't as bad as the full custody he'd been fighting for when he and Theresa had been ready to tie the knot. But it was still three nights away from home in another county, instead of a few blocks down the street. "He's a monster," she said, chopping parsley with a vengeance.

"He's not a monster. He's just angry." Angry, because his relationship with Theresa hadn't worked out. Because his business was struggling after five bodies had been exhumed from his farm. Because I was finally making enough money to support myself and the kids without him.

"Because of this young man you're seeing?"

And maybe that.

The fact that I was seeing someone had been a nagging thorn in Steven's side. He liked to pluck it out and turn it on me, calling Guy every week with some new plan to slowly whittle away at my custody.

My mother raised an eyebrow. "Georgia says this man you're seeing works part time. That he's still in school."

"Graduate school."

"He's too young for you. You should be dating someone closer to your own age. Someone stable who can provide for you and the children."

"*I* can provide for me and the children."

"If you had a husband, Steven wouldn't be threatening to take the kids. He wouldn't have a leg to stand on."

I pushed away the bowl of murdered beans. "Why are you and Dad always nagging me to find a husband? You never nag Georgia about finding a wife."

"Georgia has health insurance and retirement benefits."

I heaved a sigh and dropped my head in my hand. I had no answer for that.

"What about that nice man who works with your sister?" My mother stirred the air with her ladle, conjuring his name. "The tall one with dark hair whose partner had cancer. I met him once, years ago, when he and Georgia graduated from the Academy together. He's very handsome," she said, pitching her voice low as if this was some scandalous announcement. "And he's Catholic."

I lifted the beer to my lips to hide my blush. Detective Nicholas Anthony was, indeed, very handsome. He was also a helluva kisser. But my mother didn't need any more fodder for her marriage fantasies. It'd been a month since Nick had shown up on my front porch with a bottle of champagne and a chagrined apology for suspecting the worst of me, but my argument with him still needled me. I hated that even though my motives had been innocent, to some degree, Nick had been right. I'd lied to him to keep myself out of trouble, and I hadn't gotten around to forgiving myself for that.

"I'm not dating Georgia's coworker," I said firmly.

"Fine. Your sister says this young man you're seeing is studying to become a lawyer. Maybe *he* can help you deal with this Steven problem."

"He's not studying that kind of law." Julian was

studying criminal law. And no, the irony of our situation was not lost on me.

"Has he met the children?"

"No." Julian hadn't asked to come to my home, and I hadn't offered. We usually met at the bar where he worked. Or in his apartment. Usually in his bed, occasionally on his sofa, and once on his kitchen floor. I got up and snagged another beer from the fridge, my head lingering in the open door to hide my incriminating flush. Julian and I weren't serious. I wasn't sure exactly what we were. Only that I enjoyed his company and the sex was amazing. I didn't really want anything else right now. I had Vero, the kids, and a steady paycheck. That's all I really needed besides the occasional mind-blowing orgasm.

"Even more of a reason to put some money in savings, Finlay. A single woman can never be too prepared. You should have a nest egg."

"My nest is just fine," I said, closing the fridge and popping the cap off my beer. I didn't need any more mob money, dead bodies, or problem husbands—mine or anyone else's.

The swing doors to the kitchen burst open and my sister came through, fully suited in SWAT gear, carrying Zach under one arm. A bead of sweat trailed down her temple through the open faceplate of her helmet. "Situation resolved," she said, dumping a tightly rolled diaper in the trash can as Zach wriggled out of her arms and toddled toward the living room. She dropped into the chair beside me and dragged off her helmet.

"I knew you could handle it."

"It was definitely touch-and-go for a while. When are you going to start potty training that kid? And what's all this about Career Day at Delia's school?"

I handed her my beer. "She's supposed to bring an

adult to class on Tuesday to talk about what they do for a living."

"Why can't you go? You're the famous author."

"I'm not famous." One decent book deal had been just enough to cover my bills. It hadn't even gone to print yet. For all I knew, it could flop and I'd never get another one. "Besides, Delia already asked and her teacher said no."

"Why?"

I glanced at my mother and lowered my voice. "Apparently, the school had some concerns about the *content* of my books."

"You mean the sex?"

My mother stopped stirring. I kicked my sister under the table, barking out a swear when my toe connected with the steel toe of her boot. "What possessed you to bring SWAT gear to Thanksgiving?"

"I didn't. It's my old training gear from the Academy. Found it upstairs in the closet in my old room. Still fits," she said proudly, patting her chest plate.

"It's Velcro!"

"What's this about sex in your books?" My mother planted a hand on her hip, a dripping gravy ladle poised in the other. "Why would your books have sex in them? You told me they were mysteries."

"Thanks," I muttered, snatching my beer back from my sister.

A mischievous gleam glinted in her eye. "Didn't you read Finn's books, Ma? How could you not remember the sex?" Georgia winked at me, picking a raw bean from the bowl and popping it into her mouth.

I smacked her hand as she reached for another. "For Christ's sake, Georgia. You just changed a diaper. Did you even wash your hands?"

My mother pointed her ladle at me. "Do not take

the Lord's name in vain in my house, Finlay Grace Mc-Donnell."

"Donovan," Georgia and I corrected her in unison.

My mother gritted her teeth, the ladle scattering gravy as it swung toward my sister. "And Georgina Margaret, go wash those filthy hands!"

Georgia's eyes rolled up in her head. She punched my shoulder as she stood up and slunk from the table.

"Now what's this business about sex in your books?" my mother asked me.

"How much of them did you actually read?"

The color deepened in her cheeks. "The first chapters."

"Only the first chapters?"

"Of the first one."

My mouth fell open. I knew—and was grateful for the fact—that my father hadn't read my novels. The print was too small on those tiny paperbacks for him to bother. But I had assumed my mother, who lived for the opportunity to insert herself into my personal life, would have at least made the effort to finish one.

"The one I tried," she explained, "it didn't appeal to me. What?" she asked as I gaped at her. "I like Nora Roberts. Have you read Nora? She's really very good." She grunted as she hefted the turkey back into the oven. "See, this is another reason you should have a husband."

"I can lift my own poultry, thanks."

She looked to the ceiling, or maybe to god, as she shook open a dish towel and wiped off her hands. "Go tell your father the turkey will be ready in half an hour, and I need him to find the electric carver."

Still shaking my head, I carried my beer through the swing doors. A football game blared in the next room, where Vero and my father were settled on the couch, shouting at the TV and arguing over first downs.

"Hey, Pop. Mom needs you in the kitchen." I came up behind him and kissed his cheek. He patted my hand where it rested on his shoulder.

"Not so fast, old man," Vero teased, holding her palm out to him as he rose stiffly to his feet.

My father dug in his pocket and peeled out a twenty. "I should stick to betting online."

"You shouldn't be gambling at all. It's a bad habit. Terrible odds," she said, taking his money with a wink.

"Says the girl who just cleaned my wallet. *You* should try some of those websites. It's a big weekend for college ball. Take that twenty and put a few bucks on every game. Maybe you'll have better luck than me."

Vero's eyes narrowed thoughtfully at the twenty in her hand as my father retreated to the kitchen. She slipped the bill in her pocket with a faraway look, hardly noticing when I collapsed into the warm imprint my father had left in the cushion beside her. I wondered if Vero was thinking about her cousin, wishing she was with him watching football on his couch. Had she only agreed to spend Thanksgiving with my family because I'd asked her to? Because my mother had insisted? Was there some unspoken moral code that said you had to suffer through turkey dinner with someone's family, just because you'd buried a body together?

"You can still go to Ramón's if you're having second thoughts," I offered.

She turned to me with a look of surprise, as if the suggestion had plucked her from wherever her mind had roamed. "But your mom—"

"My mom will understand. She'll probably even pack you some turkey and pie to go." As much as my family drove me nuts, I couldn't imagine spending a holiday without them. I dragged my van keys from my pocket and dropped them in Vero's hand.

"What about you?" she asked.

"I'll catch a ride home with Georgia after the kids go to bed. Go spend the weekend with your cousin. I've got plenty to keep me busy."

Her laugh was wicked. I knew she wasn't thinking of the library when she said, "Don't do anything I wouldn't do."

CHAPTER 3

My sister dropped me off at home just before eleven. My van was in the garage and Vero's Charger was gone. She'd left a handwritten note on the counter, reminding me I had a pitch due to Sylvia on Monday, and I tucked it under a stack of bills, pretending not to think about it.

I bent in front of my open fridge, playing Tetris with the leftovers my mother had sent home with me, struggling to get the mountain of disposable Tuppers to fit. After I withdrew two beers to make room, the door still wouldn't close, and I eventually gave up, removing a carton of ice cream from the freezer and shoving the last container of cranberry sauce in its place.

Triumphant, I kicked off my shoes, grabbed a spoon from the drawer, and retreated upstairs with my beers and Ben & Jerry's, trying not to notice the stifling silence of the empty house. Vero's bedroom door was closed, like it often was at night after she'd gone to bed, but her absence felt tangible. I should have been thrilled to have the house to myself, but now that I did, I wasn't sure I liked it.

After changing into an old pair of sweats and a loose-fitting, faded T, I lay on my bed under the dim glow of the lamp on my nightstand, the open tub of ice cream resting on my chest. I sucked mint chocolate chunk off the spoon, torn between working on my pitch for Sylvia and grabbing a rare full night of sleep while I could. I didn't even know what my next book was about. Every time I sat down at my computer to work, I ended up thinking about the women's forum instead, worrying over the buried thread containing Steven's name.

I jabbed the spoon in the container and stared at the ceiling. Maybe my mom was right. Maybe I should put some money aside for a decent attorney. Maybe I should fight for full custody. But what would I say? How would I justify it? *Your Honor, I really can't let my kids spend weekends with their father because there's a bounty on his head, and I only know this because, given my recent success eliminating problem husbands, a former client thought I might be well suited for the job. And while I have no immediate plans to kill my ex-husband, I'd rather my kids not be with him if someone else decides to try.*

My phone vibrated on the nightstand. I set down the carton of ice cream and dragged the phone toward me, grinning when Julian's picture flashed on the screen.

You home? he asked.

Yes.

Up for company?

Headlights swung through the gaps in the blinds, flooding my bedroom with light. I rolled out of bed and padded to the window, pushing down a slat to find his maroon Jeep idling in my driveway.

Be right out, I texted back.

I slipped on a pair of tennis shoes, dragging a sweatshirt over my head as I descended the stairs. The air outside was sharp and cold, and I hugged my sweatshirt around myself as I hurried across the lawn. With a shiver, I threw open the passenger door of Julian's Jeep. I'd hardly had a chance to slam it closed when he leaned over the gearshift, taking my face in his hands.

The pads of his fingers were soft, the skin around his mouth smooth and freshly shaven. He smelled like nutmeg and aftershave, and the smell of woodsmoke clung to the thick wool of his sweater.

"Happy Thanksgiving," he said, grinning against my lips. He pulled back far enough to tug a knit hat over my head, brushing my hair back from my face and tucking it behind my ears. His honey-gold locks were hidden beneath a dark beanie, the soft curls peeking out from underneath it.

"What are you doing here?" I asked as I spooled one around my finger. "I thought you were spending the holiday with your parents."

"I did." His thumb traced a lazy outline around my lips. "I was on my way home. You left your hat at my apartment last week. Thought you might be missing it."

"Oh," I said, rising onto my knees and looping my arms around his neck, "I was definitely missing it."

His eyes twinkled as he reached under his seat. The driver's seat slid back on its track, dragging us with it. "Missing anything else?"

"I can think of a few things," I said, climbing over the gearshift, not caring if Mrs. Haggerty peeped out her window and gave herself a heart attack.

"I needed to see you," he murmured between kisses. His hand slid under the cocoon of my sweatshirt, drawing an icy pattern up my bare back and pausing in the middle where my bra strap should have been. He grinned, his low moan rumbling against my lips as his hands moved down to my thighs and he pulled me harder against his lap.

There was too much clothing involved. I could barely feel him through his leather bomber jacket and the thick cables of his sweater. But I was definitely feeling something through the denim of his jeans.

"Is your van in the garage?" he asked as the windows began to fog.

I choked out a laugh, remembering how things had turned out for the last man who'd gotten into the back of my van. The van *was* in the garage. But so were my children's car seats, a box of fruit snacks, and a case of baby wipes. I couldn't believe I was actually considering it.

"The kids are at my parents' for the weekend. You want to come in?" The words came out in a desperate rush, hot and sticky in the air between us, too late to take them back.

He caught my bottom lip between his teeth "What about Vero?"

"At her cousin's," I panted.

His tongue crashed into mine, and I was pretty sure I would get naked and do it on the front lawn if it got any hotter in his Jeep. He grabbed my hand as I reached for the door. "Wait. We shouldn't," he said between ragged breaths. "I can't stay. I have to get home and pack. The guys want to be on the road at six A.M."

I sat up, disoriented, my hat falling askew. "Where are you going?"

His lips were swollen, his eyes still hungry. "Our professors are away at a conference next week. They gave us a few extra days off to study for exams. Some of us are heading down to Panama City to go camping for the week."

"You're going to Florida?"

"It was an impulse trip," he said, smoothing back my flyaway hairs and fixing my cap. "My boss let me trade a few shifts at the bar. We just booked the campsite this week."

I remembered Steven's college breaks to Daytona

and Miami with his fraternity buddies. I'd never been invited, and I had never been privy to the details after. But that didn't mean I was ignorant. "Just you and the guys?"

"And a few people from school," he said. I sat back, putting a few inches between us. Julian took me gently by the chin. "We're just going to grab some sun and unwind. That's all. I'll be back in a week."

Green colored my visions of college coeds in tiny bikinis and even tinier tents. I had no right to feel jealous. Julian and I weren't serious. He'd never even been inside my house. He'd never met my kids or Vero or my ex. "Oh," I said as the flip side of that equation hit me like a slap in the face.

In the entire month that we'd been seeing each other, I'd never met any of his friends either.

"What's wrong?" he asked.

"Nothing," I said, pasting on a smile. What did I expect from him? I had two children and a job and a house I was responsible for. Had I seriously expected him to invite me along? "It's fine," I insisted. "You should go. Have a good time."

"Are you sure? Because if something's wrong, maybe we should—"

I took him by the face and kissed him. Because I didn't want him to finish that sentence. *Maybe we should stop seeing each other. Maybe we should take things slower. Maybe we should talk about it.* I didn't want to do any of those things. I wanted to have sex with him in his Jeep, and maybe even on the crumb-crusted floor of my minivan. I didn't want to think about him at the beach, in a sleeping bag with someone else.

He dragged off my hat, tossing it into the passenger seat. His fingers slid into my hair and under my shirt as he pulled me back onto his lap with a frustrated groan.

Tires squealed. We jerked apart, breathing hard, as

a truck skidded to a stop at the foot of my driveway. Its taillights glared, a livid shade of red.

I slid out of Julian's arms into the passenger seat. Julian turned, following my gaze out the back window, his eyes still smoldering as he panted, "Your ex?"

I nodded, waiting for Steven to put his foot on the gas and leave. Instead, he put the truck in park. "Shit!" I muttered.

Julian sank back against the headrest, his voice husky. "I should probably go."

"Don't. Please. Just . . . don't move," I said, holding up a finger as I threw open the door of his Jeep.

I slammed it harder than I'd intended, adjusting my sweatshirt and raking back my ruffled hair as I stormed down the driveway and met Steven at the bottom of it.

"What are you doing here? I told you, the kids are with my parents."

"Whose Jeep is that?" Steven frowned at the GMU sticker on the rear window, craning his neck to see inside it.

"A friend." I put a hand to his chest as he took a determined step toward the Jeep. "Look, I'm a little busy right now. Can't you just call me tomorrow?"

He paused, surprise coloring his cheeks. "Why's your neck all red? And what the hell happened to your hair?"

"Nothing's wrong with my hair. Can you please just—"

A car door shut behind me and Steven stiffened. I squeezed my eyes closed.

"Who the hell is this?" Steven asked as Julian came up beside me.

Julian drew me aside. "You two look like you need to talk, and I should probably get home. I've got an early morning tomorrow. Are you going to be okay if I go?"

"She'll be fine," Steven grumbled.

I nodded.

Julian dipped low, stealing a slow, lingering kiss that left me a little breathless.

"For crying out loud, kid," Steven snapped. "Don't you have a curfew or something?"

"I'll text you when I get back," Julian whispered. I melted into a puddle of frustration, seriously reconsidering that one-hundred-thousand-dollar offer to kill my ex as Julian climbed in his Jeep and drove off.

I rounded on Steven, planting my hands on my hips—better there than around his neck. "What the hell was that about?"

"I could ask you the same thing. Was that him?" he asked, throwing a finger toward the Jeep's diminishing taillights. "Was that the mystery attorney Vero keeps blathering on about? Jesus, Finn! How old is he?"

"How old is Bree?" I fired back. I doubted the perky blond assistant at his office was old enough to legally drink.

"That's none of your goddamned business!" I raised an eyebrow, but apparently the double standard was lost on him. His mouth pursed with disgust. "Is this why Delia and Zach are at your mother's for the weekend? So you can be out here in your damn pajamas, steaming up the windows of some kid's car?" His eyes narrowed on the front of my sweatshirt. "For Chrissake, Finn, you're not even wearing a bra."

I folded my arms around my chest, dimly aware of a light flicking on in Mrs. Haggerty's upstairs window. "Why are you here, Steven? It's Thanksgiving. Don't you have somewhere better to be?"

He scrubbed a hand over his short beard, masking a flinch. His parents had retired to Tampa a few years ago and his sister had relocated to Philly. Ketchup stains dotted his untucked flannel and onions soured his breath. He'd probably spent Thanksgiving eating fast food in his car.

Steven paced short, irritable lines in front of his truck, raking his hands through his untrimmed hair. He looked as horrible as he had the last time he'd shown up in my driveway in the middle of the night, when he and Theresa had been fighting and he'd come crawling back to talk.

"Bree dumped you," I said, certain I was right when he didn't bother with a snappy comeback.

"She didn't dump me," he said bitterly. "It was a business decision. I lost too many clients after the police investigation, and I couldn't afford to keep an assistant on payroll anymore. I let her go a few weeks ago." I choked on a wry laugh, shaking my head. "What?" His cheeks reddened under the glow of the streetlamp. "I offered to let her come in on an as-needed basis. It's not my fault she turned it down."

I dropped my head into my hands, whispering his name through a sigh. He'd be lucky if Bree didn't take him to court and paint *#MeToo* all over the billboard in front of his farm. I didn't even want to know how many women Steven had done this to over the years, casting them aside when they rejected his advances. He'd pulled the same crap with Vero before she came to live with us, claiming he couldn't afford to pay her, only agreeing to keep her on if she worked a little overtime in his pants. He'd fired her under the guise of a layoff when she'd flat-out refused his proposition for sex.

Arms folded around me, I headed for my front porch. "Go home, Steven."

"I don't have a home," he called after me. I stopped in the middle of the driveway, cursing myself for turning around. His nose was red, his face washed out by the harshness of the streetlight. "That house isn't home. Not without the kids."

Too bad it took him so long to figure that out. "What do you want, Steven?"

"I want them on Sunday," he pleaded. "Just for a few hours. My firs aren't big enough to cut this year, but I found a farm that has some real beauties, and I thought the kids could pick out a Christmas tree. You know, one for each house."

I rubbed my eyes, running out of excuses to keep them away from him. "Delia's got school the next morning."

A spark of hope lit his face. "I'll have them home in time for bed. I promise."

"Fine." I hunched into my sweatshirt, too exhausted to argue. "I'll feed them early. You can pick them up at five."

I turned back to my house—the house he suddenly wanted to dress with the perfect tree. The same house he'd walked away from because he'd thought the sod was greener someplace else. He was still standing in the driveway, hands in his pockets, the fog of his breath heavy in the air as he watched me shut the door.

CHAPTER 4

The library parking lot was nearly empty when the doors opened on Saturday morning, the rest of the world still probably sleeping off their turkey-induced comas and waiting for the buttons on either side of their pants to become reacquainted. Even my yoga pants had felt a little too snug when I'd slid them on that morning. Instead, I opted for the comfy pair of sweats I'd worn, telling myself it wasn't because they still smelled faintly like Julian's Jeep.

Tugging one of Vero's baseball caps low to cover my face, I circumnavigated the circulation desk, hoping the lone woman behind it couldn't smell the steaming go-cup of coffee hidden under my coat or sense the Thanksgiving leftover sandwich tucked inside my laptop bag with her super-librarian powers as I took the longest route to the farthest set of cubicles offering computers for public use. Checking to make sure no one was lurking in the stacks, I settled in front of a monitor at the back of the room.

I unpacked my sandwich and coffee and fished my phone from my computer bag. My heart skipped at a new notification on the screen. I swiped it open, but the text wasn't from Julian. It was only my mother,

reminding me to pick up the kids early tomorrow, in
time for her to make it to afternoon mass.

Curious, I tapped open my Instagram account and
searched for Julian's profile. We didn't follow each other,
but his account wasn't set to "private." I told myself
that it wasn't snooping as the mouse hovered over his
name. My pulse quickened as I clicked on his profile pic.
I don't know what I had expected or hoped to find, but
my shoulders sagged as the same photos I'd seen before
filled the screen.

I set my phone facedown on the desk, turning my
attention to the library computer. I was here to work, I
reminded myself. To find *FedUp* and write a pitch for
Sylvia. Not to spy on Julian while he was enjoying his
break from school.

Pushing Julian from my mind, I typed the address
of the forum into the search engine and logged in, using the anonymous profile Vero and I had created when
we'd first been made aware of the post. The forum
was huge, with nearly thirty thousand registered users
generating thousands of new posts each day. I scrolled
past the familiar women-centered chat rooms: *Women's
Networking, Women's Health, Divorce and Bereave-
ment Support Groups* . . . Then through the *#momlife*
groups: *Working Moms, Breastfeeding Moms, Home-
schooling Moms, Potty Training Moms* . . . I paused
over that last one, making a mental note to return to that
room later, before continuing to scroll. Vero and I had
found the more suspicious subgroups toward the bottom of the page, buried under playdate chats and book
club meetups. Like the *Thrifty Women* who dealt coupon codes like drugs, the *Momma Bears* who shared
methods for spying on their secretive teens and cheating husbands, and the *Crafty Chicks* whose "house-
cleaning tips" occasionally veered into uncomfortable

territory, with more than a few posts reading like a metaphor for dealing with a problem spouse.

The post containing Steven's name had appeared in a chat group called *Bitch Sessions*. I scrolled quickly past the newer threads, clicking on the subject line that read: *Bad Business*. This thread had started like so many of the others—with women complaining about the troublesome men in their lives—before taking an ominous turn.

> **Momma2Three:** *I feel it is my civic duty to warn all my fellow mommas not to use Vin at that new salon in Fair Oaks. I caught him texting my daughter. She's 17!!!*

> **SexyMomToTwins:** *No!!! I hope you reported him! While we're on the subject of men behaving badly, remember that massage appointment I scheduled for my sciatica at that PT office in Centreville? One of the therapists tried to feel me up. Total perv. They really need to get rid of him.*

> **Snickerdoodle:** *UGH! I'm sorry you had to go through that. Men are pigs! Case in point, a friend of mine rented an Airbnb in Rehoboth last week, and she found a freaking hidden camera in the bathroom. Not even kidding. I looked him up and the guy owns dozens of vacation rentals. I'll post a link.*

> **HarryStyles#1Fan:** *Gross.* 🤮 *So glad we have this chat so we can all look out for each other.*

> **FedUp:** *I know exactly what you mean. A real piece of work owns the Rolling Green Sod and*

Tree Farm on Green Road in Warrenton. Steven Donovan is a liar and a cheat.

PTAPrez: *Wait . . . Isn't that the farm that was on the news in October? The one where they found all those bodies?*

FedUp: *Yes, and I can think of 100 Good reasons the world would be better off without him.*

The thread died there, a disconcerting, unspoken, yet tangible silence hanging in the wake of the last reply. No one liked to be reminded that the pricey grass that covered their manicured lawn had been seeded in the same dirt as organized crime. And this post felt like more than an expression of solidarity. It reeked of ill will, the coded language of illicit business.

A real piece of work sounded an awful lot like a contract. And *100 Good reasons* sounded suspiciously like a price. Steven's full name and the location of his business had been clearly spelled out, and *the world would be better off without him* . . . well, that part was obvious.

I relaxed a little as I closed the thread. There had been no new replies since Vero's last library visit three days ago, but there was still the problem of figuring out who *FedUp* really was. I spent the next few hours dipping into rabbit holes in the forum, searching for her other posts, but as far as I could tell, this message about Steven had been *FedUp*'s only contribution. According to her profile, she had registered as a member two days before posting the job and hadn't posted since. But she was clearly still active; her last log-in had been earlier this morning.

"Who are you?" I asked, staring at *FedUp*'s scant profile. Clearly, this was a woman. Someone Steven had either lied to or cheated on. Someone with questionable moral character. My obscured reflection stared back at me from the glass, and I wondered if *FedUp* was on the other side, lurking in the shadows, waiting for someone to write back.

CHAPTER 5

On Sunday morning, I left the library for the last time with exactly zero clues about *FedUp*'s identity, and even fewer about the plot of my next book. I picked up Delia and Zach from my parents' house, relieved beyond measure when my garage door ground open and I saw Vero's Charger parked inside. Holding Zach in one arm and dragging two Rollaboards, my laptop, and the diaper bag with the other, I wrestled open the kitchen door.

"Vero!" I called out. Zach slid from my arms and toddled to the playroom. Delia tossed her coat over a chair. Vero's name echoed through the otherwise silent house. I dumped the luggage and bags on the floor, expecting her to burst into the room with a gleeful cheer after a whole weekend away from us. I called out again as I fished an empty sippy cup from the diaper bag and set it in the sink, surprised to find it full of the breakfast dishes I hadn't had time to clean before I'd rushed off to the library that morning. The coffeemaker was still half-full of cold grounds, the counter still dotted with toast crumbs.

While I hadn't intended to leave her a mess, it wasn't like Vero to walk past one without tidying up.

I stood at the bottom of the steps in the foyer, listening for the sound of a shower running upstairs or the thump of reggaeton through the walls of her room.

"Where's Vero?" Delia asked.

"She must be taking a nap. Why don't you go play with your brother," I suggested, nudging my daughter toward the playroom.

I climbed the steps to Vero's bedroom. Soft music bled through the closed door, a moody boy band ballad I'd never heard before and was sure she'd make fun of if it came on the radio in her car. I knocked, listening to the creak of her bedspring and the slow shuffle of feet on the floor. Her door opened and she peeked through the crack, wearing a mismatched pair of flannel pajamas I'm pretty sure were mine. Her eyes were ringed in day-old mascara, half-hidden behind wisps of tangled dark hair that spilled from her loose topknot.

"Who are you?" I asked, pushing open the door. "And what have you done with my nanny?"

I waited for her to remind me that she was actually my accountant, but Vero only turned back to her bed and plopped facedown onto it. I sat on the edge of her mattress, wedged my hand between her face and the pillow, and pressed my palm to her forehead. Her skin wasn't clammy or hot, but her hair smelled faintly like a dive bar.

"Your weekend with your cousin was really that good, huh?" It wouldn't be the first time she'd come home hungover after a night out with Ramón. But it was the first time she came home from her cousin's looking glum. She buried her face deeper in the pillow, and a knot of worry cinched in my chest. "You want to talk about it?"

"No," came her muffled reply.

I was pretty sure there was only one thing that would pull her out of this funk. "Then get up," I said, rising to my feet and dragging the pillow out from under her head, making her hair stand up with static. "We're going shopping."

She opened one eye, wide and uncertain. "For what?"

"Christmas presents. And Dairy Queen drive-through." Vero had never met a chili dog or a milk-shake she didn't like. "But if you're too tired to come along—"

"Don't leave," she said, bolting upright in the bed. "And do *not* buy anything without me. I'm coming with you."

Two minutes later, the shower sputtered on in her bathroom and that knot of worry finally began to unwind. Vero was obviously having trouble with her family, and as much as I loved that she felt so at home with mine, it bugged me that she didn't seem ready to confide in me about it.

After a quick run through the DQ drive-through, she started to perk up, only to wilt again as I pulled the van into the packed parking lot of the home improvement store.

"What are we doing?" she asked.

"Shopping," I answered.

"You said we were Christmas shopping. This isn't Christmas shopping," she whined as we hauled the kids out of the van and toted them into the store. "Christmas shopping is done at the mall. Or on the internet at the last minute with gingerbread and candy canes. Or on the couch in front of the Home Shopping Network in fluffy slippers and pajamas." She snatched a coupon book from a greeter by the door.

I plunked Zach into the front of a shopping cart. He wiggled in his seat, reaching his pudgy, sticky fingers toward the slow-spinning ceiling fans in the lighting aisle, his high, shrill whine building momentum the farther I pushed him in the opposite direction. I grabbed a stud finder with beeping, blinky lights off an endcap and set it in his lap, silencing him with a distraction.

Vero plucked the stud finder from his hands. "Trust me, kid. Your mom does not need one of these." She gave him a bag of Cheerios when he started to fuss.

I handed her my shopping list. "See if you can find these. Georgia wants a car care kit and Mom wants one of those window-mounted bird feeders. While you're in Lawn and Garden, we could use a snow shovel for the house. I'll head over to the tool department and grab something for my dad."

"Here," she said, surrendering her coupon guide. "Stick to the sale items. Don't spend too much. We just paid off your credit cards." She disappeared into the crowd with Delia in tow. I pushed my cart into an aisle packed with shoppers and sales associates, grabbing the last cordless drill off the island display for my dad and dropping it triumphantly in my cart. I navigated slowly past the racks of household tools. The aisle was full of women, all of them carrying printed gift lists, probably for their husbands. I wondered how many of them would have empty workbenches in their garages a year from now.

My thoughts drifted to that stupid pink trowel above the workbench in my garage—the only tool Steven had bothered to leave on the pegboard when he'd moved out. I thought about all those empty pegs and dust-filled drawers. About the lengths Vero and I had gone to just to find a damn shovel to bury a body. Weaving between the throngs of shoppers, I began plucking one of everything off the rack: screwdrivers, hammers, tape measures, flashlights, and a collection of pliers in a variety of sizes, shapes, and colors. On second thought, maybe I'd keep the cordless drill for myself. I grabbed a mega-assortment pack of Duracells and dumped them in my cart.

Zach finished his Cheerios and started whining again. Thirty minutes had passed, and I was beginning to wonder where Vero had gone when her cart rounded the aisle and pulled up alongside mine.

"Look, Mommy!" Delia said, her feet swinging from the holes in the seat. "My teeth are loose. The tooth fairy's going to come and give me lots of money." Delia pushed her front teeth with the tip of her tongue. I squinted, leaning closer to see. They hardly wiggled.

"I don't think those are quite ready to come out."

"That's why Vero got me one of these." Delia brandished a pair of pliers. I snatched them before she could wedge them into her mouth, trading her for my iPhone and dumping the tool into Vero's cart.

Vero smirked down at the contents of my basket. "Looks like someone went a little crazy with the batteries. I thought you said Julian was only gone for a week." Her voice fell conspiratorially low. "If you need some power tools, Stacey down the street just started one of those home-based adult toy businesses. Free batteries with every purchase and they offer discreet shipping."

A teenage store clerk paused his restocking to stare at us. My cheeks burned. "I don't need those kinds of tools, thankyouverymuch."

"I've seen the drawer in your nightstand, Finn, and I respectfully disagree." The clerk's eyes drew open wide. "What are you staring at?" she called out to him, drawing the attention of the other shoppers in the aisle.

When the last sets of curious eyes returned to their carts, I lowered my voice. "This has nothing to do with Julian. I'm just sick of seeing that empty pegboard every time I pull into the garage. There's no reason I should have to rely on Steven or my dad every time something breaks." Vero and I were perfectly capable of handling the occasional loose screw on our own. I reached for a double roll of duct tape and dropped it in her cart.

"Since you obviously didn't get to play house with your boyfriend, how'd the writing go?"

My grunt was noncommittal. "I spent the entire weekend searching the forum for *FedUp*."

"Any luck?"

"Not a bit."

"Me either."

I dragged my cart to a stop, grabbing Vero's and forcing it to a halt. "You checked the forum from your cousin's house?" I whispered.

"Of course not!" she said, pulling a face. "I did it from a business center in a hotel lobby."

"What hotel lobby?"

"That's not important. What's important is what I found."

I gasped. "You found *FedUp*?"

"No, but get this," she said, her head bent to mine as we slowly resumed pushing our carts. "Someone calling herself *EasyClean* has been making a fortune on that forum. A post pops up, all cryptic and vaguely worded—usually from some woman who's looking to *get rid of something big* and needs someone to *haul it away for a price*. Or some mom who's *dealing with a stubborn stain* and she's willing to pay someone to *help her clean it up*." Vero kept her voice low, punctuating each description with one-handed air quotes. "After a few days, *EasyClean* replies with a couple of carefully worded questions, until it's clear she and whoever posted the message are speaking the same language. Then *EasyClean* and her new client take the conversation private. Next thing you know, the thread dies—and I'm guessing so does the big, messy husband."

"Are you sure you're not misinterpreting all this?" I asked doubtfully. "If this *EasyClean* person *is* a contract killer, why didn't she respond to Patricia Mickler's posts?" According to Patricia, she'd spent months on that forum searching for someone willing to dispose of her husband before she finally gave up and asked me.

"*EasyClean* is a *professional*. She probably vets her targets. Would *you* have killed Harris if you'd known he was cooking the books for the mob?"

"Keep your voice down," I hissed. "And I didn't kill anyone."

"I am telling you, this *EasyClean* chick is literally cleaning up, Finn! These jobs do not come cheap. I've watched at least three of them go down in the last two weeks."

"Why didn't you say anything?"

"Not enough data to draw a pattern. I wasn't sure what I was seeing until that third job showed up, and I didn't want to worry you for nothing. It does make you wonder though . . ."

"Wonder what?"

"About all that money." Vero tapped her chin, then reached for my circular. "They have a chest freezer on clearance over in Appliances. I bet it would fit in the garage."

She laughed as I snatched the coupon guide from her. "Where is the snow shovel? And the bird feeder for my mother?"

She sighed and frowned at her cart. "I guess Delia and I got distracted."

The crowds were starting to thin as we pushed our carts down the wide center aisle toward Lawn and Garden. I checked the time on my phone. "We'll have to hurry. Steven's picking the kids up in an hour to go Christmas tree shopping."

"I can't believe you're letting them go with him," Vero muttered so the kids wouldn't hear.

"What choice do I have?" He had a legal right and an annoyingly capable attorney. "Believe me, I don't like it any more than you do, but they'll be outside in a public place. And we both checked the forum this weekend. It's been a month and no one has responded to the post, and it's buried under hundreds of new messages anyway. I'm sure the kids will be fine."

"I don't know, Finn," she said as we turned down the gardening aisle. "*EasyClean*'s been keeping very busy. What if she's already out there, scoping Steven out?"

"I seriously doubt it." Even as I said it, something twisted in my gut. I didn't like the idea of the kids being out there alone with Steven while he had a target on his back. "I mean, I can't call him and tell him he can't spend time with the kids without me. I've insisted on coming with them to every visit this month. He's starting to get suspicious."

Vero's head tipped as she scrutinized the selection of bird feeders. "Maybe there's another way to keep an eye on the kids without going with them?"

"What do you mean?"

She slid a pair of binoculars off a bird-watching display and dropped them in my cart. "Didn't you learn anything from your field trips with Detective Anthony?"

CHAPTER 6

Vero and I slouched in the front seat of an old Chevy sedan, bundled in winter coats, knit hats, and scarves, with two steaming coffees and a half-empty box of Dunkin' Donuts between us. Vero had left her Charger on the lot at Ramón's garage and borrowed a set of keys to one of his loaner cars. When Steven came to pick up the kids, I'd helped them into their coats and strapped Delia's backpack on her shoulders, waving an enthusiastic goodbye as Steven's pickup pulled out of the driveway. Then I'd grabbed my coat, locked my house, and dashed to meet Vero at the curb. We'd followed Steven's truck to the Christmas tree farm, careful to keep our distance, backing into a dark parking space at the end of the gravel lot.

Vero squinted through her binoculars. "Should we move a little closer?"

"If we get any closer, he might see us." The Christmas tree lot was packed with cars, the neat rows of precut spruces, firs, and pines illuminated by warm white lights that had been strung from wooden frames. Holiday music piped through overhead speakers, and farm attendants in elf hats wandered through the rows, collecting cash from customers and carrying trees to awaiting cars.

"There they are!" Vero said, pointing out the windshield. I sat up and set my coffee in the drink holder, leaning closer to see Delia and Zach as Vero passed me the binoculars. Zach squirmed under Steven's arm. Delia dragged him through the rows by his other. Her mouth was moving, but I couldn't make anything out.

"Turn the volume up."

Vero adjusted the bright blue knob on the receiver on the dashboard. Delia's excited chatter broke through the static, muffled by the rasp of the baby monitor as it jostled inside her backpack. I'd turned it on and zipped it inside right before Steven had picked them up. "What's the range on this thing?" Vero asked.

"According to the manufacturer, it's good for a thousand feet." I laid the binoculars on the dash, allowing myself a few sips of coffee, feeling slightly more at ease as the sounds of Delia's babbling filled the car.

"I think my mom's right," I said. "I should hire a decent divorce lawyer to handle the custody stuff. I'm completely out of my league trying to handle Steven myself."

"How much does a real attorney cost?"

"Guy gets two hundred an hour," I said, blowing steam from my cup. "Might as well do it now while there's money in the bank. I was thinking about trading in the minivan, too." I reached for a donut. Vero was unusually quiet. Too quiet. She didn't even protest when I took the only chocolate crème. "Why are you looking at me like that?"

"Like what?"

"Like something's wrong."

"Nothing's wrong." She set down her half-eaten donut, wiping a streak of powdered sugar down her pants.

"Just last week you were nagging me to buy a new car. Why are we suddenly concerned with clipping coupons and buying clearance freezers at Lowe's?"

"Do I need a reason to make economically wise choices?"

"How much is left in the account, Vero?"

Her eyes swung slowly to mine. "Before or after we went Christmas shopping?"

My jaw dropped. "You can't be serious! What about all of Irina's money?" The wealthy wife of the Russian mob enforcer had paid us a cold, hard seventy-five thousand. Literally. We'd kept it hidden in my freezer. "We couldn't possibly have spent all that money in a month!"

"We didn't. I invested it."

"Well then *un*invest it. How hard can it be to cash out a few stocks?"

"That's not how these things work, Finlay. You have to let the money sit."

"How am I supposed to pay my bills in the meanwhile? And don't say murder for hire!"

"I don't know," she said, her voice rising. "We'll use the money from your next book. The sooner you get that manuscript done, the sooner we get paid." *We.* She threw that word around as if she were the one who had to sit in front of that keyboard and write it. "When's it going to be finished anyway?"

I turned and looked out the window, catching a fleeting image of Delia and Zach running ragged between the rows of Christmas trees with Steven at their heels. "You don't want to know."

We sat in silence as the tension in the car simmered. Vero started to fidget.

"Maybe you're just burned out on romantic suspense," she said, pivoting toward me. "Maybe you need to spread your wings. You know, challenge yourself artistically. I've been reading about this new trend. There's a huge untapped market for it."

"For what?"

"Dino porn." I choked on my coffee. "I am telling

you, Finlay, I have run all the numbers, and dino porn is the next big thing."

I turned to gape at her. "How is that even possible?"

"I wondered about that, too, so I downloaded a few samples." She bent her elbows into tiny T. rex arms. "Apparently, the dino-hero's hands are pretty small, but our heroine doesn't mind, because he more than makes up for it with his super-enormous—"

"Stop!" I covered my eyes, determined not to picture it. "I don't want to know."

"Fine. But when everyone starts buying up veloci-rapterotica, don't say I never told you." Arms crossed, she fell back against her seat, both of us staring out the windshield.

Steven approached a young tree farm attendant with jingle bells on her hat and extremely generous boobs. He leaned close to point out a tree, sneaking a peek down her sweater as he reached for his wallet.

"Are you watching this?" Vero asked with a tone of disgust. "He's totally coming on to the Elf with the Shelf. He is so freaking predictable. Seriously, Finn, it wouldn't be hard to take him out. A hundred grand would buy a very nice car. And think of all the money you'd save on attorneys."

"I'll finish the book."

Vero shook her head, watching Steven through her binoculars as he flirted shamelessly with the attendant. "What did you ever see in him anyway?"

If Vero had asked me a year ago, I would have said it was Steven's charm, his drive, his confidence. But hindsight had clarified so many things about our rela-tionship. I sighed. "He was good at making me feel like I needed him."

"That's fucked up."

"Yeah, it is." I watched him give the elf his busi-ness card, certain he was asking for her number. While

Steven's back was turned, Zach toddled off, escaping between a row of trees. Delia took off after him. Steven whirled, shouting both of their names. He stuffed his wallet in his front pocket as he ran, nearly knocking over a tent pole in his hurry to catch them.

All three of them disappeared into the maze. The children's laughter trilled through the monitor.

"Where'd they go?" Vero chuckled, adjusting the focus on the binoculars.

"I'm sure he's wrangling them. They'll probably turn up in a second."

We listened as Zach's laughter faded, lost in the scuffle of Delia's backpack. Steven's shouts grew more and more distant. I reached for the monitor and turned up the volume. A moment later, their voices went silent.

"Why can't we hear them?" Vero asked.

I moved the receiver closer to the windshield. All I could make out was the rustling of the monitor. My neck prickled, and the hair on my arms stood on end. I stretched up to see deeper into the maze, but the farm beyond the lights was a labyrinth of trees, acres of them stretching into the blackness. I couldn't begin to guess where a thousand feet ended in the dark.

Delia's voice broke through the static. "Daddy, where are you?"

I gripped the receiver, my chest growing tight. "They can't have gone that far. He'll find her any minute."

"Daddy? Daddy?" Delia's voice wobbled. "I'm scared!"

Vero and I threw open our doors, our dropped cups splashing coffee over the pavement as we took off running through the parking lot. We tore through the crowd, muttering *excuse me*s and *pardon me*s as we raced around couples and families. An attendant in an elf hat jumped in front of me, motioning for me to slow down. Heart pounding, I shoved him aside. Vero raced after me into the maze of trees beyond the lit area. We split off in opposite directions, shouting the children's names. The path darkened and narrowed around me. Branches slapped my face as I ran.

"I've got Zach!" Vero called out.

"Delia!" I paused, turning in circles, ears straining for her answer.

"Mommy!" Her frantic shout came to me in stereo, through the monitor in my hand and somewhere to my right. I took off in a sprint, searching the rows as they blurred past until I spotted a flash of her bright, pink coat.

"I've got Delia!" I cried out, dropping to my knees in front of her and scooping her into my arms. Vero appeared a moment later with Zach pressed to her chest.

"Where's Steven?" she asked, her breath coming in steaming pants.

"Steven?" I called out. A low groan answered from the darkness. Vero and I carried the children toward the sound, checking each row until we spotted a figure face-down in the dirt. "Steven!" Delia bounced on my hip as I rushed to his side.

He sat up slowly, gingerly rubbing the back of his head. Vero took out her phone and aimed it toward him, washing his face in bright white light. A long stream of red flowed down his temple. "Get that out of my face! What the hell is she doing here? And what are *you* doing here?"

"What happened?" I asked.

He rose stiffly, swatting my hand away when I tried to help him to his feet. He winced as he pressed his fingers to the wound. "I don't know. It was dark. I was running after the kids. Someone hit me from behind and knocked me down. I must have cut my head when I fell."

He reached into his pocket, relief washing over him when he dug out his wallet. He patted his jeans, his shirt, his jacket pockets and frowned. "That asshole took my phone!"

Delia's wet cheeks burrowed into my neck. "I want to go home, Mommy."

Zach sniffled against Vero and sucked harder on his pacifier. Vero rubbed soothing circles on his back. "I'll take Zach and Delia to the car." Vero held out a hand as I set Delia on the ground. Steven gritted his teeth as he watched the three of them walk to the loaner car.

"Whose car is that?"

"It's not important."

"You can't drive the kids home. You don't have their car seats."

"I brought them with me, just in case."

"Just in case what? What's that supposed to mean?" I switched off the monitor and he snatched it from my hand. "What the hell is this? Were you spying on me?"

There was no point in answering that. "Vero can take the kids home. Give me your keys. I'll drive you to the ER. You might need stitches."

"I don't need stitches," he snapped.

"At least let me call Georgia. You should file a police report."

"Some punk kid mugged me, Finlay. It's not a big deal. He didn't get my wallet."

"It is a big deal! You're hurt. The kids could have been hurt. If Vero and I hadn't been here—"

"The kids would have been fine!" He glared at me, blood dripping over his eye. "I would have dusted myself off and bought the damn tree they picked out, and then I would have driven them home. But you couldn't even let me have that, could you?"

Vero flashed the headlights as she started the car. "We'll discuss this tomorrow. Please, file a police report," I begged him as I walked away. I just wanted to get my kids out of there. Steven had been mugged, but not for his money. His wallet had been in that very same pocket, which meant whoever came after him only wanted one thing—his phone. Or, more likely, the information in it . . . his schedule, his contacts, records of the places he frequented. Everything a contract killer would need to plan the perfect murder.

Vero was right. Just because no one had taken the job didn't mean they weren't planning to.

CHAPTER 7

Monday morning dawned far too early. I tossed back the blankets and sniffed. Rolling over, I spotted the culprit beside my bed. By the time I rubbed the remnants of sleep from my eyes, Zach was gone, already giggling in the hall, his business in my room clearly concluded to his satisfaction.

With a heavy sigh, I got up and hunted him down, hauling him back into my room for a diaper change. Pans clattered in the kitchen, the sound of sizzling oil and the smell of salty goodness wafting up the stairs.

"Delia!" I called out. "Time to get up and get ready for school." She stomped into my room with a scowl, brushing her spiky bangs from her eyes, the feet of her pajamas loose around her ankles and her stuffed dog dangling by his neck from one hand. I set Zach down, his legs already moving before they hit the carpet. "Smells like Vero's making breakfast. Why don't you two head downstairs."

The cordless phone lit up on the nightstand beside me. Sylvia's name flashed on the caller ID. I checked the time on my cell phone and swore, swiping away her three missed calls.

"Ooooh," Vero sang from the kitchen, probably seeing the same thing on the cordless downstairs, "someone is in trooooouble. Told you, you need to start working on that book!"

I considered the possible consequences of letting the call ring to voicemail. But knowing Sylvia, she would keep calling until I eventually picked up. I wiped sweat from my hands and pressed the phone to my ear.

"It's eight A.M.," Sylvia said before I could get a greeting out. "On Monday," she clarified.

"I know. And I'm sorry."

"I'm meeting with your editor in an hour to discuss your pitch, which is not in my inbox."

"I meant to get that to you. Really, I did. But the weekend got away from me." I scrambled down the hall to my office, as if the pitch I had neglected to come up with over the weekend would magically appear the second I opened my laptop. "And well, see . . . here's the thing." I sat down at my desk, pushing aside used sticky notes and receipts. "I've got it all in my head. I just haven't had a chance to type it up yet. I'll do it right now, I swear. I can have something to you before you meet with her at nine." I wasn't entirely sure what that something would be, but it would buy me an hour to figure it out.

"Let's get something straight, Finlay. The title on my business card does not say *Ms. Donovan's Assistant.* I am your *agent*—one you are very lucky to have, I might add. Taking dictation for an author who can't stay on top of her deadlines is not in my job description, but because I would like to get *paid,* I will do that for you. Just this once. Now," she said, her chair creaking through the phone as she settled into it, "I'm all ears. Give me everything you've got."

"Right, everything I've got." I sifted through the crumpled-up sticky notes in the trash can, frantically searching for all the horrible ideas I'd jotted down and discarded over the last month. Most of the damn notes were just grocery lists and reminders. I pulled the most recent one from my laptop screen, skimming the first item on the to-do list and chuckling darkly over the irony.

Pitch for Sylvia by Monday.

Awesome. Way to go, Finn.

Sylvia huffed impatiently as I skipped to the next item on the list.

Contact Guy to cancel visitation.

"So, there was this man . . . a father," I began slowly, gathering my scattered thoughts. "He was . . . a businessman of questionable character who'd made plenty of enemies." I closed my eyes, groping for inspiration in the dark. I needed a scary setting. A place where something suspenseful and terrifying might happen. "The man was outside . . ." I said, "hiking in a dark pine forest with his children . . . when he was attacked from behind and brutally murdered."

"Murdered how?"

"Blunt force trauma to the head?"

"Great. Keep going."

"Right . . . so . . . our assassin . . . was in a tree, stalking the man. He was supposed to be her next mark. See, he was divorced from his wife, and she'd been hiding the children from him because she knew he was dangerous."

"Gooood." Sylvia drew out the word with an encouraging lilt. I could practically hear her inching forward in her chair as I scanned the next reminder on the list.

Check lost and found at school for
Delia's missing gloves.

"But the man found her," I continued. "He kidnapped the children from their school, whisking them away to a remote cabin in the woods where he was certain no one would come looking for them."

"Bastard!" Sylvia whispered.

"Meanwhile, one of the man's enemies had become fed up."

"With what?"

"I don't know," I said, tossing the list on the desk. "I haven't figured that out yet. Whatever reasons bad guys kill for: money, jealousy, revenge, whatever . . . So this mystery enemy hired our assassin to kill the man." I rose from my chair, the words tumbling out freely as I paced, as if some clog in my brain had finally shaken loose. "Our heroine had hunted her mark, tracking him to his cabin, but when she looked through her binoculars and saw his children were with him, she knew she couldn't act. Not then. Not there. Who would care for the children if their father was dead? How could she get them to safety while keeping her own identity secret?" Sylvia had gone quiet. I wasn't entirely sure what that meant, but I pressed on, the story growing more dramatic as the pitch took on a life of its own. "Our assassin perched in the tree, wrestling with her decision as she watched the man and his children from a distance. Meanwhile, unbeknownst to her, someone else was in the woods. It had begun to snow. The forest was growing cold and dark, the visibility poor. Just as the man and his children turned back for the cabin, another killer leapt from the woods, murdering the assassin's mark and leaving the children for dead."

"No!" Sylvia gasped.

"Our heroine was forced to make a choice: expose herself and save the children from certain death as temperatures dropped and night closed in, or pursue the other killer who'd stolen her bounty."

Sylvia's voice was breathy and urgent. "What did she do?"

"She saved the children."

"I knew it!"

"But in the process of turning them over to the authorities, she was arrested for the murder herself."

"But she breaks free," Sylvia insisted.

"No, she goes to jail."

There was a sound like Sylvia's heels hitting the floor. "Wait a minute," she said, her acrylic nails clicking against the phone as she switched ears. "She goes to jail? We're already into the second act and I'm not hearing any B plot. Where's the romance? Where's the sex? How's she supposed to get it on with the hot cop if she's stuck behind bars?"

I pinched the bridge of my nose. "There is no hot cop."

"What about the cop from the first book?"

Why was everyone so hung up on the cop? "He's not in this one?"

"Why not? Everybody liked him."

"Because now she's in love with an attorney."

"And they have sex in jail?"

"I'm getting to that."

"Well, get to it a little faster. I'm picking up a cab in twelve minutes."

I slumped into my chair, dispirited and ready to rush through the rest, certain Sylvia was going to reject the whole pitch. "So she falls in love with this attorney who's been assigned to her case. He's young and smart—"

"And hot?"

"And hot."

"As hot as the cop?"

"Maybe hotter. Because he *believes* in her, Sylvia!" In her and Hanlon's razor and pizza and beer. "He

swears he's going to prove her innocence. But then . . ."
I choked, scrambling for my list.

Find attorney.

"Then her attorney goes missing," I said, smacking
the desk. "He disappears without a trace. No calls. No
texts." I left out the part where he was probably loung-
ing on a beach, slathered in baby oil, drinking beer with
a bunch of bikini-clad coeds. "And she knows in her gut
someone's abducted him—or worse—to make sure she
suffers a lifetime in prison."

"*Then* she breaks out?" Sylvia cut in.

I heaved a sigh. "Sure, why not?"

"Determined to find her hot lawyer at any cost. I love
it. That's what we're going to call it, Finn." I could hear
Sylvia's pen drop onto her desk. "*The Hit 2: At Any
Cost.*"

"Fine." She could call it whatever she wanted. If I
was lucky, maybe she'd write it for me, too.

"I've got to tell you, Finlay, I doubted you for nothing. I think you're really onto something here. It feels
very cinematic. We might be able to shop this for the
screen."

"Maybe we shouldn't—"

"I've got to run. I'm going to be late to meet with
your editor. I'll email you later and let you know what
she says." The line went dead. I slumped back against
my chair, processing everything I'd just told Sylvia,
picking the pitch apart for anything that might come
back to bite me. It seemed safe enough.

An engine rumbled outside my house.

I got up and pushed down the slats of my blinds,
groaning as I spotted the familiar pickup in the driveway.

Vero was peering out the foyer window as I came

rushing down the steps in my slippers and my robe. "What's Steven doing here?"

"I have no idea."

"If things didn't go well with Sylvia, we could always kill him," she suggested.

A rush of frigid air blew in when I opened the door. Steven stood on my porch wearing a heavy flannel, an enormous pine tree wedged in the crook of his arm. His work boots shed dirt on my foyer rug, and the tree dropped needles as he carried it over the threshold.

"Daddy!" Delia squealed, flying down the steps and throwing herself into his free arm. Heavy thumps sounded through the house as Zach rushed down after her.

"Hey, pumpkin." Steven kissed Delia's head and set her down. A bandage peeked out from under his wool cap, and a bruise colored his cheek.

"What's all this?" I grimaced as the high branches of the tree scraped against the ceiling, the top of the tree bending as he leaned it against the wall. Zach toddled over to pet it. Steven's relief was almost palpable.

"I felt bad about what happened at the tree farm last night, so I went back first thing this morning and bought the nicest one I could find."

Vero raised an eyebrow. "It's a little big, isn't it?"

He smiled up at the fir. "I can always trim it back. The girl at the tree lot said it's better to pick one that's larger than you need than to get stuck with one that doesn't fill the space."

Vero's gaze dropped to Steven's crotch. "Won't she be disappointed." She tucked her elbows close to her sides, curling her hands into dinosaur claws as she passed me on her way to the kitchen.

Steven's face reddened. "What was that about?"

"You don't want to know." I gestured to the bandage at his temple. "How are you feeling?"

He tugged off his cap, prodding the gauze. "Two stitches," he said sheepishly. He reached into his pocket and held up his cell phone. "And look what I found on the floor of my pickup this morning. Must have dropped it last night when I was getting the kids out of the truck."

Or *EasyClean* got what she needed from his phone and conveniently put it back. "Someone hurt you. You should talk to the police."

"And tell them what? That I was running in the dark and I hit my head? It was just a stupid accident, Finn. There's nothing to talk about." He sniffed the air. "Something smells good. What's for breakfast?" His cheerful tone rang a little stiff.

Delia clapped. "Vero's making soggy chips!"

Steven frowned. "She's giving the kids chips? For breakfast?"

"They're chilaquiles!" Vero snapped from the kitchen. "And no, you can't have any."

"We weren't expecting company," I explained.

"It's fine," he said through a tight smile. "I was planning to stop for pancakes after I dropped off the tree anyway. I thought maybe Delia and Zach could come with me."

"Delia's got school."

"I can drive her to school after."

I glanced out the window at his truck. For all he knew, *EasyClean* could be watching it even now.

"Please, Mommy," Delia begged, hanging on my arm. "I want to go get pancakes with Daddy!"

"You've got school in less than an hour and Vero already cooked."

"If you can call chips cooking," Steven muttered.

I gritted my teeth and nudged Delia toward the kitchen. "Go on and eat your breakfast. Take your brother with you. You're going to be late for school." Delia pouted, dragging her feet. I waited until they were out of earshot before taking Steven's arm and turning him toward the door. "Thank you for the tree. And thank you for the offer to take the kids, but it's really not a good time."

"What the hell is this about?" he asked, holding the door shut. "Every time I call, you've got some excuse why I can't see them."

"I'm not making excuses. We've just been busy."

"This is about Theresa, isn't it? You're freaked out because of the bodies they found on the farm."

"What do you want me to say, Steven?"

"Whatever Theresa was into had nothing to do with me. You know me, Finn. You know I would never have been involved in something like that."

"Do I? Because after everything that's happened between us, I wonder if I ever knew you at all."

A muscle worked in his jaw. "That's not fair. You've known me a lot longer than you've known her," he said, pointing at the kitchen. "You've got some stranger you met less than a year ago living under your roof, driving Delia to school, and spending all day with Zach! What do you really know about *her*?"

"She's their babysitter, Steven!"

"And I'm their father! I want to see my kids."

I couldn't argue that. He had every right to spend time with our children. I didn't want to keep him from Delia and Zach any more than he wanted to be apart from them. But the truth was buried in a can of worms I couldn't afford to open. "You will see them. Just not this morning." I reached around him for the door.

"I want them this weekend."

I gave an ambiguous nod. "I'll call you later this week and we can set up a time for you to come over and visit."

"No, Finn." He stood over me, his blue eyes seething. "I'm picking them up after school on Friday.

No baby monitors. No spying on me from your car. They're spending the weekend with me—the whole weekend—or else I'm calling Guy."

He gave the tree one last look as he threw open the door, slamming it behind him. I started as Vero placed her hand on my shoulder. "I knew we should have bought an extra shovel."

CHAPTER 8

The mall was busy for lunchtime on a Tuesday. Christmas songs pumped through a speaker in a potted plant beside me, the crooning lyrics drowned out by the bustle of holiday shoppers in the food court and the clatter of plastic trays. I sipped on a fountain drink, watching the ebb and flow of the crowds. Vero had suggested I get out of my office. That maybe a change of scenery—some good old-fashioned people watching and Christmas shopping—would lift me out of my slump and light a fire under my muse. Or at the very least, take my mind off the fact that Julian had been gone for four days, and he hadn't so much as texted. All I had so far was the seed of a story—a missing lawyer who'd fallen in love with his client, a hit woman on trial for a murder she didn't commit. But no matter how many hours I spent staring at my keyboard, I couldn't imagine this story having a happy ending.

My phone vibrated on the table. I reached for it, wilting a little when the number on the screen wasn't Julian's.

I pressed the phone to my ear, plugging the other with a finger. "Hey, Syl."

"I've got great news," she exclaimed. "Your editor

loved your idea. She wants to see a sample. How quickly can you get me twenty thousand words?"

Twenty thousand was almost a quarter of a book. "I don't know. Maybe by the end of the year." At the rate I was going, even that was a stretch.

"Good! I told her you'd have it to her by Monday." I choked on my soda. "That should give you plenty of time to make one tiny, little change."

"What change?"

"She wants the hot cop back in the story. Just hear me out," Sylvia said when I started to protest. "You can keep the lawyer—she liked that angle—but your readers will be expecting the cop to be in the book. It'll add some internal and external tension, and a second love interest will spice up the plot."

"Love triangles are too hard to juggle," I argued.

"Then kill one of them off in the third act. Let the other one save her and give her a steamy happily ever after. Pick whichever one you want. Just make sure the hot cop makes it into the sample. Twenty thousand by next Monday, Finlay. Don't let me down."

Sylvia disconnected.

My Auntie Anne's pretzel sat unfinished, going cold in a greasy puddle on my tray. Why did my heroine need a hero to save her? Why couldn't she just be trusted to save herself?

For that matter, when did *she* get to do the rescuing?

Tearing off a mouthful of dough with my teeth, I closed my manuscript and opened my browser, glancing over my shoulder to make sure no one was watching as I navigated to the forum. I could log in and out in less than a minute. Just long enough to check the post. No harm, no felony.

I clicked on *Bad Business,* revealing the short thread. I stopped chewing, my hand frozen over the track pad.

EasyClean: @FedUp, Steven Donovan sounds like quite a piece of work indeed. I've looked into the liar and cheat in question, and I'm in agreement. He could disappear next week and the world wouldn't miss him. 50 Good reasons is all I need to start a conversation. If you're ready to talk to someone who understands, DM me. I'm ready to listen.

A knot formed in my throat.

I stood, shoving my pretzel in my bag, preparing to pack up my laptop and head for Delia's school. Georgia was there, presenting for Career Day. I could show her the post and make up some story about how I'd gotten an anonymous note in my mailbox (it wasn't entirely a lie). I could do what I should have done weeks ago, let the police sort it out and—

I stared at the screen as a new message appeared below *EasyClean*'s reply.

FedUp: It's so kind of you to offer. I was beginning to worry I was doing this wrong. I don't have much experience with this sort of thing. I'm grateful to have someone to talk to. I'll send a message soon.

I fumbled in my computer bag for my phone and called Vero's number.

Pleasepickup, pleasepickup, pleasepickup . . .

"Someone had better be dead," she mumbled.

"You can't possibly be sleeping. It's almost eleven o'clock."

"Zach's taking a nap. I get one, too."

"*EasyClean* took the job."

Blankets rustled through the phone. Vero's harsh

whisper was suddenly clear and sharp. "What do you mean, *EasyClean* took the job?"

"I mean exactly what I said! I'm on the forum right now!" A woman at a nearby table gave me the side-eye. "We have to do something," I hissed.

"Short of putting your ex on a plane to Siberia, I don't think there's anything we can do."

"I'm picking up Delia in thirty minutes from school. Georgia's there for Career Day. I'm going to talk to my sister."

She sucked in a sharp breath. "And say what?"

"Only as much as I have to."

"No, absolutely not, Finlay!"

I dropped my voice to a harsh whisper, angling away from the woman at the table beside me. "You saw how terrified the kids were at the tree farm. I can't just stand by while someone's trying to murder their dad!"

"If the police find this post, they'll be all over this forum, and you know exactly where that will lead them. This is the same damn forum Patricia Mickler used when she was looking for someone to kill Harris, before she found *you*. That case is closed, Finlay. Feliks is in jail, and we're off the hook. But if you blab this to your sister now, that investigation could be reopened before Feliks even goes to trial. And we could both go to prison for murder."

I wiped sweat from my lip. Vero was right. It would be a huge risk involving the police in this, but I had to do something. Once *FedUp* and *EasyClean* moved their conversation off the group chat, I'd have no way of following it.

"Finlay?" It was the same tone Vero used when my children were too quiet. When we both knew they were up to no good. "What are you doing?"

I pulled my laptop closer and clicked *Reply in Thread*.

"You should come home," she said sternly. "We should talk about this."

My hands flew over the keys. It was the most I'd written in weeks. Because there was only one way I was going to let this scene play out.

> ***Anonymous2****: @FedUp: Sounds like you'd benefit from talking with a real professional. I've helped several women eliminate unwanted stress from their lives, and I'm confident I can assist with this particular problem. I don't need any Good reasons up front to start a conversation. DM me. We'll work it out.*

"Finn, we have to be smart about this. Whatever you're doing, stop."

I clicked *Submit,* pushing my laptop away from me with a shuddering exhale.

The phone went deathly silent. "Tell me you didn't reply."

"It was the only thing I could think of!" I needed time. Time to think. Time to figure out who *FedUp* was. Maybe this would buy me enough.

"Where are you?" Vero asked.

"In the eatery at the mall."

"On your laptop?"

"Yes, on my laptop!"

"Jesus, Finn! What were you thinking?"

"*You* were the one who said you wanted to buy a chest freezer!"

"I was not suggesting you take an offer to kill your ex from the open Wi-Fi at the food court!"

I slammed my laptop closed with a gasp, my eyes darting to the tables around me. What had I done?

"Listen to me, Finlay," Vero said with a forced calm. "Log off the forum right this minute. Pick up Delia from

Career Day and do not breathe a word of this to your sister. We will deal with this ourselves. Just like we did before."

I swallowed hard against the memories of dead bodies. Of the weight of a man's life. Of endless hours of shoveling by moonlight.

Just like we did before was exactly what I was afraid of.

CHAPTER 9

A chill wind sliced through the open buttons of my coat as I cut across the packed parking lot of Delia's preschool. As I wove between cars, I searched for my sister's shiny blue Impala, but it was nowhere in sight. Digging my cell phone from my bag, I stood outside the front of the school, scrolling through the calls and messages I'd thumbed off while I'd been panicking in the food court. My heart stuttered when I skimmed the first of four missed text messages, all from Georgia. The first had come nearly an hour ago.

> *Emergency at work. Stuck on a scene. Dumbass #1 shot his brother in the foot. Dumbass #2 retaliated. Need to run them to the ER before booking. Not going to make it to school in time. Can someone else cover?*

The second had come five minutes after.

> *How about Vero? Accounting is cool, right?*

Then . . .

> *Never mind. Forget I said that.*

Her last message had come more than forty minutes ago.

Don't worry about Career Day. Tell Delia I've got it covered.

I rushed through the doors into the crowded lobby, muttering apologies as I nudged myself between a dad in an orange construction vest and a mom in blue scrubs. Stretching up on my toes, I peered inside Delia's classroom. She stood at the front of the room beside her teacher, anxiously twirling a spike of her hair. I sagged with relief when I spotted an imposing figure in a padded SWAT uniform and helmet standing among the parents. A few moms whispered to one another, their gazes dropping appreciatively over the long legs of Georgia's uniform as she cut a careful path through the cheering kids sitting crisscross on the rug, but my focus was rooted on Delia's wide grin.

The applause quieted as Delia's guest paused beside her and turned toward the class, reaching up to unfasten the SWAT helmet. When it lifted, two dark eyes—eyes that definitely did not belong to my sister—skimmed over the faces in the room, locking on mine. Nick tucked his helmet under his arm. A shy dimple cut into his cheek as several of the moms angled for a better view. Their shameless gazes climbed the length of his uniform, lingering over the holsters hugging his thighs and the formfitting tactical vest cinched around his chest.

Delia's teacher read from a clipboard, silencing their whispers. "Class, Delia Donovan has invited a special guest to meet us today. This is Detective Anthony with the Fairfax County Police Department. Mr. Anthony is with a special division that monitors organized crime. I know we probably have many questions for the detective, but I do ask that parents keep the content appropriately suited to our young audience members." The teacher looked at the parents over the rims of her glasses, lifting a brow at the whispering moms, making a few of them giggle.

The children arched up on their knees on the rug, arms held high. Delia picked one of her friends to ask the first question. The room hushed to listen, the deep timbre of Nick's voice casting a spell over the room. Delia gazed up at him with an admiration she usually reserved for her father—as if he could fix anything. Last time I saw Nick, he'd asked me out and I'd gently turned him down. And here he was, standing in front of my daughter's classmates in SWAT armor, the hero I never asked for and probably didn't deserve.

My phone vibrated in my hand. Georgia's name flashed on the screen. I stepped back from the crowded doorway, lifting the phone to my ear.

"Did he make it?" she asked.

"Yes. What the hell is he doing here?"

She expelled a relieved breath, the sound muffled by the garble of walkie-talkies and buzzing doors in the background. "I didn't know what else to do. I couldn't reach you and I didn't want to mess up Delia's Career Day."

"And Nick just conveniently offered to show up at her preschool in tactical gear?"

"Not exactly. The gear was my idea. It looks cooler than jeans and a Henley. I thought it might impress Delia's friends."

I managed a begrudging thank-you. "You owe me for this," I added. "Big-time."

"Why? I was doing you a favor."

"Volunteering for Career Day or sending Nick in your place?" My brain snagged on that last thought. "Wait . . . Did Mom put you up to this?"

"No," Georgia sputtered. "Of course not."

"She did! I can't believe you let her talk you into this. God, Georgia. This is so awkward!"

"Only as awkward as you make it."

"What if I tell Nick I'm planning to murder you?"

"Yeah, that would definitely make things weird. Look, I've got to go finish booking Thing One and Thing Two. Call you later."

"You owe me!" I said again as my sister disconnected. Nick grinned at me through the open door of Delia's classroom, watching me over the children's heads, causing a few curious moms to look over their shoulders at me. I was going to make Georgia change so many diapers for this.

"Smooth, huh?" I turned at the raspy voice behind me. The man shook his head as he watched Nick over my shoulder. "He's got every one of them eating out of the palm of his hand. Even the kids." The man jiggled a set of keys, or maybe some loose change in his pants pockets, the spread of his open jacket revealing the butt end of a sidearm and the glimmer of a badge. I was still struggling to place him when his blue eyes jumped to mine. "Sorry," he said, extending a hand. "I should have introduced myself. I'm Joey Balafonte." At my vacant stare, he jutted his chin toward the classroom. "I'm Nick's partner."

"Oh," I blurted as I rushed to shake his hand.

The end of a toothpick poked from the corner of his smile. He was in plain clothes, like Nick usually wore, but his color palette was noticeably lighter: thick fair hair hinting at gray around his temples, a French-blue shirt, and pale gray slacks. The faint scent of cigarette smoke clung to his tan leather jacket. He was handsome, but not in the same lean and dangerously rugged way as Nick. More like Steven, with his boy-next-door good looks and a slight softening around the middle. He didn't look like someone who'd been undergoing cancer treatments. "I thought you were on leave," I said delicately.

"You must be thinking of Charlie. No," he said, his smile turning down at the edges. "Charlie's not back to work yet, but we're all pulling for him. I'm Nick's new partner. And you must be the infamous Finlay Donovan." Joey's astute cop eyes skimmed over me the same way my sister's often did, like a lint roller picking up the little things others never bothered to notice. He chuckled quietly, sliding the toothpick to the other side of his mouth. "Even if Nick wasn't staring at me like he'd like to take off my head for speaking to you right now, I'd still be able to pick you out of a crowd. He talks about you all the damn time."

The class erupted in applause, signaling the end of Nick's presentation. He glanced our way, a warning to Joey in the sharp edge of his smile. Joey nudged me with his elbow. "See what I mean? He's worried I'm spilling all his humiliating secrets."

"What's he afraid you might say?"

Joey leaned close to my ear as a line of parents funneled out of the room. "That I'm shitty company on a stakeout and he had a lot more fun with you."

Blood rushed to my cheeks as Delia took Nick's hand, dragging him toward me through the crowd. When they reached us, she threw her arms around his legs, her whispered "thank you" making my heart flutter.

A loaded silence fell between the two of us as she raced off to collect her backpack from her cubby. This close, he seemed taller than I remembered, thanks to the extra inch or two in his boots and the way my daughter had looked at him just now, elevating him to something more than human.

The dimple in his cheek made a slow appearance, as if he knew. "It's good to see you, Finlay."

"You, too." I hitched my bag higher on my shoulder,

trying not to stare at the way his uniform hugged his frame, but I was eye level with his chest. Averting my eyes only managed to land them on one of his equally impressive biceps. And lowering them was . . . definitely out of the question. I looked up at him through my lashes, my breath catching on the soft curl of his smile. "Thanks for doing this. You really didn't have to."

He nodded toward the line of cubbies down the hall, where Delia was shrugging on her coat. "I was glad to. She's a great kid." It was generous of him to say so after she'd called him an asshole a month ago, repeating her father's low opinion of Nick after Delia told him we were dating. Which we weren't. Not technically. Not unless you counted making out like jackrabbits in the front seat of his cruiser during a stakeout.

My neck grew slightly sweaty at the memory.

Nick's blush suggested maybe he was remembering the same thing.

Joey slapped a hand on Nick's shoulder. "I'm going outside to grab a smoke. I'll wait for you in the car." He smiled at me around his toothpick. "Nice to finally meet you, Finlay. Don't be too tough on him, huh?" With a wink, he melted into the crowd.

I waited through a series of awkward pauses as a few of the fathers who'd been Career Day guests stopped to shake Nick's hand. Some of the moms patted his arm, their fingers resting a moment too long on his biceps as they thanked him for coming.

"You really were great in there," I said when his line of fans had finally dwindled. "It meant a lot to Delia. I'm grateful."

He tipped his head. "Grateful enough to let me call you sometime?"

I glanced at the cluster of moms by the cubbies who were pretending not to eavesdrop as they wrangled their children into coats.

"Sorry, that was out of line," he said, turning his back to them. "I just thought maybe we could catch up." He fidgeted with his helmet, palming it in the broad stretch of his hand. A hand that had felt really good cupping my backside in his car a month ago. "You could call it research, if you want. You know, ask me questions about your book." Nick looked around and lowered his voice. "I read that one you signed for Pete in the lab. He let me borrow it under threat of bodily harm if I didn't return it. It was pretty good."

I struggled to remember which of my novels the young forensic tech had asked me to sign. A vision of the half-nude cover model hit me, and I nearly swallowed my tongue as I remembered a few of the scenes in the book. "Oh, god. You read that?"

Amusement simmered in the low heat of his smile. "Georgia says you're working on a new one. I'd love to hear about it."

"I don't know if that's a good idea. I'm sort of—" A kid stumbled into the back of Nick's legs, knocking him a step closer to me. The enticing aromas of coffee and spearmint tangled with the spice of his aftershave. If I closed my eyes, I'd probably smell the upholstery of his car. My mouth went dry. "Sure. Okay."

His dark eyes lit as he backed toward the exit, navigating the crowded hall without tearing his gaze from me. Or maybe people just naturally parted for him. "Tell Delia I had fun today. I'll call you." He sank his teeth into his lip to hide his grin as he turned and slipped out the door.

CHAPTER 10

My breath came back to me in a rush. What had I done? Had I seriously just agreed to go to dinner with Nick? When he called—*if* he called—I would just have to explain that I'd made a mistake. Clearly, I'd been impaired when I'd made that decision. I couldn't possibly be expected to think straight when he'd been standing so close.

I turned for Delia's cubby, the hair on the back of my neck rising when I spotted a woman crouching beside my daughter. Her straight blond hair curtained her face, but I was sure she wasn't a teacher at the school, and she didn't resemble any of the moms I knew in passing. I maneuvered toward them, stepping around the last of the lingering children, picking up my pace as I caught a glimpse of a cell phone held between them. They both waved to someone on the screen.

"What's going on here?" The woman jerked upright, her hand landing protectively on Delia's as she spun around. She lowered her phone and pressed it to her thigh.

But not before I recognized the face on the screen.

"Hello?" Theresa's voice grew impatient, muffled by the woman's leg. "I can't see anything, Aimee. Are you even there? I told you, I don't care about some stupid

Career Day." A heavy sigh burst from the phone. "If you can hear me, just come over. *General Hospital* starts in an hour and I need you to stop by Harris Teeter; we're out of Ben and Jerry's—"

Theresa's best friend, Aimee Reynolds, stared back at me, wide-eyed and guilty as she thumbed off her phone. I reached for my daughter and gently pulled her to me.

Delia bounced, tugging on my pants. "Mommy! Aunt Aimee came to see me!"

"Um, hi, Finlay," she said, tucking away her phone and extending her hand. "I'm—"

"I know who you are." I'd seen Aimee before. I'd watched from a distance while Vero had confronted her at a makeup counter in the mall. Aimee and Theresa had been sorority sisters, inseparable since college. Photos of them, arm in arm, were framed in Theresa's office and on the walls of her house.

She withdrew her hand when I didn't take it. "You're probably wondering what I'm doing here. It's just . . ." She glanced down at Delia and lowered her voice. "I haven't seen the kids since . . . you know." Delia's head tipped up, her blue eyes curious.

"Sweetie," I said to Delia, "why don't you use the bathroom before we go?"

Aimee gave her a reassuring smile. "Don't worry. I'll be here when you get back." She bit her lip as Delia skipped off down the hall, her eyes pleading with me as if suddenly she wasn't sure. "I'm sorry, Finlay. I know I should have asked if it was okay to come, but I haven't seen the kids in a month. Not since Theresa was arrested."

"Theresa and Steven aren't engaged anymore. She isn't their—"

"I *know* who Theresa is," Aimee said, her voice sharpening. "I was the one she called from a restaurant bathroom, crying and covered in soup. I was the one who brought her a towel and washed French onion out of her hair."

"I'd just found out she'd been sleeping with my husband!"

"And it was my SUV she borrowed when her car was in the shop because *you* decided to retaliate by stuffing Play-Doh up her tailpipe!" She drew a steadying breath, lowering her raised voice. "Don't make her out to be the only bad guy in that story. When it involves lying and cheating, there are always two."

"Regardless of my feelings toward Theresa, her relationship with Steven is over. She has zero reasons to talk with my children, even through the phone. Neither do you."

Aimee's eyes shimmered, her voice unsteady when she spoke. "I don't know if Steven told you, but I used to see them every weekend. I used to take them to the park. Delia and I would give each other manicures and make cookies. And I just . . ." A tear fell, and she scraped it from her cheek. "I just miss them. My husband and I . . . we don't have kids of our own. He never really wanted them, and Delia's so great. We had a lot of fun together." She sniffled. "I know this all probably sounds silly to you."

I hated that it didn't.

"Look," she added quickly as I opened my mouth to ask her to leave, "I know you and Theresa don't get along, and I don't blame you. What happened between her and Steven must have hurt, and I wouldn't be surprised if you hate me because of it. I mean, I get it; she's my best friend. But no matter how badly she screwed up, she always will be. We share everything. Or at least we did, until this whole mess with Feliks." Aimee shuddered. "Steven's still pissed at me. He hasn't returned my calls since I saw him at the jail that night. He blames me for not telling him that Feliks and Theresa were involved, but Theresa didn't tell me everything . . . at least, not about that." She flushed with guilt as her eyes lifted to mine. "What he's doing—cutting me off from Delia and Zach because he's mad at her—it's not fair. I had to see them one last time. It didn't feel right, disappearing from their lives. All I wanted to do was say goodbye." She released a long, shaky breath and wiped her eyes. "Is Zach here?" she asked, peeking around me.

"He's with his babysitter today." I registered her quiet flinch. I was still struggling to process this new version of her. Not Theresa's sorority sister Aimee, the woman my husband's lover had confided in while he'd been cheating on me, but my children's *Aunt* Aimee. The woman who had babysat them on Sundays and polished Delia's nails. The woman who showed up at Career Day, even though Theresa couldn't be bothered to care.

A sad smile bloomed on Aimee's face as Delia emerged from the bathroom.

"Come on, Delia." I scooped her backpack from the floor. "It's time to go. Say goodbye to Aunt Aimee."

Aimee gave me a small nod, letting me know she understood. She took Delia's hand, watching me askance as we walked to the parking lot with Delia between us. Aimee's eyes squeezed shut when we got to the van, a tear slipping free as she hugged Delia tight. She gave my daughter one last kiss on the cheek, her pain palpable as Delia climbed into her car seat.

After an awkward silence, Aimee and I settled on a handshake. Her lower lip quivered. "Will you tell Zach I said goodbye?"

Something inside me broke at the anguish in her voice. Even if Zach was too young to understand or care, I didn't want to be the one to deliver that message. Delia twisted in her car seat, watching us through the window. I cleared a lump of emotion from my throat. "You said you and Theresa used to tell each other everything. Do you still?"

Aimee frowned. "What do you mean?"

"If you're willing not to say anything to Theresa—no more video calls, no meetups with her, or trips to her home—then I won't tell Steven I invited you to visit the kids."

Aimee's eyes snapped to mine, clearly wrestling with the wrongness of what I'd just asked of her; it was like asking me to keep a secret from Vero. Honestly, I wasn't sure I could. But keeping Theresa out of the children's lives was a point I wasn't willing to budge on. "I can do that," she said after a tense pause. "I'm off work this coming Saturday. I could come over then, if it's okay with you."

Steven had been firm about spending the weekend with the children. But after what I'd just seen on the forum, I had no intention of letting that happen. Aimee might not be my favorite person, but it was obvious she loved my children. They'd be far safer with her than with Steven.

I opened a new contact and handed her my phone. "Saturday will be fine."

CHAPTER 11

Never go back to the scene of a crime. It's simple common sense if you want to get away with murder. Right up there with don't wrap a corpse in your shower curtain, don't buy four gallons of bleach and a shovel with your credit card, and don't keep a chest freezer in your garage. Why Vero had insisted on returning to the mall that afternoon was a mystery, even to me. And yet, that's exactly where we found ourselves at four o'clock.

We wove between the crowds of shoppers, cutting through the long tail of the line of families waiting to have their pictures taken with Santa. The children's play area behind Santa's workshop was packed with frazzled childcare workers and shrieking toddlers. After we checked the kids in, signed the release forms, and left the attendant our phone numbers, Vero dragged me to a distant corner of the mall, where she pulled me into a computer repair shop.

"What are we doing here?" I asked.

"Just trust me."

The kid behind the counter couldn't have been out of high school. He hunched on a stool, his elbow perched beside the register, his head resting in the cradle of his hand and a name badge pinned to the front of his graphic T. He studied his phone through a mop of tangled hair as shrill guitar riffs ripped from a speaker behind him.

Vero knocked on the counter. "Hello?"

The kid looked up, confused, as if he wasn't sure what day it was or how he'd gotten there. The stool creaked under him as he reached to turn down the volume, exposing a roll of his preternaturally white belly. "Can I help you?"

"We'd like to talk to someone in your Geek Squad . . ." Vero tipped her head to read his name badge. "Derek."

He grimaced, turning the stereo back up. "Try down the street at Best Buy."

"Believe me, I'd love nothing better than to be anywhere else," Vero said over the music, "but our kids are in the play area and we can't leave the mall." His heavy-lidded eyes lifted from his phone, sliding from Vero to me before dropping back to the screen. Vero knocked harder on the counter. "Hello! I said I'm having an issue and I need tech support. Do you have anyone here who knows what they're doing?"

One eyebrow might have raised a little, as if it couldn't be bothered to drag itself any higher. "What's the issue?"

"It's a security problem."

He lowered the music with a heavy sigh. "I'll need to see the device."

Vero studied him down the length of her nose. "Why?"

"This isn't a self-help line, lady. You want me to fix your shit, you give me the device and pay by the hour." He held out a hand. There was a smear of chocolate on his thumb. I cringed as I drew my brand-new laptop from my bag and handed it over to him.

"You said it's a security problem?" he asked, opening my screen.

"More like a question," I began cautiously. "I was wondering . . . how secure is my laptop if I'm on an open Wi-Fi, like the one in the food court?"

His hands flew over the track pad. "Depends."

"On what?"

"What were you doing? Paying bills, sending emails, surfing for porn . . . ?" His disinterested gaze climbed to Vero's chest. By the look on his face, it hadn't been worth the effort.

I maneuvered between Vero and the counter before she decided to smash my laptop over his head. "Let's say I was on a chat board, and I posted a message anonymously. Would someone be able to trace that message back to this computer?"

He shrugged. "Some rando in the seat next to you? Probably not. Someone who knows what they're doing? Maybe."

"Let's assume it's someone who knows what they're doing. How long would it take them to trace that post back to me?"

"Don't know," he said as he clicked through my device. Derek barely had time to pull back his hands before Vero reached across the counter and slammed my laptop closed. He shook out a fingertip, glaring at her. "It's not a simple question, lady! The answer depends on a lot of things."

"What things?" she asked.

He huffed, as if the answers should be obvious. "I don't know. Like, a lot of things: the browser, the network, the website, how your computer is registered . . ."

"Is there a way to keep someone from finding out it was me?"

"Look," he said, raising his hands, "I'm just a hardware guy. You'd need to talk to someone who knows networking and shit."

"Is there someone like that here?" I asked. "Someone who could . . . you know . . . make a problem like this go away?"

Derek looked back and forth between us, his gaze lingering on Vero's designer sunglasses, then to the Charger logo on the fancy key fob dangling from her knockoff Prada purse. His pudgy index finger absently traced the Apple insignia on the cover of my laptop as he darted a glance at the EMPLOYEES ONLY door behind him and lowered his voice. "I *might* know a guy." He fished a worn leather wallet on a chain from his back pocket, retrieving a business card from its folds. He pushed it across the counter. There was no name on either side when I turned it over. Just a phone number on plain white card stock. "Ask for Cam."

Vero studied her nails and muttered, "Is he twelve, too?"

I shot her a look. "She means, is he any good?"

Derek glanced once more to the door behind him, then rested his elbows on the counter and whispered, "Last year, I got catfished by some chick online. She talked me into sending her a dick pic." Vero made a gagging sound, and I stepped hard on her toe. "This chick posted it on a bunch of sites," he continued. "She thought she'd covered her tracks, but Cam found her in less than an hour. He hacked into her accounts and pulled down all the pics before too many people saw my junk." The kid nodded, a hushed reverence in his voice when he said, "Yeah, he's good."

Vero didn't look convinced, but I didn't care how old Cam was. *Good* was what I needed right now.

Derek held out a hand. "That'll be forty bucks."

"Forty?" Vero tore off her sunglasses, her eyes bugging out of her head. "Are you kidding?"

I pulled my credit card from my wallet, eager to get my computer back and leave.

"Sorry," he said. "Card reader's down. Cash only."

"You're a *tech repair* shop! How is your card reader down?" Vero tacked on a few expletives as I scraped two twenties from the bottom of the diaper bag. The kid took them without offering a receipt. "Let me guess," she deadpanned. "Your printer's down, too. Help desk, my ass," she grumbled.

Derek smirked and stuffed the bills in his pocket. "Good luck," he said as he dumped the laptop in my hands.

My answering laugh was wry. Luck and I? We didn't exactly have the best track record.

I tucked Cam's card in my pocket, hoping he was lucky enough for both of us.

CHAPTER 12

Vero wrestled the key into the lock to Ramón's garage, her breath billowing out in quick bursts around her quiet swears when the key stuck. With a final wrench, we tumbled inside, rubbing our arms against the cold night air. My sister had agreed to keep Delia and Zach for the night, payback for sending Nick to Career Day. I could think of a million other things I'd rather be doing on my child-free night, most of them involving Julian and body heat under a pile of warm blankets, but he was still incommunicado on a hot beach in Florida, and I was freezing my ass off with Vero in an empty garage.

She snapped on a light in the waiting room. It was as stark and uninviting as I remembered—a handful of plastic chairs around a low, wobbly table and fluorescent lights framed in a ceiling of yellowing dropped tiles. Ramón's shop had closed two hours ago, but Vero had a copy of his key and insisted her cousin wouldn't mind if we used it after hours; I had no intention of inviting a mysterious hacker to my house.

Vero rubbed her arms, making a beeline for the thermostat. A moment later, the heat clicked on, the smell of propane sifting through the duct above my head, the memories it stirred making me shudder.

I gasped and clutched my chest when a notification pinged on my phone.

"Someone's a little jumpy," Vero said, rubbing her hands together for warmth.

"Can you blame me?" The last time I'd been in this room, Feliks Zhirov's goon had pressed a knife to my throat and forced me into an interrogation with his boss. I'd avoided the garage since. I tapped my screen, hoping to find a pleasantly distracting message from Julian, but it was only a text from Aimee, thanking me for letting her spend time with the kids and confirming that she'd come by the house on Saturday.

A car door slammed outside. Knuckles rapped against the front window. I tucked away my phone and opened the door, frowning at the lanky teenage boy waiting on the step under the security light. Oily blond bangs swept over his eyes. He shook them aside to glare at me.

"You want to take a picture or something?" His hands were tucked into the pockets of an old army jacket that had been inked all over in Sharpie, the name above the breast pocket completely blacked out.

"You must be Cam?" I asked, hoping I was wrong.

"And you must be a genius. You gonna let me in?"

"Right." I stepped aside. His light eyes raked over the hot rod magazines, the water cooler, and the shadowy hall that led to Ramón's office before he came inside.

"We alone?" he asked. He didn't give off any threatening vibes. If anything, he seemed jumpier than I did, careful to leave a few feet between us as he scanned his surroundings.

The heels of Vero's boots clicked down the hall toward us and Cam inched back a step. "She's a friend," I said.

Vero came to an abrupt halt in front of him, hands

planted on her hips, her long ponytail tipped to one side. "*This* is Cam? He's a freaking kid."

Cam gestured between us. "You two must be in Mensa together."

I shot Vero a look, warning her not to say whatever was about to fly out of her mouth. "We can talk in the office," I suggested.

"I'll talk here." The metal legs of a chair screeched as Cam dragged it a short distance from the others before sitting down. He slouched in his seat, the outline of his tight fists clear against the inside of his pockets. Vero and I sat across the low melamine table from him.

"You got my number from the shop?"

"The one in the mall," I clarified. "The young man working behind the counter said you helped him with a rather sensitive privacy issue. I'm hoping you can help me with more of a security problem."

Cam sucked a tooth, watching us from under his bangs. He leaned back, legs outstretched and crossed at the ankles. "I get two hundred for the house call, plus fifty per hour. Hardware and software installs cost an extra hundred per hour, plus parts."

Vero's jaw fell open. I thought she might come out of her chair. "Two hundred dollars just to show up?"

"Two fifty," he corrected her. "Your hour started three minutes ago."

"That's some first-class, grade A bull—"

I slapped a hand over Vero's lap, holding her down. "That's fine. I have cash." I just needed this problem to go away. I dug in my purse for his two hundred and fifty dollars and reached across the table, crumpling it into his hand.

He stuffed the money in the front pocket of his jeans. Arms crossed, he looked down his nose at me. "What kind of security problem?"

"There's a forum," I explained. "A message board I read sometimes. I don't normally post there, but—"

"Is it private?" he cut in. "You log in to it with a password?"

"Yes. But I made an anonymous username."

"Tied to your real email address?"

"No, I used a dummy account."

He tipped his head. "Where were you when you set up the dummy email account?"

"The public library."

Cam nodded once, like I'd passed some kind of test. "Ever log in to that dummy email account at home?"

"Never." I'd only ever used that email account once, the day I set it up. I'd created it for the sole purpose of joining this specific forum to spy on *FedUp*.

"How about at work?"

I shook my head, not bothering to explain that my home and work were the same place. I hadn't even given Cam my name, reluctant to share any personal information with him. And to his credit, he hadn't asked.

He watched me, his hitched thumbs tapping against his chest. "So what's the problem?"

I glanced at Vero. Her jaw was locked tight, her pursed lips scowling as she picked the polish off a long pink fingernail. Her shoulder bobbed once.

"Earlier this week," I explained, "I logged in to the forum while I was at the mall, on the open Wi-Fi at the food court. I posted a reply to one of the threads. It contained information that was very . . . personal . . . and now I'm concerned that someone might be able to track that post back to me."

He raised an eyebrow, his critical gaze sliding over me, as if he were picturing me naked and wasn't impressed. "What browser were you using?"

"The one that came on my laptop . . . Safari, I think?"

He gave a slight shake of his head, as if that answer disappointed him. He jerked his chin toward the laptop bag beside my chair. "Where'd you get the device?"

"I ordered it online."

"New?"

"Refurbished."

"From the manufacturer?"

"No, from eBay."

His subtle nod suggested I had gained back some ground. "Did you register it?"

"No, I don't think so." The man I'd bought it from assured me he had wiped it of all his old files. He had given me a password to get past the lock screen, and I hadn't gone through the hassle of changing it. But something told me that confessing this wouldn't win me any points with Cam. "I think it's still registered to the person who owned it before."

"You're good." Cam unfolded his arms and pushed out of his chair.

"Wait," I sputtered, shooting to my feet. "That's it? I'm good? What does that mean? You didn't even look at my computer."

He shrugged. "Crowded mall. Open Wi-Fi. Anonymous account. No log-ins to the email account that could be tied back to your home or office. You're clean," he said, jamming his hands in his pockets. "Don't post or check that email from anywhere that can be traced back to you, and you're golden."

"You charged two hundred fifty dollars for 'don't check that account from home'?" Vero's laugh was harsh. "I could have Googled that!"

"Fine, you want your money's worth? Here's some advice. Don't post nudes from the goddamn food court. And if you want to stay off the radar, then next time you're at the library or whatever, download a dark web browser so you won't get caught doing it. Use it when you're posting *personal* shit you don't want tracked."

"This dark web browser," I asked, blocking his exit, "can it hide me from professional hackers?" Like the cyber forensic guys Georgia drank with on Thursday nights. The ones that busted kiddie porn rings, local terrorist cells, and big-time internet scammers. I was pretty sure it would take them all of two seconds to find me.

"As long as you don't do anything stupid."

"*That* doesn't bode well," Vero muttered.

A car horn beeped outside. "That's my ride. Pleasure doing business with you."

"Wait," I said as Cam reached for the door. If he knew how to keep people from tracking me, maybe he knew how to track someone else. "If I give you an email address, would you be able to figure out who the account belongs to?"

He shrugged. "It'll be another fifty for a search."

Vero grabbed my hand as I reached in my purse. "What the hell are you doing? You think money grows on trees?"

"What's wrong with you?" I hissed. She'd been acting strangely about money, ever since she came home from her weekend with Ramón.

The car's horn blared outside. A muscle clenched in Vero's jaw.

"Look, ladies. If you hold on to that fifty any longer, I'm going to have to start charging you interest."

Vero let go of my hand, swearing quietly when Cam took the cash. I shuffled through the piles of magazines and found a chewed-up ballpoint pen. Tearing the edge off the cover of an issue of *Sports Illustrated,* I scribbled *FedUp*'s email address on it and handed it to him.

"How long will it take?" I asked.

"Depends," he said, slipping it in his pocket. "I'll be

in touch." The bells jangled as the door closed behind him.

Vero shook her head. "I don't trust that little shit."

The worst part was, neither did I.

CHAPTER 13

Later that night, Vero and I sat on the carpet in the living room, a bowl of popcorn between us and a mountain of Christmas lights piled around us on the floor. The house was blissfully quiet, and I hated to admit it, but the tree Steven had brought was rather lovely, filling the room with fresh pine smells. Vero had brought up the dusty Christmas boxes from the basement and was working through the tangles in the glittering green ropes. Earlier, she'd propped the tree in a stand, perching on a chair to trim the tall tips. She had a way of getting things to fit—of quietly smoothing down edges to make our prickly, disorganized life work.

I frowned at the three stockings she'd hung on the mantel. I didn't care what Steven said. Vero and I might not have known each other for long, or even very well, when she'd stumbled into the garage and helped me bury a body, but she was family now. I made a mental note to stop at the mall this week to purchase an extra stocking.

"Has she posted yet?" Vero asked as she bent over her work, lights strewn over her arms.

I checked my phone again. "Not yet."

We'd spent the last few hours Googling the dark web browsers Cam had recommended, figuring out how to download them to each of our laptops and phones. After that, we'd logged in to the women's forum to see if *FedUp* had responded, but there had been no activity on the thread since I'd posted my offer at the food court. A single direct message had been waiting in my inbox—two words from *EasyClean: Back off.*

"You seem tense," Vero said as I snapped the cap off one of Delia's magic markers.

"Of course I'm tense. What if *FedUp* hasn't written back to me because she's already hired *EasyClean*?"

"Doubt it. *EasyClean* wouldn't waste time messaging you if she knew she had the job. She's just trying to scare you off. You sure that's all that's bugging you?"

"What else would be bugging me?" I tested a marker against the long sheet of art paper I'd unspooled across the carpet. It was dried out.

"Heard from Julian yet?"

"No." I ground my teeth as the nub of the marker tore through the paper. Five days had passed since he'd left for Florida, and still not a peep. "He said he'd text when he gets home."

"When's that?"

"I didn't ask." Vero raised an eyebrow. "What? I'm not his mother. I'm his . . ." Hell, I didn't know what I was to Julian. "And don't you dare make any more wisecracks about my age."

She shoved a handful of popcorn in her smug, grinning mouth. "So are you going to go out with Nick?" she asked, wagging her eyebrows.

I'd made the mistake of telling Vero about Nick's casual invitation to catch up sometime. Ever since, she'd been hovering over my cell phone, waiting for him to call. Although, if I was being honest with myself, I might have been hovering a little more than usual, too. I wasn't entirely sure if I was checking for texts from

Julian or from Nick. Or which of those two possibili-
ties I was more anxious about.

"I'm pretty sure catching up with Nick would be a
mistake."

"I disagree. I think your editor's onto something.
Who's going to keep your heroine company while her
attorney is missing? A second love interest would definitely spice things up."

My phone pinged. Vero dove for it, her hand closing
around it before mine could, her body twisting away
from me as she punched in my passcode. Her eyes
bugged wide.

"Daaaaaaamn!" she breathed, holding my phone out
of reach as I lunged for it. "Who do I have to kill to
get forty percent of that?" My stomach did a strange
little flip when I saw Julian on the screen. I grabbed
the phone from her and fell back against the side of the
couch, my mouth going dry as I stared at Julian's selfie.
Sand peppered his shoulders. His rose-gold chest was
slick with seawater and sweat, and the low waistband
of his board shorts revealed a tantalizing sliver of the
taut pale skin underneath, probably just to torture me.

*Wish you were here. Home in a few days. Will text
when I'm back.* His sun-bleached curls were wild, his
smile roguish.

I glanced down at my sweats and smoothed down
my mom-bun. At least I was wearing pants. Still, I was
pretty sure any selfie I took right now would pale in
comparison. For a second, I considered the possibility
that a selfie without pants might be a more equitable
response. But then I remembered what Cam had said
in the garage about not doing anything stupid online,
and I was pretty sure texting nudes to Julian would fall
squarely in that category.

I settled on a flame emoji and typed, *Can't wait. See
you soon.*

Ignoring Vero's smirk, I saved the image to my camera roll, shamelessly wondering if the resolution was high enough to make it a screen saver on my laptop.

"We should check his Instagram. I bet there'll be more," Vero suggested.

I locked my phone and set it facedown behind me. "No, we shouldn't. That would be creepy and wrong."

"Don't even tell me you're not curious."

"If you're so curious, check them from *your* phone."

"*I* don't have an account," she reminded me, reaching around me and plucking my phone off the floor.

"Why not?" I asked. It had always seemed strange to me that someone as stunning and fashionable as Vero wouldn't have a single social media account. I was pretty sure if she posted a selfie now, even in her flannel pajamas, she'd have a thousand followers within an hour.

"Because I don't need the whole world knowing my business."

"What about your friends?"

"You and Ramón know where to find me." Her brow furrowed as she typed in my password and scrolled around. "Huh," she said, frowning at the screen. "Julian's account is set to *private*."

"No, it's not. I was just on it a few days ago."

"I thought you said it was creepy and wrong."

"Give me that." I took the phone, surprised to see Vero was right. With the exception of his thumbnail pic and a one-line bio, Julian's account was locked. "That's strange. Why would he change his settings now?"

Vero's eyes crinkled with sympathy, as if the answer should have been obvious. Julian was on a road trip with his friends, drinking and cutting loose at the beach. And I was here, stalking my ex and buying batteries for power tools.

"Whatever. I have more important things to worry

about." Ignoring the ache in my throat, I tossed my phone on the carpet and picked up a marker, determined not to think about Julian or what he was doing. "Like this *EasyClean* person and what she plans to do to my ex-husband."

I snapped off the cap and wrote Steven's name in angry red letters across the top of the long sheet of paper between us. Beside it, I wrote a date: October 29. Below that, I drew two vertical lines, dividing the paper into three sections.

"What are you doing?" Vero asked around a mouthful of popcorn.

"What I should have done a month ago. I'm going to figure out who *FedUp* is and find a way to stop her."

"How are you going to do that?"

"The same way I write a story."

"Not showering for days while you hoover gummy bears in your pajamas and swear at your laptop?"

"No," I said irritably, "I'm plotting Steven's murder."

"Thank you, baby Jesus, it's about damn time."

Vero ducked, giggling as I threw the marker at her head. "Not literally. I'm making a list of everyone Steven's managed to piss off. Then I'll figure out which one of them has the strongest motive to kill him."

Vero's laughter quieted as she surveyed the length of paper. "I hate to break it to you, Finn, but you're going to need another roll."

"We have to start somewhere." I labeled the three sections. "People usually murder for one of three reasons: love, money, or revenge." Under the revenge section, I wrote Theresa's name. "*FedUp* first posted about Steven on October 29, two days after Theresa was arrested." Steven and Theresa's relationship had already been on shaky ground, but according to Georgia, they'd had a nasty fight in the police station and Steven had called off the engagement the night she was booked. The next morning, Steven had moved out of her house, taken back her two-carat engagement ring, and withdrawn his money from their joint checking accounts.

Vero shook her head, chewing thoughtfully on a popcorn kernel as she worked through a tangle in the lights. "There's no way Theresa could have written that post. She was still in jail."

Vero had a point. Aimee had posted bail, but that had taken days. Theresa wouldn't have had unfettered access to a computer while in custody or, for that matter, enough privacy and time to pull it off.

Vero jutted her chin at my chart. "Who else do you have?"

"As far as spurned lovers? The only one I know of is Bree."

Vero glanced up from her Christmas lights, wrinkling her nose as I wrote Bree's name under the "love" column. "Why would Bree want to kill Steven? I thought she was crazy about him."

"I'm sure she was. Right up until he laid her off. Steven said he lost some big clients after news of the murder investigation broke, and he had to cut back on payroll. He let her go a few weeks ago."

Vero tipped her head as if she was working out the math. "The timing doesn't add up. The news broke on Monday night. The ad was posted on the women's forum two days later. Even if his clients started bailing right away, he wouldn't have laid Bree off that fast; he's too selfish for that. He would have needed her to field all the phone calls while he dealt with the police. And where's someone like Bree going to get her hands on a hundred Gs? There's no way a twenty-year-old office assistant could afford to pay someone like *EasyClean*. No," Vero said, shaking her head as she tapped a long nail against the second column on the paper. "Follow the money. It always comes down to money. Who stands to benefit if Steven drops dead?"

"The kids are the beneficiaries on his life insurance accounts."

Vero chuckled darkly. "That makes you suspect number one in column two. Think hard. Who else?"

"Steven didn't have any other assets. Every penny he had went into the farm."

My phone chimed. Vero dove to grab it before I could stop her. "Ooooh, I bet it's Nick," she said with a wicked grin. Her face fell as she thumbed on the screen.

"What's wrong?" I asked. "Who is it?"

"*FedUp* . . . she posted a reply on the thread."

I scooted close, reading over her shoulder.

FedUp: *@EasyClean and @Anonymous2, Thank you for your replies. You're both very kind to offer, and I am interested in chatting with either of you, but it's a stressful time of year. There's so much to do before Christmas, and so few days left to handle it all. I'm sure you understand. Perhaps we can connect after it's over? When you've wrapped up your holiday plans, I hope one of you will send me another message.*

Vero frowned at the screen. "*I am interested in chatting with either of you . . .* ? What's that supposed to mean?"

I reread the post. *There's so much to do before Christmas, and so few days left to handle it all.* "I think she's hiring us both. Whoever handles Steven gets the money." *FedUp* was increasing the stakes, winner takes all. Then adding a ticking clock by giving us a deadline. "She wants it done by Christmas."

"That's more than three weeks away."

A new post appeared at the bottom of the thread.

EasyClean: @FedUp, I completely understand that time is of the essence. My preparations are already under way. You'll hear from me soon.

Vero was right. Money was the biggest motivator of all. And if *EasyClean* thought she had a lot of money to lose, I had no doubt she'd work quickly. Which meant I had to be quicker. I had to figure out *FedUp*'s true identity and persuade her to call off the job.

Snapping the cap back on the marker, I considered the possible plotlines unfolding in front of me.

Three motives.

Three directions the story could go.

But only one setting they all had in common.

I rolled up the paper and got to my feet. "Get dressed. We're going to the farm."

CHAPTER 14

The last time Vero and I had driven this dirt road in the dark, we had three thousand feet of Cling Wrap, a flashlight, and a shovel in the trunk, along with a solid plan for moving a decomposing body. This time, I didn't feel nearly as prepared.

"Give me your credit card," Vero whispered. We'd parked her Charger in the shadows behind Steven's trailer before we'd realized we had no way of getting in.

"Why my credit card? Why can't you use one of yours?"

"I don't have one." She reached back, her hand open and waiting as I dug out my American Express card. I slapped it into her palm, angling my phone's flashlight closer to the lock as she wedged the card between the door and the frame.

"Are you sure you know what you're doing?"

"Of course I know what I'm doing. I saw it on YouTu—" The credit card snapped. Vero extracted what was left of it and held it up to the light.

I yanked it from her hand and jammed it back in my coat pocket. "There's got to be another way in."

"Short of busting a window?"

We'd already tried all the locks and the set of keys we'd found tucked in the visor of the run-down Ford

Steven used as a farm truck. I knelt in the mulch by the door, shining my light over the mums and winter cabbages, searching for the missing piece of my credit card. This was pointless, maybe we should just . . .

My light glinted off the metal nozzle of a hose bib.

"What are you doing?" Vero asked as I stared at the front of the trailer, my light making a slow pass over the siding and trim. Steven had to have a key hidden out here somewhere; he always did. My ex-husband was no Boy Scout, but he was always prepared. His uncanny planning and organizational skills were how he managed to live with one woman while sleeping with another, sliding in and out of doors unnoticed. He always had an exit strategy.

And he always had a key.

My light landed on a concrete splash block under a downspout at the far corner of the trailer. When I lifted the edge, a glint of silver winked back at me from a depression in the mulch. "Thank you, Mrs. Haggerty," I whispered. Vero raised an eyebrow as I wiped the key on my jeans. "Steven used to leave a key outside our house for Theresa when they were having an affair," I explained as I slipped it in the lock. "Mrs. Haggerty saw her sneaking it from the splash block under our drain. He's a creature of habit."

"He's a sleazeball is what he is."

I stepped inside the darkened trailer. Vero bumped into my back as I froze beside a flashing red light on a keypad on the wall. "What's that?" she asked as the red light and I blinked at each other.

"A security system."

"You said he didn't have a security system."

My stomach took a nosedive as the light blinked faster. "Apparently, he has one now."

"What do we do?" she asked, her popcorn breath hot on the back of my neck.

"We need a code to disarm it."

"What's the code?"

"How the hell do I know?"

"You knew where he kept the key!"

"That was different! We never had a security system in the house."

"Did Theresa have one at her place?"

"No. Steven hated them." Probably because they made it too hard to come and go without being tracked.

"Okay, think," Vero said, pushing me toward the panel. "The codes for these things are usually four digits, right? What number would Steven pick?"

"I don't know," I sputtered as the red light sped up.

"Try the code to your garage door."

I punched in the four-digit code to the garage door. The panel stopped flashing.

"Did it work?" Vero whispered. The only sound was the tick of the clock on the wall and the thermostat clicking on.

"I think so," I said through a shaky exhale. I closed the door behind us. With my phone light held aloft, I cut a swath through the shadows to Bree's old desk and switched on her lamp. The soft glow of the bulb felt brighter than it was, and I hoped no one could see it from the road. "Let's get what we came for and get out of here. Steven's accounting books are probably in his office. See what you can find in his desk. I'll search the one out here for anything suspicious."

The hardwood planks creaked under Vero's feet as she crept down the hall. A lamp snapped on in Steven's office, and I heard the fast glide of file drawers and the frantic rustling of folders as Vero searched. I pulled aside Bree's desk chair, hurriedly opening and closing drawers, rummaging through them for anything personal she might have left behind . . . anything that might help me find her. If Steven had made any enemies through his work, his assistant was likely to know.

A message book sat open beside the phone, the kind with a spiral binding and perforated tear-away sheets that left duplicate copies on thin yellow film. I flipped through a few dozen messages, but none of them jumped out as odd. As I set the message book back in its place, I noticed a plastic file box marked TIME CARDS beside the phone.

I thumbed through the index cards where Steven's hourly employees clocked in and out of their shifts, pausing on the only woman's name in the box: Breanna Fuller. This had to be Bree.

I snapped a photo of the card with my phone, capturing her contact information and the times and dates of her most recent shifts. Her last day of work was a Saturday . . . October 26?

That couldn't be right.

That was the day Nick and I had come, pretending to shop for sod, when Bree had given us directions to the fescue field. The day *before* the police dug up the bodies. But Steven said he'd let her go *after* the news broke.

I turned over the card, but the back was empty. Her last day of work had been about a month ago. Steven had always been an excellent liar, but why bother lying about this?

The clock on the wall ticked. I stuffed the card back in the box and moved to a set of file drawers. A pile of personal items had been tucked inside, and I rifled through them. A pair of faux leather gloves, a collapsible umbrella, a tube of lip gloss, a bottle of sparkly blue nail polish . . . I paused, withdrawing a well-worn copy of a familiar romantic suspense novel—one of *my* novels. The edges of the book were stamped, property of the local public library. I flipped clumsily to the back cover and fished the library card from its sleeve. The book was weeks overdue. If these were Bree's things, why hadn't she come back for them? And of all the romantic suspense novels she could have checked out of the library, why had she chosen one of mine?

A photo slipped free of the book's pages. Bree's fresh face smiled back at me. Steven's arm was slung over her shoulder, the photo folded on either side of them so only the two of them were shown in the frame. I unfolded the sides, revealing the rest of the image. Another older man I didn't recognize stood to Bree's right, his arm around her waist. He was tall, a good ten or fifteen years older than Steven, with a strong jaw and handsome features, his light hair receding just enough from his temples to reveal tanned smile lines around amiable blue eyes. He looked familiar, maybe because he oozed the same unshakable confidence as my ex-husband. While he and Steven didn't necessarily look alike, there was an *alikeness* to them, and Bree looked radiantly happy bookended by their arms.

To Steven's other side, a thin middle-aged man with shaggy graying hair stood slightly apart, as if he'd been caught up in the pull of the other three and unwittingly captured in the moment. His close-lipped smile was tight, his face angled away, as if to downplay the large, dark mole high on his right cheek. While the blond man looked familiar for reasons I couldn't entirely place, I had no idea who this man might be. Whoever these men were, they were clearly important to both Bree and Steven.

I tucked the photo in my pocket as a shrill ring rattled the room.

I swung toward the phone on Bree's desk. The caller ID lit up: *Incoming call from Homesafe Security.*

"Finn? Are you seeing this?" Vero's voice was tense,

suggesting she was seeing the same thing I was on the phone on Steven's desk.

"It's the monitoring company. We have to answer it."

"Then they'll know we're here!"

"If we don't pick up, they send the cops!" The phone rang again. My heart pounded as I reached for it. I held it to my ear and covered the receiver, speaking through my fingers. "Hello?"

"This is Homesafe Security. We're responding to an alarm. With whom am I speaking?"

My panicked eyes scanned the desk, landing on the box of time cards as the woman waited for my answer. All the names in the box had belonged to men, except for one. I cleared my throat, adjusting the pitch of my voice to match Bree's bubbly lilt. "This is Bree. Bree Fuller. I'm the administrative assistant. Sorry to disturb you. I totally forgot my . . . umbrella."

Your umbrella? Seriously? Vero mouthed beside me.

"When I came back to get it, I forgot the alarm was set. But it's all fine here. Really. Nothing's wrong," I said through a nervous laugh.

"That's fine, Bree. I'll just need your verbal code word, authorizing us to void the alarm."

"My verbal code word?" I turned to Vero. Her eyes went wide.

"Ma'am, do you need me to send an officer to your location? Are you in distress?"

"Yes, I mean no!" I slapped a hand over my face. "No, I am not in distress. You absolutely do not need to send an officer here." Vero rushed to the window, peering through the blinds.

"Then I do need you to confirm the six-letter safe word to dismiss the alarm."

My tongue froze against the roof of my mouth. What safe word would Steven use? The silence dragged on as

I counted off letters. *Delia* was too short. *Theresa* was too long.

"Finlay!" Vero hissed. *Hang up the phone! We have to go!* she mouthed.

"Thank you," the woman said cheerily. "That's all I needed. I'll let dispatch know to cancel the request for a property check."

I stared at the phone as the monitoring service disconnected, still trying to piece together what had just happened. The only word that had been spoken, even faintly, was my name. But it had six letters.

Had my name been Steven's safe word?

"How much time do we have before the cops get here?" Vero asked, pulling me out of a daze.

"They're not coming," I said. She sagged against the wall and pressed a hand to her chest. "Did you find Steven's books?"

Vero held up her phone.

"Good. Let's get out of here."

CHAPTER 15

I switched off Bree's desk lamp, nearly tripping over Vero in the dark as I turned to go. She stood motionless beside the front window, staring down the long gravel road toward the entrance of the farm. A glare skated over the glass as headlights swung toward the trailer.

"Shit!" Vero ducked. "Is it Steven?"

I peered around her through the slats. "I don't think so." The lights were still too far away to know for sure, but they seemed too low to the ground to be Steven's pickup.

The beams cut through the glass, shining right at us. We dropped to the floor, our backs pressed to the wall under the window as shadows stretched across the room. I shut my eyes, listening to the steady, slow crunch of gravel under tires. Both of us gasped as the headlights extinguished and the trailer went black.

I twisted up onto my knees and peeked between the blinds. The dark outline of a sedan crept steadily closer.

"You think it's the cops?" Vero asked.

I swung back around, palms sweaty against the floor. The lady at the security company had said she would cancel the alarm, but maybe I hadn't given her the safe word fast enough. "They're probably just doing a quick check of the place. We parked behind the trailer. They can't see your car from the parking lot. If we're quiet, maybe they'll go."

"You think they saw the lights from the road?"

"I don't know." The car hadn't turned onto the gravel road until after I'd switched off the desk lamp, but the trees along the edge of the property were bare of leaves and the night was clear. It was anyone's guess what the police might have seen from the road if they'd been looking this way.

"Come on!" Vero said, grabbing my hand. "We'll jump out the back window."

"We can't leave! They're too close." Even if we did manage to make it to the car, they'd see our taillights if we tried to escape through the rear of the farm, the way we'd come. "Let's just stay calm. They might not even get out of their car. It's safer to stay hidden and wait until they're gone."

We pressed our backs to the wall as the car crawled to a stop in front of the trailer. I listened for the telltale squawk of a police radio through the thin window glass above our heads, but all I heard was the low purr of the engine as it idled.

A car door clicked open. A foot crunched down. Then another. Vero squeezed my hand as the footsteps grew closer, stopping right behind us. Vero made the sign of the cross, her mouth moving in prayer through an excruciating silence. We both gasped as a long, forceful stream of fluid spattered against the siding.

"Is he pissing?" Vero hissed. I clapped a hand over her mouth as the spatter waned to a slow dribble. A pause followed, broken by the familiar scrape of a cigarette lighter. Vero tore my fingers away from her face and whispered, "Is he seriously taking a smoke break now?"

I tipped my head back, eyes squeezed shut. It could

take him a full five minutes to finish that damn cigarette. And if he happened to walk around the trailer
while he did, he might spot Vero's car. Or worse, peer
inside the back windows and see us.

"Just stay still," I whispered, clutching her hand as
the lighter scraped again. "It's dark in here. He probably can't see any—"

The window shattered. We hit the floor as shards
rained over our heads and glass smashed against the opposite wall. The car's engine roared outside, its tires
spinning, the spray of gravel against the siding lost in a
sudden *whoosh*.

The room erupted in flames around us. I pushed up
on my knees, dragging Vero up beside me, coughing
as the air thickened with fumes. Black smoke poured
through the broken window. I waved it from my face in
time to catch the flash of taillights fishtailing onto the
road.

Vero tugged me toward the door. "We have to go!"

I turned back to the room. The fire was already
climbing the walls, its fingers curling over the arms of
the sofa, staining the ceiling black. I darted feverish
glances around the office, wondering what, if anything,
I could save. This trailer held everything Steven had
worked for, and it was going up in flames before my
eyes.

Vero grabbed me by my coat, shouting over the
crackle and hiss. "We have to get out of here, Finlay!
Now!"

The smoke chased us as we stumbled out of the
trailer. Vero rushed to get the car while I locked the door
behind us. My hands shook as I fought with the key, the
metal already hot. The Charger's engine growled to life,
the headlights painting eerie beams through the thick
pockets of smoke as it rounded the corner.

"Get in!" she shouted. I ran for the passenger side,

slamming the door as Vero made a tight turn and sped toward the back entrance of the farm, both of us breathing hard as bright yellow flames flickered through the smoke behind us. "What the hell just happened?"

"Someone firebombed Steven's office, that's what happened!" I gripped the dashboard as the Charger raced past the barren field Vero and I had dug up a month ago. The line of cedars at the rear of the property loomed ahead, and she slowed at the end of the gravel road, careful not to leave skid marks as she turned onto the asphalt.

The Charger picked up speed, hugging the winding road too tightly. Everything inside the car smelled like charcoal, and my throat grew tight around my swallow.

"Pull over," I said, bile threatening to rise as the car soared over another bump.

Vero's eyes narrowed on the curves ahead. "We can't stop here."

"I said, pull over!" My hands tightened on the passenger door. The tires squealed, kicking up smoke as the car skidded to a stop on the narrow shoulder. I flung open the door, heaving the meager contents of my stomach into the ditch.

When it was over, I rested my sweaty forehead on my smoke-blackened hands, my elbows braced on my knees and my butt perched on the edge of Vero's bucket seat, waiting for the feeling to pass as I remembered the way the flames had curled around the sofa.

"Steven slept on that couch," I said, my voice ragged with acid and smoke.

I could feel Vero's tension fill the car as she pieced together the bits I hadn't said. Steven had only moved into his new house a few days ago. Up until last week, Steven had been living in that trailer. Sleeping on that couch. The only address *FedUp* had shared in the post was for the farm. If *EasyClean* had staked Steven out before taking the job, like Vero suspected, she would have known he'd been sleeping in his office.

A tongue of orange flames licked the sky in the distance, clouds of black smoke smudging out the stars. I wondered if Steven's security system was tied to his smoke detectors. If it would alert the authorities in time for anything from his office to be spared, or if it would all burn to the ground before anyone reported the fire.

I wiped the last of the sickness from my mouth and shut the passenger door.

"Whoever *EasyClean* is, she wasn't exactly neat." Vero shook her head at the flames. "You and I would have done a much better job."

I raised an eyebrow at her soot-smeared face.

She held up her hands; they were as filthy as the rest of her. "I'm just saying, for one hundred grand, you expect a person to be professional. Thank you, by the way, for not puking in my car. See? Neat," she added, gesturing to me, as if my ability to avoid vomiting on her upholstery should be a bullet on my résumé. My dark laugh brought tears to my eyes, and I wiped them with my sleeve.

Vero put the car in gear and eased us back onto the road. "Did you get anything from Bree's desk?"

"I found her name and address on her time card and a few odds and ends she left in a drawer. Her last day of work was the twenty-sixth of October." Vero threw me a meaningful glance, probably thinking the same thing I was. Steven hadn't been entirely forthcoming about *when* he'd laid Bree off. Which meant he probably hadn't been honest about *why* either. "How about you? Did you find anything in Steven's books?"

"I didn't have time to read them, but I took a bunch of photos of his transactions over the last few months. And I snapped some pics of the bills in his inbox. We can go through them at home. Maybe we'll dig something up." At my wince, she shrugged. "Sorry. Bad pun."

A siren wailed in the distance. Vero checked her rearview mirror and I turned in my seat. Red-and-white flashing lights flickered through the trees behind us, racing toward the farm. There wasn't likely to be much left standing, but at least Steven hadn't been sleeping there—or worse, passed out drunk on the sofa in his office—when the fire started.

"You think the cops will talk to the security company?" Vero asked.

I thunked my head against the window, clapping a hand over my eyes. The fire marshal would need a day or two to collect evidence. And the police would need time to obtain a warrant to talk to the security company. But Steven . . . he could request a report from the security monitoring service within a matter of hours. He could pass that information along to the detectives if he wanted to speed up the investigation. "The record of my conversation with the security company will lead them right to Bree."

"If she didn't hire *EasyClean* to roast Steven, she doesn't have anything to worry about."

"What if she did?" I still wasn't convinced Bree was entirely innocent. "I need to talk to her before the police do. Steven's hiding something. He lied about the reason he fired her, and as far as I can tell, she hasn't been back to the farm since; all of her personal stuff is still sitting in a file drawer. If she was upset enough not to go back for her things, then maybe she was angry enough to pay someone to kill him."

"You seriously think she's responsible for this?"

"I don't know, but if she is, I need to convince her to call off the job before the police have a chance to arrest her."

CHAPTER 16

My cell phone rang early the next morning as I pulled my minivan onto a dirt lane through a winter-gray farm. The frosted fields were lined with fences and dotted with cows. "Hey, Georgia," I answered, my voice bobbing with the frozen ruts in the road. "Did Delia make it to school?"

"I just dropped her off. I'm on my way to work. I left Zach at your place with Vero. Did Steven call you?"

"No, why?"

"Someone made a bonfire of his sales office at the farm last night."

"What do you mean?" I tried to infuse the question with a reasonable degree of surprise.

"The trailer's gone. Someone burned it down."

"Wow. Do they have any idea who it was?"

"The fire marshal's still there. My contacts at Fauquier PD won't have his official report for another couple of days, but all signs point to arson. They're putting a couple of detectives on it. That's all I was able to get out of him."

Those detectives would likely be here in a matter of hours. "Will you let me know if you hear anything else?"

"I'm all over it," Georgia assured me. "In the meanwhile, you should call Steven's attorney. Ask him to suspend visitation until the investigation is wrapped up. This was no accident, Finn, and I don't think the kids should stay at Steven's place until we know what happened."

"I'll handle it. Thanks, Georgia." I disconnected, slowing the van as a sprawling farmhouse came into view. Its crisp white siding dripped with icicle lights, and garlands dressed the rails of a wraparound porch. I parked alongside an ivory Lincoln Continental and a red Volkswagen bug I recognized as Bree's. Hugging my coat around me, I climbed the porch steps and rang the bell. Wispy hot glue webs trailed from holly berries and sleigh bells on a homemade wreath on the door. Warm smells oozed from the house when the door swung open—spiced apples and bacon, the rich scent of cinnamon rolls wafting from the oven.

"Hello." The woman who answered bore a striking resemblance to Bree. Her smile was polite but uncertain, as if she was struggling to place me. She wiped her hands on her jeans, leaving a patch of tiny dish bubbles to dissipate into the pale blue denim.

"Hi, I'm looking for Bree. Is she home?" I peeked over her shoulder into a wide, inviting foyer adorned with country landscapes and quaint hand-painted crafts. I had looked up the address on Bree's time card, only mildly surprised to find her still living at home with her parents. I'd known that Bree was enrolled in community college from scouring public records, but it wasn't until I was standing in front of her mother that the age gap between us felt quite so wide.

"Oh, of course!" She held out a hand, her short nails stained with Christmas-colored craft paint. "I'm Melissa. Would you like to come in . . . ?" She inclined her head, waiting for me to offer my name.

"Finlay," I said, taking her hand. It was warm, still damp from washing. Her lips thinned as she registered my name.

"You're Steven's wife."

"Ex-wife." My mouth pursed as I corrected her. The "ex" had always held a sour bite coming out.

Some of the warmth leeched from her smile. "I see. Bree's probably out at the barn," she said, pointing at an outbuilding past the fence. "You're welcome to find her." She let go of my hand, her invitation to come in quietly withdrawn.

"Thank you," I said, stepping off her porch. I didn't blame Melissa for closing the door, or for watching me through the slit between her living room curtains as I turned for the pasture. She clearly knew enough about Steven to dislike anyone with the last name of Donovan.

Ducking under a fence rail, I headed toward the barn. The metal rooster perched on its roof spun a few circles one way, then the other, the wind uncertain as I approached the wide barn doors. I inched one open. The air inside was warm and musty, thick with the smells of hay and manure.

"Bree?" My voice echoed from the shadowy corners of the loft.

"In here." I wandered deeper into the barn, uncertain which direction her voice had come from. Pigs rooted in their stalls and goats bleated at me as I passed a wall studded with nails and hooks, each one holding a rake or a shovel. On the other side of the wall, Bree sat on an overturned bucket with her back to me. She picked at a knot in a length of rope where it looped around an old tire swing.

"Hi, Mrs. Donovan," she said without looking up. Her phone sat on the floor beside her. Her mother must have told her I was here. "Guess you heard I'm not working at the sod farm anymore." She kept her head down, pretending to be engrossed in her task. Her voice was flat, absent of that optimistic high note that always seemed to punctuate her sentences.

"Steven mentioned it a few days ago. He said the farm's been struggling and he had to let some people go."

Her snort was dry. "Typical," she said under her breath.

"Steven's never been the most forthright man," I admitted. Bree had nothing to say about that, but I could sense something shift. She hadn't once looked at me since I stepped inside that barn, but I felt a sudden curiosity under that prickly demeanor. I gestured to a column of buckets against the wall. "Mind if I sit down?"

She shrugged. I dragged one from the stack and set it upside down, taking a seat beside her.

"So I guess I'm not the only one." Her short nails dug into the stubborn knot. They were bitten to the quick, raw and pink, her pale face clean of her usual makeup.

"The only one Steven's ever hurt? No," I said gently, "not by a long shot."

A muscle tightened in her jaw. I wasn't sure if this information made her feel better or worse, but she deserved this much. I reached into my purse and withdrew the photo I'd found in her library book, feeling her gaze shift as I held it out to her. "You left this at the trailer. It looked special. I thought you might want it back."

She let go of the swing. Her eyes lifted slowly to mine. I saw a faint reflection of myself—the me from a year ago—in the hollows inside them. "Thanks," she said, setting the photo facedown beside her phone. "Is that why you came? It's a pretty long drive. You could have mailed it." I didn't think she was sassing me. Sarcasm didn't seem to fit with Bree. This felt more like a nudge, an invitation to a conversation she didn't want to admit she needed to have.

"I thought maybe you'd want to talk about what happened with Steven."

"It had nothing to do with the farm," she said through a heavy sigh. "Or the bad press or lost clients or Theresa's arrest. We were having problems long before that."

"What kind of problems?"

She picked at the fraying end of the rope, thinking. "I was trying to be patient. Things had been going really well for us since my dad got me the job at the farm. Steven and I . . . we connected instantly. And things just sort of happened from there." Her cheeks flushed when I raised an eyebrow. "It wasn't like that. Not like you're thinking. Steven *knew* Theresa was involved with someone else. He'd suspected it for a while, and it was making him crazy. Some nights he'd get drunk and that's all he wanted to talk about. He said that's why it was fine that we were sleeping—" Bree's mouth snapped shut. She gnawed her lip. "He said that's why it was fine that we were spending so much time together, because Theresa was cheating, too. I thought for sure if I just waited, eventually he'd call off the engagement and we could be together without having to keep it a secret anymore. But the longer I waited, the less sure I was that Theresa was the one he was really hung up on." She glanced up at me through her lashes.

A shocked laugh burst out of me. "You thought he was hung up on me?"

"Maybe," she said defensively. "I mean, you do have kids together. And you're a lot nicer than Theresa, even if she is prettier than you." Bree's hand shot up to cover her mouth. "Sorry, Mrs. Donovan. I swear I didn't mean it that way."

"It's okay," I said, my laughter turning soft. "Theresa's prettier than most people. I'm sure that's why Steven left me to begin with."

Bree frowned, worrying her lip between her teeth.

"He'll never admit it, but he's always snooping around, checking up on you."

My laughter died. "Checking up how?"

"You know, fixing your garage and paying your bills and stalking your social media to see if you're dating anyone. For weeks, he had some bee in his bonnet because he got some crazy idea you were dating an underwear model." She rolled her eyes. "Then you came to the farm that Sunday with Nick." Her eyes brightened as she remembered him, the same starstruck expression I'd seen on the faces of women who'd ogled him in the hallway at Delia's school. "You two looked so happy, and he was obviously so into you. And I thought, here was my chance. You were moving on with this amazing guy, and Theresa was having an affair with someone else. I thought for sure this was it. So I called Steven right after you left the office." She ducked her head. "Maybe it was petty, but I couldn't wait to tell him you and Nick were shopping for sod together—that you two were really serious. But when I did, Steven blew up. He came rushing out to the farm the second I told him. He had a freaking meltdown in the trailer, then he stormed out. He didn't call me for two whole days. Granted," she said, holding up her hands, "he was dealing with a lot. I mean, Theresa had been arrested and the police were all over the trailer with warrants, shutting down the office and digging up the farm. By the time he finally got around to calling me on Tuesday, it was to tell me not to bother coming back."

I uttered something that sounded like *I'm sorry*. At least, I think I did. My head was still stuck on what she'd said earlier, that the emergency Steven had responded to at the farm that day was the simple fact that he thought I was there buying sod with someone else. "And you think the reason he fired you had something to do with me?"

She nodded. "He's still in love with you. I knew it back in October, when he ordered the security system and he made you his safe word."

I schooled the recognition from my face. "His safe word?"

"When you accidentally trip the alarm," she explained, "it's the word you're supposed to tell the monitoring company to let them know everything is okay. Steven's safe word was *Finlay*. I suspect maybe in the back of his mind, he just figured you'd always be there in case things with Theresa didn't work out. I think that's why he got so freaked out about Nick."

Because I was his safety net whenever he tripped, and he was afraid if I was seeing someone else, I wouldn't be there to catch him anymore. All this time he'd been gloating about how I needed him—to pay my bills and fix my garage and babysit our kids—when maybe it had really been the other way around.

I rested my elbows on my knees, until our shoulders were almost touching. "You know that Steven and I are over, right? His horrible behavior has never been about you or me. Or even Theresa," I said quietly. "It's about his own insecurities. That's all."

"I know," she said. "My mom told me the same thing, that our breakup didn't have anything to do with me and I should just let him go. But that doesn't make it any easier. I just keep thinking maybe he'll change his mind." Her eyes lifted to mine. "Is that stupid?"

It was hard not to look at her and see Delia, all her misplaced hope and optimism. I didn't want to hurt Bree's feelings, but lying to her didn't seem right. "Maybe not stupid. But definitely not smart." She dropped her head and picked at the frays in her rope. "Can I ask you something?"

Her nod was slight, wary.

"You said Steven ordered the security system in

October. Was that because of everything that happened with Theresa and Feliks Zhirov?"

"No. It was before all of that. He ordered it because of the phone calls."

"Phone calls?"

"Someone was harassing him, calling him all the time. It went on for months. By the fall, it had gotten really bad. Steven was a little freaked out about it."

"Who was it?"

"I don't know. The calls always came to his cell phone. Whenever they did, Steven closed his door. There was a lot of shouting, and Steven would get angry and hang up."

"Do you know what the caller wanted?"

"Steven said it was some crazy person who thought Steven owed her something."

Her. "So it was a woman?"

"I think so. I mean . . . I overheard Steven call her a selfish bitch once." Her brows pulled together. "You don't think he was involved with someone else, do you?"

"Not that I know of," I said thoughtfully. I wouldn't put it past Steven, but until I knew for sure Bree was incapable of harming him, I didn't want to give her any more ammunition to try. "But Steven mentioned he was having some financial problems at the farm. Do you know of anyone who might have had a gripe with him—a client or a supplier? Someone he owed money to?"

"No." She gave a firm shake of her head. "Steven was good about paying his bills. His clients and suppliers all loved him."

"Can you think of anyone who might have had a reason to be angry with him?"

"If you mean someone who could have been angry enough to start the fire, then no; I can't think of anyone."

"The fire?" Bree had said she hadn't had any contact with Steven since he'd laid her off. So how did she know about the fire? Had the police been here already?

She pushed to her feet and wiped straw dust from her thighs. Taking my bucket as I stood, she stacked it with the others. "You didn't hear? Someone set fire to the sales trailer at Steven's farm last night. My older brother's a volunteer at the fire department. He got the call after midnight. He said there wasn't much left standing by the time they put it out." Bree must have mistaken my silence for surprise. Her cheeks reddened. "When you came by, I just figured you knew. I thought maybe that's why you were here."

"To see if you were angry enough to have lit the match?"

She nodded. "My brother asked me the same thing."

"What did you tell him?"

"That I was here, watching TV with my dad all night. I'm not gonna lie," she added, "I was plenty mad when Steven let me go. But I didn't set that fire. My brother said the police will probably want to come and talk to me about it anyway, just to be sure."

"And what will you tell them?"

"The truth," she said. "That I love him."

Bree gave me a small wave goodbye, her unlaced boots falling softly against the dirt as she retreated back to the warm glow of her parents' house.

CHAPTER 17

In my hurry to get to Bree's that morning, I'd forgotten the Pop-Tart I'd left on the counter, and my stomach had been growling since Melissa had opened her door, all those warm, luscious breakfast smells pouring out and taunting me. Somehow, I'd lost my appetite during our conversation in the barn, and I couldn't muster the desire to stop on the way home for fast food. All I could think about as I turned onto my street was the reheated cup of coffee and Pop-Tart I hoped might be waiting for me.

My foot slammed on the brake less than a block from my house.

A strange sedan was parked in my driveway. Judging by the extra antennas on the roof, I was pretty sure it belonged to a cop.

No. This could not be happening. The fire had only occurred last night. In a different county. The police hadn't even talked to Bree yet, and Vero and I hadn't left anything at the trailer that could have led the cops here first. Had we?

As I eased the car into the driveway, my mind whirled over what Vero might have already confessed to them. Or what alibi she might have managed to come up with on the fly. Before I left for Bree's, I'd washed our soot-stained clothes from the night before, but what about our shoes? We'd probably left evidence all over Vero's car.

I parked the van, closing the garage door behind me, prepared to turn the police away if they hadn't come with a warrant. My feet jolted to a stop as I stumbled into the kitchen.

Nick sat at my table, deep lines of concentration cutting into his brow. Delia sat on her knees in the chair opposite him. Propped on her elbows, she leaned across the table, watching him through the few remaining empty holes in her yellow Connect Four rack. Nick didn't look up from their game, but I could feel the flick of his eyes as he registered my arrival.

Vero leaned against the counter behind them, grinning as she dried her hands on a dish towel.

No handcuffs. No warrants.

Nick's partner, Joey, sat on the couch in the living room, his head tipped back, eyes closed, mouth open, his chest rising and falling in the slow, steady rhythm of sleep. Zach sat beside him, his attention glued to the TV as *Blue's Clues* played softly in the background.

Vero pressed a finger to her lips as I closed the door, jutting her chin toward the table where my daughter and Nick were engaged in a game of strategy. Or maybe a test of wills.

"The detective came looking for you," she whispered, too softly to be heard over the clatter of discs into the frame. "I told him you were out and you'd call him when you got home, but then Delia spotted him before he could get away."

A mug of coffee steamed on the table in front of Nick. The open foil of the last Pop-Tart in the house—my Pop-Tart—glimmered beside it. He held a red disc poised over the top of the rack. One eyebrow rose as he glanced over at Delia and let the piece fall. "Connect Four."

Delia's jaw dropped. "You won?"

"It's about time!" He leaned back in his chair, stuffing a corner of my Pop-Tart into his mouth and talking around it. "You've been clobbering me for the last half hour."

She snapped open the lever at the bottom of the rack, sending a shower of red and black discs over the table. "Let's play again."

Vero pulled Delia's chair back from the table, forcing her to abandon the pile of black discs she'd gathered toward her. "I've got a better idea. Let's let your mom and Nick play a round." My daughter blinked up at me, as if she'd only just realized I was home. She opened her mouth to object, but Vero held out the last of my Pop-Tart, bribing her from the kitchen.

"Be careful," Delia warned me. "He's sneaky." She trotted away with a smug Vero in tow.

"Up for a game?" Nick laced his fingers together behind his head, his dark eyes twinkling as I sat in Delia's abandoned seat.

"New car?" I dropped a black disc into the frame, watching it plunk and settle on the bottom. Nick let a red one slide from his fingers, right on top of mine.

"It's Joey's."

"He seems nice." I didn't know many men who could sit through an episode of *Blue's Clues*.

"He talks too damn much."

"I heard that," Joey grumbled from the couch.

"He's been moonlighting as a mall cop at night and helping his mom on the weekends," Nick explained. "He conked out on your sofa about thirty minutes ago. I figured it couldn't hurt to stay and play a few rounds with Delia while he grabs a few *z*'s."

"It's fine. I just wasn't expecting a visit. You said you'd call."

He watched me position another disc over the frame. "I heard about the fire at the farm."

My hand froze around my game piece. "Oh?"

"I wanted to make sure you and the kids were doing okay."

"We're fine," I said cautiously. "Do the police know anything yet?"

"No idea. The farm's not in my jurisdiction. But I can ask around the lab. Maybe Pete's heard something. Give me a day or two to nose around and see what I can find out. If you're free on Saturday, maybe I could fill you in over dinner."

My throat tightened as I looked up at him. There was nothing platonic in the way he was watching me over his coffee as he sipped. "Just dinner," I clarified. "It wouldn't be like a date."

"Not if you don't want it to be."

"Because I'm seeing someone," I rushed to add.

"A lawyer. I know. Vero told me."

"What else did she tell you?"

He set down his mug. "That you're not in a committed relationship, and he's out of town for the week." I made a mental note to murder Vero in her sleep.

Nick toyed with a disc, dragging it slowly back and forth across the frame as he picked the perfect place to drop it, boxing me in. "I was planning to check out this new restaurant with Joey on Saturday night, but he's ditching me—"

"For my mother," Joey interjected. "I promised I'd take her to bingo."

"—and I thought maybe you'd want to go."

"Please go with him, Finlay," Joey begged, "or I'll never hear the end of it."

I kept my eyes glued to the game, afraid if I looked up again, I'd agree to something I shouldn't. "Oh, wow, Saturday . . . That's not a lot of time. Vero's usually off, and I don't have a sitter."

"Yes, she does," Vero called from the top of the stairs.

"I don't have anything to wear."

"Yes, you do!" she shouted.

That's it. I was definitely going to kill her.

Nick leaned closer and whispered, "We could always have dinner at my place. I've been told I make a decent chili, and my biscuits are pretty amazing, too." The disc slipped from my fingers. I scrambled to catch it as it clattered toward the edge of the table. His hand caught mine as it closed around the runaway game piece. "It's just dinner." His eyes fell to my mouth as he slowly let go.

Just dinner. I could do that. Only to get an update on the arson investigation.

"Okay," I said.

His eyebrows shot up as I slipped the token in the rack. "So that's a yes?"

"Yes. But maybe we should skip the chili and try the restaurant instead." The last thing I needed was to be tempted by his biscuits.

"Then it's a date . . . I mean . . . definitely *not* a date." He held up his hands, the picture of innocence as he dropped a final token into the frame, connecting a line of four. He took a last long sip from his mug as he stood, setting it in the sink on his way out of the kitchen. "Thanks for the coffee, Vero!" he called from the foyer.

"Anytime, Detective," she sang back.

"Thank god," Joey whispered in my ear as he reached for his jacket. "The guy's been insufferable. If you didn't say yes, I was going to have to shoot him." He slipped a toothpick between his teeth and winked at me as he opened the door.

"You're leaving?" Delia cried out, scrambling down the stairs as Nick shrugged on his coat.

"Gotta go, Dee, but thanks for the game." She wrapped herself like an octopus around his legs. "Keep practicing. I'll be back in a few days for a rematch."

He scooped her up and planted a kiss on her head. I'm pretty sure confetti exploded from my ovaries as he set her gently on her feet. "I'll pick you up at six," he told me on his way out.

"Wait," I said, running to catch him on the front stoop. "What should I wear?"

His grin was a little wicked. "Surprise me."

My breath rushed out of me as he ducked into Joey's car.

I was full of far too many surprises. And I was certain they weren't the kind Nick was hoping for.

I was still staring at the game board when Vero wandered into the kitchen.

"Fantasizing about your hot date?" she asked.

"It's not a date."

"Sure, it's not," she teased, rinsing Nick's mug and setting it in the dishwasher. "How did things go with Bree?"

I slumped in a chair, taking a cautious sip of the coffee I'd left on the counter that morning. "I'm pretty sure she's not *FedUp*; she's still in love with Steven." Vero stuck a finger in her mouth and made a gagging noise. "But she did mention something suspicious. She said Steven ordered the security system before all this business with Feliks. Apparently, some woman had been harassing him, calling his cell phone and making demands."

"Did Bree have any idea who it was?"

"No, but she said the calls were frequent. She said they started over the summer and got worse through the fall. She said Steven ordered the security system in the early part of October. If we can get our hands on his mobile and look through his call history, maybe we can figure out which number belongs to this mystery woman."

"How do you plan to do that?"

I drew my finger through the Pop-Tart crumbs on the table as I considered that. "The same way we sneak things away from the kids—we use a distraction."

CHAPTER 18

An hour later, Vero and I stared at the mess we'd made on the kitchen floor. The cabinet doors under the kitchen sink had been flung wide, all the chemicals, detergents, and cleaning supplies removed and displayed across the countertop. A puddle spread from the bottom of the cabinet, dripping over the lip onto the floor where an artfully arranged landscape of bath towels had been scattered to collect it.

Vero squatted to inspect the pipe fitting I'd loosened. "Who would have thought a plumbing wrench could be so handy?"

A truck door slammed outside. I thrust the wrench into Vero's hands. "Steven's here. Hide this somewhere. I'll keep him distracted in the kitchen. You take his phone and see what you can find."

I took my time unlocking the front door. Steven stepped inside, carrying a leather tote bag of tools. "I can't stay long. I've got a meeting in an hour," he said, toeing off a pair of muddy work boots.

"It's probably just a leak. Thanks for coming." I stole a glance at his jeans as he shrugged off his coat. No obvious bulges in the pockets. His phone was probably inside his jacket. "You didn't have to bring your tools.

I've got a few here if you want to go check out the garage."

When I looked up, Steven was smirking, as if he'd caught me peeking at his jeans. "If you had the tools you needed here, Finn, you wouldn't have called me." He rolled up his sleeves and carried his bag to the kitchen. Vero was waiting inside, her hip cocked against the stove, arms crossed and jaw already set to fight.

"Hello, Steven."

"Vero." He spared her a cool glance as he set his tools on a dry patch of floor beside the open cabinet. Flipping on a flashlight, he ducked to look inside. I signaled to Vero over his head, pointing behind me to the coatrack. She nodded. Steven's voice came from under the sink. "I can already see the problem, Finn. Just a couple of loose fittings."

"How long will it take you to fix them?" Vero would need at least ten minutes to copy the numbers from his phone.

Steven pulled his head from the cabinet. I hated that cocky grin, all the assumptions behind it. He tapped his flashlight on his palm as he scrutinized me with mild interest. "Those threads are pretty grimy. I could take them apart and clean them a bit. Put some fresh plumber's tape on them. By the time I'm done, they'll be good as new."

Vero rolled her eyes behind him.

"That'd be great," I said.

Steven reached in his bag for his plumber's wrench. "Hey, Vero," he called over his shoulder as he rummaged through his tools. "Why don't you make yourself useful and clean up that water under the sink. I don't want to get my clothes wet."

I cringed at the dangerous tilt of her head.

"Sure, Steven." Her furious eyes met mine as she squatted to wipe the puddle under the sink. "Why don't you go get me a few extra towels, Finlay. I'm betting we're going to need them."

Vero tossed the wet towels aside with a flourish as Steven lowered himself to the floor. *Go!* she mouthed to me, shooing me from the kitchen when his head disappeared under the sink.

Shit! This was not the plan.

I rushed to the coatrack and dug inside Steven's pockets, scurrying up the stairs to my room with his phone. I thumbed it on as I grabbed the last handful of shower towels from my bathroom, tossing them down the stairs into Vero's waiting arms. She carried them into the kitchen with a devilish grin.

I stole back to my room with Steven's phone, pausing over the lock screen as Steven and Vero bickered downstairs. He was a creature of habit, I reminded myself, trying our old joint ATM PIN first. When that didn't work, I tried the four-digit code to the garage. The home screen opened, revealing a menu.

Tools clanked against pipes downstairs, their argument building to a crescendo in the kitchen. Vero's voice rang out, alerting Delia and Zach their father was here for a visit. Delighted screams tore through the house. The children's feet thundered down the steps.

Scrolling frantically through Steven's call log, I skimmed past the familiar names, pausing only on the incoming calls from women. There had been one outgoing call to *Bree's House,* in the late hours of Thanksgiving night. Nothing else stood out to me in recent weeks.

I scrolled further back in time, to early October, when Bree had said the calls had been frequent, but most of the calls were to or from Bree—outgoing calls to *Bree's Cell,* incoming from both her cell and her house, the calls coming and going at all hours of the day and night, interspersed with routine calls from Steven's work associates, Theresa, and me—no unusual patterns of incoming calls I could identify. At least, nothing that jumped out as threatening or suspicious.

The cacophony grew louder downstairs, the children's laughter escalating until it was almost frantic. I rushed down the steps, slipping Steven's phone into his coat pocket on my way back to the kitchen.

As I rounded the corner, a shout of alarm erupted from under the sink. Steven sat up fast, smacking his head against the bottom of the drain as he reached protectively for his groin. Zach was climbing between his thighs, squealing with delight at the handful of Cheerios Vero had poured over Steven's crotch. Steven lifted our son aside as he extricated himself from the cabinet, livid and dripping. Vero sat on the counter beside the running sink, wearing a remorseless grin. She shoveled a handful of Cheerios into her mouth as water flowed through the opening in the drain and the children stomped gleefully in the fresh puddles on the floor.

Every towel in the kitchen was soaked. I pulled the dishrag off the handle on the stove and handed it to Steven. Slowly, he wiped sink water from his face. A vein bulged in his temple, his skin an apoplectic shade of red as he bent over his knees.

"Vero, why don't you go take the kids upstairs to dry off," I suggested. "I'll help Steven finish up here." I was certain there would be a murder in my house if she and Steven were in the same room for one more minute. Steven glared at her as she jumped off the counter and led the children from the kitchen.

"Sorry about that," I said, rushing to turn off the faucet.

Steven straightened with a groan, unfurling his hand and pressing its contents into mine. "This was stuck in your trap. Looks like a SIM card from a cell phone." I stared down at the mangled SIM card Vero and I had dropped into the garbage disposal last month.

"Wow, that's strange," I said, tucking it away with a nervous laugh as Steven kicked aside a pile of sodden towels and eased back under the cabinet. "I wonder how that got in there."

"Probably your damn babysitter. She's going to destroy your disposal dumping that kind of stuff down there. And if she does, I'm not coming back to fix it." I held the flashlight for him as he wrapped the disconnected pieces of the drain in purple tape and threaded them back together. "That girl's a menace. She's irresponsible, Finn."

"She's not irresponsible. She's a big help to me and she's amazing with the kids."

"Case in point," he argued, gesturing to the counter above his head, "she shouldn't be storing all these cleaning supplies together."

"We have childproof locks on all the cabinets." He should have known, since he was the one who'd installed them.

"At the very least, you should have a decent fire extinguisher under here. That oven cleaner is nasty stuff. You'll start a house fire if you're not careful."

I snapped off the flashlight as he climbed out from under my sink. "You're seriously going to lecture me about fire safety right now?"

He dumped his tools in his bag, muttering my sister's name like a swear. "Your sister told you, didn't she?" I fixed him with a sharp look. "It's nowhere near as bad as she probably made it sound. It was probably just some delinquent kids, sneaking around on an empty farm and screwing around with matches. The only reason the police are looking into it is because the insurance company won't process a claim unless I file a report."

"Fine. But until we know for certain that fire wasn't targeted at you, I'm sure we can both agree that the kids will be safer at my house."

"My house is perfectly safe!"

"Really? Are you sure? Because someone doused your trailer in accelerant and tossed a Molotov cocktail through the window at your couch!" I snapped my mouth shut. The children's bedroom door shut quietly upstairs, a floorboard squeaking on the top step where Vero was probably listening.

Steven's eyes narrowed. "The cops didn't say anything about accelerant. Did Georgia tell you that?"

"She called me first thing this morning. Which is more than I can say for you." Steven and Georgia hated each other. I was pretty sure they wouldn't compare notes.

"If it makes you feel better, I have an appointment with the security monitoring company today. In a couple of hours, I'll know who's responsible for that fire, and this will all be over anyway. Your sister has no business getting involved."

"She's their *aunt,* Steven. And she has serious reservations about letting the kids spend the night at your house."

"She's not even a parent!"

"No, she's a cop! And I trust her judgment on this! So either you and I can handle this between the two of us, or I can ask my attorney to get involved."

His laugh was cutting. "Who? The kid in the Jeep?"

"No, Steven. The one I will hire and pay to deliver a court order to Guy, informing him that there was an attempt made on your life and he is to suspend all visitation until this is sorted out."

"Fine!" He snatched up his tools and stormed from the kitchen. "Have it your way. But you're overreacting." He shoved his arms in the sleeves of his coat and jerked open the door. "No one was trying to kill me, Finn. The only person who hates me that much is you."

I opened my mouth to argue, but he slammed the door behind him.

I flipped the lock and rested my head against the frame as Vero padded down the stairs. "What did you find on his phone?" she asked.

"Nothing," I said, following her into the kitchen. She handed me a broom. With a weary sigh, I swept the soggy Cheerios off the floor. "Just a lot of calls to and from Bree that ended the week he laid her off. And one call to her house last week. Probably a drunken attempt at a booty call," I said, remembering how lost and alone he'd looked, standing in my driveway on Thanksgiving night. "He must have deleted any records of the mystery woman's calls."

"Then we're back to square one," Vero said, scooping up an armful of sopping towels and dropping them into a laundry basket.

I dumped the Cheerios into the trash can as Vero knelt to return the cleaning chemicals to their place under the cabinet. "There has to be something we overlooked in his trailer. Did you find any leads in Steven's books?"

"Nothing that jumped out. He was current on all of his bills as far as I could tell." Her eyes narrowed thoughtfully as she stowed the last of the bottles. "Except now that I think about it, there was one statement that seemed odd."

"Odd how?"

She closed the cabinet door, dusting off her hands and rising slowly to her feet. "Steven's been renting a five-by-eight storage unit since August."

"But in August he was living at Theresa's house. Why would he have needed a storage unit?"

"Exactly."

"You think he was hiding something from her?"

She arched an eyebrow. "It wouldn't surprise me. He is a lying dirtbag, but he's also cheap. So why would he pay for storage when he has those huge sheds for his tractors at his farm. Why not keep his pervy, man-cave crap there? Why rent a storage unit an hour away. In *West Virginia*?"

"West Virginia?"

"The best place to hide a dirty secret is across a state line, Finn. Whatever Steven's hiding in that storage unit must be important."

Vero was right. This was definitely suspicious. "Do you know where the storage unit is?"

"I have a photo of the invoice. It's got the unit number on it and everything."

The police would probably be investigating the fire for days. I doubted *EasyClean* would be foolish enough to make a move until the dust settled. "Are you up for a road trip on Saturday?"

"Can your mom watch the kids?"

"No need," I said, remembering my conversation with Aimee, "I've already got a sitter."

CHAPTER 19

My sister pulled off her coat on Saturday morning and stared at me across my foyer as if I'd sprouted a second head.

"Let me get this straight. You want me to *babysit* your *babysitter.*"

"No. Sort of." I peered through the sidelights as Aimee's SUV passed the house. We'd agreed that it might be better if she parked on the next block so Mrs. Haggerty wouldn't have a record of her being here. I didn't trust Steven or his attorney not to exploit the all-seeing eye of the neighborhood watch for the express purpose of making my life difficult.

Vero was waiting for me in her Charger at the playground down the street. Aimee and Vero had met before, a month ago, when we'd infiltrated her workplace at Macy's in a misguided sting operation that involved Vero pretending to be a cop and asking a lot of murder-y questions while I'd hidden behind a rack of clothes. Given Aimee's innocence, I was pretty sure Aimee wouldn't react well to seeing Vero in my house. "Aimee is an old friend of Theresa's," I explained. "She and the kids spent a lot of time together while Theresa and Steven were engaged, and I promised Delia her Aunt Aimee could visit. Except I have somewhere I really need to be."

"And you don't trust her to be alone with the kids."

Aimee crossed the yard wearing comfy-looking sweatpants and an old pair of sneakers. She had a DVD in one hand and a grocery bag in the other. Nothing about her reminded me of Theresa, and I wondered if maybe I'd been overreacting when I'd asked my sister to come. I pulled the curtain closed and turned to my sister. "It's not that I think she would do anything wrong. It's just—"

"She's Theresa's friend. I get it." Georgia set her hands on her hips, assuming a very cop-like pose. "How do you want me to roll? Street-side surveillance or up close and personal?"

The doorbell rang. "Up close is fine. She's bringing a movie and snacks. You can stay and hang out. Just . . . don't mention Theresa or the trial in front of the kids."

Delia came tearing into the foyer, a blinding pink blur, the second I opened the door. Zach's eyes flew open wide. "MeeMee!" he screamed and leapt into her arms. The children were all over her, squealing and hanging from her legs, peeking into her grocery bag and reaching for the video. After a quick round of introductions over the ruckus, Georgia relieved Aimee of her grocery bag, and Delia and Zach dragged Aimee off to the playroom.

I bit my lip, listening to her dote on them in the next room. "I feel a little silly, asking you to stay," I said to my sister. "If you have other things you'd rather be doing—"

Georgia made a dismissive sound. "Are you kidding? Who doesn't want to make Rice Krispie Treats and watch . . ." She snuck a peek at the DVD. ". . . *Trolls World Tour*?" She grimaced.

"You're the best, Georgia," I said, wrapping her in a hug. "I'm sorry for all the names I called you last week."

She patted my back. "Thanks. I think."

I grabbed my purse and coat and dashed out to meet Vero, locking the door behind me.

Vero handed me her phone as we drove. I scrolled through the photos she'd taken of Steven's books.

"I don't see a passcode for the storage unit on any of these invoices."

"I called the place. They use padlocks."

"Maybe we should pull over and find a hardware store. We can probably get one of those bolt cutter things. Or maybe a hacksaw."

Vero shook her head. "Then someone will know we broke in. We don't want to be too obvious."

"How else do you plan to get in? Flash your boobs and ask the guy behind the counter for the key?"

She rolled her eyes at me. "After my brief conversation on the phone with Phyllis today, I doubt she'd be impressed. But don't worry. I've got another way in."

An hour later, Vero slowed, easing the Charger onto the crumbling shoulder of a rural road and turning in to a gravel parking lot. A high chain-link fence bordered the property, surrounding a small brick house with a neon OPEN sign in the window and several rows of run-down storage garages. Vero parked the Charger just outside the fence.

"What are we waiting for?" I asked when she slumped in her seat, checking her phone.

She shot off a quick text message. A notification pinged, and she glanced up at her rearview mirror. "That."

A white panel van pulled alongside us. The window rolled down. The passenger dragged his mirrored sunglasses down the bridge of his nose, his dark eyes twinkling as he smirked at us over the rims. "You owe me big-time, V."

"You lost that bet, fair and square. All I did was cash in."

"Yeah, well, if I start hearing banjos, I'm outta here." His eyes skated to me. Then past me to the rows of storage garages behind us. He looked vaguely familiar, though I couldn't place why. "What's the unit number?" he asked.

"Seventy-three."

"Give us a minute to scope it out." The passenger slid his glasses back in place as the driver pulled forward and parked in front of us.

"Who's that?" I asked as the two men got out of the van, both close in age to Vero if a bit older.

Vero ducked her head to watch as they slipped between the gap in the gate. "My cousin and his friend."

"That's Ramón?" I'd seen Ramón from a distance, when he'd towed Theresa's car once, but I'd been fleeing the scene, running too fast in the opposite direction to get a good look at him at the time. All I remembered was his dark, closely cropped hair and the baggy blue coveralls he'd been wearing. "How have I never met him?" Vero had dropped off my van at his garage for repairs. I'd talked to him on the phone when he called to tell me it was ready. But when I'd gone to pick it up, Ramón's office had been empty, and Feliks and Andrei were there waiting for me. Ramón had felt so bad about what had happened that night, he'd discounted my balance and delivered the van to my house. I hadn't been home at the time, and Vero had paid the bill.

Vero shrugged. "He's not here for a social call. He's going to get us inside Steven's storage unit, and then he's leaving," she said firmly. She checked her phone. "That's him. Let's go."

We left the Charger at the curb, and I followed Vero through the gate toward the last row of garages. Crushed cans and empty oil pints littered the fence line.

BEWARE OF DOG signs had been zip-tied to the rusted chain links.

"This place is a dump," I said, my sneakers crunching on broken glass. "I thought you said it was a climate-controlled unit."

Vero dodged a pile of fly-ridden dog turds. "Steven's been paying extra for electric. I assumed that meant it was climate-controlled, but this place isn't exactly the Ritz." We rounded the last row of storage units and found Ramón's friend kneeling in front of a dented steel door, a padlock cupped in one hand and a pick in the other while Ramón looked on.

"Lucky for you," Ramón's friend said without looking up. "Fancy storage places have cameras."

I glanced up at the eaves above the garages, then up to the single security lamp mounted on a pole at the end of the row. He was right. No surveillance cameras. The garages didn't even have power of their own. A thick orange extension cord snaked out from under the door of Steven's storage unit. Daisy-chained to another extension cord, it barely reached the electrical outlet under the rental office window.

Ramón's friend bent over the lock, his glasses perched on his head. His dark hair was pulled back in an elastic band at the nape of his neck, showing off deep bronzed skin and the dark edges of the tattoos that peeked out from the collar of his black T-shirt.

"Your mom called my apartment this morning," Ramón said over the quiet scrape of the pick in the lock. "Said someone came around her place yesterday looking for you."

Vero was silent for a long moment, the shift of her body language so subtle I would have missed it if I wasn't so on edge. "Who?"

"He wouldn't leave a name."

"What did she tell him?"

"I'm done being your damn go-between, V. She's still pissed that you didn't show for Thanksgiving dinner. It's been a month since you talked to her. Call her yourself and ask."

"A month?" I asked. "Why haven't you talked to your mother in a month? And I thought you said—"

"Ignore my cousin," Vero said through her teeth. "His mom dropped him on his head when he was a baby. He's got a shitty memory and he failed basic math." She broke into rapid-fire Spanish and smacked Ramón's arm. Ramón fired back a retort, and Ramón's friend's shoulders shook with silent laughter. "You shut up, Javi!" Vero snapped at him.

"How long will this take?" she asked, changing the subject. A tiny click issued from the padlock. With a quick snap of his wrist, Javi popped the lock open. He slipped his pick in his back pocket as he rose and sauntered toward Vero. Chin high, she took a half step back.

"Good to see you, V." He tilted his head, giving her a casual perusal. "Where've you been hiding?"

"I don't remember inviting you."

A slow grin spread across his face. "Thought you might need someone with particular skills."

"Ramón could have handled it."

"Wasn't talking about the lock."

Vero blushed. She crossed her arms over her chest. "When I need someone with skills, I'll be sure not to call you."

Ramón shook his head as he held out a hand to me. "Ignore them. She and Javier have been like this since we were kids. You must be the famous Finlay Donovan." Faint grease stains colored his cuticles, and the pads of his fingers were calloused where they gripped mine. This close, I could see the family resemblances between him and Vero. Flawless skin, full lips, and a jaw that could double as a steak knife.

"I've lost count of all the favors I owe you. Thanks for fixing my van. And for the save at Theresa's house last month. You really didn't have to mark down my bill."

"Yes, he did," Vero cut in, shouldering past Javi toward the open lock.

Ramón's smile grew a little sheepish in her wake. "I'm sorry about what happened that night with Zhirov. I'm glad you're okay."

"She's fine," Vero said, plucking the open padlock from the door. "Speaking of the garage, don't you two have somewhere you need to be?"

Ramón gave her a heavy dose of side-eye. "It was nice meeting you, Finlay. And watch out for this one," he said, inclining his head toward his cousin. "She's a bad influence."

"Goodbye, Ramón," she said pointedly.

Javi winked at her. "I'll wait in my van for a few minutes, just in case you need me."

Vero watched him from the corner of her eye as he walked to the van, her gaze drifting down to his backside before turning away.

"What's the story with you two?" I asked.

"There is no story."

"I don't believe you."

"He's my cousin's best friend. It was a long time ago."

"So there is a story," I said as Vero bent to grab the handle of the metal door. "I don't get it. Why don't you want me to get to know your cousin or his friend? Or, for that matter, anyone else in your family."

"There's nothing to know," she said, putting her shoulder into the door. "A little help, please?"

The track had rusted stuck, and we both grunted as we struggled to open it. "What was all that about somebody looking for you?" I asked.

"Nothing," she said through her teeth as she pushed. "My cousin's just being dramatic." The door made a horrible shriek as we dragged it open.

Vero dusted off her hands and froze.

"Finlay?" I followed her stare into the open garage and went still beside her. "Do you remember that night we went to dig up Harris," she asked, "and I told you that keeping a chest freezer in a garage was probably a bad idea?"

"Uh-huh," I said.

"I think I should tell you . . . my feelings on the matter haven't changed."

The storage unit was empty, except for one thing.

My gaze followed the orange extension cord deep into the shadowy recess of the garage, where a chest freezer hummed quietly in the corner.

"Don't be ridiculous," I said, my breath a little thin. "It's hunting season. Steven goes shooting with a lot of his clients . . . you know . . . like playing golf, but with a gun. The freezer's probably full of deer meat he couldn't fit in his freezer at home."

"And he keeps it in a storage unit in some Podunk town in West Virginia?"

"Sure." I swallowed.

"Then you can check it." She pushed me toward the freezer.

Steeling myself, I crossed the dusty concrete in three quick strides. The chest looked perfectly normal. Shiny and white, all except for a long scratch and a dent on one side, and a bright orange clearance sticker from a used appliance shop that no one had bothered to remove.

Vero peeked over my shoulder as I lifted the lid.

"See?" I exhaled pure relief at the parcels wrapped in butcher paper inside. "Venison." Grabbing the package closest to the top, I held it aloft for Vero to see. The tape peeled away from the ice-crusted brown paper, and the contents fell back into the freezer with a muffled thud.

Vero and I lurched, our chests rising and falling fast.

"That's not venison, Finlay!" Vero wrung her hands, wiping them up and down the leg of her jeans as if she'd been the one to touch it. "That's a head. And it didn't belong to a deer!"

"I can see that!" I was pretty sure I was going to puke.

"Whose is it?"

The features were blue, discolored by frost and distorted by rigor mortis. And yet, I had the horrible feeling I'd seen the same face before. I leaned closer, my head angled away, sneaking another reluctant glance out of the corner of my eye. The man's frozen salt-and-pepper bangs had parted, revealing wide, sightless eyes, and a dark mole stared back at me from his frost-dulled cheek.

"I recognize him," I said into the back of my hand. Because vomiting on the dead guy was probably a bad idea. "He was in the photo I took from Bree's desk."

"Why is he in pieces in your ex-husband's storage unit?"

"I don't know!"

"You don't think . . ." Vero and I locked eyes. I thought back to the day I returned the photo to Bree. How she had hardly looked at it before turning it face-down beside her. Had Steven rented this storage unit, or had Bree rented it for herself and billed it to the farm?

"What are you doing?" Vero asked in a strangled voice as I reached for my phone.

"I'm calling Steven."

"You can't do that! We can't tell anybody! They'll want to know how we knew it was here!"

"We can't just leave it!" A wave of panic washed over me. My finger hovered over Steven's number. Vero was right. There had to be a way to figure out for certain who this man was, and more importantly, who'd put him here.

Vero's shoulders relaxed as I shoved the phone back in my pocket. She swatted at my hands as I reached for hers instead. "Stay here," I said, taking her phone as I left the garage.

"Finlay! Where are you going?" she hissed as I followed the signs for the rental office. I paused in front of the office door, rubbing my hands on my pant legs, the ghost of a chill still seeping through my fingers where they'd touched the dead man's head. Drawing in a deep breath, I pushed the door open.

A daytime soap opera played on the TV behind the counter. The air inside smelled like cigarettes and burned coffee. A woman—presumably Phyllis—held a cigarette between two hot pink fingernails, the long thread of ash dangling precariously over the open mouth of a soda can. She glanced up at me over the rims of her glasses, her eyes moving back and forth between me and the TV.

"Help you?" she asked.

"I hope so," I said, pulling up a photo of the invoice Vero had taken on her phone. "I'm an accountant with . . ." My mind whirled, grasping onto the name of the only accounting agency I knew. "Mickler and Associates." As soon as the words were out of my mouth, I wished I could take them back. Phyllis didn't glance up from her soap opera. With any luck, she wouldn't even remember. "I'm conducting an audit for a client at the Rolling Green Sod and Tree Farm. I have a copy of an invoice for a storage unit, and my employer would like to know who authorized the charges. I was wondering if you could tell me the name of the person who opened the account?"

Phyllis took a long drag, huffing out smoke. "If you got an invoice, you got all the info we do. Billing address and credit card is the only info we keep on file."

"Maybe you remember talking with the person who opened the account? It's unit seventy-three."

"Do I look like Google? I got a hundred units out there," she said, pointing her cigarette toward the window. "People open and close accounts all the time. And we got a privacy policy. I don't ask, and I don't—"

I slid a twenty across the counter. Phyllis tapped the ash off her cigarette onto the floor, watching me with renewed interest. "It's the unit with the extension cord," I said, leaving the bill in front of her.

"Seventy-three, you say?" She turned her swivel chair toward the counter, her pink nails scraping over the cash. "I might remember something about her. But it's been a while."

"So it was a woman?" Relief flooded through me. At least it wasn't Steven. "Do you remember the woman's name?"

"Didn't ask."

"Do you remember what she looked like?"

Phyllis shrugged, her heavy-lidded eyes dipping back to my purse. "Memory's a little foggy."

I fished another bill from my wallet and slapped it down on the counter. As she reached for it, I slid it out of reach.

Phyllis's lips pursed. "She was blond. Pretty girl."

One hand planted firmly on the twenty, I Googled Bree's name with the other. "Is this her?" I asked, showing Phyllis the social media profile photo I'd enlarged on Vero's phone.

She lowered her chin, staring at the picture of Bree

over the rims of her glasses. Her jowls swung as she
shook her head. "Nah. That's not her," she said, tugging
the edge of the bill.

I clamped down harder. "Are you sure?"

Phyllis pointed to a sign on the wall: CUSTOMERS
MUST HAVE VALID DRIVER'S LICENSE AND BE 18 YEARS
OLD TO RENT. "Girl in that photo looks too young to buy
beer. I would have asked to see some ID. Woman who
rented that unit was older."

"How much older?"

Phyllis's eyes raked over my face. "'Bout your age,
I guess."

"And you just let her rent a unit without asking her
for any identification?"

"She rolled up in here in a fancy BMW, flashing a
company credit card. Offered to pay double if we let her
run an extension cord. Figured she was good for it."

Phyllis dragged the bill out from under my hand as
I stood there, breath catching on that small detail. Theresa was blond, my age, and drove a BMW. And she
would have had access to Steven's company credit card.
I dragged up an image of Theresa on Vero's phone. "Is
this her?"

Phyllis studied it, risking another hopeful glance at
my purse. I tucked it behind me.

With an aggrieved grunt, she said, "Yeah, that's her."

So the storage unit, and the dismembered man inside it, belonged to Theresa. But there was no way she
could have gotten him, or that freezer, in there alone.
Had she and Steven put him there together? Is that why
he was still paying the bill? "Do you remember who was
with her?"

"Never saw anyone. She paid and left. Next day,
the unit started drawing some amps, so she must have
come back to plug something in, but I ain't seen her
since." Phyllis turned to an old PC beside her register.

She drew her glasses down her nose, her press-on nails tapping on the keys as she squinted at the screen. She rotated it toward me, pointing at a billing record. "That credit card we have on file expired a week ago. If you talk to her, you let her know she needs to call in and update her card or else I gotta pull the plug and empty her unit."

"The payments are automatically charged to the card?" A bill that small could easily go unnoticed in a business as large as Steven's. He might not even have known he was paying for it.

"Every month," Phyllis said. "Next payment's due on the fifteenth. Unless you want to handle it for her."

The only cash I had left in my purse was a twenty. And I sure as hell wasn't giving Phyllis my credit card.

Steven had cut off Theresa's access to his accounts a month ago. She probably had no idea the card had expired. Her trial would be held in a matter of weeks, and if she went to prison, who would pay the bill? I couldn't confront Steven about the freezer; his only option would be to pay Phyllis or move the body, and both would make him an accessory to the crime, if he wasn't one already. But if Phyllis pulled the plug and emptied that storage unit, Steven would be the first person the police would come looking for. And when the police came asking questions, Phyllis would surely remember me. The only way to make sure the police didn't find this garage and cart Steven and I *both* off to jail was to make sure there was no body here to find.

"Do you have any garbage bags?"

Phyllis dug under a shelf and slapped a box of extra-large trash bags on the counter. As I reached for it, she tugged it back. With a begrudged "thanks," I handed her the last twenty from my purse, snatching the entire box and tucking it under my arm before walking out the door. I carried the bags to the storage unit, checking over my shoulder to make sure the slats in the window blinds hadn't moved. Vero waited inside the bay door, pacing and wringing her hands.

"Well?" she asked.

She jumped as I shook out a garbage bag and flung open the freezer door. "Call Ramón. Ask him how much he'd charge to haul a freezer to the dump."

CHAPTER 20

Vero's knuckles were white around the steering wheel, her eyes flicking regularly to her rearview mirror as she drove us back to South Riding. We'd long since lost sight of Javi's van. Once we'd emptied and bagged the contents of the freezer, Vero had called her cousin, and after a heated, whispered conversation between them, he'd agreed to haul the freezer to the car crusher behind his garage.

Later, I would ask Vero where she'd spent her Thanksgiving. And why things seemed so tense between her and Ramón. All I wanted to do now was take a bottle of bleach to my hands and wipe away any traces of the dead man whose thawing parts were currently rolling around in trash bags in Vero's trunk.

My phone vibrated. Cam's cell number flashed on the screen. I put the phone on speaker and held it between Vero and me.

"What did you find?" I asked Cam.

"Nothing useful," he said over the chatter of voices in the background. I could have sworn I heard a locker door slam.

"What do you mean, nothing useful? You said you could track her."

"I said I'd search. And I did."

"And?" The tension of the day had strained my temper to the breaking point. "You must have found *something* we can use to find her."

"It'd better be fifty somethings," Vero muttered.

"This *FedUp* person you're looking for is a ghost," Cam said. "There's no record of anyone using that email address anywhere else. I searched the shit out of it, even checked variations. It's not tied to any personal or social media accounts, no business profiles . . . nothing. Just that one forum you told me about."

"I thought you were supposed to be good at this?" Vero snapped.

Cam's voice dropped, low and muffled, as if he'd cupped a hand around the speaker. "Look, lady. I'm a hacker. Not a cop. I dug as deep as I could go. But this *FedUp* person was careful. They didn't want to be found." A bell rang in the background. "I've got to go," Cam said. "We done?"

"Yeah. Wait, no!" I said before he had a chance to disconnect. "Can we try another email?"

"That'll be another fifty."

"I'm good for it," I insisted. Vero threw me an exasperated look.

There was rustling in the background, the slam of a locker door, and the drone of a voice over a loudspeaker. "Text me the address." Cam ended the call.

I texted him the address tied to *EasyClean*'s profile.

"What makes you think he's going to have an easier time finding *EasyClean*?" Vero asked, her eyes fixed on the road. "If I was taking hit jobs online, I wouldn't be running all over the internet waving my IP address around."

"It's worth a shot," I said.

"You might think it's worth a shot, but I'm betting my forty percent just flew out the damn window."

"What other choice did I have? You heard what he

said, *FedUp* is a ghost! She didn't leave any tracks for us to follow."

Vero leaned on the brake as we veered off the interstate. We both flinched at the thud that resonated from the trunk.

"Slow down," I said. "The last thing we need is to be pulled over."

"I cannot believe I let you talk me into this. We should have left him in the freezer and padlocked it shut. Cops pull over sports cars. No one pulls over repair trucks. And now I have a melting corpsicle dripping dead-guy juice in my trunk."

The Charger eased to a stop alongside the curb in front of Theresa's house.

"You sure she's here?" Vero peeped over the rims of her sunglasses at the three-story townhome. Theresa's blue BMW was parked in the driveway, but the blinds in every window were shut.

"Georgia said she's on house arrest until Feliks's trial. Where else could she be?"

Vero got out and popped the trunk. With a grimace, I hauled out the smallest of the bags, tucking it under my arm. I tried not to think about the fact that the contents of the bag felt a little softer than they had ninety minutes ago.

A set of curtains parted in a window upstairs as we approached the house. I caught a glimpse of Theresa's long blond hair a second before the curtains snapped shut. Vero rang the doorbell. Seconds ticked by, and when nothing else seemed to move inside the house, I considered the possibility that Theresa might not answer.

Vero leapt back as the door flew open. A blast of stale, stuffy air rushed out.

"What the hell do you want?" Theresa braced a hand on the doorframe. Her sallow skin was free of makeup, her hair hanging in long, limp strands over an oversized T-shirt, the baggy legs of her sweatpants dragging on the hardwood floor. Her bare feet peeked out from under them, the flaking red polish of a grown-out pedicure staining the middles of her toenails. She crossed her arms, concealing her empty ring finger and pinning me with a cold glare.

"We need to talk." I stepped to the door, but Theresa didn't budge.

"We have nothing to say to one another."

I loosened the drawstring of the trash bag under my arm, nudging down the plastic to reveal the head inside. "Oh, I'm pretty sure we do."

Theresa's eyes went wide. "Where did you get that?"

"I think you know."

She grabbed the door, preparing to slam it in my face. I thrust a foot in the gap.

"I told you," she said through clenched teeth as she leaned all her weight against the door, "I have nothing to say to you."

"Fine!" I jerked my foot from the opening. "I'll just leave all this here and we'll go." I dumped the contents of the bag in the middle of her front stoop. The hair on the corpse had thawed, clinging like tangled seaweed to the condensation on his forehead. His dead-eyed, slack-jawed face gaped at her. "Your lease at the storage place is up, by the way. I told Phyllis you weren't interested in renewing. We took the liberty of cleaning out the unit for you."

Vero grabbed another trash bag from the trunk. The weight of the body parts packaged inside strained the plastic, creating macabre outlines as she carried it to Theresa's stoop.

Theresa stiffened. "What are you doing?"

Vero turned the bag upside down, shaking it out with a flourish. The color drained from Theresa's face as

the contents fell to the concrete with a series of sickening thumps. She gaped at the piles of butcher paper, at
the dark stains where the brown wrapping had grown
soggy. Her throat worked with her rising panic as we retreated to Vero's car. "Wait! Where are you going? You
can't just leave those here!"

"I don't see why not," I said, slamming the trunk
closed. "According to Phyllis, they belong to you."

"What am I supposed to do with them?" she asked,
gesticulating wildly.

Vero shrugged. "I don't know, but I suggest you put
him in the fridge until you figure it out."

"I can't put those in my refrigerator! They won't fit!"

Vero chuckled. "I've seen that fancy Sub-Zero in
your kitchen. That bitch could probably hold the entire
meat department at Costco."

Theresa's eyes narrowed to slits. "When were you in
my kitchen?"

"Forget it!" I said as I threw open the passenger door.
"We're not cleaning up your mess. If it won't fit in your
fridge, you can take it to the dump."

Vero ducked into the driver's seat and put the keys
in the ignition.

"Stop! Please!" Theresa yanked up the hem of her
sweatpants, thrusting her right foot out the door, revealing a thick black tracking device around her ankle. "I
can't go to the dump. I can't even leave my house!"

My jaw fell open. Vero's dark giggle built into an
outright guffaw. "Try the shed. Maybe Steven left you
a shovel. You can bury him in your backyard." She
turned the key, revving the engine.

"Okay, fine!" Theresa cried out. "You can come inside, but you can't leave those here!" She pointed to the
thawing parcels on her stoop.

Vero raised an eyebrow, deferring to me. I shut the
passenger door and crossed the lawn, ducking to put

the head back in its bag as I shouldered my way past Theresa and carried it into her house. The engine cut off behind me. Vero picked up a few more parcels before following me inside. Theresa pulled a face, gathering up the last of them and dropping them indelicately on her kitchen floor.

Theresa stared numbly at the piles of brown paper. She grabbed a tub of disinfectant wipes from the cabinet under the sink and handed one to each of us. We stood beside the marble table in her kitchenette, frantically wiping our hands with matching expressions of disgust. She collected our used-up towelettes, pinching them between two fingers and hurling them into the trash bin.

"If I tell you what I know, do you promise to take it all with you?" She jutted her chin at the floor.

"That depends," I said. "How is Steven involved?"

Theresa's green eyes bored into me, her arms crossed stubbornly over her sweatshirt. "He's not involved. I rented the storage unit without him."

"Are you telling me he had no idea what you were keeping in there?"

"Bree gets all the monthly statements. I doubt he even looks at them."

"He fired Bree last month."

Theresa's thin lips parted with surprise. "Does Steven know about the storage unit?"

"That's what I'm trying to figure out. Who is he?" I asked, pointing to the bags.

Her jaw rocked back and forth through her hesitant pause. "He was one of Steven's silent partners in the farm."

I blinked at her. "Steven never mentioned any business partners."

"That's why they're called *silent*. How do you think he bought all that land? With his mountains of cash? Or maybe his stellar credit?" she asked scornfully. "Why would he finance the farm through a bank, knowing full well he was going to divorce you? He'd have to be an idiot to give you that kind of legal claim to it."

"Wait . . ." I held up a hand, certain I'd misunderstood. "Are you telling me he bought the farm *before* the divorce?"

"Someone give the lady a prize," Theresa cooed. "Finlay finally gets it."

I wanted to smack the haughty smirk from her face, but she was right about one thing. I did finally get it. It didn't matter that Mrs. Haggerty caught them screwing in my house. Steven had been plotting to leave me anyway, and Theresa knew it.

Theresa shrugged, her expression cool. "Steven hired me to find him a silent partner. Someone willing to put down the cash for the farm and transfer the deed to his name after the divorce was settled. I found him two."

"I thought *you* were his partner. That it was *your* money that helped pay for the farm." Theresa's lips pursed. I tilted my head as all the clues came together. "He didn't want to partner with you, did he?" I asked, certain I was right when she averted her eyes. "That's why he kept stalling the wedding date. That's why you agreed to take custody of my kids. Because it was the only way you could get him to agree to marry you. So you could stake a claim over his farm."

"I loved him!" she shot back.

"Which you so clearly demonstrated by boning Feliks Zhirov in the back of his car."

"Daaaamn," Vero whispered.

Theresa's mouth snapped shut.

"What's his name?" I asked, pointing at the dead guy.

She ground her teeth. "Carl Westover. He and his cousin, Ted, paid for the land. They drafted a private contract with Steven, agreeing to turn the property over to him once he'd earned enough to buy them out. The agreement gave Steven the right to farm the land and run the business as he pleased, as long as the profits were being distributed to the partners in accordance with their contract."

"Let me guess," Vero said. "Steven did something to piss them off and the deal went sour."

"No." Theresa shot Vero a nasty look. "Everything was going great. The farm was making money. More than any of us had expected. Between Steven's business plan and my real estate contacts, we were able to secure some of the area's biggest developers as clients. He was on track to pay off the farm in less than five years."

"So what happened?" I asked.

Theresa paled. She stared at the packages on the floor, shaking her head. "He'll kill me if he finds out I told anyone."

Vero nudged the pile with her foot. "I promise, this guy isn't doing any talking."

"Not him, you idiot! Feliks Zhirov!"

My body recoiled at the name. "Feliks did this?"

Theresa nodded.

"But you told the police Feliks had nothing to do with Steven's business. You told them Steven didn't know Feliks was using the farm."

"He didn't." Her voice broke. "Because I never told Feliks that Steven had an ownership interest in it. I wanted to keep Steven out of it. So I gave Feliks the name of one of Steven's partners instead. I figured if one of them consented to letting Feliks use the land, that would be enough. And if they were making money off the deal, why would they refuse?" Theresa drew a shuddering breath. "I took Feliks to see Carl. Carl and Steven weren't as close; they hardly even talked. Carl and his wife had recently split up, and Carl had a lot of medical bills. I knew he was struggling financially. I thought he'd be more likely to take the money and less likely to tell the others, but . . ."

"But Carl refused," I guessed.

Theresa nodded. "Carl said he had seen Feliks on the news. He said he didn't want his good name soiled by doing business with criminals . . . only that's not exactly what Carl called him."

"So Feliks killed him."

Theresa swatted away a tear. "Andrei slit Carl's throat. On Feliks's orders."

Of course he did. Because Feliks never did his own dirty work. But now Andrei was dead, Feliks was in jail, and Theresa was stuck holding the bag—literally.

"So you and Feliks made an agreement to let him use the farm. And you never told Steven or the other partner?"

She shook her head. "I didn't want anyone else to die. I told Feliks I had a close relationship with the person who owned the land. I told him I could get him and his men in and out of the farm whenever he needed to use it, and he didn't need to speak to anyone else. Feliks agreed."

"And you were more than happy to take his money." Vero tsked.

"If you and Feliks came to an agreement," I asked Theresa, "why didn't the two of you just bury Carl on the farm with the other bodies?"

"I told the police the truth. I never knew Feliks was using the farm to bury bodies." She choked out a dark laugh. "Believe me, if I had, that would have made my life a whole lot easier. I never would have been stuck dealing with this!"

Theresa covered her mouth with a trembling hand,

as if she'd said too much. But something didn't make sense. If Feliks and Andrei killed Carl, why had Theresa gotten stuck with the body? Why risk leaving an amateur to clean up the evidence of their crime? Unless . . .

"They killed him and left," I said, picturing the scene playing out in my mind as if it were a chapter in my own book. "Feliks left you to deal with the body because he wanted you to be culpable. If you were an accessory to the crime, you'd be a fool to report it, so he made you clean it up. And you didn't think to use the farm. Instead, you took Carl across the state line."

"And used Steven's credit card to pay for it," Vero added, "so you could pin the murder on your fiancé if the police ever found Carl's remains."

Theresa turned away.

Vero was right. Steven's future interest in the farm could be seen as a motive for killing Carl. He was the perfect patsy.

"Wow," I said, unsure if I was disgusted or impressed. "That's real love and commitment for you."

"I was scared! They killed a man in front of me. I didn't know what to do!"

"So you found the answer in Feliks Zhirov's wallet?"

"More like in his pants," Vero muttered.

"There's one thing I still don't understand," I said. "If Andrei slit Carl's throat and they left you to clean up the body, then how did Carl end up in all these pieces?"

Theresa winced. "Oh, god. You didn't . . ."

Vero blanched. "So glad I skipped lunch."

"What did you expect me to do, Finlay! They'd left me alone in a house with a corpse! Have you ever tried to lift a dead body?"

"All it would have taken was some table linens and a skateboard," Vero said under her breath. I shot her a look.

"I couldn't leave him there! Someone would have found him and called the police. And he was so heavy!" Theresa's confession spilled out of her as if a dam had broken. "I couldn't carry him to my car. Not in one piece."

"Why didn't you tell the police about this when Feliks was arrested?" I asked. "You could have told them Andrei and Feliks killed Carl when you gave your statement. Feliks is behind bars. He isn't a threat anymore." And one more count of murder, with an eyewitness to testify, would have made the DA's case against Feliks airtight.

Theresa laughed. "You're kidding, right? This is *Feliks Zhirov* we're talking about. He won't serve a day of prison time. If his lawyer doesn't get the case kicked out for some stupid technicality, Feliks will find his own way out, and when he does, I have no doubt he will personally take down anyone who had a hand in his arrest. I told the police I had no idea there had been any bodies at the farm, and that was the truth. I never accused Feliks of murdering anyone, and I don't plan to start now. He would only come after us." Theresa's cheeks flushed a guilty shade of red.

"Us?" I asked. Theresa had never cared about my well-being before. And she certainly had no reason to care about Vero's. Why start now?

Unless *we* weren't the *us* she was worried about.

"How'd you get the freezer to West Virginia?" I asked. The trunk of her sporty BMW was far too small to hold such a large appliance.

She raised her chin defiantly. "Steven's farm truck."

"Steven's farm truck has restricted license plates. It's not registered to drive on the highway. You could have been pulled over and searched." Theresa would have been a fool to take that kind of risk with a dismembered corpse in the open bed of the truck. That freezer had been nearly four feet long. Even empty, it must have weighed over a hundred pounds. "Who helped you move it?" I demanded.

Theresa's watery green eyes leapt between Vero and me. "Don't tell me you wouldn't do the same for each other. That if she asked you, you wouldn't do something like this for her?"

My breath caught as Theresa's meaning became clear. She was talking about me and Vero. About our friendship. About the crazy things we would do for each other. She had no idea how right she was.

"Aimee?" I whispered.

"Please don't turn her in," Theresa begged. "She was only trying to help! I called her from Carl's house. I didn't know what else to do. It was Aimee's idea to put him in the freezer. She said she knew where to take Carl. How to make him disappear."

My heart lurched. Vero's nails dug into my arm.

Theresa reached for me, tripping over the trash bags as I bolted for the door. "Where are you going?" she cried. "You can't leave! You can't leave him here! You can't—"

I didn't even think about the body as Vero and I sprinted to her car.

CHAPTER 21

I was out of the Charger before Vero put it in park, my mind too scrambled to think as I unlocked my front door. What if my sister had been chopped into tiny pieces? What if my children were gone? What if they were all stuffed into shiny black trash bags in the back of Aimee's car?

I threw open the door to a rush of warm air and the smell of burnt popcorn. The living room was dark, the TV left on, the closing credits of a movie scrolling down the screen.

I burst into the kitchen. The microwave door had been left ajar. A burned bag of singed, cold popcorn had been abandoned in the sink.

"Georgia!" I called out. No one answered.

"Finlay?" Vero's voice was low and choked. She stood in front of the pantry, pointing at a trail of red droplets on the floor.

I followed them from the pantry to the stairwell, gasping when they led to a bright red smear on the wall. The stain was the size and shape of a tiny hand, traveling up the stairwell the same way Delia's and Zach's handprints did after they'd eaten something sticky or trailed in dirt from the playground. "No!" I surged up the stairs with Vero on my heels. My sister's voice carried from the end of the hall, and I chased the sound of it into my bedroom.

Vero grabbed my arm and jerked me to a stop. "Listen," she whispered.

"You don't have to do this." Georgia's voice was muted through the bathroom door. "If you hold them hostage, you're only hurting yourself."

A muffled cry of distress came from inside the bathroom. I tried the knob, a strangled, terrified sound escaping me when I realized the door was locked.

I reached for the key we kept hidden above the doorframe. Vero dragged me backward and held a finger to her lips. "Your sister is in there," she whispered.

"So are my children!" I whispered back.

"Georgia's a trained professional. Whatever's going on in there, she's qualified to handle it."

Zach let loose an angry howl. Vero clapped a hand over my mouth before I could call out to him.

"I've heard your list of demands," my sister said in a carefully measured voice, "and I am prepared to be reasonable. But you need to give me something in return. A show of good faith. That's all I'm asking."

My throat tightened. I couldn't breathe. I pried Vero's hand from my mouth, dragging in a shuddering gasp. Aimee was in there with my kids. She was holding them hostage. Theresa must have called her and told her we knew about Carl the second we'd left her house. This was all my fault.

Zach whimpered through the door, and my heart ripped to pieces. "We have to go in there," I whispered.

"What if Aimee panics? She might hurt them."

"They're already hurt!" They must have fought her off in the kitchen. They must have run to my room to escape, and she'd trapped them. Cornered them in my bathroom and locked the door.

"Take it easy," my sister pleaded. "I know you want out of here. I know you're afraid to give up control of the situation, and I get it. I do. But you need to let them go. Let's start with one. Just one. Let one of them go, and I'll give you what you want."

"It won't stop bleeding," Delia cried.

Vero gripped my hand. Her lip trembled.

"It'll stop soon, Delia. I promise." There was an undercurrent of tension in my sister's voice, as if she was barely holding it together. "It'll be okay. But right now, I need to help your brother."

Zach cried out. I couldn't take it anymore. I tore out of Vero's arms. With shaking hands, I grabbed the key from the top of the doorframe, jabbed it into the lock, and threw open the door, my chest heaving.

Vero slammed into my back as I lurched to a stop. Zach's cries fell abruptly silent, and three heads turned to look at me.

"Hey," Georgia said with obvious relief, "I didn't hear you come home." My sister sat cross-legged on the floor in front of my toilet, an open bag of fruit snacks in one hand and a single orange gummy held aloft in the other. Zach perched on Delia's old potty training insert in front of her, red-faced and furious.

"What's going on in here?" I asked through ragged breaths.

"Potty training," Georgia said proudly. Zach whined, teetering on the knife-edge of a tantrum as he grabbed for the fruit snack Georgia held out of reach. "Nope. I told you, buddy. This is a negotiation. You don't get to make any demands until you drop me a deuce."

"What's a deuth?" Delia asked.

I followed the red trail on the floor to my bathtub. Delia's head peeked out from a mountain of pink-stained bubbles. "Look, Mommy!" She flashed me a wide, gap-toothed smile. Her tongue poked through the bloody space where her front teeth used to be. "I loth'd my teeth!"

I sagged, holding myself up against the counter as Vero doubled over laughing behind me.

"What?" My sister scowled at us. "What's so funny? I read all the potty training blogs. This is how you're supposed to do it."

Vero snorted, clutching her chest and rubbing tears from her eyes. She pulled it together long enough to pat me on the shoulder. "I'll get the carpet cleaner and the Magic Eraser."

"Where's Aimee?" I pulled Zach off the potty seat as Vero went off in search of cleaning supplies. He squealed like a pissed-off pig and wriggled out of my arms, waddling out the door after Vero, an angry circle imprinted on his butt.

"You just missed her," Georgia said. "She got a phone call a few minutes ago. Tore out of here like her hair was on fire. Must have been an emergency." She rose stiffly to her feet, peering into the empty toilet. With a disappointed shake of her head, she popped the fruit snack in her mouth.

Exhausted and numb, I dropped to my knees beside the bathtub and planted a kiss on Delia's suds-covered head. "What happened to Delia's teeth?" I asked my sister.

"She got tired of wiggling them and decided she didn't want to wait for them to fall out on their own. Aimee was busy making the popcorn. I was up here with Zach. We didn't see Delia tie her teeth to the pantry door and kick it closed. She nearly gave Aimee a heart attack with all the screaming and the blood. It's a good thing I was here. I don't think Aimee could handle the gore."

An anxious laugh bubbled out of me. I hauled Delia from the bathtub and wrapped her in a towel. "Those teeth weren't ready to come out, sweetie. Why would you do that? That must have hurt."

She blinked up at me as I rubbed a towel over her hair. Her tongue poked through the hole where her teeth used to be, making all of her *s*'s sound like a lisp. "Vero thaid it'th not enough to want thomething. She thaid you have to make your own luck. Now the tooth fairy ith going to come, and I'll get two hundred dollarth."

"Two hundred dollars?" I laughed. "I don't think the tooth fairy carries that kind of cash."

"But I need it to help Vero."

"Why does Vero need help?"

"I heard her talking on the phone. She thaid if she can't get two hundred, she'll be in big trouble."

My face fell. "What kind of trouble?"

"A man got really mad at her becauth she lotht a marker. I told her she can have my purple one becauth I don't like purple, but she thaid that won't help. She needth a really big one."

I stared after Delia as she hobbled out the door in her towel.

"What was that all about?" Georgia asked.

"No idea," I said, pulling the plug on the drain. "I'd better go put a diaper on Zach before he releases a hostage on the floor."

My sister laughed. "I'll go see if Vero needs any help cleaning up the crime scene."

"If only you could," I said to myself when she was gone.

I found Zach hiding in his room, one hand braced on the wall, assuming the pose. "Oh, no you don't!" I scooped him up and wrangled him into a Huggie.

When I carried him downstairs, Georgia was already mopping blood off the floor. Her nose wrinkled when I came into the kitchen. "Don't take this the wrong way,

Finn, but I can stay and keep an eye on the kids for a few more minutes if you want to grab a shower."

"Where's Vero?" I set Zach down, and he toddled toward the living room.

"Looking for carpet cleaner in the garage."

We both turned as Vero burst into the kitchen. She set down a bottle of upholstery cleaner, put an arm around Georgia, and ushered her to the door, grabbing my sister's coat from the rack and shoving it into her arms. "Thanks so much for watching the kids, Georgia. I'll take it from here." She took my sister's keys from the counter and pushed them into her hand.

I turned sharply to Vero. "Georgia offered to stay and help clean up."

Vero pinched my elbow hard. "Can I have a word with you in the kitchen?" She held up a finger to my sister as she forced me into the next room.

"What are you doing?" I asked, shaking off her grip.

"Georgia needs to go."

"Why?"

Vero whispered through clenched teeth. "Because Carl Westover's torso is still in my trunk."

For a moment, I forgot how to breathe. "Oh, god."

I turned back for the foyer and cleared my throat. "Thanks so much for all your help, Georgia, but there's no need to stay."

"Are you sure?" Georgia's forehead wrinkled as Vero swung the door wide for her.

"Totally sure. Yep. We're good here."

"Okay. But you'd better grab that shower soon. Isn't Nick picking you up at six?"

"What?" I felt the blood drain from my face.

"You know, for your date?"

Vero and I both turned toward the clock. *Oh, no.* I'd forgotten all about Nick. "It's not a date," I said between increasingly tight breaths.

"It's totally a date." Vero pushed my sister out the door. "You'd better be going so she can get ready."

"I knew it!" my sister said as Vero shut it in her face.

"What do we do?" I asked, clutching my chest. Was I having a heart attack? This must be a heart attack. I had less than thirty minutes to figure out what to do with Carl.

"You take a shower and get ready for Nick. I'll drive back to Theresa's and be back before you leave. Go," she said, shoving me toward the stairs. "I'll handle Carl." Vero grabbed her keys and rushed out the kitchen door.

The kids were peacefully engrossed with their toys, but if I didn't get dinner on the table soon, there was sure to be a mutiny. I preheated the oven, grabbed bags of chicken nuggets and tater tots from the freezer, and washed my hands no less than five times before pouring the frozen lumps into a metal baking tray. The sound of them hitting the pan made my stomach turn. I slid the pan into the oven, set the timer, and raced upstairs to the shower.

After scrubbing every inch of skin with scalding hot water, I came out of the bathroom to find one of Vero's dresses hanging on my closet door. A pair of matching heels had been tossed to the floor under it.

I toweled off quickly and wiggled into the dress. It was far sexier than anything I owned—a deep sapphire blue with a plunging neckline and a clingy wrap waist, the soft material just forgiving enough to fit me—but as I frowned at the contents of my own closet, it was painfully clear I had no other options.

I adjusted it around my curves, ran some curling mousse through my hair, and spritzed on some floral body spray, hoping I didn't smell like a corpse in a funeral home. After a few swipes of mascara and lip gloss, I slipped on Vero's heels and searched for my phone.

Shit. Where was my phone?

I must have left it in my purse. Which was still in Vero's car.

I slung a handbag over my arm as I scurried down the stairs.

My knees locked on the last step as I caught a whiff of Nick's cologne. It mingled with the aroma of tater tot grease. Delia's high voice came from the kitchen, re-laying the story of how she lost her teeth, followed by Nick's deep, rumbling laugh.

I pressed my back against the wall. I could do this. I just needed to keep it together through dinner. I took a deep breath and smoothed the front of my dress, heels clicking with more confidence than I felt as I walked into the kitchen. Everyone turned to look at me. Every-one except Vero.

She stood in front of the oven, her shoulders stiff as she scooped tots onto melamine plates.

"Wow." Nick leaned back in his chair, taking me in.

My laugh was high and a little panicked. "You told me to surprise you."

Vero set the children's plates down on the table. Her dark eyes pierced me over Nick's head. "Did you get my message? I've been texting you."

"No, I must have left my phone in your car."

"You should probably go get it." She handed me her car keys with a pointed look. "Don't forget to check the trunk."

I cleared my throat. "Good idea." My phone had probably fallen out while we were hauling out the trash bags. I could feel the heat of Nick's gaze trailing me as I crossed the kitchen and slipped into the garage. The trunk of the Charger popped open when I clicked the key fob. I lifted the lid and swore.

Carl—or at least one very big piece of him—was still inside.

"Damn you, Theresa." I groped under the edges of the trash bag for my phone. She'd probably refused to answer her door, for the same reason Feliks refused to take Carl after he'd killed him. Because if Vero and I were stuck with a piece of Carl, we were a lot less likely to tell anyone about him.

I slammed the trunk and stormed to the passenger side door, dropping into the bucket seat and fishing my purse from underneath it. I searched inside, but my phone wasn't there. It wasn't in my room. It wasn't in Vero's car. The only other place it could be was . . .

Fuck!

I dropped my head to the dashboard. I couldn't go back to Theresa's now. Not without rousing Nick's suspicions.

I got out of the car, locking it behind me. The sooner I got Nick out of here, the better. I'd pretend everything was fine. We'd go to dinner, and Vero and I would deal with Carl and Theresa when I got home.

Vero was waiting by the door when I returned to the kitchen. "Did you find your phone?"

Nick's back was to us. Delia giggled as he snuck a tater tot from her plate, but I had no doubt his cop-brain would quietly register every word, even if he was only half listening.

I handed her the keys. "It wasn't in your car. I must have left it at the *neighbor's* house when we dropped by this afternoon."

"I don't think so," Vero said, locking eyes with me. "I just *left* the neighbor's house, and no one was home."

No one was home? How was that possible? Theresa was on house arrest. Where else could she be? "What do you mean?" I asked in a low voice.

"Just what I said," Vero said through her teeth. "I knocked on her door, and when no one answered, I let myself in. The door was *unlocked*. Our *neighbor* wasn't there. Neither was her *guest*."

"Her guest?" Vero answered my confused look with a pantomimed chopping motion.

Carl? No!

She nodded.

But Theresa wouldn't have been stupid enough to risk leaving her house, even to get rid of the body. "Are you sure she wasn't in the backyard? You know . . . *mulching* her *flower beds*?"

Vero shook her head, darting a cautious glance at Nick, but he and Delia were preoccupied, negotiating for another tot. "They definitely were not there. I looked *everywhere*. For *both* of them," she said, pointing at the refrigerator door. "Her guest was definitely gone. And I definitely didn't see your phone. But our neighbor left a rather large piece of *jewelry* sitting out on the kitchen counter." Vero pointed to her ankle. "I didn't want to take a chance that someone *else* might let themselves in and *find* it, so I tidied up," she said, holding up a tube of Clorox wipes, "and I locked her door behind me."

Oh, this was not good.

Aimee must have gone straight to Theresa's house at the same time we were rushing home, taking a different route from the adjacent block where her SUV had been parked. She and Theresa had probably panicked. They must have taken off the ankle monitor and run, desperate to get rid of the body, leaving me and Vero with the biggest piece of it. It wouldn't be long before the police showed up and realized Theresa was gone.

At least Vero had wiped any trace of us from Theresa's kitchen.

Nick's chair slid back from the table. "We should probably go," he said, checking his watch. "We have reservations at seven, and I have a quick stop I need to make on the way. I promise, I won't keep her out too late."

Vero's laugh was slightly manic. "Don't worry about me, Detective. I've got plenty to keep me busy here."

I kissed my children as Nick's arm came around me, his hand firm against the small of my back as he escorted me to his car.

CHAPTER 22

Nick's car hadn't had time to cool in the few short minutes it had been parked in my driveway, but he angled the vents toward me and cranked up the heat, probably because I was shivering. I stole a glance at Theresa's town house as we rolled by. The windows were all dark except for a single light in the kitchen. Theresa's BMW was still parked in the driveway. Wherever Theresa and Aimee had gone, they must have taken Aimee's SUV.

"You okay?" Nick asked.

I dragged my attention from the dim glow in Theresa's kitchen window. "I'm fine. Did you get a chance to talk to Pete?"

"A bit. He just got the file, so there's not much to talk about yet. The fire was started by a crude incendiary device, using turpentine as an accelerant. That's pretty much all he could tell me."

"Turpentine? You mean, like paint thinner?" Nick nodded. "Great, that could be anyone."

"Maybe," he said as he turned off my street. "But the most promising evidence didn't come through the lab."

"What do you mean?"

"The security company logged a call just before the fire. Someone tripped the alarm. Apparently, they have a recording, but Steven's dragging his feet. He hasn't given the monitoring company authorization to share it."

"Why not?"

He shrugged. "It's possible he knows the person and he's trying to protect them. If the investigators want the recording, they can always pull a warrant."

"Did they find anything else?"

"Just a piece of a broken credit card, recovered from the weeds just outside the fire perimeter. It might have been used to try to break in. They also found some high-performance tire treads in the mud behind the trailer. None of Steven's employees drive sports cars, so it's possible the impressions were made by the arsonist's vehicle."

Perfect. The three most compelling pieces of evidence they'd found were left by me and Vero.

"You sure you're okay?" Nick's eyes skated to me before sliding back to the road. "You look a little pale."

"I'm probably just hungry. I haven't eaten since breakfast."

"Good," he said with a furtive smile. "This restaurant we're going to is supposed to be pretty amazing. I just have one quick stop to make before we head to dinner. Need to talk to a CI. Figured you wouldn't mind coming along."

Nick's attention was focused on the road, and I took a moment to see the things I'd been too stressed to notice when he'd picked me up a few minutes ago. His leather jacket was slung over the center console, his usual Henley and jeans swapped out for a crisply pressed French-blue dress shirt and a tie. His hair looked freshly cut, his face was clean-shaven, and the spicy scent of his cologne was warm and heavy in the car. Everything about his appearance suggested he was dressed for a date, except for the holster around his shoulders and the gun hugging his side.

I raised an eyebrow. "I thought the identities of confidential informants were supposed to be a secret."

He gave a thoughtful dip of his chin. "They are."

"I thought you didn't trust me." The last time he'd allowed me to tag along on secret police business, it had blown up in his face; he'd accused me of using both him and his case as fodder for my books.

He eased the car to a stop as the traffic light in front of us turned yellow, washing his face in a pale amber glow. He shook his head and sighed. "I said a lot of things that day, most of which I wish I hadn't. I wasn't angry with you, Finlay. I was angry at myself. You were right. I made the choice to involve you in the case, and the blame for that falls squarely on me."

"So you want to do it all over again?" I teased him. "I thought you would have learned from your mistake."

"I never said I regretted it." His sideways glance lingered as the color of the light changed. I cleared my throat, nodding at the green traffic signal and the empty lane in front of us, relieved when he finally dragged his attention back to the road.

"Who's your CI?" I asked, admittedly curious as we turned onto a dark residential street. The homes on both sides were obscured by old trees, their front yards shrouded in dead leaves and cheap lawn ornaments, their driveways riddled with cars in various stages of disrepair.

"Not mine. The kid's one of Joey's informants, but Joe's off visiting his mother this weekend and I didn't see a reason to bug him."

I turned to Nick, surprised. "Kid? What did he do?"

"Joey busted him for identity theft about a year ago. He's a small fish, but he swims in a pretty murky pond—online drugs and weapons dealers, internet sex trafficking, cyber-fraud . . . Joey got him a deal. Probation and community service. In return, the kid keeps his nose out of trouble and feeds us leads on the big fish as he finds them. He called me a few hours ago. Said he found some nasty stuff online. He thinks it might have ties to Zhirov's outfit. I didn't want to wait until Joey gets back to check it out."

"Feliks Zhirov? But he's in jail."

"Never stopped him before. He's got his hands in everything, and his reach is pretty far. The more evidence I can pile onto the DA's lap, the less likely Feliks is to walk when he finally goes to trial. We're chasing every possible lead. I'm not taking any chances with that asshole."

I suppressed a shudder. Patricia Mickler once told me that Feliks had eyes and ears everywhere. I'd heard Nick make similar comments before, and I'd always assumed he was being hyperbolic. But after my conversation with Theresa over Carl's dismembered body, I wasn't so sure. Even knowing Feliks was securely behind bars, Theresa had been terrified to cross him.

That day in Ramón's garage, Feliks had warned me he'd be keeping an eye on me. Now, as I watched the shadows deepen around the car, I wondered if he still was.

Nick's car came to a stop in the driveway of a ramshackle split-level. A TV flickered through the sheer curtains as a figure pulled the fabric back to stare at us.

"Wait here," Nick said, leaving the ignition on.

He shrugged on his jacket and got out of the car, his long legs taking slow, easy bites of the cracked front walk as he approached the house. Light spilled over the front steps as someone opened the door. A lean figure in a dark hoodie slipped out, checking both ways down the street before meeting Nick halfway to the car.

I slouched low in my seat, keenly aware that I shouldn't be here, but Joey's CI didn't seem to notice me through the tinted windows of Nick's car. The engine purred quietly, muting their greeting. Nick's hands were planted on his hips, the CI's shoved deep in his pockets as they spoke, their heads bent close. I reached for the window button, tempted to crack it open just enough to catch a little of their conversation. But at the last second, I pulled my hand away. The simple fact that Nick had brought me here felt like an olive branch—a demonstration of trust. Trust I wanted to be worthy of.

Until the CI pushed back his hood.

Cam's crown of bleached-blond hair caught the brash yellow light of the window behind him. My mind raced. Back to what Nick had said about Cam's murky pond. About the kinds of leads Cam fed to Joey.

. . . he's found some nasty stuff online.

Oh, no.

I pressed the window button, holding my breath as it hummed down an inch, just enough for a few words to slip through the crack.

". . . some kind of moms' group or something," Cam said in a low voice.

"Moms' group?"

"I know, right?"

No, this was not good. If Cam told Nick where to find the women's forum, Nick would dig until he found a bone.

"If you're bullshitting me—"

"I'm serious, man. It all seems normal on the surface, but some shady deals are going down. I'm not just talking dime-bags of weed. I found someone trying to move cases of ARs . . . high-dollar hookers . . . contract hits . . . pretty sure the whole site is a front . . ."

No. No, no, no! I couldn't let Cam give Nick any names. Not *FedUp.* Not *EasyClean.*

And definitely not mine.

I reached for my purse before I remembered my phone was gone. I had no way to text Cam. No way to warn him to keep his big mouth shut. I rolled my window down a few more inches, praying Nick couldn't hear the hum over the idling engine.

"Who runs it?" he asked.

Cam jerked his chin toward Nick's jacket pocket.

Nick muttered something under his breath as he reached for his wallet and plucked out a few bills. Cam looked up and down the street before taking them and stuffing them in his pocket.

"I did some digging around," he said. "The names were all Russian. Been watching the news about that guy you busted last month. Thought the information might be worth something to you."

"And you thought you'd wait until Joey was out of town to hit me up for beer money."

Cam threw up his hands. "Fine. If you don't want my intel, I guess we're done."

Nick grabbed Cam's elbow as he turned for the door. "Depends on the quality of the intel."

Cam shrugged. "Hosting, site admin, domain registry, member profiles, user logs . . . I've got it all, plus a back door in."

"What's it gonna cost me?"

"I give you everything I have, and then Joey and I are done. I've stayed out of trouble—no hacking, no ditching, and no scamming—just like we agreed. I want out of probation and I want the cops off my . . ." Cam's eyes flicked in my direction. I watched them darken as he recognized me through the window gap. I had enough dirt on Cam to blow his cozy deal with Joey and send him back for a nice long stint in juvie, and Cam knew it.

I drew a finger across my neck.

His Adam's apple bobbed. He cleared his throat, jamming his fists deeper in his pockets as I quickly rolled my window up.

Nick turned toward the car and frowned. I shrank back in my seat, hidden behind the tinted glass. He reached once more for his wallet, holding a few bills just out of Cam's reach as he bent low to meet the hacker's eyes. I knew that look. It was a lecture. A warning. Cam shot a quick glance at my window as he folded the money into his pocket and disappeared inside his house.

Nick circled around the car and dropped into the driver's seat.

"What did you find out?" I asked, peeking at the screen of his cell phone as he fired off a quick text to Joey. He slipped his phone in his pocket and backed out of Cam's driveway.

"Maybe nothing. The kid's probably working me."

"Then why'd you pay him?"

"Because on the off chance he's telling the truth, a lead like that could be a gold mine." I paid closer attention to our route this time, committing the street names and turns to memory as Nick wound our way out of Cam's neighborhood. "He says he found some online chat group that might be a front for organized crime."

"Did he tell you how he found it?"

Nick's lips twitched, curling up on one side. "He says he stumbled on it by accident."

"You don't believe him?"

"Seventeen-year-old hackers don't stumble into women's chat rooms by accident. He probably boosted some unsuspecting lady's phone and found it while he was rooting around in her accounts."

"Do you believe any of it?"

Nick shrugged as he turned back onto the highway. "He knew I was working the Zhirov case. I'm guessing he found a few moms selling Xanax online and fig- ured he'd make a quick buck off me while Joey's out of town. The kid's going to send me everything he found tomorrow. It should only take the cyber guys a few days to flush it out. It's probably nothing."

I rested my head against the window as we reached the interstate. I had to call Cam before he sent those leads to Nick. But Cam's number was in my phone, and my phone was with Theresa.

Or, more likely, it was buried in a shallow grave with Carl.

CHAPTER 23

My mind was still spinning when Nick pulled into a parking space in front of a strip mall in Arlington. The name on the red awning of the restaurant said KVASS, and white lights glittered from the potted evergreens flanking the door. Rich, savory smells wafted through it as Nick held it open for me. My stomach rumbled as a host in a suit jacket and tie guided us to our booth.

I slid into the bench across from Nick, only half listening as a maître d' with a thick accent welcomed us to the restaurant.

"Can I get you anything to drink, miss?" He held a leather folio in front of me. "A bottle of wine, perhaps?"

I flipped open the menu, skimming the drinks, the nervous bob of my knee hidden under the long silk table linens and the dim lighting of the dining room. "I think I'm going to need something stronger."

"May I suggest the vodka sampler. We have an exceptional selection of—"

"Perfect," I said, closing the folio and passing it to Nick.

Nick's mouth quirked up. He glanced at the name badge on the man's lapel. "Just a beer for me, Sergei. And how about an order of piroshki with that?"

Our host nodded as he lit the single votive in the

middle of our table. "Ivan will be your server this evening. He'll be with you shortly to review this evening's specials." I set aside the dinner menu, too distracted to focus on the descriptions of the entrées when Ivan arrived to take our orders. Soft music played. The restaurant hummed with quiet conversations and the dull clatter and hiss of cooking sounds through the service doors from the kitchen. Silver clinked against fancy blue-and-white plates.

Who was I kidding? This was definitely a date.

"Rough day?" Nick asked, ducking his head to catch my eyes.

"You could say that."

"Things not going well with your new book?"

"Not exactly," I said as our server slid a tray of gleaming shot glasses in front of me. "I'm pretty sure the entire plot's gone off the rails." As soon as the waiter was gone, I downed the first one. My eyes watered, and I quickly chased it with another.

"Maybe I can help," Nick offered, taking a slow pull off his beer. A slightly hysterical laugh bubbled out of me as I reached for a piroshki. "I'm serious," he said, toying lazily with the fancy imported bottle in his hand. "Ask me anything."

"Anything?"

He rested his elbows on the table, his teeth sinking into his lower lip as he watched me eat. "Anything."

It felt like a loaded question. But he was offering. "Okay," I said, clearing my throat. "So, this website your CI told you about. What happens if the cyber guys find something?"

Nick slumped back in his seat, shaking his head. He set down his beer, threading his fingers behind his neck. "You really want to talk about that?"

"Why not? You offered to help me with research for my book."

"From what I read, you had the crime angles all figured out. I thought maybe I could help you with the other stuff."

"What other stuff?"

"You know, the romantic bits."

I stopped chewing. "What's wrong with my romantic bits?"

"Nothing." His gaze fell to the plunging neckline of my dress as he nursed a long, slow sip. "I admit it. That book Pete let me borrow was pretty hot. Especially the part during the stakeout, when she made out with the cop in the front seat of his car, and then she climbed on his lap and—"

"Just dinner." My face warmed and I slugged down another shot.

He grinned into his beer. "Right. Just dinner."

His eyes flicked over the room. "I did say you could ask me anything." I paused, my piroshki poised halfway to my lips as he leaned his elbows on the table and lowered his voice. "If the kid's right and the forum is being used as a front, we'll probably send an undercover in. We'll set up a sting, make a few arrests, and find a canary. Then we'll dangle a deal in front of them and hope they sing." Nick leaned back in his seat, lips pressed shut as our waiter approached the table with the rest of our meal. Ivan placed a heaping plate of stroganoff in front of me, and it was all I could do to keep from kissing him.

Nick waited for Ivan to leave before continuing. "Joey's back in the office on Monday. Hopefully by then, I'll know what we're dealing with." He forked into his chicken Kiev, his eyes roving around the restaurant as he ate. "What's your new book about anyway?" he asked between bites.

"It's just the next book in the series. The same

character. You know . . . a hit woman . . . getting framed . . . solving crimes."

"Is the hotshot cop still in the picture?"

I gave a tentative nod. "He's in the story. For now."

"For now?"

"It's still a rough draft."

"How about the lawyer?"

Our eyes caught across the table. How much had Vero told him when he'd been sitting at my kitchen table while I was with Bree? I twirled my fork through my noodles. "He went missing."

"Is she looking for him?"

"I don't know. It's a little early in the story for that. Maybe she's worrying for nothing."

"Maybe not. She's smart. She should trust her instincts."

"And do what?"

He shrugged. "She could ask the cop for help."

I laughed, the vodka dissolving the walls I'd been holding up. "I don't think that'd be a good idea. She and the cop have a history. He's too close to her. There'd be a clear conflict of interest."

"Oh, he's definitely interested." I lifted my eyes and found Nick watching me across the table. I didn't think it was the beer that had roughened his voice. Or the candlelight that made his irises darken. We definitely weren't talking about my book anymore.

With a thoughtful pause, I set down my fork. I certainly didn't want his help finding Julian. But maybe he could help me find someone else. "Let's say my character did want to search for a missing person on her own . . . someone who didn't want to be found. How might the cop suggest she go about it?"

His brow creased. "Are you sure that's a good idea? She might not like what she finds."

"You said *anything*."

A resigned sigh escaped him. He set down his fork and wiped his mouth with his napkin. "Has she checked the location services on his phone?"

"No luck."

"Social media accounts?"

"Dead ends." Aimee knew how to keep a low profile. Vero and I had tried to find her through social media before, but she'd been a ghost online. And Theresa had shut down all of her own accounts after her arrest made national headlines.

Nick's frown deepened. "If your heroine was really close with this missing person and she had access to his bank records, she could track his spending. Credit charges, gas cards, ATM withdrawals . . ."

I had no access to Theresa's banking information. I seriously doubted she and Steven still shared any accounts. I shook my head and his worry lines softened.

"Look," he said after a thoughtful pause, "I know you said your heroine doesn't want any help, but if she knows anyone this missing person might feel close to, maybe she and her cop friend could try to stake them out."

I laughed, reaching for the last shot of vodka as I pictured Theresa speeding off in Aimee's SUV. "I'm pretty sure they ran off together."

Nick took my wrist as I lifted the glass. "If you ask me, Finn, you're better off without him."

His touch lingered. We stared at each other across the table. Nick still thought we were talking about Julian. I opened my mouth to correct him when his gaze flicked to the door of the restaurant behind me. A muscle tensed in his cheek, and he let go of my hand. I turned in my seat to see what had stolen his attention so fully.

A statuesque brunette in a designer coat and perilously high heels strutted into the dining room, the long waves of her hair bouncing as she walked. She was stunning, polished in a way that reeked of money and power, with the same confident swagger I'd seen in Irina Borovkov. To Nick's credit, his gaze never dropped below her face. With a smug smile, she signaled for the maître d'. He glanced at our table as she whispered in his ear.

"This should be interesting," Nick muttered as the maître d' retreated to his station and picked up a phone.

"Clearly, you two know each other." I set down the last shot and slid it toward him.

He declined, pushing away his plate as if he'd suddenly lost his appetite. "You could say that."

The woman stopped beside our table, tossing her Jaguar keys into her handbag. She pushed her tortoise-shell glasses in place with a stiff middle finger, and Nick barked out a laugh.

"Kat," he greeted her, strangling the neck of his beer.

"Detective. I trust you're enjoying your meal." Her rich voice seemed to match the rest of her. Sophisticated and sharp, with the hint of an accent.

"I was until you got here."

"Aren't you going to introduce me to your friend?"

Nick ran his tongue over the edges of his teeth. "Kat. Finn. Finn. Kat."

She reached out with her left hand, forcing me to switch mine to match. Her heavy signet ring squeezed a little too hard. "It's a pleasure to meet you," she said sweetly. "I've heard so much about you."

Nick tensed.

"Oh?" I asked, looking between them. "How do you two know each other?"

"Work," they answered in unison.

Nick's eyes burned, that muscle in his cheek still

twitching. He opened his mouth to speak when a buzzing sound came from the pocket of his coat. He reached inside it for his cell, his eyes lifting to mine as he pressed it to his ear. "Hey, Vero. Everything okay? . . . Yeah, she's right here." Nick passed me the phone. "There's a hallway by the restrooms. I'll order us some coffee and dessert. Take your time," he said, cutting a sideways glance at Kat.

I felt the weight of several pairs of eyes on me as I carried the phone into the ladies' room.

"What's wrong?" I asked Vero, my heart already racing as I considered all the reasons she might have called. "Are the kids okay?"

"The kids are fine. They've been in bed for an hour, but we have a problem."

"What problem?"

"Which part do you want first?"

"It's a multipart problem?"

"I've been busy," she said, her voice clipped.

"What's the first part?"

"We got an email from *EasyClean*."

"An email?"

"Through the address you used to set up the account."

"What did she say?"

"She said she has dibs on the job, and you'd better step off if you know what's good for you. So *I* said—"

"You replied to her?!"

"—that if she wanted the money, she was gonna have to work for it because *Anonymous2* backs down for nobody—"

"Tell me you didn't."

"I'm paraphrasing for the sake of brevity . . . Then *she* said, game on, bitch. And *I* said, bring it—"

"Jesus."

"She threatened you, Finn! What else was I supposed to do?"

"Maybe not make it worse?" I needed more vodka. "What's the second part?"

"I still haven't located your phone."

The line went quiet as she waited for me to put the pieces of our problem together. Every message Vero and *EasyClean* had exchanged would have popped up as a notification on my smartphone. "We have to find that phone, Vero."

"I tried calling it, but Theresa didn't answer. And your locator service is turned off."

I slumped back against the wall. We'd turned off the GPS the night we'd snuck onto the farm to dig up a body and I'd never bothered turning it back on.

"Look at the bright side. At least Theresa didn't break the circuit when she took off her monitor."

"How'd she manage that?"

"I wondered the same thing, so I Googled it. Guess what I found?"

"A YouTube tutorial?"

"That video was eye-opening, Finn. You never know when a butter knife will come in handy. We should consider keeping one in the garage."

"Noted," I said, pinching the vodka headache blooming behind my eyes.

"I plugged the ankle monitor into the charger in Theresa's kitchen. That should buy us some time to figure out what to do with Carl. I want that dude out of my trunk before he starts to smell."

"He was in deep freeze for months, Vero. He's practically a mummy. He won't smell," I assured her. "Not yet."

"Great. My car's probably cursed."

"We'll deal with him when I get home. Meanwhile,

no more emails to *EasyClean*. I have to get back to the table before Nick comes looking for me."

"Bring cash," she said before she disconnected. "Delia's waiting on the tooth fairy."

I braced myself against the vanity and frowned at myself in the mirror, certain this day could not possibly get any worse. I didn't have any money left. All I had in my purse was a broken credit card and a tube of lip gloss. I swiped on a fresh coat of it and fluffed my hair, feeling flat and colorless in Kat's wake. If she worked with Nick, then she also worked with Georgia, which would explain how she'd apparently heard so much about me. She and Nick obviously had some unpleasant history, which bugged me for reasons I didn't want to think about.

I tossed my lip gloss in my purse and headed back to the dining room. The air in the restaurant seemed to hum with tension. Nothing I could put my finger on. Just something about the stiffness of the waitstaff. The way their gazes all seemed stuck on the far side of the room.

I slowed as I noticed the maître d' standing beside our table, wearing a stern expression. Two waiters, both unusually large in stature, hovered behind him. Nick smirked up at them as I approached, his arm slung carelessly over the back of the booth. "What?" he asked. "No dessert?"

The maître d' set a leather folio in front of Nick. "Your meal is on the house tonight, courtesy of the owner, with the understanding that you will not return."

Nick stood, yanking his wallet from his pocket. He dropped a handful of crisp bills on the table. More than enough to cover the meal and a generous tip. "Oh, I'll definitely be back," he growled. "Tell the owner dinner was unforgettable."

He took my coat from the booth and held it open

for me. Sliding his hand in mine, he towed me from the restaurant, glaring at Kat's table as we passed.

"What was that all about?" I asked, handing him back his phone as the door closed behind us.

"That was a message."

"I thought it was a date."

He paused in the middle of the parking lot, tugging me gently to a halt. A triumphant smile rode the thin line of his lips. "Was it? I seem to recall you insisting it was only dinner."

When I didn't answer, he started purposefully toward his car.

"Who was that woman?"

"Why? Are you jealous?"

I scowled. "Why would I be jealous? Of course I'm not jealous." Okay, fine. Maybe I was jealous. But only just a little.

Mercifully, he let it go. "That was Zhirov's star attorney," he explained, opening the passenger side door of his car and ducking into it before I had the chance. He felt around under the front seat for a box of disposable gloves, peeled two sets from the box, and handed one to me. "If I have a nemesis, I guess you could say Kat is it. This restaurant just opened two weeks ago. I had a feeling it was one of Zhirov's fronts. Feliks must have heard I was here checking out his new digs and sent his watchdog to warn me off. Come on," he said, taking my hand with brisk steps and leading me behind the strip mall.

I tripped on a pothole, struggling to keep up. "This restaurant belongs to Feliks?"

"Apparently so."

"*That's* why you brought me here? Just to goad him?"

"It was the only way I could be sure he's involved." He dragged on his gloves and pushed back the lid of the dumpster behind the restaurant.

"What are you doing?" I asked as he hauled himself over the top.

He reached back for me with an impish grin. "Just a little digging around. You want in?"

"No!"

"Suit yourself." He disappeared inside, bags and cans crunching under him.

"What are you looking for?" I called over the top.

"Anything that's not related to food."

"Is this legal?"

He laughed. "Aren't you the woman who had to call a tow truck to rescue her from a botched B and E?"

"*I'm* not a police officer," I reminded him. "And that house didn't belong to Feliks Zhirov." I whirled as a dead bolt slid open behind me. "Someone's coming!" I whispered.

"Give me your hands!" Nick grabbed me as I reached for him, hauling me over the side of the dumpster. I landed on my butt in a pile of trash. He ducked beside me and held a finger in front of his lips.

A door flung open. Footsteps scraped against the pavement. We shielded our heads as two giant trash bags flew over the lid and landed beside us. Nick waited for the back door to the restaurant to click shut before rolling onto his knees and reaching for the bags. Unknotting one, he sifted through the contents. "Perfect timing," he murmured. "Shake the tree and all the rotten fruit falls out."

"What is it?" I asked, peeking over his shoulder.

"Delivery receipts. Feliks uses his own shipping and supply companies. His companies all feed and launder for one another. I'm betting most of these receipts come from businesses he owns under other names. It should be easier to trace them back to Zhirov, now that I know where to look. Kat's probably in there now, cracking the whip, making sure they get rid of any bread crumbs, in case I come back with a warrant to search the place." He retied the bags, slinging them over the top of the dumpster to the street below.

I stood up, my heels sinking into the trash as I brushed something I hoped was coffee grounds from my coat. Nick laced his fingers together and hoisted me out. He landed softly on his feet beside me and stripped off his gloves, tossing them back over the lip.

"I cannot believe you brought me here to go digging around in the trash."

"Come on!" he said, hefting the bags. "You can't tell me you're not having fun."

I rolled my eyes and turned for the car. Nick caught up to me. He dropped the bags as he reached for my arm. Turning me gently toward him, he boxed me in between his body and the side of the restaurant. "I brought you here," he said, his voice falling low, "because you wouldn't let me make you dinner at my place. *You* were the one who made me promise it wasn't a date."

I laughed as he plucked a piece of trash from my hair. He threaded his fingers in mine with a tenderness I hadn't expected from him. Our laughter quieted, and a heavy thought seemed to pull on his brow.

"That's not the only reason I invited you," he confessed into the narrowing space between us. "Last month, when you came with me to the lab, and to the farm, and on the stakeout . . . when I busted you coming out of Theresa's house . . ." He shook his head, as if that memory still surprised him. "That was the most fun I've had with anyone in a long time. Don't get me wrong. Joey's a great partner. But I wanted *you* riding along with me tonight. I wanted you there when I picked a fight with Zhirov's attorney and went diving in his dumpster. Call it dinner. Call it a date. Call it research for a book. Call it whatever the hell you want, Finn. Whatever it was between us, I miss it." It was hard to breathe when he was standing this close. Close enough to smell the warm hops on his breath over the stench of garbage on our clothes. "I'm sorry our date got cut short," he said, his thumb tracing lazy patterns over mine. "I'd love to make it up to you. Maybe over dessert at my place?"

My belly was pleasantly full, and my muscles were warm and loose from the vodka. And I had no desire whatsoever to go home and deal with Carl. As much as I hated to admit it, I'd had fun tonight. I slid my hand from Nick's before I agreed to something I'd regret.

"I should probably get home. But thank you for dinner," I said, hugging my coat around me. "Or maybe I should thank Feliks."

Nick laughed, a hint of disappointment in his smile. "Right, I promised. Just dinner this time." He leaned close, bending to pick up the bags, his breath warm against my ear, making me shiver when he said, "But next time, Finn, I'm not making any promises."

CHAPTER 24

A single light was on in the living room when Nick dropped me off in front of my house. He idled in my driveway as I walked to my door, watching as I fumbled in my handbag for my house keys. As I slid them into the lock and turned the knob, a gas station receipt slipped from the doorframe. I bent to catch it before the wind could blow it from the porch, my steps faltering when I recognized the handwriting on the back.

I waved goodbye to Nick and ducked inside, silently slipping off my shoes and setting my handbag on the hall table when I noticed Vero sleeping on the couch. Her body was curled around a library book, the reading lamp still on beside her. I carried the note to the kitchen and held it under the night-light above the stove.

Just got back. Tried to call. Your mailbox is full. Talk tomorrow?—J

I read it again. No *sorry I disappeared for a week*? No *had a great time but I wished you were there*? What did *talk tomorrow* mean? If there had been a kissy emoji or a flame, maybe I'd have a better grasp of the subtext. But after being gone for a week and locking me out of his profile, *talk tomorrow* felt disappointingly . . . casual.

I reached for the house phone, my fingers hovering

over the keypad. I'd never called him from my home phone before. I'd never even given him the number. My cell phone felt secure and private, only my own. Calling him from my house line felt like an invitation inside my home.

I reached to put the phone back in the cradle when I noticed the message light flashing. I held the phone to my ear, wincing at the horrid smell coming from my coat sleeve.

Finlay, it's Sylvia. I haven't gotten your twenty thousand words yet. They're due by Monday, and I expect them to be fabulous. And don't forget the hot cop.

"Fat chance of that," I whispered. Monday was less than two days away. She would have to settle for ten thousand crappy ones. The only two men I wanted to think about right now were far from hot, and their names were Ben and Jerry. I took a spoon from the drawer and opened my freezer, head tipped curiously as I stared inside.

The food was gone, the frozen waffles, vegetable medleys, and nuggets all mysteriously absent. And worse, there was no trace of my Cherry Garcia anywhere. What had Vero done with all the food? On second thought, I wasn't sure I wanted to know.

I shut the freezer and trudged to the coffee maker.

A sticky note hung from the pot. Vero had scribbled a dollar sign and the outline of a tooth. I swore quietly, set the coffee to brew, and tiptoed upstairs to the laundry closet to shed my foul-smelling clothes.

An overly sweet aroma wafted out as I slid open the door. Two heavy-duty air fresheners—the kind we used to mask the smell of Zach's diaper pail—sat on the shelf over the machines. The mountain of unwashed towels we'd used to sop up water from the kitchen was piled beside them, mildewing on the floor. I stripped off Vero's dress and lifted the lid of the washer. Bags of frozen broccoli and peas, loose cubes from the ice maker, and a pint of Chunky Monkey stared back at me. The corner of a black trash bag peeked out from under the tater tots.

With a shudder, I shut the lid, my fantasies of taking Ben and Jerry to bed officially ruined by the crime scene that had once been my washing machine.

The dryer, thankfully, contained nothing of Carl. I reached inside, dragged out a wrinkled T-shirt and pulled it over my head, then scraped a few crumpled dollar bills from the lint catcher. A small plastic disc slipped out with them. It was thinner and smoother than the ones in Delia's game. I turned it over, squinting at the logo in the dim light of the dryer—THE ROYAL FLUSH CASINO HOTEL.

I frowned at the poker chip in my hand. Vero said she'd checked the forum over Thanksgiving weekend from a business center in a hotel. And she hadn't spent the weekend with Ramón. Was this where she'd gone? If so, why hadn't she told me?

Creeping into Delia's room, I tucked the stiff bills under her pillow. It wasn't the two hundred dollars she was expecting, but it was better than an IOU for a cash advance from my broken credit card. I paused beside her bed, toying with the black chip from the casino as I watched my daughter sleep, remembering what she'd said about Vero losing a marker and making someone mad. Those words had resonated with the same ominous tone as Vero's hushed conversation with Ramón that morning, when he'd told her someone had gone to her mother's house looking for her.

A seed of worry planted itself inside me as I wondered what it all meant. Brushing back Delia's hair, I placed a kiss on her head before tiptoeing to the hall.

I paused in front of Vero's bedroom, standing at her cracked bedroom door, listening to the house.

*You've got some stranger you met less than a year
ago living under your roof . . . What do you really know
about her?*

Quietly, I nudged her door open. It hadn't been
locked, I told myself. And this was my house, after all.
Vero had more than once admitted to snooping around
in my laptop and my nightstand. I was only going to
leave the casino chip on her desk, where she'd be sure
to find it.

I switched on the small lamp on her desk. The surface was piled with accounting textbooks, the nightstand stacked with self-help manuals she'd checked out
of the library, about smart goal setting and thinking
big. The wall beside her bed was covered with pictures
Zach and Delia had drawn for her.

I set the plastic chip on her desk. My hand slid down
to the drawer and drew it open. Pens, pencils, note-
books, and calculators were neatly arranged inside, and
I quietly slid it shut. I turned toward her nightstand,
peeping through one eye as I opened that, too.

A framed photograph rested inside it.

I lifted it out, angling it toward the light. A young
Vero and Ramón smiled back at me, along with two
women who, based on obvious resemblances, could only
be their mothers. The glass in the frame was clean, the
stand intact, a tiny crack in the wood carefully glued
back together. This photo was clearly precious to Vero,
and I couldn't help but wonder why she kept it in a
drawer.

I returned it to its place, standing beside her neatly
made bed as I turned a slow circle around the room,
hungry to learn more about her. To understand why
she'd kept so much of herself hidden when she knew
everything there was to know about me. The closet was
open, her endless supply of trendy brand-name clothes
neatly packed to fit on the rod above a row of brightly

colored shoes. A stack of books perched on a high shelf: probability and statistics, odds and profits, algorithms for winning, the mathematics of chance . . . and a photo album. I pulled it down, careful not to disrupt the rest of the stack.

Sitting on the edge of Vero's bed, I thumbed through the early pages of her baby book, skipping ahead toward the more recent photos at the back. There were dozens of pictures of Vero and her mother, her aunt, and her cousin. Several of her extended family. Even a few of her friends from high school. I flipped through photos of her homecoming, prom, and graduation, noting the honor society adornment on her gown. I turned the page. A loose piece of paper stuck to the clear plastic film.

Congratulations! You've been accepted to the University of Maryland Robert H. Smith School of Business.

Along with a full-tuition merit scholarship for all four years.

The last name on the letter wasn't one I recognized.

Veronica R. Ramirez.

Not Veronica Ruiz.

If Vero had earned a full ride to a major university in Maryland, what was she doing taking community college classes here in Virginia? Why had she agreed to help me dispose of a body for money, claiming she needed it because she was buried in student loans?

The best place to hide a dirty secret is across a state line.

But what dirty secrets was Vero hiding?

The scent of brewing coffee drifted up from the kitchen. I slipped the photo album back in its place. I hadn't found anything about this mysterious marker Delia claimed Vero had lost, and yet I felt like I had learned more than I was entitled to.

When I crept downstairs, Vero was still fast asleep on the couch. Careful not to rouse her, I drew a warm blanket over her and switched off the lamp. Her laptop awoke on the coffee table, casting a pale blue glow over her sleeping face as a notification popped up on the screen. I angled the laptop toward me. The page was opened to the mail program I'd used to set up the account on the forum, on a message Vero must have sent to *FedUp* while I'd been out with Nick.

> *Dear FedUp, It's very important that I speak with you. Can we meet for coffee? I promise to be discreet.—Anonymous2*

A response had appeared below it.

> *Dear Anonymous2, I'm sorry. I really don't have time right now. I thought I made it clear, I prefer to chat after the holiday. Please contact me then. Sincerely, FedUp*

In Vero's defense, I hadn't expressly told her not to email *FedUp*. And there hadn't been anything too incriminating in the message itself. *FedUp* obviously wasn't willing to talk until the job was done, but at least Vero had tried.

I checked the locks on the front door on my way to the kitchen. Then I fixed myself a cup of coffee strong enough to raise the dead. I had eight hours until morning. Eight hours to start drafting a sample of my story. Eight hours to figure out how to delete my posts from the forum and what to do with Carl. And maybe, if I was lucky, a few precious hours to sleep.

I retreated to my office, opened my laptop, and started typing. About the defense lawyer who'd disappeared without a trace. About the assassin who'd lost her mark and evaded capture. About the only friend in the world she could trust to help her, a woman with too many secrets of her own. About a star witness to a murder who'd mysteriously gone missing—a woman who could put the heroine in prison for life—and a cop from her past, who was determined to find her.

CHAPTER 25

Irina Borovkov wasn't an easy woman to find. I had only ever met Irina in two places: Panera and her fitness club. When I'd asked the receptionist at the health club if Irina was in, she'd informed me Irina didn't usually come on Sundays. And I didn't take Irina Borovkov for the type of woman who'd hang out in a crowded sandwich shop. At least, not without a compelling reason, like murder for hire.

So I'd called the only other place I could think to try: the front desk of the extravagant high-rise address she'd written on the slip of paper she'd given me when she'd asked me to kill her husband. The bellman who answered had placed me on hold for a discomforting length of time, then returned with instructions to proceed to this address.

A few heads turned behind the pristine glass walls of the showroom as my minivan rolled onto the international car lot. The rattle in my engine had grown more pronounced during the short drive, and I wasn't sure if it was the grinding noise or the filthy, frumpy appearance of the thing that had attracted their disdainful attention. I eased into an empty space between two sleek sports cars that, even used, were probably worth more than the bounty on my ex-husband. Careful not to bump their doors with my own, I angled clumsily out of my van and headed for the showroom.

A man in a tailored suit stepped in my path as I reached the sidewalk. His mouth pursed, the shape growing increasingly sour as he made a slow perusal of my gym clothes. "May I help you?" His smile was doubtful.

"I'm meeting someone here. I'll just wait inside." I moved to step around him.

"Perhaps you'd be more comfortable waiting in your vehicle." I jerked my hand back as he reached for my arm, clearly intending to steer me away. "The showroom is for customers only."

"She is a customer, Alan. She's with me." We both turned at the sound of the woman's voice. In a pair of burgundy stilettos, Irina Borovkov stood eye to eye with him, the collar of her fur coat ruffling with the breeze. She scraped a strand of her dark hair from the corner of her deep red lips with a perfectly manicured fingernail. Alan's throat bobbed against his collar, his neck reddening to match his tie.

"Of course, Mrs. Borovkov. My apologies," he stammered.

"Be a dear and fetch me the keys to the Spider. My friend and I will be taking it for a test drive."

"Right away. The silver one has just been waxed. I'll have it brought around."

"The black one," she corrected him, stripping off her gloves and sliding them into the pockets of her fur.

"Of course." His head bobbed as he disappeared into the showroom.

"Thank you for meeting me," I said when Alan was gone. "I need to speak with you about—"

Irina held up a hand, gesturing discreetly toward a large man in black cargo pants and a black leather jacket standing a few feet behind her. A tiny device hugged his right ear, and there were several suspicious bulges under his jacket.

"Not here," she said in a low voice as the sleek black hood of an Alfa Romeo swung around the side of the showroom and parked at the curb. The salesman stepped out of a car that was worthy of James Bond. "Thank you, Alan," she purred as he held the door open for her.

"Of course, Mrs. Borovkov. Keep it as long as you like."

That was it? No *may we see your license and proof of insurance to make sure you're not on a wanted list?* No *sorry, it's our policy to have a salesperson ride with you so you're not tempted to steal it?* Just *here are your keys to this very expensive car, Mrs. Borovkov. Drive it to California if you'd like. We probably won't miss it.*

She winked at me as she slid into the driver's seat. With a nod of her chin, she gestured for me to get in. The man in the leather jacket beat me to the passenger door, his grip tight on my arm. Irina leaned over the console. "Wait here, Sasha. We won't be long."

Sasha looked at me askance, his hand slowly falling away from me as Irina continued speaking to him in Russian. He stepped away from the passenger door, holding it open for me, his eyebrows arched with surprise as I got in and slammed it shut. "Why is he looking at me like that?"

"He is concerned for my safety." Irina gunned the engine, leaving Sasha in a cloud of tire smoke as the Spider peeled out of the lot. "I don't normally go anywhere without my bodyguards."

"What did you tell him?"

"I explained that you are a highly skilled assassin. I told him he could wait here, or we could ask Alan to bring us a larger vehicle so he could join us. But I warned him that you may not take kindly to being asked to sit in the back seat behind him." Her grin was wicked.

An attractive man in a BMW in the next lane surveyed Irina with obvious interest as we eased to a stop at a red light. She spared him a cool glance as he gave his engine a low rev. Irina returned it with a louder one. I held fast to the door handle as the light changed and her stiletto came down hard on the gas, forcing the man in the BMW into a turn lane. She watched him fishtail in her rearview mirror through the daggerlike points of her raven-black bangs, her smile triumphant.

"I apologize for Sasha's behavior," she said as the car accelerated. "Feliks's men take their jobs very seriously."

"Your bodyguards work for Feliks?"

"Feliks has insisted on employing them ever since Andrei's body was found."

I gasped, squeezing my eyes shut as she urged the Spider through a changing light, missing the bumper of a tractor trailer by inches and nearly clipping an Audi. Maybe I wouldn't vomit if I couldn't see my death playing out in front of me. I peeked at her sideways. "I don't understand. I thought you cooperated with the police after Andrei's death? Why would Feliks want to protect you?"

She let her attention drift from the road to me. "Do not make the mistake of assuming he does so for *my* protection. He knows I was forced to walk a very fine line with the police. I did nothing to hinder their investigation of Andrei, but I did nothing to further their case against Feliks. I gave them only what they asked. It's in Feliks's best interest to make sure it remains this way."

"So he's using them to watch you?"

Her obsidian eyes returned to the road. "Let's just say it's better if you and I have these conversations alone. I can't dismiss Feliks's men long without drawing suspicion. So, let's get to the point, shall we? To what do I owe the pleasure of your visit?"

"I need to talk to you about a certain website. The one your friend was using when she was looking for a . . ." I swallowed as we swerved onto the merge ramp to the interstate. "When she was looking for someone to take care of her husband."

"You can speak freely, Ms. Donovan. It's why I asked you to meet me here. I chose the car myself. Alan had no time to prepare for my arrival, so you can rest assured there are no listening devices."

I clutched my seat belt as the car cut across three lanes of traffic. "I need you to speak with the person who runs the women's forum."

"And what makes you think *I* know the identity of this person?"

"Because the police are already sniffing around the website. According to my source, they think it belongs to Feliks Zhirov."

Irina's face gave away nothing, but her languorous pose became disconcertingly still. Her foot relaxed on the accelerator, and I pulled myself upright in my seat as the speedometer slowed to eighty. "By source, I assume you're referring to your friend, Detective Anthony."

"And others." She was too smart to fall for a lie. But I could at least distribute the suspicion, and hopefully keep Nick from being the sole target of Feliks's ire when word of the sting inevitably got back to him.

"Why should any of this concern me?"

"Because if the police dig deep enough, they'll find my profile on that forum. The only way to make sure they don't is to take the entire site down." The implication hung heavy between us. Irina had paid me a lot of money to dispose of her horrible husband, and Feliks hadn't yet gone to trial for it.

"How will speaking to Feliks change any of this?"

"So Feliks *does* run the site?"

"I don't recall saying that."

"You didn't deny it."

Irina stayed quiet for an uncomfortably long time as she weaved the Spider in and out of traffic. I squeezed my eyes closed, my shoulder slamming into the car door as she took an exit way too fast.

"*If,*" she finally said, "Feliks did run this forum— and I'm not suggesting he does—why would he be foolish enough to entertain such a request? A site like that is worth a great deal to his business. It would cost him more than you can imagine to take it down."

"Maybe," I admitted, "but an investigation into that forum will cost him a lot more than that. The last thing Feliks wants is the police digging around that site. And the last thing you and I need is for Feliks to figure out that I buried your husband and you let Feliks take the fall. If you tip him off that the police are investigating the forum, he'll have to work fast to cover his tracks. Hopefully, he'll shut the entire site down before he looks too closely at what he's erasing."

"Feliks is no fool," Irina cautioned. "He will want to know how I came by this information." She shook her head through a pause. "No, I cannot be the one to speak with him about this."

I braced myself against the dash, only realizing where we were as the Spider came to a screeching halt in front of the dealership.

"Go home, Ms. Donovan," she said, as Sasha and Alan rushed from the showroom.

"That's it? But what about all that stuff you said at the health club a month ago? About women helping women and sticking together—"

"I said, go *home*," she said firmly. Her voice dropped low as Sasha appeared beside the Spider and opened her door. "I'll be in touch." Irina smiled up at him, placing

her hand on his arm as she stepped gracefully out of
the driver's seat and dropped the key in Alan's waiting
palm. Neither of them bothered to help me out of the
car.

CHAPTER 26

I sat in my van in the parking lot of the dealership, my head against the steering wheel, fighting the lingering car sickness after my test-drive with Irina.

On the positive side, I had confirmed that the women's forum belonged to Feliks.

On the downside, Irina's refusal to help me hadn't left me any better off.

Hazy winter sunlight beat through the windshield. Lifting my head, I checked the time on the dashboard clock, surprised to find it was already noon. I sighed as I considered my options: go home and scarf down a box of Oreos with Vero, or drive to Julian's apartment and see if he was home. He'd been the one who suggested we talk today, and I couldn't exactly call him since I hadn't replaced my phone.

A death rattle reverberated through the van as I turned the key in the ignition. I headed toward Julian's apartment complex before I could change my mind. My heart rate kicked up when I spotted his Jeep in the parking lot. Coat pulled tightly around me, I knocked on his door. A TV blared inside, the voice of a sports announcer leaking through the walls. I knocked again, louder this time. My breath rushed out of me in a white puff as the door swung open.

A young woman stood in the threshold wearing an oversized sweatshirt over leggings and a pair of fuzzy socks. The sounds of a football game roared out around her. More voices billowed from inside. The smell of pizza and garlic bread. The crackle of a beer can. A collective cheer as the announcer called a touchdown.

"Can I help you?" The girl's nose was freckled and peeling, her auburn hair pulled back in a careless ponytail. Her green eyes widened, waiting for me to say something. I checked the number beside the door, even though I recognized the furniture and posters inside.

"Is Julian here?"

Her sun-kissed forehead wrinkled as if she was trying to place me. She held the door open and moved to let me by. "Go ahead in. He's in his room."

I thanked her and stepped inside. Open pizza boxes covered the kitchen counters and crushed cans overflowed the recycling bin on the floor. The sofa and love seat were crammed with bodies. A few heads turned from the flat-screen TV as the door shut behind me. The girl's curious stare was heavy on my back, watching me pick my way to Julian's bedroom. The fact that she hadn't pointed out which one was his felt like a test, but it was too late to pretend I hadn't been here before.

His door was cracked. I held up my hand but couldn't make myself knock. I couldn't get past the idea that he'd locked down his accounts. That there were things about his life he didn't want me to know. I turned, ready to slip quietly out of his apartment, when his door opened.

"Hey!" I spun around as Julian dragged a T-shirt over his head. His curls were wild and slept on, his bare feet poking out from under the shredded hems of a faded pair of jeans. He rubbed his eyes, as if he'd just woken up. "I wasn't expecting you. What are you doing here?" He drew me in for an awkward hug. His T-shirt smelled faintly of sun lotion, and his eyes were a mix of whisky and sea-foam against the sun-bleached streaks in his hair.

Tucked in the hollow of his chest, I met the curious gazes of his friends. My cheeks warmed, and I pushed out of his embrace. "Sorry," I said over the blare of the TV, "I would have called, but I lost my phone. I thought maybe you were trying to reach me." I shook my head. How stupid did that sound?

Julian took my hand and led me into his bedroom, closing the door behind him so it was barely cracked. I took in the disarray of his room: his rumpled sheets and the stacks of law books on his dresser. A duffel bag lay open at the foot of his bed, its sand-crusted contents spilling onto the floor.

"I *was* trying to call." He pulled me close, wrapping his arms around my waist. "I dropped by your place when I rolled into town last night. I left you a note."

"I saw."

"I would have knocked, but I was afraid I'd wake you. Besides, I couldn't stay. The bar was short-staffed and my boss asked me to cover. I left your place and went straight to The Lush." His frown deepened. He brushed my hair back from my face. "Everything okay?"

"Fine." I couldn't make my smile hold a convincing shape. There was a dead guy in my washing machine (or, at least, part of one, which might actually be worse). Someone was trying to murder my ex, there was a suntanned girl in Julian's kitchen, his social media accounts were set to private, and he wanted to have a *talk*.

A sudden cheer erupted in the living room. Someone pounded on the wall and shouted, "Get out here, Baker! You're missing the second half of the game!" Julian rolled his eyes. Murmurs rose over the dimmed volume of the TV commercials, followed by laughter. "Who's the cougar?" one of them asked.

"She's kind of hot," said another.

"She's no one," a female voice chimed in. "Just someone he met at the bar. They're not serious."

I pulled out of Julian's arms, my cheeks flaming. "I didn't know you were having a party. I can go."

He held fast to my hand, turning my face to his. "Don't pay any attention to them. My roommate invited a few people over to watch the game. They're just trying to get under my skin." He toed the door shut, inciting another round of laughter from the next room. These were probably the same friends he'd gone to the beach with. An uncomfortable feeling I wasn't ready to name left my stomach unsettled when I pictured Julian spending the week with the cute redhead who'd answered his door.

"I can come back when you don't have company."

He shook his head as he backed me gently against the wall. His mouth grazed mine and his eyes drifted closed. "They have really short attention spans. Two more minutes and they'll forget you're even here."

I tried to relax into him, but I couldn't shake the feeling that I *shouldn't* be. The closed door. Their stares and laughter. The fact that none of them knew my name or who I was. It all pointed to the fact that I didn't belong here. For all the same reasons I hadn't invited him to my house to meet my kids—because we were both compartmentalizing this. Us. The pieces of our lives that didn't fit in the same box.

"Parker's out of town next weekend," he whispered against my ear. "I'll have the place to myself if you want to stay."

His warm breath drew goose bumps over my skin. A thrill rippled through me at the prospect of spending a weekend with him. Julian had mentioned Parker before, but he had only ever brought me here when we were alone. And I'd never stayed the night. "Your room-mate wouldn't mind?"

"No," he said, trailing kisses down my neck, "she's cool."

She? I felt the blood drain from my face. My lips parted, but words wouldn't come. The cute redhead who'd answered the door . . . *that* was Parker—his roommate?

"Why did you lock your Instagram account?" I blurted.

Julian pulled back to look at me and frowned. "That had nothing to do with you, Finn." He traced my cheek with his thumb. "Some of the guys I went camping with weren't thinking about what they were posting. I'm in my last year of law school. In a few months, I'll be graduating and applying for jobs, and the last thing I need is to have a firm see me tagged in someone's Insta-gram pic, doing keg stands with a bunch of drunken idiots." I looked down at the floor. If he was worried about potential employers knowing he'd cut loose on a beach trip, what would they think if they knew he was sleeping with a divorced single mother with a body in her washing machine? He tipped my chin up. "I don't have anything to hide from you, and I'm not trying to hide you from anyone else. Parker's just a roommate. It's not what you're thinking. We dated for less than a min-ute before she graduated last year, and I thought we'd clawed each other's eyes out the whole time."

"So you've always had a thing for older women?" I joked, feeling like a fool.

"No. I have a thing for smart women." He towed me with him toward his bed, perching on the edge of it and drawing me onto his lap. "Mature women who are hon-est with themselves about what they want and aren't afraid of it." I felt like an impostor as he leaned in for a kiss. It didn't feel honest and fearless when we were hiding in his room.

"I should go," I insisted.

"Stay," he murmured.

"I gave Vero the night off, and I have to get home to my kids." His grip loosened on my waist. That one sentence seemed to stretch the distance between us. I climbed off his lap. His mouth turned down as our hands slid apart.

He stood and followed me to his bedroom door. "I'll walk you out."

"I can manage."

"How can I reach you?"

"I'll get a new phone this weekend."

He bit his lip, as if there was something he wanted to say. "Call me later?" When I nodded, he dipped low for another kiss. His mouth was teasing and warm, beer and sand and sunshine, and I couldn't resist drawing out that short, bittersweet taste of him before leaving his room.

I showed myself to the door, ignoring the appraising looks, stepping over someone's abandoned shoes and resisting the urge to carry the greasy paper plates on the floor to the trash can. Parker glanced my way and I pasted on a smile, feeling guilty for reasons I couldn't put my finger on. As if I had come looking for something in this apartment that never should have been mine.

CHAPTER 27

My mother's Buick was parked in front of my house when I arrived home from Julian's. Mrs. Haggerty, who must have heard the rattle in my engine, peeled back her curtains as I turned in to my driveway, and I offered her a good-natured wave. She wasn't horrible, I reminded myself. She was just lonely and bored. In another thirty or forty years, that could be me—the old lady who lived in a big house all alone, who joined the neighborhood watch just to keep life interesting. Hopefully because I didn't still have a dead guy in my washing machine.

As I reached for the kitchen door, I noticed the trash can lid was askew. I lifted it to find it full of empty five-gallon bags—the kind ice cubes were sold in for parties. Dripping cartons of Ben & Jerry's, bags of soggy vegetables, and thawed tater tots filled the bottom of the bin. My washing machine probably looked like a beer cooler, but at least Carl was cold.

I settled the lid on the can and pushed open the kitchen door. My mother stood at my counter, unloading bags of groceries. One of Vero's scented candles burned on the kitchen table, probably to mask any hint of Carl.

"Hey, Ma," I said, planting a kiss on her cheek. "This is a surprise. What's all this?"

"I'm making dinner."

"Why?"

"Do I need a reason to cook for my grandchildren?"

"Not as long as I get to eat, too. What are you making?"

"Pot roast," she said, emptying a bag of carrots and digging in my cabinets for a cutting board. My mouth watered. My mother's pot roast was, arguably, better than sex. The smell of it, cooking low and slow in the oven, was the nearest I'd come to a tantric experience.

Vero sat at the kitchen table, nibbling on a cookie. Zach perched on her lap, his face dusted with crumbs, his hands reaching greedily for a plate piled high with snickerdoodles. I gave each of my children a kiss and took a cookie for myself.

"Have a seat," my mother said, cracking open a bottle of red wine. Only a third of a cup went into her recipe. The rest she poured into two glasses, setting one in front of me and one in front of Vero.

"I could get used to this," Vero said, holding Zach's wiggly bottom in place with one hand while she washed down her cookie with the other. I sank back into my chair, my body going warm and languid as the wine softened the edges of my very rough day.

Oil sizzled on the stove, the kitchen filling with the savory smells of garlic and onion powder as Mom seared the roast. She fell into a steady rhythm of peeling and chopping. After a few minutes, she confiscated the plate of cookies from the table, wiping the children's hands and sending them off to play.

"So," she said, layering the meat and vegetables into the roasting pan. "How was your date with Nicholas?"

And there it was.

Of course she had a reason for coming over unannounced and making me dinner. Nicholas, she called him. No one else called him that. It sounded like a pet name, as if she'd already adopted him into the family.

"It wasn't a date, Ma."

"Yes, it was," Vero said around her cookie. "Come on, Finlay. Tell us all about it. I'm dying to know if you sampled his biscuits."

Wine sprayed out my nose. I risked a glance at my mother as I reached for a napkin, but she was engrossed in her task, her head engulfed in a cloud of red wine steam as she poured a long thread of it into the pan.

"Vero says he took you out to dinner. I hope you wore a dress." My mother's expression was doubtful.

"Vero needs to learn to keep her big mouth shut." She dodged as I crumpled my napkin and threw it at her.

"Finlay borrowed one of mine," Vero informed her. "She looked like a million bucks. Or at least a hundred grand." My mother glanced up with a puzzled expression. If Vero kept this up, I was going to cut her off.

My mother pointed the business end of her wooden spatula at me. "You shouldn't have to borrow nice clothes. You should have called. I would have taken you shopping. See, this is why you should set aside some money. These advances you're making on your books are all very uncertain. What if no one buys them? What if your publisher decides they don't want you to write them anymore?"

"Gee, thanks, Ma. I've never stared at my ceiling all night, wondering about any of that."

"I'm just saying, now that you have Vero to help you, you'd have time to apply for a government job."

Vero smirked. "Personally, I've always felt there was better money in contract work."

If I'd had a knife, I would have thrown it at her.

"The whole idea of it just seems very unstable," my

mother said, setting the roast in the oven. "How will you ever retire? You'll be writing books until you're eighty."

"I'll be fine. I have a very responsible accountant. Vero's handling all my investments. She won't let me die old and broke."

Vero's smile turned down behind her wineglass. As I opened my mouth to ask her what was wrong, the house phone rang. Vero reached for it and passed it over. Steven's number flashed on the caller ID. I waited for the last possible ring before forcing myself to answer him. "Hey, Steven." I sensed my mother's ears perking as she dried and put away the dishes, her slow, quiet movements the only clue she was listening.

"Where've you been?" Steven asked. "I've been trying your cell all day."

"I lost it yesterday."

"You could have called last night to let me know."

"I was busy."

"With what?"

"None of your business." I jumped as my mother slammed a cabinet.

"What was it?" he goaded. "A hot date? I thought your boyfriend was out of town."

I rubbed my eyes, already exhausted by the conversation. "What do you want, Steven?"

"I want the kids next weekend."

"We've discussed this already. I don't want them going to your house."

"Then I'll come to yours. I'll stay in your guest room."

"That's Vero's room."

"Then I'll sleep on the couch."

If he did that, Vero would probably learn to make Molotov cocktails on YouTube and light the sofa on fire herself. "The kids won't even be here. They're scheduled to spend the weekend with my parents."

"Again?"

I mouthed an apology to my mom. I hadn't even asked her.

"I'm not falling for that crap. I know what you're doing. You're making excuses to keep them away from me."

"They're not excuses—"

My mother grabbed the phone from my hand. "Steven," she said through a saccharine smile, "so good to hear from you." She tucked the phone between her ear and her shoulder, scrubbing the counter with unnecessary force. "Finlay tells me you'd like to spend time with the children. I think that's just *wonderful*. Delia and Zach are staying with Paul and me next weekend so Finlay can spend time with her new boyfriend." My mother called out to me, "Which one was it, sweetheart? The police officer or the law student? They're both so handsome, I get them mixed up."

"Savage," Vero whispered.

"There's plenty of room with us, Steven. And we haven't seen you in *far* too long. Why don't you pack a bag and come for the weekend? Then you and I can have a nice *long* chat. It's *way* overdue." I cringed. "What's that? You'd like to speak to Finlay? Hold on, dear." My mother's smile was bitter as she thrust out the phone.

"Yes?" I cupped a hand over the receiver so he wouldn't hear Vero giggling.

"This is not over, Finn."

With a weary sigh, I said, "It never is."

The line disconnected. I set the phone in the cradle and slumped into my chair, refilling my glass with the last dregs of the bottle. Vero stood up and stretched. "I'm going to put the kids in a bath. Don't have too much fun without me."

My mother folded her dish towel, settling into Vero's empty chair once we were alone. "You're handling

Steven all wrong, sweetheart. There's no sense locking horns with an ox. Fighting with him only gives him exactly what he wants."

"What's that?"

"Your attention," she said with a sympathetic smile. "He's like a toddler, Finlay. He's done playing with his toy, but he doesn't want anyone else to have it, and he's going to throw a tantrum until he gets his way." She sighed as she tucked a lock of hair behind my ear. "He doesn't deserve you. He never did. Find someone else. Someone who makes you happy. Someone worthy of you and the children."

I swirled the wine in my glass. Nick and Julian both made me happy, I supposed. But I wasn't entirely sure I was worthy of either of them. I turned to my mother. "How did you know Dad was the one?"

My mother laughed. "Who says I ever did? Most days, I'm still not sure."

"But not because you didn't really *know* him," I clarified. "I mean, Dad was always honest with you, right?"

My mom's hand closed softly over mine. "All couples have secrets, Finlay. You don't have to tell each other everything to know what's in each other's hearts. But the kinds of secrets Steven was keeping . . . those weren't the same kind."

"So Dad never cheated?"

"Not unless you count that once with Jennifer Aniston." At my dubious look, my mother's grin became wry. "Your father fell for one of those internet scams. He clicked a link in an email offering to show him Jennifer Aniston's breasts. He learned his lesson the hard way," she said with a shake of her head. "Your father contracted a nasty virus and I had to hire one of those nerd people—you know, the ones that drive those tiny cars—to come to the house and clean it all up. She was a very nice girl; discreet," she said, "but very expensive. I made your father pay for it."

I drank the last of my wine, still chuckling to myself, having learned more about my parents' relationship than I cared to. Maybe she was right. Maybe sometimes we were better off not knowing.

The house was beginning to smell good. The table and high chair had been set for four. The prep dishes were all washed and put away, and the dishwasher hummed a soothing rhythm.

"Thanks, Ma," I said, feeling the weight of the day ease a little.

My mother stood and slipped on her coat.

"You're not staying for dinner?"

"No, I have to get home and heat up leftovers for your father. He thinks I'm out Christmas shopping. If he knew I made a pot roast that wasn't for him, I'd never hear the end of it. I'll pick up the kids on Friday after school."

"You don't have to do that."

"I want to. If they're with me, Steven won't bother you." She bent to kiss my cheek. "Give Nicholas a call. Go out and have some fun. But if you're going to try his biscuits, be sure to use protection."

Upstairs in the bathroom, Vero cackled.

I rolled my eyes to the ceiling. "Goodbye, Ma."

I followed her to the door, resting my head against it as I locked it behind her.

CHAPTER 28

The one piece of advice no one ever gives you when you divorce is never take a shower when all the towels are in the laundry. I'm pretty sure it's right up there with check to make sure there's toilet paper before pulling down your pants and never accept an offer to murder your ex while using public Wi-Fi.

Vero had let me sleep in after a second long night of writing. By four in the morning, I'd managed to eke out a messy draft of a few opening chapters, which I had emailed to Sylvia without bothering to proofread before falling into a brief and fitful sleep. By the time I'd rolled out of bed at nine, Vero and the kids had already left to take Delia to school. I'd been relieved to wake up to a quiet and empty house, but as I shut off the water and stood in the shower, groping for a towel on the empty hanger, the inevitability of my situation sank in with cold, sharp teeth.

Arms folded around myself, I slunk out of my bedroom, goose bumps pebbling my bare, wet skin. A wave of cinnamon apple air freshener and *eau de slowly thawing dead guy* washed over me as I opened the door to the laundry closet at the end of the hall. I reached inside the empty dryer and swore.

My mother would insist this was some form of

divine retribution, punishment from god for keeping a dead body in my house. Honestly, I'd rather pray the rosary. Someplace warm. With clothes on.

Crossing the hall, I grabbed a marginally clean Disney Princess towel from the hanger in the children's bathroom. Shivering, I wrapped it around me and knotted the ends of the tiny pink swatch around my chest.

A floorboard creaked down the hall. I paused, head tipped toward the sound of the furnace clicking on. Warmth drifted from the register above my head to combat a sudden icy draft that was creeping up the stairs, as if a door had been left open. I stiffened at the familiar telltale squeak of the riser on the top step.

Searching the bathroom for a weapon, I cursed myself for the childproof locks on all the cabinets. As the slow tread of footsteps grew closer, I grabbed the only pointy object I could find. With my toilet plunger poised to strike, I pressed my back against the bathroom wall. Breath held, I listened as, one by one, the bedroom doors swung slowly open. A dark shadow fell over the carpet beside me. With a feral yell, I raised the plunger over my head and leapt into the hall. My scream died in my throat as I stared down the barrel of a gun.

"Christ, Finn!" Nick lowered his weapon and bent over his knees. "You scared the crap out of me!"

I clutched the towel to my chest. "What the hell are you doing in my house?"

His eyes climbed my bare, dripping legs, and his cheeks flushed scarlet. I tugged down the bottom of the towel, glad I'd bothered to shave. He averted his eyes. "I can explain," he said in a strained voice. "See, I was down the street at Theresa's when dispatch called with a 10–66. I recognized the address as yours, so I rushed over to check it out."

"10–66?"

"Right, sorry," he said, still flustered. "Mrs. Haggerty called nine-one-one. She told the operator she saw someone suspicious outside your house. I did a quick check of the yard and didn't see anyone, but—"

A door flew open downstairs, crashing into a wall. Nick whirled, gun aimed down the stairwell into the foyer.

I peeped around his shoulder. Joey stood at the foot of the stairs. His wide eyes jumped from Nick to me, and a slow smile spread over his face as he lowered his weapon. "Maybe I should come back later?"

"It's not what it looks like," Nick said, hands raised as my sister burst into the house behind Joey. Her eyebrows leapt toward the ceiling when she spotted me behind Nick, wearing nothing but Delia's towel. "Well, that escalated quickly."

Vero rushed into the house with Zach on her hip. "What's with all the blue lights? Where's Finlay? Is everything o . . . *oh*!" Vero slapped a hand over Zach's eyes. "Finn, why are there three armed cops in the house? And why are you naked?" Nick, Georgia, and Joey all holstered their weapons.

"I'm not naked! I just took a shower, and all the grown-up towels are in the *wash*," I said with a piercing look at Vero. "And the police are here because Mrs. Haggerty is a busybody. She thought she saw someone suspicious prowling around outside." Vero held Zach tighter against her body and glanced out the open front door. I tugged the hem of my towel to cover myself. "As you can see, this was all just a false alarm. There was no 10–99."

"Sixty-six," my sister corrected me.

"Whatever. Obviously, Mrs. Haggerty was mistaken. There's nothing suspicious going on here, so you can all go back to whatever it was you were doing."

"I'm not so sure," Joey said, exchanging a look with

Nick. "I did a quick check around the house and found this on the front porch. Aside from her name, it's unmarked." Nick descended the stairs, taking a fat brown envelope from Joey. Vero peered over Joey's shoulder to see it. From the top step, I could clearly make out my name, printed on the envelope in bold, indelible ink. I recognized that handwriting. And by the shocked look on Vero's face, she did, too.

I raced down the steps as Vero snatched it from Joey's hand. "These must be the adult toys Finlay ordered. Stacey down the street does catalog parties. You know, like Tupperware but with batteries." She showcased the front of the envelope. "See? They even offer discreet packaging to guarantee your privacy."

Three sets of eyes shot to me. Nick cleared his throat as he reached for the envelope. "I should probably check it out first."

"They are not sex toys!" I yanked it away from him. "It's probably just . . . you know . . . copyedits. My editor must have sent them by courier." Nick's eyes twinkled a little, the curl of his smile becoming wolfish as his gaze drifted down. I jerked the towel higher. Then lower. Struggling to adequately conceal all the cold, damp flesh on display.

I raised my chin to restore some modicum of my dignity. "I'm going to get dressed. When I come back down, I want all of you out of my house."

Envelope clutched to my body, I bolted up the stairs.

"Finn, wait." Nick caught up to me in the hall just outside my room. He maneuvered past me and performed a quick search inside, then moved deftly through the entire second floor, checking every bedroom. He reached for the laundry closet, wrinkling his nose.

"Do you smell something?"

I grabbed him by the arm, jerking him toward me.

"Wet towels! I forgot all about them and they started to mold." My hair dripped, a cold bead of water trailing over my collarbone. Nick's dark eyes followed it. Then down, to where my hand still rested loosely on his arm. I let go, but it did nothing to break the sudden swell of tension between us. "There are no perps hiding in the laundry closet. Mrs. Haggerty probably saw someone deliver the package and overreacted. You don't have to search the house."

The wall was at my back. My bedroom door was open beside me. Enough room between us that I could have slipped inside and shut him out. If I wanted to.

"I owe you an apology," he said, his voice a little husky. "I swear, I didn't mean to bust into your home like that. Your car was in the driveway. When I knocked and you didn't answer, I thought . . ." He rubbed the day-old stubble on his face. "After the gas leak at Steven's this morning, when dispatch called and said someone was creeping around your house, I assumed the worst."

"Gas leak?" My stomach bottomed out. "What gas leak?"

He swore under his breath. "I'm sorry, Finn. I figured Georgia already told you."

"Told me what?"

"Steven's fine," he assured me. "But Fauquier PD were out at Steven's place this morning. There was a gas leak in his house. Thankfully, Steven found it and shut off the main before anyone got hurt, but the gas company thinks the line might have been tampered with. Given what they know about the fire at his trailer, they're looking into the possibility that it may have been intentional."

I crushed the envelope to my chest. "Where's Steven now?"

"He's at home. The EMTs suggested he get checked at the ER, but he insisted on being at his house when the gas company came out to inspect the lines. I asked a couple of off-duty uniforms to head over to his place. They'll stay and keep an eye on things until we know what happened."

I sagged against the wall. It had to have been *Easy-Clean*. How many times could she miss before she finally succeeded in killing him?

Zach babbled downstairs. Kitchen drawers opened and closed. The microwave beeped, and the strong herbed smell of leftover pot roast filled the house. It was a little early for lunch, and I wondered if Vero was doing it just to mask the faint scent that had begun creeping from the washer.

"I should go," Nick said, hitching a thumb toward the stairs. "Joey's waiting for me back at Theresa's."

"Why? What's going on?"

"Theresa disappeared." The kitchen noises stopped, as if Vero was listening. "We found her ankle monitor in her house. It looks like she may have been gone for a few days. We're not sure exactly how long. We're talking to her neighbors, but so far, no one remembers seeing her leave. Until I figure out where she is, and what's going on with Joey's CI, I want you to be careful. I have a bad feeling this is all connected somehow."

I clutched the knot in my towel. "What happened to Joey's CI?"

"He never called with that intel he promised me yesterday. Joey went to his house to follow up on it this morning, but the kid wasn't there. The attendance office at his school says he never showed up. I sent a car out to his house a couple of hours ago to talk to his grandmother. No one's heard from him since we saw him on Saturday." When I'd drawn my finger across my neck and warned him not to say a word about me. Cam must have decided his probation wasn't worth the risk of turning over what he knew about the forum. Nick shook his head. "I'm starting to think Joey's CI may have been onto something. If he's right about that forum, then Theresa, Steven, and the kid all have a link to Zhirov, and I don't like it."

"You think Feliks Zhirov had something to do with what happened to Steven?"

"I can't rule it out. Until then, I want you to be more careful. You really shouldn't leave your front door unlocked."

"What do you mean? It's always . . ." I glanced to the stairs. I clearly remembered locking the front door after my mother had left yesterday. And this morning, Vero would have left through the garage.

The brush of Nick's fingertips startled me back to the moment. He reached for a strand of dripping hair, tucking it behind my shoulder before it could soak through the envelope I was holding. "I'm sorry I scared you before."

"I'm fine," I said through a shiver.

"You sure you don't want me to open this mystery package for you before I go? Just to make sure there isn't anything in it I should be concerned about?" His eyes lit with a dangerous degree of interest.

I moved it behind my back, my face warming. "They're just copyedits. Really, you can forget this whole incident ever happened."

"Believe me, nothing about this incident was forgettable. I'll call you later," he promised with a smirk. He hollered goodbye to Vero from the foyer, reminding her to lock up after him.

I slipped into my room and shut my door, throwing the envelope on the bed and rubbing my hands on Delia's towel. It felt cleaner than the envelope with my name written in Irina Borovkov's handwriting.

I heard the snap of Zach's high chair buckles in the kitchen, then the scatter of dry Cheerios against the plastic tray. Feet scurried up the stairs, and Vero threw open my door.

"Is everyone gone?" I asked.

She nodded. "What's in the package?"

We walked to the edge of the bed, staring at the brown envelope. I tore it open and turned it upside down. A long brunette wig spilled out, fanning over the comforter, a business card tangled in its shimmering dark waves. Vero picked it up. "Who's Ekatarina Rybakov?"

The fine print under the name read *Attorney at Law*. I shook out the envelope. A handwritten note fluttered out.

Attorney visiting hours daily, 7 A.M.—10 P.M.
Bowling League practice every Tuesday, 8–10 P.M.

"What do you think it means?" Vero asked.

I picked up the wig. The strands fell into place, assuming a familiar shape around my hand. The odd pieces of Irina's package snapped together with a startling clarity.

"Oh, no," I whispered. The woman Nick had argued with at Kvass on Saturday night—her name had been Kat. "I think Ekatarina Rybakov is Feliks Zhirov's attorney."

A finger of fear trailed down my spine. Irina had no intention of passing a message to Feliks. She was going to make me deliver it myself.

CHAPTER 29

On Tuesday night, Vero stood in front of me in my bathroom and fussed with my hair, her eyes skipping back and forth between the strands of the dark wig and the photo on her cell phone. She held the image of Ekatarina Rybakov out in front of her.

"I'm not sure if this is the dumbest thing you've ever done, or the most badass thing you've ever done."

"Definitely the dumbest." I tried to keep my mouth still as she smeared my lips with deep red lipstick.

"What are you going to do if you get caught?"

Truthfully, I'd been so worried about getting into the jail, I hadn't even thought about what I would do once I made it inside. But failure wasn't an option. With both Cam and Theresa missing, Nick would tear the internet apart trying to find a connection between Feliks and the forum, and there was only one person with the power to take it down before Nick found it. "I'm not going to get caught."

"If you keep fidgeting like that, your wig's gonna come off, and then yes, you'll definitely get caught. Hold still," she said, shoving me back down to sit on the lid of the toilet while she rummaged in her cosmetic bag. "I've got some bobby pins in here."

"No pins." I'd been in the jail once before with my sister. She'd come with me one night when Steven had been hauled in, belligerent and drunk beyond reason after he'd picked a fight at a bar. Georgia had signed me in, escorting me past the usual filters so I could wait with Steven until they released him. I distinctly remembered being thoroughly searched. "Pins might set off the metal detector."

"Then stop messing with it." Vero swatted my hands away as I tried to slip a finger under the wig to scratch my scalp. "You look great. How's your accent?"

"Crap. I didn't think of that." I cleared my throat, making it low and breathy. "Hello," I said in my best impression of Irina. "My name is Ekatarina Rybakov."

Vero grimaced. "You sound like Angelina Jolie and Vladimir Putin made a baby. Just pretend you have laryngitis. Sign in, get through security, and don't make small talk."

"Right."

"Here's your business card."

"What about ID? What if they ask me for a license or something?"

"Just waltz in like you own the place. Nobody wants to argue with a bitchy woman who could sue their pants off. Keep your glasses on and try not to make direct eye contact with anyone." Ekatarina "Kat" Rybakov and I were apparently close in age, but that's about where our similarities ended. According to Kat's photo online, she had startling dark eyes that matched her tumbling brunette locks. And while the wig was a perfect match to Kat's hair, my eyes were far too light to pass under close scrutiny.

"How do I look?" Vero's sleek gray pencil skirt was perilously tight, and the stiletto heels I'd borrowed from her closet should have come with their own insurance policy. I was probably going to break an ankle. But Kat was nearly five foot eight, and Vero insisted I'd need the added height.

She opened an extra button on my blouse. The neckline flared, revealing a hint of the black lace cups of my bra. "What are you doing?"

"Giving the guards a distraction so they don't notice your face." She shoved aside my hand and straightened the strand of pearls over my collarbones. "Quit trying to cover them up. You look hot."

"I don't want to look hot. I want to look like Kat."

"Kat *is* hot. Feliks obviously has a type. He likes his women smart, beautiful, and confident. Just pretend you're Theresa."

"That's what got me into this mess. And Theresa got caught."

"Stop messing with your hair! Here, put these on." Vero slid a pair of dollar-store readers onto my nose. They were a close match to the glasses Kat had been wearing in her pictures.

I did a slow turn in front of the mirror, checking to make sure my wig was straight and there weren't any runs in my stockings.

"If I don't make it out . . ."

"Relax. Feliks isn't going to murder you in jail. There are far too many cameras."

"And if I get arrested for impersonating a lawyer?"

She gave me a reassuring pat. "I've got the kids. And your sister will bail you out. Here, I bought you a new cell phone and programmed all your emergency numbers for you. Text me when you get there." She dropped the phone into a knockoff messenger bag she used for school and slung it over my shoulder. "Remember, you're a badass bitch. You don't take shit from anyone. Not even Feliks Zhirov."

"Right." My heels seemed to plant themselves in the

carpet, digging all the way into the pad. Vero put her hand in the middle of my back and pushed me toward the door.

It was almost nine o'clock by the time I pulled into the parking lot of the county jail. Early enough that it would still be permissible for a lawyer to visit, but late enough that the real Ekaterina Rybakov should be well into her bowling league match.

As I touched up my lipstick in my visor mirror, a horrible thought gripped me. Feliks's star attorney would know every bit of protocol. She'd know where to go once she got inside, how to fill out forms, and how to answer any questions. As I drew my new phone from Vero's messenger bag and dialed Julian's number by memory, I wasn't sure if I was calling for information or just the comfort of hearing his voice.

"Hello?" His favorite songs played softly in the background, his voice deep and relaxed. I could picture him sitting up in bed, his back against the headboard, studying by the white glow of the Christmas lights he'd tacked along the edges of his room.

"Hi, it's me." I closed the visor mirror; it felt too much like a lie. "I finally got a new phone."

"I was hoping you'd call." There was a thump, like a textbook falling closed. "I hated not being able to reach you yesterday. I wanted to apologize for what happened when you came by on Sunday. My friends . . . they weren't trying to be assholes. They were just giving me a hard time. I still really want to see you this weekend. Think you can make it?"

I couldn't make myself answer that. So much had happened in the last few days, I couldn't begin to imagine how it would all get resolved before Friday. "Actually, there's another reason I called. I was hoping I could ask you a legal question. For my book."

"Sure." The music in the background quieted, the silence narrowing until it felt like we were in the same room. "How can I help?"

My mouth went dry. I hated how easy he was making this. I'd never lied to him like this before—not since that night when I'd told him everything. Julian had been the one person aside from Vero who knew all my most horrible secrets. But if he'd been worried a few Instagram photos might compromise his future, what would he think if he knew what I was about to do? "I'm having trouble with a scene. My character is an attorney, and she's visiting her client in jail. I need to know the process—what happens from the time she walks into the jail to the time she leaves—so I can accurately describe it."

"Well," he said, his box spring squeaking. I could picture him lying back on his mattress, one hand behind his head. "There's usually a visitation desk where she'd be asked to sign in. She'll surrender any personal effects they don't allow inside—keys, phones, sharp objects, hardback books, anything that can be made into a tool or a weapon. She'll be asked for her license or some form of identification."

"Would a business card work?"

"No, it would have to be government-issued. A photo ID."

I shook out my hands, resisting the urge to start the van and drive home. This was exactly what I was afraid of. "Then what?"

"From there, she would pass through security—metal detectors and maybe a pat-down. Then an officer would escort her to a meeting room, and she'd be given a set amount of time to speak privately with her client."

"There wouldn't be a guard in the room?"

"No, but there might be one outside."

A terrifying image flitted through my mind. "Would her client be restrained?"

"Possibly, if the client was known to be dangerous, or if the attorney requested it because she felt unsafe." Feliks wouldn't pose a risk to his attorney. And he definitely wouldn't want anyone listening to their conversation. Which meant I would be alone in a room with him. No shackles. No cuffs.

"Finn, are you okay? You sound stressed."

I glanced up, catching my reflection in the rearview mirror. "I'm fine! It's just . . . you know, this damn book. Sylvia's really breathing down my neck. Deadlines and all . . . I should probably get back to work."

"Okay," he said, the words still tinged with worry. "Call me later if you need to talk anything through."

"I will. And Julian? Thanks. For everything," I added before he could disconnect. In case I never got another chance to tell him.

CHAPTER 30

My heels clicked with purpose over the tiled entry of the jail. Resisting the urge to conceal my face, I held my chin high, swiping away a long dark strand of the wig as it blew into my eyes. I could do this. My name was Ekatarina Rybakov. I was Feliks Zhirov's personal attorney, here to review some court documents with my client. I clung to my messenger bag. The papers inside were copies of Vero's last accounting exam. Delia had scribbled smiley faces on them with watercolor markers, and I was pretty sure the green blob was a booger of Zach's. Hopefully, the guard would be too busy trying to look down my blouse to notice.

The attendant at the counter was an older woman with thinning gray hair and red-framed glasses. She handed me a basket without looking up. Her name badge said OFFICER LOIS PYLE.

"Keys, cell phone, anything in your pockets," she droned, sliding a clipboard across the counter. I surrendered all my personal belongings and signed the form using Kat's name. "ID?"

I snapped the edge of Kat's business card as I set it in front of her. Officer Pyle's eyes slid to it, then back to her screen. "I'll need to see some identification."

The fact that she didn't seem to know Kat person-

ally felt like a small victory. I studied my nails, chan-
neling Theresa's unflappable inner bitch. Vero had glued
on falsies and polished them a deep blood-red, the same
color I'd seen Kat wearing in the restaurant. "I left my
license in the pocket of my other suit. It's currently at
the dry cleaner's, enjoying a hot tumble. Which is more
than I can say for myself. And yet, duty calls, so here I
am. If we could just get on with it."

"I can't let you in without ID."

"Believe me, I'd love nothing more than to give you
one. As it is, I'll be spending all day at the DMV tomorrow having mine replaced." I pushed the business card
toward her and tapped Kat's name. "I'm in this place almost every damn day for this man. You can look me
up. I was just here yesterday." It was a gamble, but I was
willing to bet an empire as big as Feliks's would require
daily briefings at the minimum.

Officer Pyle glared at my card. With a huff, she typed
something into her computer. My heart stopped as her
fingers paused over the keys. She raised an eyebrow.

"Go on," she grumbled. "But next time, bring your
ID."

I nearly melted into a puddle of relief. With a curt
nod, I surrendered my messenger bag, turned on my
heel, and sashayed to the metal detector, my file in hand
and stilettos snapping.

I shifted uneasily as the officer inspected my file, but
he was more concerned with removing the tiny staple
from the papers than what was written on them. I was
instructed to wait for an escort. Doors buzzed, jangling
my already-spent nerves as they clanked open and I was
guided into the jail. Officers gossiped loudly in the cor-
ridors and I averted my eyes, praying I didn't know any
of them. Their chatter quieted as I passed. Hopefully
Vero was right and they were too busy staring at my ass
to notice anything else about me.

My toes and heels were already blistering, the balls of my feet aching from the stiff leather shoes, but I was far too nervous to sit when my escort deposited me in an empty meeting room. I paced the length of it, freezing when the door opened.

"A little late for a visit, Katya." Feliks Zhirov paused just inside the room. His coal-black eyes surveilled me through a fringe of tousled bangs, the tightening of his lips framed by a thick shadow of dark scruff. He was taller, leaner than I remembered, his coldly handsome features cut sharp. In his baggy orange jumpsuit, without his smooth-shaved face and gel-styled hair, without his fancy cuff links and tailored suit, Feliks looked far more dangerous somehow . . . less like the man who ordered the hits, and more like the man who killed with his own hands.

"Professional visitation ends at ten," the officer said, oblivious to the flare of tension in the room. "Knock when you're ready, and someone will escort you out."

Feliks nodded once for both of us. My breath caught as the officer stepped out and closed the door. A single set of restraints bound Feliks's wrists, connected loosely by a chain around his jumpsuit. Feliks strolled toward the table where I stood, his movements almost predatory, his dark eyes missing nothing as he took a seat. "To what do I owe the pleasure of your company, Ms. Donovan?" His voice was silken and dangerous. I glanced up at the camera on the ceiling and Feliks's gaze followed, a slight smile tugging at his cheek. "They do not record our conversations. Only our behavior." I swallowed when his piercing eyes settled on my throat.

"We have a mutual problem." I took a seat across from him, keenly aware that I couldn't see his hands under the table. It didn't matter that there was a camera recording every movement he made. I had no doubt Feliks would reach across the gap and strangle me if I gave him a reason to try.

"By mutual problem, you must be referring to Detective Anthony." His lip twitched at my surprise. "Tell me, did you enjoy your meal? Vodka, piroshki, stroganoff . . . all outstanding, I'm sure. I understand the detective was planning to spring for dessert. He must be very fond of you. And yet, I admit, when I last inquired about your relationship with him, I was skeptical of your answer."

"You asked why I was with him that day. I told you. It wasn't a lie." Not entirely.

"Does the good detective know about the young law student who's been warming your bed?"

The breath punched out of me. Nick said Feliks had a long reach, but the only way he could have known about my relationship with Julian was if one of his goons had been tailing me. A shiver ran through me as I remembered Nick's mention of my unlocked door.

Feliks's leer fell over me like a hot, close breath. "I must admit to a certain . . . curiosity about you. Tell me, what is this mutual problem that warrants such a daring visit?"

"The police know about your website."

His shrug was careless. "I have many websites."

"They know about the women's forum." Feliks's irises turned a violent shade of black. I wasn't sure if I should feel terrified or victorious that I'd managed to surprise him.

"How did they come by the information?"

"One of their confidential informants found it."

"His name?"

"I don't know it." Cam might be a criminal, but he was just a kid. I wouldn't offer up a juvenile to be shredded by a monster. "All I know is that he traced the site back to one of your shell companies. A cyber-crimes unit is already looking into it."

"If you and Detective Anthony are so close, why are you telling me this?"

"Let's just say, you and I both have good reasons to want to keep the police from finding that forum."

Feliks arched an eyebrow. "Do tell, Ms. Donovan."

"I'd rather not."

His slight smile was cocky. "Perhaps I will leave the forum for Detective Anthony to find, if only to satisfy my own curiosity about you."

"You won't."

"You seem very confident. What makes you so sure?"

"Because I know how Carl Westover died. And I know who has his body."

His perfect stillness sent a chill through me. His grin turned hard. His restraints clanked as he lifted his hands to the table, moving slowly enough not to rattle the guards. Fingers laced, he leaned toward me and whispered, "You're playing a very dangerous game, Ms. Donovan."

"I found Carl Westover in a freezer in West Virginia," I explained in a low voice. "Theresa told me everything before she disappeared with Carl . . . or at least, *most* of Carl. I have one very identifiable piece of him. I've hidden it where no one will find it. But in case anything happens to me or my family, I've left a letter explaining everything to the police. I propose a deal. You delete the forum—all of it—and I won't put Carl's torso in Theresa's BMW, park it in front of your restaurant, and call the paparazzi." I let the rest simmer in the subtext between us. The discovery of Carl Westover's body would be the nail in the coffin at his trial. If the police could prove he murdered Carl for refusing to let the mob use the farm, it would blow Kat's already shaky defense to pieces. Feliks's only play was to take the entire forum down.

His shoulders shook with silent laughter. He scratched the scruff on his jaw. "Anything else?"

"That, and you and your people stay out of my house and away from my family."

"I see no need to visit your home or your family; you haven't given me a reason to." The word *yet* hung unspoken. Strangely, I believed him. He was too arrogant to lie, and Feliks's truths were a far more effective weapon. He cocked his head. "Is that all?"

I opened my file and slid Vero's accounting exam across the table, pointing to the small letters I'd printed next to a blob of red crayon. "This is the handle of a user on your forum. I need to know this person's real name and how to find them."

His eyes dipped to the paper between us. If he recognized *EasyClean*'s handle, his face gave nothing away. "Your demands are mutually exclusive, Ms. Donovan. A search like this will take some time. Once the site is down, all of its user information will disappear along with it. It seems you have a choice: I can take the site down, or I can try to find this *EasyClean* for you. Which will you choose?" The question was punctuated with a curious lilt, as if he knew he was backing me into a corner and he was eager to watch me squirm. The longer I paused to think about my answer, the more that curiosity seemed to sharpen. I didn't like the way it cut like a scalpel through my façade.

"Take down the site," I said, sliding the paper off the table. "I'll find *EasyClean* myself."

Feliks smiled as if my answer surprised him. "I have no doubt you will. And I'm sure you will honor your end of our agreement." He stood, his chains rattling softly against the front of his jumpsuit. "You are a fascinating woman, Ms. Donovan. I'm curious to see how this little game of yours plays out." He gave me a lingering last look before rapping on the door.

CHAPTER 31

An officer led Feliks back to his cell. Another met me at the door. I followed my escort through the building, conversations quieting at the snap of my heels. A muttered obscenity earned a few laughs behind my back. Kat was an enemy in this place . . . the woman committed, either by duty or by kinship, to defend the indefensible acts of a man who'd slipped through the cracks in the system far too many times. The wig itched, and I was more than ready to take it off.

A cluster of uniformed officers turned to stare as I entered the lobby. I pushed my glasses up my nose, obscuring their view of my face, giving them a wide berth as I strode to the counter to sign out.

A cold rain greeted me as I pushed through the doors to the parking lot. Security lights glowed, gleaming off the wet pavement. Head ducked against the drizzle, I hurried toward my van. I'd hidden it on the far side of the lot, as away from the lighted areas as I could manage, tucked behind a maintenance truck. A car door slammed somewhere ahead of me. Taillights flashed and a lock chirped as a tall shadow slipped out from between two parked cars, his back hunched against the rain. I kept my head down as we passed each other.

"What gives, Rybakov?" I stumbled at the sound of Nick's voice. "What? No insults tonight? I don't know if I should be concerned or disappointed."

I stiffened, keenly aware of how close we were standing. I angled my face away and kept walking, picking up my pace, desperate to put space between us as his footsteps splashed in the puddles toward the jail.

Suddenly they paused. His soles scraped the pavement as if he was turning around. "It's a little late for a meet and greet, isn't it, Counselor?" I skidded to a stop. My heart thudded in my ears as I heard him take a few steps closer. "If I didn't know my case was airtight, I might think you and Zhirov were up to something."

My mind raced. What would Kat do?

Keeping my back to him, I thrust my right hand in the air, saluting him with my raised middle finger. He barked out a laugh as I started briskly toward the maintenance truck.

"You always did have a way with words, Rybakov," Nick called after me. "See you in court, Counselor."

When the door to the jail clicked closed, I ducked behind my van, peeking through its windows to make sure Nick was gone. My hands shook as I fished in my bag for my keys. Trembling, I unlocked the door and melted into the driver's seat.

That was close. Too close.

I sighed with relief when the engine started. Cold air blasted from the vents, and I cranked the heat, cupping my hands in front of the fins. A dim light issued from my open purse, and I reached inside it for my phone.

"How'd it go?" Vero asked in a low voice. The kids were long asleep. In the background, I could hear the squeak of the pantry door and the telltale rustle of a bag.

"Terrifying."

"Did you make it in to see Feliks?"

"Yeah, but I ran into Nick on the way out."

Vero gasped. "Did he recognize you?"

"No, thank god."

"What did Feliks say?"

"Apparently, we have a deal. Did you dig up any information on Carl?"

"Nothing helpful. As far as I can tell, in the four months he's been dead, not a single person has reported him missing. Don't you think that's odd?"

"Theresa mentioned that Carl and his wife had split up. Maybe she didn't know anything was wrong."

"But why wouldn't Steven be looking for him?"

"Theresa said Carl and Steven weren't close. Were you able to figure out who the other silent partner was?"

"I'm not certain, but I have a pretty good guess. Theresa said the other partner's name was Ted, which is a common nickname for Edward. When I Googled Carl, another name kept popping up. Turns out, Carl owned a few farms with his cousin, Edward Fuller."

"Fuller. As in Bree Fuller?" I couldn't believe I hadn't made the connection before. Bree had been in the photo, sandwiched between the three of them. And she'd said her father had been the one to get her the job at the farm. But if Ted Fuller and Carl Westover were cousins, why hadn't he reported Carl missing either?

My phone vibrated. I drew the phone from my ear, swearing at Steven's name on the screen.

"I have to take this," I told Vero.

"Pick up some chips and ice cream on the way. I'll keep looking and see what I can dig up on Carl's wife."

I clicked over to Steven. "What the hell are you trying to pull?" he shouted.

I squeezed my eyes shut, struggling to hold the reins on my temper. "I don't know what you're talking about."

"All this drama about arsonists trying to blow up my house . . . it's all one big plot you've concocted in your head. And now I've got cops all over my property, convinced someone's trying to kill me."

"Did you ever stop to think maybe someone *is* trying to kill you?"

"That's a load of horseshit! I heard the security recording. You and I both know who set that fire."

I gripped the steering wheel. "Look, I admit I was at the farm that night, but I swear, Steven, I didn't start that fire. You have to believe me."

"I don't have to believe anything—not a word you just said or the voice on that stupid recording! But so help me, if you pull one more stunt like this last one, I'm going to tell the cops it was you in my trailer!"

Rain spattered the windshield. "Wait . . . they don't know?"

"Of course, they don't know! You think I want my children to see their mother sent to prison for arson? I told them I didn't recognize the woman's voice on that recording, but if you insist on spreading all these wild conspiracy theories, convincing the police that some psycho is out to kill me just so you have an excuse to keep the kids away from me, I'm going to get Guy involved and then I'm calling your sister."

"You wouldn't."

"Watch me." Silence fell like a hammer, the windshield wipers making angry passes back and forth. "I'm serious, Finlay. Back off and stay the hell off my property. As soon as the dust settles on this mess, I want my weekends with Zach and Delia back."

"But Steven, it's not—"

Click.

I tossed the cell phone in the cupholder. The van had grown uncomfortably warm, and I dragged the wig from my head. My wet shoes stuck to the blisters on my feet. I was drenched through my clothes, and all I wanted was to go home.

The van rattled in protest as I put it in gear and nosed out of my hiding space behind the maintenance truck. My headlights cut a swath through the heavy mist as I navigated toward the only open gate to the street. As I rounded the building, I slammed on my brakes. Blue lights flickered through the steady slap of my windshield wipers. Two cruisers blocked the exit in front of me, their doors thrown open, officers kneeling behind them with their weapons drawn.

Nick stood behind them, squinting at my windshield, a radio clutched to his lips, the hard lines of his face captured in the glare of my headlights.

"Turn off your engine and step out of the vehicle with your hands up."

CHAPTER 32

Nick escorted me into the station himself, his grip firm on my arm as he guided me through a side door and deposited me into an interrogation room.

"Do you want me to call Georgia?" he asked as he unfastened my cuffs.

"No. Please," I added, rubbing my wrists as he folded the cuffs into the pocket of his jacket. He pulled out a chair and directed me to sit, his eyes raking over my drenched overcoat and heels. My reflection was jarring in the dark mirror on the wall, my wet hair plastered to my forehead and long smears of mascara streaking from my eyes. "Not Georgia."

"Do you have someone you can call?" A muscle worked in his jaw. "An attorney?"

"Do I need one?"

Nick's lips thinned as he handed me his phone and turned away. Arms folded, he leaned against the two-way mirror. My heart stuttered when I thought of my children waking up in the morning without me.

I dialed Julian's number. Part of me hoped he wouldn't answer. The other part of me nearly cried out with relief when he did. Glasses clinked over the loud hum of conversation in the background.

"Hello?" Julian asked cautiously, as if he recognized

the number. He and Nick had spoken before, when Nick had been questioning witnesses during the Mickler investigation at The Lush.

"Hey, it's Finlay," I said, trying to keep my voice steady. A long beat of silence followed. The background noise of the bar hushed to a soft murmur before falling away, as if he'd stepped outside.

"Are you okay?"

"I'm okay."

"Where are you?"

My eyes lifted to Nick's. He pushed off the wall, his movements stiff as he left the room, the door swinging closed behind him.

"I need a favor," I said, my throat thick. "I'm at the police station. I need a lawyer. I didn't know who else to call." I couldn't face my sister. Not yet.

"Are you alone?"

"Yes."

"What happened?" Julian's voice was tense.

"I can't really talk about it right now."

"Finlay, I haven't even finished law school. I can't represent you."

"I know. And I would never ask you to do that. But I thought maybe you'd know a defense attorney? Someone who could help me tonight?"

He swore quietly. "Let me make a few calls. Are you going to be all right? Do you need me to come pick you up?" Another question lingered in the subtext. Were they going to let me go? Or would they keep me here?

"I'm okay. I'll find a ride home." I lifted my head as the door cracked open and Nick stepped inside. "Thank you," I whispered and disconnected, careful to delete the record of the call from the phone before sliding it across the table toward Nick. I pressed my mouth closed until the silence was too much to take. "How did you know it was me?" I asked.

He braced his hands against the table. The fluorescent lighting was harsh, revealing the thick, dark stubble on his jaw and the shadows under his eyes. "You flipped me off with your right hand. Kat's a southpaw. And she wouldn't be caught dead without her signet ring; it's Feliks's seal." He worried his lip with his teeth. "If I'd known it was you, I wouldn't have called for backup. What were you thinking, Finn?"

There was no right answer for that. Instead, I asked, "Does my sister know?"

He shook his head, his shoulders heavy. "She's not going to."

"What do you mean?"

"No one's going to tell her."

"How can you be sure?" There had been four cops with him when they caught me leaving the parking lot. This department gossiped around the watercooler like a bunch of politicians. Someone was bound to tell her. And when they did, she was going to bust that door down and throttle me herself. And then she'd tell our mother, which might actually be worse.

"No one's going to talk about it," Nick said. "Not you. Not me. And not any of the other officers who were with me."

"Why?"

"Because we all agreed not to." Nick pushed himself upright. "Lois Pyle has been with this department for thirty years. Her retirement party is next month. If anyone found out she let you in without checking your ID, she'd lose her job. None of us want to see that happen. If anyone asks, you were here conducting research for a book. It was all cleared with me ahead of time. Just a little role-play to get the full experience. That's all."

"Why would you do that? You could get in a lot of trouble."

"Yeah, well, maybe I should." He scrubbed a hand

over his face. "This is all my fault. If I hadn't told you my suspicions about Feliks's involvement yesterday, you never would have pulled a stunt like this. I swear, Finn, I'm handling it. We've already ruled out one suspect—"

"What suspect?"

His jaw locked, as if he was wrestling with how much to tell me. "Fauquier PD brought Bree Fuller in this morning for questioning. The security company said a woman triggered the security system in the trailer just before the fire. When the company called, the woman identified herself as Bree. The investigators thought they had an open-and-shut case, but apparently the real Bree had an alibi. Her parents confirmed she was home with them, watching TV. Her alibi was verified with a photo. Her mom had taken a picture of Bree and her dad in their living room that night, and Bree had posted it to her social media. The metadata from the original photo on Bree's phone says it was taken around the same time the security company alerted the police to the fire."

"So they still have no idea who started it?"

"That's why I came in tonight. Lois Pyle knows a few people who work at the station in Fauquier County. I asked her to make a few calls for me. She said they released Bree about an hour ago. I promised you I'd keep an eye on things, and that's what I'm doing. Now we know we're dealing with a female suspect. And we know she has some intimate knowledge of Steven's business and personal life. Given the fact that Theresa ditched her ankle monitor, and her best friend was reported missing by her husband, my money is on Theresa Hall and Aimee Reynolds."

"Aimee Reynolds?"

"She hasn't been home since Saturday night, and her husband says she cleaned out their savings account. I'm guessing she and Theresa are involved in this together."

Aimee Reynolds.

Aimee, who would do anything for Theresa, including disposing of a body. Aimee, who knew how to maneuver quietly online. Who knew how to make a problem disappear. Who'd been fighting with Steven over the kids. Who'd just cleaned out her bank accounts. Probably to pay *EasyClean* to finish the job.

Nick took me by the shoulder as I launched out of my chair. "I know what you're thinking, but there's no reason to panic. I've got an unmarked watching Steven's place and a tail on him everywhere he goes. Joey's there now until I can find a team to cover shifts around the clock. We're going to do everything we can to make sure Steven's safe until we find Theresa and Aimee and figure out who set that fire." He guided me gently back into my seat, releasing a frustrated sigh. "You could have gotten yourself killed tonight. I know you were scared. That you only did what you did to protect your family. But you don't negotiate with terrorists, Finn, and that's exactly what Feliks is. No matter what he says, you can't trust anything he promises." Nick took the chair opposite mine and spun it across the floor until it was right in front of me. Sinking into it, he braced his elbows on his knees, his head heavy and close to mine. "What did Zhirov say when you asked him about the attempts on Steven's life?"

My mouth opened and closed again. Nick thought I'd come here to negotiate for Steven's life. "N-nothing," I stammered.

"Did he say anything at all about who might have been behind them?"

"No."

The tension slipped from his shoulders. "Good."

"Good? Why would that be good?"

"Because if he didn't confess anything that can be used against him in court, then maybe Kat won't press charges against you." A moment passed as he let that sink in. He cupped my chin, dipping his head to meet my eyes. "I'm going to let you walk out of here, Finn. And none of us are going to say a word about this. Hopefully, Kat and Feliks won't either. But you have to swear to me that next time you're scared, you'll come to me. I know you're worried about Steven, but promise me you'll let the professionals handle it."

I nodded into his palm, nearly leaping out of my skin when someone rapped on the door. Nick dropped his hand as one of the officers who'd dragged me from my van an hour ago poked his head into the room. "Her lawyer's here."

Without a word, Nick rose from his chair and stepped out into the hall. Through the gap, I watched his shoulders fall as if a weight had been lifted off them. As if maybe he'd expected someone else. His body obscured my view of whichever public defender Julian had managed to rustle up to help me. All I could make out was a pair of crisp black slacks and simple black ballet flats through the gap between Nick's legs.

"Thanks for coming," he said as they shook hands. "I'm sorry to drag you out here so late for nothing. This was all just a big misunderstanding."

"Oh?" The woman's voice sounded skeptical.

"See, Ms. Donovan is a writer. She was here doing some research. She cleared it with me ahead of time, but a few of my uniforms didn't get the memo, and they must have misread the situation."

"Really? I was told you were the one who took her into custody?" Auburn hair framed the familiar pair of wide green eyes that peered around his shoulder through the crack in the door. My stomach bottomed out.

Nick cleared his throat. "Ms. Donovan requested that her experience be as authentic as possible."

"And that necessitated handcuffs, impounding her vehicle, and a call to an attorney?" Parker stepped around him and pushed open the door, pausing abruptly when her eyes met mine. Recognition lit like a slow fuse.

"I know how this must look," he said, following her into the room. "But it was all a big misunderstanding. Ms. Donovan isn't being charged with a crime."

"Then why is she in an interrogation room?"

Nick held up his hands. "You're absolutely right. I made a bad call letting it go this far, but like I said, she's not in any trouble." He stood close to me, resting a hand on my shoulder. "It's late. I'm sure she'd like to get home."

Parker's eyes narrowed as they skipped back and forth between us. "If you don't mind, I'd like to speak with my client."

Nick looked reluctantly to me. When I nodded, he left us alone, pulling the door closed behind him.

I wrapped my arms around myself to fend off a chill. "Thank you for coming," I said quietly.

Julian's roommate didn't bother to return my uncomfortable smile. We both knew she hadn't come for me. She set her messenger bag on the table. Neither one of us sat down. "Mind telling me exactly what's going on?"

"Detective Anthony already did. I was doing research for a book, and we all got carried away. That's all."

"Impersonating an attorney? Sneaking into a jail? Carried away? Yeah, I'd say so. If that detective wasn't covering for you, you'd be spending the night behind bars." She tipped her head as she studied me. "Is there something going on between the two of you I should know about?"

"With all due respect, that's none of your business."

"I disagree. Julian is my friend. He's a good person,

if a little too trusting. He doesn't deserve to be used *or* lied to."

"Then it's a good thing I'm not doing either."

Her laughter was sharp and joyless. "Julian was right. You're a hot mess. Do us both a favor. Next time you're in trouble, don't call him. He's got a really bright future ahead of him, and he's better off without you." She yanked her messenger bag off the table. I didn't bother to argue as she jerked the door open and stormed out.

Nick slipped into the interrogation room, carrying his coat.

"Come on," he said, holding it open for me. "I'll drive you home." He tugged the warm leather close around me and led me out through a side door. Parker stood on the sidewalk in the rain, her cell phone pressed to her ear as she wrestled with her umbrella. Our eyes caught as Nick wrapped his arm around me and escorted me to his car.

CHAPTER 33

Nick was painfully quiet during the short drive to my house. It was nearly one in the morning when he pulled into my driveway, both of us staring numbly out the windshield, the car still running. Mrs. Haggerty's house was dark, but in my side mirror, I could have sworn I caught the flash of a curtain being pulled back in an upstairs window.

"I'll get your van back to you in the morning," he said after a long silence. "Joey and I will drive it over. It's better if you don't go back to the station. We don't want anyone asking questions."

He had nothing to worry about. I had no interest in ever going back there. With a nod, I unlatched my seat belt. "Thank you for the ride home."

"Yeah, well, I didn't see anyone else showing up for you." There was a ragged, weary edge on his tone, but an edge nonetheless.

"I know you're angry with me. You didn't have to do what you did for me tonight."

He turned to me, his shocked eyes wide and bright in the light from my kitchen window. "I wasn't just angry with you, Finn. I was terrified! You just put yourself on Feliks Zhirov's radar. There was no way I was letting you spend the night in that place. And there was no way I was letting you drive yourself home."

"I'll be fine."

"Yeah, you will." His focus shifted to his rearview mirror as an unmarked police car rolled past my driveway and eased to a stop. His voice softened. "Officer Roddy's going to be keeping an eye on your house until I'm certain Zhirov's not going to be a problem."

"You don't have to do that," I argued.

"I'm not walking away just because shit gets messy. Your missing lawyer should have shown up for you tonight."

I winced, Parker's parting words still bouncing around like shrapnel in my head. "It's complicated."

He whirled in his seat to face me. "No, Finn, it's actually pretty simple. You deserve someone who's going to stick around."

"And you want to be that person?" I fired back.

He clenched his teeth and looked away.

I slipped off his jacket and reached for the door. "It's late. I should go."

"Finn, wait—"

"Thank you. For everything." I got out of the car before he had a chance to respond. The cold wind cut through my damp clothes, and my hands shook as I fumbled with my key in the dark. The front door flew open before I managed to get it into the lock.

Vero threw her arms around me. "You're not in jail!"

"Not yet," I said through her hair, struggling to breathe despite her vise grip around my neck.

"I was so worried when you didn't come home. Then Nick called and told me you were being held, and I freaked out and ate a whole bag of Oreos." She squeezed me tighter and whispered, "I have to know, was it just like in your book? Did you have wild, hot prison sex before he busted you out?"

I pulled back to gawk at her. Her mascara had run in long black streaks down her face, and cookie crumbs dusted the corners of her smile. "Were you snooping on my computer?"

"It's not snooping. As your accountant, I have a vested interest in the success of your book. I love it, by the way."

Nick's headlights swung over us as he backed down the driveway. I turned to see his car idling beside Officer Roddy's, their windows rolled down.

"Why is Officer Roddy parked outside?" Vero asked.

"You don't want to know." I pulled the door shut as quietly as I could, so I wouldn't wake the kids.

Vero helped me out of my rain-sodden coat. "You're freezing. Go dry off and warm up. And then come right back down here and tell me all about the handcuffs."

I shook my head as I retreated to my room, peeling off my damp clothes and changing into a pair of warm flannel pajamas. I sat on the edge of my bed, my head in my hands. My phone blinked beside me. Reluctantly, I picked it up and read the text message from Julian.

Bar's closing. Heading home soon. Call me when you can. Worried about you.

The message had come before Parker had shown up at the station.

I put the phone down. Picked it up again and stared at his message before dialing his number.

He answered on the first ring. "You okay?" He sounded wide-awake. Exhausted.

"Yeah. I made it home."

"I heard." The line was quiet too long.

"What else did you hear?"

"Enough to know it wasn't the whole story. Want to come over and tell me what really happened?"

I walked to the window and pulled back the edge of the blinds, craning my neck to see the dark outline of Officer Roddy's sedan down the block. I settled onto my bed and lay back on my pillows, one arm thrown over my head, staring at the ceiling. "I can't."

"Then I'll come to you."

"Please don't."

"Why not?"

"Because there's an unmarked police car watching my house."

"Detective Anthony's?" There was a little flint in his tone, a friction I'd never felt from him before.

"No. One of his friends is parked down the street."

"Finlay, what's going on?"

"It's nothing."

"Getting caught sneaking into a jail isn't nothing. Neither is police surveillance on your house. Who were you there to see tonight? Was it Zhirov?" I pressed my lips tight. Nick and I had agreed not to tell anyone. Too many people's jobs were on the line, not to mention Julian's future if anyone found out he'd helped me, knowingly or not. "That call you made to me earlier . . . the questions you asked me. You weren't at the jail to research a book. You went there to talk to him. Why?"

"I can't tell you."

"I thought we were being honest with each other."

"Plausible deniability. The less you know, the less you have to hide."

"I already told you, I'm not hiding anything. And you don't have to hide from me. Just, *damnit*, Finlay, don't lie."

Those words hit me like a punch to the gut. "I'm not lying. I just can't tell you everything. And believe me, you don't want me to."

"Don't tell me what I want."

I bristled at the sharpness of his tone. "My life isn't

some cute, curated Instagram page, Julian! You're right, it's a hot freaking mess! It comes with baby gates and childproof locks. It comes with car seats and diapers, and a controlling ex-husband, and a meddling, nosy, opinionated mother, and a sister who's a cop! It comes with things I've done that you probably don't want to know about. And maybe it's better that there are parts of it you can't see right now. Because if you were really being honest with yourself, you'd admit that it all scares you and you don't want to be tagged in a frame with any of that."

The line went silent. "What is it you think I want from you?"

"That's what I keep asking myself." I blew out a shaky sigh and slung an arm over my face. "I'm a single mom in my thirties, Julian. I've got two kids and a questionable job. You're a gorgeous, young bachelor with a promising career and your whole life ahead of you. I don't even have health insurance." I squeezed my eyes shut against the burn building behind them.

"Is that it?" His quiet voice was rough with emotion. "You don't think you're good enough, so you're just going to write us off?" I couldn't make myself speak past the lump in my throat. "You're right. You've got a lot you need to sort out, Finlay, but not the things you're worried about. Maybe I'm not the only one who isn't being honest with myself."

After a long pause, the call disconnected. I held the phone to my ear, wishing I could take so many things back.

There was a soft knock as Vero cracked open my door. She poked her head in, her dark ponytail swishing through the opening. "Want some company?"

She didn't wait for an answer before creeping into my room in her fuzzy slippers and flannel pajama robe and setting a hot mug of cocoa in my hands. It was filled to the brim with marshmallows. She climbed into my bed and pushed herself back against the headrest beside me. I took a sip of my drink and coughed, a trail of liquor burning fire down my throat.

Vero laughed quietly into her mug. "Figured you could use it. Want to talk about it?"

"I think we just broke up. But I'm not sure which one of us did the breaking." I filled Vero in on everything that had happened after Nick caught me leaving the jail, up through the part where Parker showed up to represent me.

"Well," she said, wiping marshmallow from her lip, "that explains why Julian was so upset."

"Because I used him for information so I could do something illegal?"

"No, because he's jealous."

"He's not jealous. He's pissed."

"He's frustrated, Finn, because he couldn't be the one to rescue you and Nick was. He sent Parker thinking he was going to be your hero, and she probably turned around and told him Nick had you covered. And now you're not telling Julian what really happened, so he's feeling helpless to do anything about it."

"Just because I ask for help doesn't mean I want to be saved."

She shrugged. "What can I say? Men are fragile. Give him some time. He'll come around." She pulled a half-pint of bourbon from the pocket of her robe and poured another finger of it into my hot chocolate before putting another splash in her own. "You think Feliks is going to hold up his end of the bargain?"

"I didn't leave him much of a choice."

"Assuming he takes the website down, what do we do next?"

"We have to find Theresa and Aimee before the police do."

"You really think Aimee is *FedUp*?"

"She has to be. She has the means to hire someone like *EasyClean,* she hates Steven, and the timing of the ad makes sense—Steven had just dumped Theresa. Aimee's best friend was alone behind bars, and she could more easily pin Carl's murder on Steven if he wasn't alive to defend himself." If I was right and Aimee was *FedUp,* then finding her was the key to solving all our problems. We could recover my lost phone, get rid of our piece of Carl, and use what we knew about Aimee's involvement in his murder to persuade her to contact *EasyClean* and call off the job. The plan would have been perfect, if I only knew where to start.

CHAPTER 34

I woke up early the next morning to find my van parked in my driveway and a message from Nick on my phone, letting me know he'd left the keys under the floor mat. I shuffled outside in my pajamas and slippers to grab them, waving to Officer Roddy's daytime replacement before pulling the van into the garage and closing it inside.

As I was settling down at the kitchen table with my first cup of coffee, there was a hard knock on my front door. Peeking through the kitchen curtains, I spotted my sister's car. I closed my eyes and uttered a swear. It had taken less than twenty-four hours for the gossip to find her. With a sigh, I flung open the door.

"Hey, Finn!" Georgia clapped my shoulder as she pushed her way inside. "Get the kids ready to go."

"They're already ready to go. Vero's taking Delia to school."

"She's not going to school. I've got the next two days off. I'm taking the kids to my place."

"Your place?" I asked, immediately suspicious of her enthusiastic tone. "Why? I mean . . . not that I'm complaining, but you do realize there would be diapers involved." I followed her to the kitchen as she helped herself to a cup of coffee and a handful of dry cereal from the pantry.

"Nick called me this morning. He told me that someone wants to off your ex-husband. And while I imagine the list of candidates must be pretty long, he's got some theory that Feliks Zhirov is connected to the whole thing. Something about a post he found online."

The ad. Nick must have found the forum last night. Georgia shrugged, popping a handful of Cheerios in her mouth and talking around it. "Nick's got good instincts. If he's worried enough to put an officer on your house, then it's probably smart to have the kids stay somewhere else for a while. Nick's got his partner covering Steven's place and he can't afford the manpower to put another rotation at Mom and Dad's, so he suggested I keep the kids for a couple of days until he can get the whole thing sorted out."

"And that's all he mentioned?" I asked cautiously.

"That and some tirade about a website disappearing from the internet this morning. He seemed pretty worked up about it."

The forum. Feliks must have had his people take it down overnight.

It was done. We'd done it. Now all we had to do was track down Theresa and Aimee before Nick did. "Do you know where Nick is now?" If he'd gone home to get some sleep, that would buy us a solid head start.

"He's chasing down a lead on that missing CI he's been looking for."

I set down my coffee. "He has a lead?"

Georgia shrugged. "Sounds like it. He hung up before I had a chance to ask him about it. You know how he gets."

I knew, all right. Enough to know Nick definitely wasn't home sleeping.

"I'll go get the kids." I excused myself from the

kitchen and raced up the stairs, nearly knocking Vero over where she stood eavesdropping in the hall. "Did you hear that?" I asked, dragging her into my bedroom. "Cam probably still has copies of everything he found on that women's forum. If Nick finds him and gets his hands on those files, everything we risked last night was for nothing."

"We have to find Cam before Nick does," Vero whispered.

"But Nick said Cam hasn't been at home or at school."

Vero shook her head. "When someone's in trouble, they don't hide where they're supposed to be. Not at home, not with family. They lay low with a friend. Or maybe an accomplice—someone who has just as much to lose if they're found."

Like Aimee and Theresa. Or Vero and me. She'd moved into my home right after we'd buried a body. "Who would someone like Cam hide with?"

"Pack up the kids," Vero said, grabbing a hoodie from my dresser drawer and tossing it in my hands. "I'll wait for you in the Charger at the playground. Get rid of your sister and leave through the backyard. I've got a pretty good idea where to find our missing hacker."

An hour later, Vero banged her knuckles on the counter in the tech shop. Derek sat behind the register, staring at his phone.

"We're looking for Cam," Vero said brusquely.

"Don't know him," Derek replied without looking up.

"Last time we were here, you gave us his card," I reminded him. "You told us he could help us fix a network problem."

"Sorry. Doesn't ring any bells."

Vero got close to his face and raised her voice.

"Let me jog your memory, *Derek*. He's about your age. Blond. Skinny. Smart-ass. And, according to you, he has a talent for cleaning up ugly dick pics."

Two girls in the accessory aisle stood on their toes to peer over the divider at us. Derek ducked lower on his stool. "I have no idea what you're talking about."

"I don't know why you're bothering to cover for that little shit. Especially after he offered to sell me your nudes."

Derek's head snapped up. He dropped his phone on the counter, knocking over his stool as he stood and shoved his way through the EMPLOYEES ONLY door behind him. Vero and I rushed after him as he threw open a door to a break area containing a kitchenette and a ratty sofa. Cam was inside, seated at a plastic table, holding a large Slurpee to the side of his face.

"What the hell, man?" Derek shouted.

Cam sprung from his chair. A deep gash sliced across his cheek and his left eye was swollen shut. His other went wide when he saw me. He held his Slurpee protectively close as Derek surged toward him and backed him into the corner.

"That was easy," Vero said, and slipped out of the room.

"I paid you to get rid of those pics!" Derek knocked the Slurpee from Cam's hand, spraying the wall with orange ice.

"Hey, I was drinking that!"

Derek grabbed Cam by the collar, holding him up by the neck until the tips of his toes were the only thing touching the floor. A chime rang somewhere in the shop. Derek swore, releasing Cam with a shove. "You're lucky I have a customer, asshole. But you and I? We're not finished." Derek lumbered out of the break room. Vero slipped in behind him, slammed the door, and threw the lock. Cam stiffened, pressing back into the corner as Derek realized his mistake and started pounding on the door.

"He's not the sharpest tool in the garage," Vero said, dusting off her hands.

I turned to the refrigerator and rummaged in the freezer, plucking out a Lean Cuisine and holding the box against the bruise on Cam's face. He winced, jerking away from me. "Who did this to you?" I asked.

He snatched the frozen dinner from me and pressed it gingerly to his cheek.

"I'm not telling you shit. I'm already in enough trouble because of you."

"Was it Feliks? Did his people do this?"

"Look," he said, dropping into his chair. "That forum was bad news. I, for one, am going to forget I ever found it. And if you know what's good for you, so will you."

I sat in front of him, fussing over the cut on his cheek around the box of frozen noodles. I'd been so careful not to reveal Cam's name to Feliks, only that the tip had come from a CI. If Feliks knew Cam was the informant—that he had records of the forum—Cam was lucky to be alive. "I need the information you were going to give to Detective Anthony."

"Sorry. No can do."

"You owe us fifty dollars," Vero reminded him.

Cam gestured to his face. "I earned that fifty dollars!" He turned away as my eyes raked over his bruises.

"You found something on *EasyClean*, didn't you?" I asked, my suspicions confirmed by his grimace. "If you know who *EasyClean* is, you have to tell us. It's a matter of life and death, Cam. We had a deal!"

"I don't have to tell you anything." Cam flinched as Derek shouted his name through the door.

"You don't want to talk? Suit yourself. We'll just leave you and your buddy Derek to catch up." Vero turned for the door, hand poised to flip the lock.

"Okay, I'll talk!" Cam dropped the Lean Cuisine, eying the emergency exit on the other side of the room. "But I can't do it here. I'll come with you, but I want a safe place to stay. Somewhere no one will find me. That's the only way I'm giving you those files."

"Fine," I said. "You can stay with Vero's cousin."

Vero whirled on me. "No!"

"What am I supposed to do?" I argued. "Take him to my sister's?"

"I want a hotel room," Cam demanded. "A nice one. With free breakfast and unlimited internet. And I want another Slurpee."

"Deal." It was a better idea than letting him crash on my couch. "Let's go."

We followed Cam through the emergency exit into the bright afternoon sunshine of the parking lot. Derek's shouts faded behind us as the door drifted shut. Vero took a moment to orient herself as she clicked her remote. Her Charger's lights flashed a few rows away from us. Cam hunched into his jacket, his eyes roving furtively over the parking lot as he ducked into Vero's car. He sank low in the back seat as Vero started the engine. I twisted in mine. "Now, talk. Who is she?"

Cam clammed up, his eyes narrowed on his phone in his lap. Clearly, he had no intention of making good on our deal until he was safely inside his cushy hotel room with his Slurpee, I directed Vero to pull over at a 7-Eleven, where I bought Cam an extra-large bright orange beverage. He sucked down a few long sips, then pressed the frosty cup to his cheek.

"Where to now?" Vero asked.

"I'll take the Ritz-Carlton for five hundred, Alex," Cam muttered from the back seat.

"There's a Holiday Inn Express across the street," I suggested.

"Apparently my health and safety mean nothing to you."

Vero shook her head. "We need a motel. Someplace that takes cash, where no one's likely to remember him."

"How about this? It's not far from here." I held out my phone, revealing a photo of a small single-story structure with a few dozen rooms that opened to a parking lot. There was a liquor store on one side and an adult novelty store on the other.

"Perfect," Vero said. "Let's go."

Cam engrossed himself in videos on his phone, slurping slush through his straw with an annoying degree of force as I navigated the way to the motel. Vero pulled the Charger around back where it wasn't easily spotted from the road. "I'll go inside and get the whiz kid a room." She held out her hand. I dug around in the messenger bag I'd borrowed from her the night before, shoving aside the brunette wig and dredging out my wallet. I slapped a few twenties in her palm and she got out, leaving the car running.

"We agreed you'd take me someplace nice," Cam said. "This place is a dump."

"Have you seen your face?" I asked, angling the rearview mirror to look at him. "And when was the last time you bathed? You look like a runaway. If we take you someplace nice, the front desk clerk will call the police. They're looking for you, by the way."

This shut him up. He sank lower in his seat, glaring out the window. "Can I ask you something?"

"Maybe."

"You keep saying *her* and *she*. What makes you so sure *EasyClean* is a chick?"

"Because it's a women's forum. You know, for *women*."

"It's also the internet. Anyone can be anyone. Who do you think convinced Derek to send his dick pics in the first place?"

"Wait," I said, twisting in my seat, "you're telling me you catfished your own friend into sending nudes, just so you could charge him to clean up the mess?"

"I know, right?" He actually looked proud of himself. "Never assume you know who you're dealing with online."

"I don't have to assume anything. In a few minutes, you'll have your hotel room and you're going to tell me everything."

"You going to get that?" Cam nodded at the ringing cell phone in my lap. Nick's name flashed on the screen.

I killed the engine and pocketed the key fob. "Stay here," I told Cam. "I'll be back in a minute." I carried my phone around the side of the building before connecting the call. "Nick?"

"Hey, have you heard from Steven?" A police siren *whooped* twice in the background and Nick leaned on his horn.

The hair stood up on my arms. "Why? What's wrong?"

"He's okay. But there was an accident."

"What kind of accident?"

"A tire blew on his pickup. He managed to run it into a ditch. He hit a tree, but it doesn't look like there was much damage. Joey and I just came from the site of the wreck. I couldn't tell much from the tire that blew, but one of the others looked like it might have been slashed."

Damnit! "Where is he?"

"I was hoping he was with you."

"I thought you said you had people watching him?"

"I did. But he got angry. Said he didn't want any cops on his property. Joey was camped out as close to the house as he could get, but Steven must have left from the back. By the time my guys found his truck, he was gone. The tow driver remembered him getting into a van."

My throat tightened. "What kind of van?"

"We don't know. The tow driver said he was too busy trying to get the truck out of the ditch to notice. That's all he remembered. I thought maybe Steven had called you for a ride."

"No," I said, pacing, "I haven't heard from him."

Nick swore under his breath. "Maybe it was a ride service. Lots of taxis and Ubers use vans. Did the kids make it to Georgia's?"

"She picked them up this morning."

"Good." Some of the tension left his voice. "I've got eyes on your place, just in case Steven's headed that way. Roddy's to contact me or Joey the second anyone spots him. If you hear from Steven, I want you to call me. Until I know what we're dealing with, I want you to stay home and keep your doors locked. Joey's heading back to Steven's house in case he turns up there. I'm heading to the station to put out a BOLO. I'll come by your place as soon as I know more. And Finn?"

"Yeah?"

"I'm going to find him. I promise." Nick disconnected.

More than anything, I wanted to believe that.

My hands shook as I dialed Steven's number. It rolled straight to voicemail. "Steven, it's Finn. Call me as soon as you get this."

I thumbed off my phone, pacing the alley behind the motel. If *EasyClean* had abducted Steven, then I had a better shot at finding him myself. As soon as Vero was done paying for the room, I'd make Cam tell me everything he knew.

Vero's engine rumbled to life. I ran around the

building to meet her. The Charger screeched to a halt inches from my knees. Cam's eyes widened behind the steering wheel. They leapt to his rearview mirror as Vero bolted out of the lobby. Cam cut the wheel hard and hit the gas, tires squealing as he peeled out of the parking lot.

"He stole my car!" Vero shrieked. "You left him alone with the key?!"

"I didn't!" I snapped, waving the fob in front of her. "I took it with me. The only thing he had was his Slurpee and his cell."

"And YouTube," she said, snatching the keys from my hand. "He had YouTube on his phone. That little shit must have taught himself to hot-wire my car! That's it." She dragged her phone from her pocket. "I'm calling the police."

I ripped the phone from her hand. "You can't do that! What will you tell them? That we just bought a room for a kid who's hiding from the cops? Cam knows too much about us. You can't report him. We have more important things to worry about."

"What could be more important than my car!"

"Nick just called. Steven's gone missing. And I'm pretty sure *EasyClean*'s got him."

CHAPTER 35

Vero and I took an Uber home from the motel. We needed a car to search for Cam, and the van was all we had left. The driver dropped us off at the park at the end of our street, and Vero and I cut through the neighbors' backyards, sneaking behind the house to the side door of the garage to avoid being noticed by Officer Roddy and Mrs. Haggerty.

Vero put her key in the lock. "That's strange," she whispered.

"What's strange?"

"It's unlocked." Vero inched the door open. From behind the hulking shadow of my minivan came a series of metallic *clank*s. "Someone's in there," she whispered. "What do we do?"

"I'll go in this way," I said. "You circle around from the kitchen." Vero nodded and tiptoed toward the sliding door at the back of the house.

I slipped into the garage and crouched behind my van, peering around it. A figure stood with his back to me in front of my workbench, examining my new tools under the dim halo of light from the naked bulb above his head. I crept closer until I could see him in profile. Steven studied my plumber's wrench and tossed it down with an infuriated sigh. He reached for my brand-new utility knife, bending over it to inspect the blade. I wasn't sure if I was relieved or pissed that he was alive.

I stood up and shouted, "What are you doing here?"

Steven swore. The knife fell onto the bench with a loud thump and he whirled around, clutching his chest. He pointed a finger at the tools as he stalked toward me. "You and I are going to talk about this. I know what you're trying to do, but this has gone way too far, Finlay. You have the entire police force thinking someone is out to kill me!"

"Someone *is* out to kill you! That's what I've been trying to tell you!"

"This has to stop. Right now. Before someone gets hurt."

"What are you doing?" I backed into the side of the van as he reached for me.

"I'm taking you to the police station."

"You can't do that!" I slapped his hand away.

"We're going to sit down with your very concerned detective friend, and you're going to tell him it was *your* voice on that security recording the night of the fire. You're going to tell him everything. That you and that nanny of yours knocked me down at the tree farm and pretended to mug me, just so you could pressure me into filing a damn police report."

"What? I didn't pretend to mug you!" I backed away from him as we circled around the garage.

"I found that spying app you put on my cell phone, by the way. Nice touch. A real step up from the baby monitor in Delia's backpack."

"What spying app?"

"But messing with my gas line and slicing my tires? Just to make it look like someone was out to get me? To make it look like our children weren't safe with me? That's crossing the line. You're going to explain to

Nick that this ridiculous post he found on the internet was just one big made-up story *you* concocted so that you won't have to share custody with me."

My back smacked into the hood of my van. I felt my way around it, inching toward the door as he closed the distance between us. "I readily admit that was me on the recording, but I didn't set that fire! And I didn't do any of those other things either. I am telling you, someone wants you dead! And believe it or not, for once it's not me! That post Nick found is real, Steven!"

He grabbed my arm and dragged me out from behind the fender. "As real as the rest of your stories." My sneakers squeaked against the concrete as I dug in my heels. "Don't worry," he said, clenching his teeth as I leveraged my weight against him. "I'll tell your cop friend I don't want to press charges. I'll tell him we're working it out between the three of us . . . you, me, and my lawyer. Guy can meet us down at the station right now. Once you've set things straight with the police, we'll figure everything out." He gripped my arm tightly with one hand as I shoved at him. His other reached into his pocket for his phone.

"You have no idea what's going to happen if you do this!" I said, prying at his fingers as he scrolled through his contacts.

"I know exactly what's going to happen. That detective friend of yours isn't going to arrest you. I'm not an idiot; I've seen the way he looks at you. And Georgia's going to swoop in and defend you, just like she always has." He started dialing. A sliver of light sliced through a crack in the kitchen door behind him. "Let's get this over with, Finn. It's time to face up to what you've——"

A thud echoed through the garage as my favorite All-Clad pan bounced off the back of Steven's head. His phone slipped from his hand as he fell sideways onto the concrete.

Vero bent over her knees, breathing hard. "You have
no idea how long I've wanted to do that." She nudged
him with the toe of her shoe. His shallow breaths were
warm on my cheek as I hovered over him, checking for
a pulse. "Is he dead?" Vero asked.

"He's fine."

"Want me to hit him again?"

I glared at her as I picked up his phone, making sure
he hadn't had time to dial his attorney before I set it on
the workbench. The drawers were all open, my new
tools scattered over its surface. An assortment of blunt
instruments and screwdrivers had been meticulously
sorted, and the box cutter was open, the guts emptied of
blades. "I can't believe him. He was looking for *proof*
that I've been making all this up." The prowler Mrs.
Haggerty had seen wasn't one of Feliks's men; it was
Steven. Nick had found my door unlocked right after
the gas leak at Steven's house. Steven must have come
snooping around and been scared off by the police. "He
thinks *I* wrote that post on the forum. Meanwhile, *Easy-
Clean* is still out there. And my only lead for figuring
out who's really trying to kill him just drove off in your
car."

Vero held up the pan. "Don't take this the wrong
way, but I have an idea."

I knew that tone. It was the same one she'd used
when we sat on this very floor and came up with a plan
to dispose of Harris Mickler. She'd been holding that
same damn pan, and that same scheming gleam in her
eye hadn't led to anything good. "Put it down."

"Hear me out," she said, setting it aside. "*EasyClean*
is a contract killer. She—or he," Vero conceded, "is only
after Steven for the money. And *FedUp* is only offering
to pay one of you—whoever gets to Steven first. All
we have to do is convince *FedUp* that the job is done.

Then we claim the money. Once the money is claimed, *EasyClean* disappears."

"And what happens when *FedUp* realizes Steven's still alive?"

"Too late. By then, we have the cash. What's *FedUp* going to do, report it to the cops? She can't go to the police with this. What the hell would she say? *I offered someone a hundred Gs to kill a guy, but I got hustled. Could you please find my money for me?* No way!

"All we have to do is take a few proof-of-death photos and find a safe place to stash your ex for a couple of days while we contact *FedUp* and arrange to collect the money. When she shows up to pay us, we'll know exactly who she is, and we can use that as leverage to make sure she never tries it again. By the time she figures out she's been duped, the forum's gone, *EasyClean*'s out of the picture, Steven is safe, and *I* have a brand-new car. That is nonnegotiable, by the way," she said, leveling a chipped fingernail at me.

Steven's mouth hung open, his face slack with sleep. I gnawed my lip. It wasn't a terrible idea. "What if we get caught? Nick knows about the post on the forum. He knows someone is trying to kill Steven for money."

"That's the beauty of it. Don't you see? Steven's not dead," she reminded me. "No body, no murder. No murder, no foul. At worst, you're guilty of manipulating the situation to save your ex-husband's life."

She had a point. And it was better than letting *Easy-Clean* finish the job. "How are we supposed to keep Steven out of sight? There's no way he's going to agree to this."

Vero grabbed a roll of duct tape off the workbench and tossed it to me.

"Have you lost your mind?" I sputtered. "We can't hide him here! Not with Nick and Georgia barging in whenever they suspect something's wrong. We're lucky they haven't found Carl! And how would I explain to Delia and Zach why their father is duct-taped in the basement?"

"Who says we have to keep him here?" Vero plucked the motel key from her pocket and dangled it in front of me. "It's already paid for. Cam isn't using it. Silly to let it go to waste."

CHAPTER 36

I sat on the garage floor, hunched over Steven's phone as Vero hauled Steven onto his back and unzipped his coat. Frowning down at him, she lifted one lifeless arm above his head and bent one of his legs at an odd angle. "What are you doing?"

"Staging a crime scene." She opened a bottle of raspberry syrup and squirted a puddle of it in the middle of Steven's sweatshirt. Then she doused the end of a long screwdriver and dotted some syrup around him on the floor, leaving sticky fingerprints on its handle. She dropped the murder weapon beside him. "There!" She licked her thumb with a satisfied grin and got busy snapping pictures of our victim. "Grab the tape. I think he's coming to."

I set Steven's phone on the workbench and tore a long strip of duct tape from the roll. Vero and I worked fast as Steven began to stir, taping his wrists together behind his back and securing a few feet of the stuff around his ankles. The last piece I slapped over his mouth, which felt better than it probably should have. Together, we hauled him into the rear of my minivan and shut the door.

I rested against it, wiping sweat from my brow. The van shuddered with Steven's furious thumps as he fully awoke. A muffled shout penetrated the door. "He's going to kill me when this is over."

"I don't think so." Vero panted beside me. "I'm pretty sure Bree was right. He's crazy about you."

"How do you figure that?"

"Think about it, Finn. The guy thinks you beat him over the head, burned down his office, flooded his house with gas, and slashed his tires, and he still hasn't gone to the cops. He let Bree spend an entire day in custody for a crime he *knew* she didn't commit, all because he didn't want the person in those handcuffs to be you."

"But you saw him just now. He was ready to drag me kicking and screaming to the police station."

"A, he wasn't going to drag you anywhere, because there's no way I'd let him take you. And B, the only reason he was trying to make you go to the station is because he didn't want to be the bad guy who called the cops and turned you in. He wanted *you* to do it yourself. And he was planning to take you straight to Nick and your sister, because he knew they wouldn't arrest you if he didn't press charges."

The van had gone still, and I wondered if Steven could hear us.

"Come on," Vero said, pushing off the door, "we should email these pictures to *FedUp* and get Sleeping Beauty to the motel before anyone comes looking for him." A series of thumps shook the van. "Any luck with the app on Steven's phone?"

I trudged to the workbench to find it. "No, it's one of those tracking apps parents use to spy on their teenagers. You need a password to disable it. *EasyClean* must have installed it after mugging Steven for his phone."

"The phone can't send a signal without power. Turn it off. We'll figure it out later."

Steven's screen lit with a message as I picked it up.

"That's weird," I said. Vero came up behind me,

watching over my shoulder as I tapped the notification. "It's a meeting reminder. But that can't be right. Steven's calendar says he's scheduled to attend a Fourth Quarter Profit and Loss Meeting two hours from now."

"With who?"

"Ted Fuller and Carl." Our eyes locked over the phone. I lowered my voice. "How can Steven have a meeting with his silent partners if one of them is dead?"

"They must have scheduled the meeting before Carl was murdered."

"No. The meeting invitation just went out this morning."

"Ted must have scheduled it. It's the only explanation. Maybe Theresa was telling the truth and Ted doesn't know about Carl."

"I don't think so," I said, holding the phone between us so she could see what I was seeing. "Ted isn't listed as the event organizer. He hasn't even confirmed he'll attend yet. The invitation was sent by Carl's assistant."

"Carl's assistant?" Vero took the phone from me to see for herself. "If Carl had an employee, why wouldn't this person have told anyone their boss was missing, especially if said boss wasn't around for months to cut them a paycheck?" Vero narrowed her eyes at the screen. "And why would they schedule the meeting at Carl's house? Are you thinking what I'm thinking?"

"That whoever sent this invitation already knows Carl is dead." This sounded too much like a setup. And besides us, there were only three people alive who knew what had happened to Carl—Theresa, Aimee, and Feliks. "What if Aimee set up a dummy account, posing as Carl's assistant? Maybe she and *EasyClean* are working together; she lures him to the scene, and *Easy-Clean* takes him out."

"Or maybe she figured she could do it quicker and cheaper on her own. Think about it . . . She posted the job to the forum while Theresa was in jail, and she responded to both offers while Theresa was stuck at home with an ankle monitor. But now Aimee has her wingman back. What does she need *EasyClean* for? She's not exactly squeamish when it comes to blood. And *EasyClean*'s already botched three attempts." Vero shook her head. "I think Aimee got spooked when we showed up with Carl and she wants Steven handled fast. And if she and Theresa take him out, she doesn't have to pay anyone."

"Then why include Ted in the meeting? If she intends to murder Steven, why invite a witness?"

"Ted hasn't confirmed he'll be there. What if she never really sent him an invitation? Maybe this is all just staging. You know, part of the ruse. Maybe Aimee set up the e-vite to make it look like it was a meeting of the partners, so Steven wouldn't suspect anything was out of the ordinary."

The more I thought about it, the more it all made sense.

"I'm sending those pics to *FedUp* before she weasels her way out of paying us."

"Wait," I said as Vero reached for her cell. "That meeting is in less than two hours. Steven won't be there, but whoever invited him doesn't know that." I powered off Steven's phone, tapping it against my chin. "Don't send those photos just yet. I have a better idea."

It was almost dusk when Vero and I arrived at the motel, with Steven duct-taped in the back and Carl in his bag on the floorboard. I had crouched in the back seat as Vero drove my van out of the garage. She'd waved to Officer Roddy as we'd left, leaving him to assume I was still safely inside my house.

Vero checked the number on the key and backed the van as close to the motel room door as she could manage. We scanned the parking lot and the closed curtains in the neighboring windows, making sure there were no witnesses as we hefted Steven from the back of the van and shoved him inside our room. He teetered on his bound ankles before falling to the carpet with a thud.

"Do we have to lift him to the bed?" Vero panted, bent over her knees. Steven writhed in his duct tape restraints, his eyes shooting daggers at me as I put the DO NOT DISTURB sign on the door and drew the heavy drapes closed. The room was a dump. The wallpaper was peeling from the walls, and there were yellow stains on the popcorn ceiling. I didn't want to imagine what kinds of horrors were hidden by the funky 1970s patterns in the carpet, but I also didn't think we could muster the strength to lift him onto the bed.

"We should at least move him away from the door." We dragged him by his armpits into the gap between the beds. I tucked a pillow under his head and turned on the TV, cranking up the volume and changing the channel to ESPN. "Ready?" I asked Vero, brushing off my hands and reaching for my keys. Steven's eyes flew open wide. His breathing became panicked and ragged as we headed for the door. "Sorry, Steven. Believe me, this definitely beats the alternative. I'll be back in a few hours to check on you."

The TV drowned out his thrashing as Vero and I left and pulled the door closed. I climbed into the driver's seat, pausing before putting the key in the ignition.

"You're feeling guilty," Vero said, buckling herself in. "Don't. He was manhandling you in your own damn garage. Meanwhile, you're trying to save his sorry, miserable life. You have nothing to feel guilty about. Now come on. We've got a body to get rid of."

With a resigned sigh, I turned the key. A familiar clicking sound mocked me from the engine.

"No! No, no, no!" Vero breathed.

I tried the key again. Nothing happened.

"What do we do?" Vero asked.

"I don't know!"

"We can't exactly call Triple A. We've got Carl!"

"We'll leave the van here and rent a car. There must be a rental place around here somewhere." I groped behind my seat for the messenger bag I'd taken to the jail the night before. I rummaged inside it, turned it upside down, and dumped out the folder and the wig. "My wallet. I must have left it in my coat."

"Don't panic. I'll text Ramón and have him bring us a loaner." Vero and her cousin exchanged a few quick text messages. She dropped her phone in the drink holder with a swear. "He's halfway to an accident in Leesburg and he's stuck in traffic. It'll be at least two hours before he can get here."

"That meeting at Carl's house is in just over an hour! We can't wait that long!"

"This isn't *Weekend at Bernie's,* Finn! We can't prop Carl between us in the back seat of an Uber!" She crossed her arms and sank back with a huff. "When I find Cam, I'm going to kill him myself. We need a car. Preferably a fast one." She wrinkled her nose. "I think our mummy's starting to thaw."

I stuffed the contents of the messenger bag back inside, pausing over the wig. It was long and dark, a perfect match to Kat's cut and style. But close enough to Irina's color and length to pass for hers in the dark. The gray December sky was already deepening toward sunset.

"Call an Uber," I said as an idea took root. "Give Ramón the address of the motel. Tell him we'll leave the keys in the van. Ask him to tow it to his shop."

"What about Carl?"

"We'll be back in plenty of time to pick up Carl before Ramón gets here. With any luck, we can still get to that meeting before it starts."

"Where the heck are we going?"

I handed Vero the wig. "We're going to find a very fast car."

CHAPTER 37

The Uber driver dropped us off a block away from the international auto lot just before dark. The towering lampposts cast halos over the cars, and the bright lights of the showroom reflected off their sleek hoods. Vero's mouth parted around a soft *oh*.

I stepped in front of her, breaking the spell as I dragged the wig over her head and smoothed down the edges. "Stick to the section of the lot farthest from the showroom. Pick something fast but practical. An SUV or something. Text me the color and model. Whatever happens, don't let any salespeople approach you and don't talk to anyone. Pretend to be on an important phone call. I'll handle the rest."

"What are you going to do?"

"I'm going to get the keys." I started toward the dealership. Vero jogged to catch up.

"And you think they're just going to *give* you the keys to one of these cars without asking for ID?"

"No, they're going to give them to Irina Borovkov. Go." I nudged Vero toward the lot and headed toward the showroom.

As I reached for the glass door, it swung open for me. Alan stood aside, an uncertain smile on his face.

"Good evening, Miss . . ." His face flushed red with embarrassment. "I'm sorry, I don't recall your name."

"Probably because I'm not important." I looked down my nose at him as my phone buzzed in my pocket. "I'm here with Irina Borovkov. She would like to take the . . ." I snuck a peek at my phone. ". . . Superleggera Volante in Modern Minimalist . . ." I checked my phone again. Was that seriously the name of a color? ". . . for a drive."

"The *Superleggera*?" A swell of panic rose inside me when Alan's eyebrows shot up. I wasn't sure what a Superleggera was. But anything with *minimalist* in the title couldn't be that bad, right? "Are you sure?" he asked.

I held out my hand for the keys.

"Of course. I'll have the vehicle brought around for her." His smile was brittle as he turned toward a phone on the reception desk.

"No!" I rushed to stop him before he could lift it off the cradle. "I mean . . . Mrs. Borovkov is already waiting at the car. She asked me to bring her the key. She's on a very important phone call and cannot be disturbed."

Alan glanced through the huge front windows, presumably toward the car in question. Vero's posture was almost regal. She stood with her back to the showroom, cast in silhouette, her dark wig blowing in the breeze and her phone pressed to her ear.

"Did I mention she's in a hurry?"

Alan cleared his throat and adjusted his tie. "Very well," he said in a low voice. "Wait here, please." He disappeared into an office. A moment later, he returned and discreetly slid a key fob into my hand as he shook it. "Please tell Mrs. Borovkov we hope she enjoys her test drive."

I fled the showroom with a muttered "thanks," frantically pushing buttons on the fob until lights flashed and an engine roared on. The taillights of a sleek matte black sports car burned a hot, bright red. Vero made a sound that bordered on erotic as she eased into the driver's seat. My heart raced as I ducked into the passenger side and locked the door. I stared at the dashboard, unable to form words. The exterior of the car was a giant phallus, and the interior looked like Darth Vader's bathroom.

"I told you to pick something practical!"

"You also told me to pick something fast. This baby has over seven hundred horsepower."

"We don't need seven hundred horsepower! We need room for Carl!"

Her eyes drifted closed as she revved the engine. "Shhhh, I think I'm having a religious experience."

"You can pray to the car later. We need to get out of here before we attract any more attention." I twisted in my seat to see Alan watching us from the sidewalk.

"Don't worry. I picked a very subdued color. See? *Minimalist.*" Vero handed me a spec sheet from the glove box. "We'll be far less noticeable in the dark."

My breath felt thin when I saw the price at the bottom of the page. "Vero! This car is worth three *hundred* thousand dollars!"

Vero threw the car in gear. "You told me to channel my inner Irina. And Irina Borovkov gives zero fucks." Vero hit the gas, swinging the Aston Martin out of its parking space. Alan raised his arm against the glare of our headlights as Vero gunned it, our tires leaving him in a cloud of smoke as we tore out of the parking lot.

CHAPTER 38

Vero and I raced back to the motel and transferred the bag containing Carl from the minivan into the trunk of the Aston Martin. I left the van keys under the seat, along with Steven's phone, and pocketed the hotel key, resisting the urge to unlock the room and check on him. We had a long night ahead of us, and I wasn't sure how long we could keep the car before Alan grew anxious and called Irina.

As I'd feared, the car attracted a lot of attention until we were several miles west of the city, where the twelve lanes of the interstate narrowed to six and the darkness thickened to conceal us. Vero navigated toward Carl's address as I studied Google's satellite image of his five-acre plot on my phone. The lot appeared to be heavily wooded. The western side of the property bordered a rural road and a country store.

"We can park behind that little market. There's a clearing in the trees about an acre in. We should have a clean line of sight to the rear of the house."

We took the rural road that ran alongside Carl's property, dimming the headlights as we pulled in behind the store. We left Carl in the trunk and locked the doors, using the light of our phones to see our way through the woods. Dead leaves and frosted ground crackled under our shoes.

"I think we're close," I said after we'd hiked a good distance, pausing to consult the GPS on my phone before turning it off. We picked our way through the trees in the dark. The clearing ahead was small, the ground irregular and mounded. The trees thinned on the far side of it, and through them, we could make out the lit windows of a house. "There it is," I said, pointing to a sprawling rambler down a shallow hill.

"Ow!" Vero jolted to a stop, hopping up and down on one leg and grabbing her foot. "What the hell was that?" I looked around her, but hardly a wisp of moonlight filtered through the dense pockets of clouds. I could barely make out Vero's features beside me, much less the ground.

I switched on my phone light, careful to keep the beam pointed down. It bounced off a shiny surface, the reflection nearly blinding me. I blinked down at a thick slab of glossy marble.

"This isn't a clearing. It's a private cemetery." I aimed my light left, then right, counting four grave markers. "These must belong to Carl's family." The frozen ground crunched as Vero and I walked between the headstones, shining the beam over the names.

"You must be kidding. This is perfect!" Vero said.

"What do you mean?"

"Remember in one of your books, how you said the heroine hid a body in a grave that belonged to someone else? We can bury Carl right here with his family. It's the one place no one would think to look."

I stumbled as my foot sank into a patch of soft dirt. Kicking away a drift of dead leaves, I ran my hand over the loose soil. "This grave is fresh," I said. But if Carl and his wife had been estranged and he'd lived here alone, who would have come here so recently to bury someone? I knelt and scraped a layer of dead leaves from the grave marker.

CARL R. WESTOVER
BELOVED HUSBAND AND STEPFATHER,
FOUGHT HIS CANCER WITH
GRACE AND COURAGE.

"Um, Finlay? Why does Carl already have a head-stone?"

And why was the death date under the inscription four months old—close to the date when Carl was actually murdered? "I don't know."

"You think he's actually buried here?"

"He must be." The more I thought about it, the more it made a sick kind of sense. Theresa and Aimee must have hidden Carl's body in plain sight, right in his own family plot, with an epitaph that would smooth over any questions about the cause of his death. "Theresa and Aimee must have planned this months ago," I said, "right after Carl was murdered."

"What do you mean?"

"Engraved headstones take weeks—sometimes months—to order. This headstone was purchased long before we found Carl in the storage unit. The storage unit was probably a temporary solution. They must have been planning to retrieve the body and move it here when the headstone was done, but Theresa got stuck on house arrest and they were forced to wait. They must have panicked when we left Carl in Theresa's kitchen, and they came straight here. Carl's vacant house would have been the perfect place to hide from the police."

"And the grave site was already prepped for his body."

"Which means Theresa and Aimee are here. They have to be the ones who invited Steven to the meeting."

I checked the clock on my phone. "It's almost time. Let's get a closer look."

Vero and I turned off the light and crept to the edge of the trees behind Carl's rambler. We laid on our bellies in the grass. A handful of lights were on inside the house. Someone had been careful to pay the electric bills. A shadow moved inside a large bay window. Vero pulled a set of binoculars from the pocket of her coat and held them out to me.

"Where'd you get these?"

"Took them from the garage before we left. Thought they'd come in handy."

I held the binoculars to my eyes, elbows braced on the frosty ground as I adjusted the focus. The knobs were still sticky with donut sugar from the tree farm.

"What do you see?" Vero whispered.

"Someone's in the kitchen. A woman. She's in front of the stove. I think she's cooking." Two vehicles were parked along the side of the house—a small sedan and an SUV that must have been Aimee's.

I swung the binoculars back toward the bay window. The woman at the stove turned as another woman entered the kitchen. "It's definitely Aimee. And Theresa is with her. They're pulling down plates from a cabinet. Wineglasses. Utensils from a drawer. Aimee's bringing food to the table. Theresa's pouring two . . . no, three glasses of wine. There are three places set." They'd gone to a lot of trouble to set the stage for their little setup.

"Steven's supposed to show up any minute. What do we do?" Vero asked.

"Send those photos to *FedUp*."

"Now? But then they'll know Steven's not coming."

"And we'll see it the very moment Aimee gets the message. We'll know for certain she's *FedUp*." And then we'd knock on the door and confront her.

Vero dragged her phone from her pocket. The

screen illuminated her face as she typed out a message. "These pics actually came out pretty convincing. The raspberry syrup was a nice touch." There was a *whoosh*ing sound as the email was sent.

Then the chilling cock of a shotgun behind us.

Vero froze. I didn't dare move.

I kept my eyes trained straight ahead, through the binoculars at the scene in the kitchen, though I had suddenly lost all interest in whatever Aimee and Theresa were doing inside.

"This is private property. You're trespassing." I didn't recognize the voice of the woman behind me, but she spoke with the authority of someone who knew exactly where the boundary lines were and precisely where we'd crossed them. As if she owned the place.

"Mrs. Westover?" I asked carefully, hoping I was right. "I can explain."

"And you will. Get up. Slowly. And keep your hands where I can see them."

I snuck a last peek through the kitchen window, before lowering the binoculars. Aimee's phone sat on the table beside her, the screen still dark. She never so much as glanced at it as she and Theresa spooned food onto their plates and started eating.

Vero pushed onto her hands and knees.

"Go on," the woman said, prodding me between the shoulder blades with the barrel of her gun. Vero looked at me askance as we rose to our feet and the woman nudged us toward the house. I guess we knew who the third glass of wine was for. Carl and his wife may have been estranged, but she was no stranger to his empty home.

We marched through the frosty grass in silence. Mrs. Westover called out as we neared the house. Theresa's and Aimee's heads snapped up, their eyes darting to the window. Theresa shot to her feet and met us at the door.

"What the hell are they doing here?" Her face paled as if she'd seen a ghost. Aimee's fork dropped to her plate with a clatter.

"Saw a light up on the hill. By the graveyard." The woman pushed us into the kitchen with a bump of her shotgun. "Sit down," she barked, directing us to the table.

Aimee gawked at us as Vero and I took seats across from her. Her phone was still dark on the table beside her. Her eyes were welling as if she might cry. "Finlay, what are you doing here?" she asked, a slight tremble in her voice.

"I was going to ask you the same thing."

"You know exactly what we're doing here," Theresa snapped, making Aimee jump in her seat. "We needed a place to hide, and no one was going to look for us here. No one except you, obviously. Because somehow, you continue to be the bane of my freaking existence!"

"This is her? This is Steven's ex-wife?" Mrs. Westover asked.

Theresa threw up her hands for dramatic effect. "Mom, please! I can't deal with this now."

Mom?

"Hold up a minute," Vero said, looking between Theresa and Mrs. Westover. "If Carl's wife is your mom, then Carl is your—Jesus, Theresa. You chopped up your *dad*?"

"Stepdad!" Theresa argued. "He was my *step*father. And for your information, I never even lived with the man. My mother married him after I left for college. Lord only knows why," she added, rolling her eyes. "Obviously, Carl and I were never close. And before you ask, no, Feliks had no idea Carl was related to me when he killed him, and I wasn't about to offer up that information to him after what he did. Feliks doesn't like loose ends, and the last thing I wanted was for him to come after my mom."

"It doesn't matter," Mrs. Westover said firmly, dragging out a chair at the head of the table and plunking herself into it. "I told you, I can handle this Feliks person. And I can handle the police. It's all handled, Theresa. You're not going to prison for that man. It's over. Carl's buried and in the ground." Mrs. Westover jabbed her finger on the table. "As far as everyone outside this room is concerned, Theresa's stepfather died of cancer in August. I have a death certificate to prove it."

Vero chuckled darkly. "The doc who signed off on *that* was missing a big piece of information. Pretty sure it's in the trunk of our—ow!" She yelped as I kicked her under the table.

"How did you manage to get a death certificate?" I asked. If Theresa and her mother could get away with burying the body without the police suspecting anything was amiss with Carl, then that solved one of our more pressing problems.

"It's all about who you know," Theresa said coyly.

"Who you know, or who you sleep with?" Vero muttered. Wine splashed over the table as Theresa launched at her.

"That's enough!" Mrs. Westover shouted. The rest of us stilled, stunned silent by the sudden appearance of her mom-voice. No one reached for the overturned wine bottle as the contents slowly dribbled out. "Sit down!" she said to her daughter, her tone leaving no room for argument. Theresa slid into the empty chair beside Aimee with a huff.

Mrs. Westover got up and brought a fresh bottle of red from the cabinet. Then two more glasses. She uncorked it, pouring a little into each before topping off her own. "Carl was dying of cancer," she explained.

"His doctor had given him only a few months to live. That was why Theresa took Feliks to see her stepfather in the first place. Carl's treatments were expensive, and his insurance didn't cover much. Theresa thought he could use the money. She had no way of knowing that Carl would refuse. Or that Feliks would hurt him. Theresa is not at fault. She was swept into all this. I don't blame her for what happened to my husband, and I won't see her go to prison for what that horrible man did to him.

"Carl's doctor is a very old friend," she continued. "I told him that Carl passed peacefully, at home with me, and I asked him for a favor. He gave me the death certificate and I ordered the headstone." She rested the shotgun across her lap. "Carl is where he was meant to be, and that's all that's important now. When people ask for him, we'll explain that he passed quietly with his family and he didn't want any fuss. There's no reason for anyone to go looking for him."

"Maybe not, but they'll be looking for your daughter," I argued. "Theresa violated her house arrest. The police are actively searching for her, and they know Aimee is with her. They can't hide here forever."

"No, they can't," she agreed. "We've already discussed it. Theresa will turn herself over to the authorities tomorrow. When they ask why she ran, she'll simply say that Feliks threatened her and she feared for her life. If she turns herself in and follows through with her plea bargain as planned, the DA isn't likely to bring up any new charges against her. Her testimony is too important to the prosecution's case."

Theresa paled. Mrs. Westover closed a hand over her daughter's. Aimee looked like she might be sick. "I don't want to go back," Theresa whispered to her mother, her lower lip trembling. "What if Aimee and I leave town instead? She has all that money she cashed out of her accounts. Enough for us to live on for a while."

"One hundred grand could go a long way," Vero agreed. "Especially if you don't have to give it to someone else."

Theresa pulled a face. "What are you talking about?"

Aimee turned away.

"Theresa doesn't know, does she?" I asked.

Aimee's wide eyes leapt between Vero's and mine and her voice shook. "What do you mean?"

"We know you're *FedUp*," Vero said. "We know you tried to hire someone to murder Steven."

Aimee's mouth fell open. Theresa's brow pinched as she pivoted toward her friend. "Aimee, what is she talking about?"

"I don't know," Aimee stammered. "I mean, I am fed up with Steven. He's a total asshole, and he wouldn't let me see Delia and Zach, but I never asked anyone to hurt him!"

"Check her phone," Vero insisted. "You'll see. She'll have an email from *Anonymous2* with pictures of the crime scene. Oh, by the way," Vero said, turning to Aimee, "in case you haven't figured it out, Steven's not coming to your little ambush, so you can send a message to *EasyClean* and tell them the deal's off."

Theresa gasped. Tears sprang to her eyes. "Steven's dead? Who's *EasyClean*? Aimee, what are they talking about?"

"I have no idea!" Aimee cried.

Theresa lunged for Aimee's phone. She scrolled, her eyes glistening as they moved over the screen. "I don't see anything. There's nothing here but text messages back and forth to her husband." Theresa turned to Aimee with a look of disgust. "You've been texting your husband? You told me no one knew we were here!"

"I'm sorry!" Aimee said. "He kept messaging me! He said he missed me and he was worried!"

"Your husband is the king of all assholes, Aimee! I guarantee the only thing he was worried about was the money you cashed out of your joint accounts to help me! You're not seriously considering giving it back to him!"

Aimee winced.

Vero grabbed the phone from Theresa. "There has to be a message here. I sent it myself. There were pictures and everything." Aimee and Theresa stared at Vero with stunned expressions as she scrolled through Aimee's phone. She pushed the cell phone back across the table. "I don't understand. If you're not *FedUp*, then who ordered the hit on Steven?"

"And who set up the meeting?" I asked.

"What meeting?" Theresa, Aimee, and Mrs. Westover asked in unison.

We all turned toward the front window as headlights cut through the trees. A pickup truck rolled up the long gravel driveway toward the house, triggering the motion sensors on the front porch lights as it slowed to a stop. The engine cut off and the headlamps extinguished. The dim light of a cell phone screen illuminated the driver in a soft blue glow as he typed a quick message. He squinted up at the house as his screen went dark.

Vero's phone vibrated. The screen lit with an email from *FedUp*. Vero held it up for me to read.

> *Anonymous2, Why would you send me this horrible picture? Is this your idea of a joke? I don't have any money, and if you contact me again, I'm reporting you to the police.*

"I think we just got stiffed," Vero said. Her eyes lifted to the window as the man got out of his truck.

Mrs. Westover rose from her chair, peeking around the curtains as he strode slowly toward the house. Her face paled as she turned to her daughter. "What on earth is Ted Fuller doing here?"

CHAPTER 39

"What do you think he wants?" Theresa asked her mother as Bree's father climbed the front porch steps.

"I don't know," Mrs. Westover said in a low voice. "I haven't spoken to Ted since their last meeting back in June. He and Carl had a falling-out about the sod farm."

"What did they argue about?" I asked hurriedly.

"Ted didn't like the way the profits were being divided. He wanted more of the shares since he'd taken a more active role in running the farm—he'd been working closely with Steven. But Carl and I told him we wouldn't amend the deal. A contract is a contract, and Carl couldn't help the fact that he was ill. He wasn't in any position to walk away from his share, but Ted didn't see it that way. I don't think they ever reconciled. Ted and Steven ran the business, and the direct deposits appeared in Carl's account every month, just like the original contract said they would."

"Then why's he here?" Theresa asked.

Ted's footsteps thumped slowly toward the door. A sickening feeling of dread settled in the pit of my stomach. I had a pretty good idea why Ted was here. And I was pretty sure it wasn't because he was invited to some mystery meeting. "Someone posing as Carl's assistant sent an e-vite to Steven and Ted, inviting them both here for a meeting." Every head turned to me. "That's why Vero and I came. We thought it was Aimee, trying to lure Steven here to kill him." Aimee frowned. "It's a long story," I said apologetically. "No offense."

"None taken." She looked a little queasy.

"But if Aimee didn't set up a meeting with Steven and Ted, who did?" Mrs. Westover asked.

The doorbell rang. Nobody moved to answer it.

Mrs. Westover reached for her shotgun. "There are five of us and only one of him. We'll get him inside and get to the bottom of this." Mrs. Westover unlocked the dead bolt and cracked the door, holding her shotgun out of sight behind it. We all crept closer to listen.

"Barbara!" Ted sounded breathless, as if the sight of her had knocked the wind out of him. "I didn't expect to see you here."

"I could say the same about you. Haven't seen you here in quite a while. Awfully late for a visit, isn't it?" she asked bitterly.

"I apologize. I know I should have called. Steven's running late, too. He just sent me a message. Said he got tied up with some car trouble, but he's on his way."

Vero grabbed my arm. "Tied up? Car trouble?" she whispered.

That couldn't have been a coincidence. We'd left his cell phone in the van and the keys for Ramón. Leave it to Steven to know exactly how to get my van running. "Steven must have gotten himself out of the motel room."

Ted's voice turned suspicious. "Is someone else in there with you?"

Mrs. Westover swung the shotgun into her arms, nudging the door open with her foot.

Ted raised his hands slowly, taking a cautious step back from the door, his brow furrowing with confusion. "Barbara, I know Carl was real upset after our last meeting, but I'm sure we can work something out just as soon as Steven gets here."

"Carl passed away this past summer, Ted. But I'm guessing you already figured that out." Barbara stepped out onto the porch, the gun leveled at his chest. "Is that what this mysterious meeting is all about? You planning to get rid of your last business partner and take the farm for yourself? Maybe you want to talk to Steven's ex-wife about that idea first." Barbara jerked her head in my direction. Ted's eyes widened when they spotted me behind her. "Come on inside, Ted. Seems we have a few things to clear up."

Barbara stepped aside, letting Ted enter the house first. She kept the shotgun pointed at his back as she directed him to the kitchen table. The rest of us circled around it as he sat, like a jury awaiting a confession.

"I'm sorry, Barbara," he began, his throat tight with emotion. "I had no idea Carl had passed. I should have called or come by sooner. I should never have left things the way I did. I didn't realize his illness was so advanced."

"Carl didn't want anyone feeling sorry for him. He was a good man. I can't say the same about you."

"I don't know what to say for myself," he admitted quietly.

"Why don't you start by telling us who is *FedUp*?" I suggested. I wanted to hear him confess that he'd posted the ad on the forum. That he was responsible for all these attempts on Steven's life. That Ted scheduled this meeting to lure Steven here so *EasyClean* could finish the job. "Start with the fire at the farm and go from there."

His head snapped up. "You know about that?"

Vero crossed her arms over her chest, drumming her nails. "We know a whole lot of things."

Ted swallowed hard. "Please understand, my wife

never meant to hurt anyone when she set that fire. Melissa was just angry with me. She'd been pestering me to cut ties with Steven for a long time, but Steven and I had a deal, and I'm a man of my word."

I shook my head, confused. "Your wife set Steven's trailer on fire? Why?"

Ted's cheeks flushed, and he looked down at the table. "Last spring, I asked Steven to hire my daughter to work in the office a few days per week as part of our agreement. Only, Bree developed a bit of a crush, and Steven . . . well, you know Steven." Ted's eyes lifted apologetically to mine.

"Hello! I'm right here." Theresa waved her hands at me and Ted. "Does anyone care that he was engaged to *me* at the time?"

Vero grabbed the open wine bottle and thrust it in Theresa's hand. "No. But have a consolation prize. You," she said to Ted, "keep talking."

He drew a breath and continued. "Melissa was livid when she figured out Steven and Bree were romantically involved. She insisted we tell Bree she couldn't work for him anymore, but my daughter's a grown woman, and I didn't think it was our place to dictate her relationships."

Vero made a sound of disgust. "More like the farm was making money, so you decided to overlook the fact that a philandering creep was taking advantage of your daughter."

Ted admitted his guilt with a tight nod. "Melissa called him incessantly. She hounded him all summer, demanding he terminate Bree's employment. She wanted an end to whatever relationship they had. Melissa finally got her way after that whole mess in October, when Steven had an excuse to lay Bree off.

"Bree was miserable. She stayed in bed for days crying, and the farm was losing money hand over fist, but Melissa was finally happy. That lasted for about a month, until Steven had a few drinks one night—Thanksgiving, I think it was—and he called our house at an indecent hour, looking for Bree." That must have been the booty call I'd seen on his call log when I'd snooped through his phone. The call he'd made to Bree's home number, not her cell.

"Bree had already gone to bed," Ted continued. "Melissa saw his number on the caller ID and didn't bother answering the phone, so Steven left a voicemail message, telling Bree he missed her and he'd made a mistake. He said he had a new place of his own and he wanted to see her." Vero looked at me, her eyebrow raised. That was the night Steven had shown up in my driveway and caught me making out with Julian. When he'd told me that his new house didn't feel like home because me and the kids weren't in it.

"Go on," I said to Ted.

"Melissa was furious. She demanded that I terminate the partnership. She said the farm was losing money after the scandal anyway, and since Bree wasn't working there anymore, there was no reason to maintain a relationship with Steven, business or otherwise. When I refused, she got angry with me. She set fire to the trailer to make a point, that she would lay waste to that farm—and our business—before she would let that man destroy our daughter. Family over profit. It was only a trailer she'd said. Our daughter's future was far more important than a lost investment."

"She could have killed someone," I said, remembering the ravenous speed with which the fire had devoured Steven's couch.

"No," Ted insisted with a vehement shake of his head "She knew that trailer was empty. Steven's truck wasn't even there. Melissa knew he was living someplace else. She would never have set the fire if she thought someone would get hurt. This was just her way of putting her foot down and reminding me of my priorities."

"So she hired someone else to do her dirty work," Vero said skeptically.

Ted looked puzzled. "I don't understand," he said, turning to me for an answer.

"We think your wife hired a contract killer to murder my ex-husband." I watched his expression morph from confusion to disbelief.

"Melissa?" He laughed, a small sound of wonder that grew into an almost hysterical outburst. "Never! You don't know my wife. She could never do something like that."

"I hate to say it," Mrs. Westover said, lowering her shotgun to her side, "but he's right. I've known Melissa Fuller for years. I could see her destroying property to teach an unscrupulous man a lesson and protect her daughter, but I can't see her taking a life. It just doesn't fit."

"She did something foolish in a moment of weakness," Ted insisted, "but she realized her mistake when the police came to the house with a warrant for Bree. Melissa will never forgive herself for that. She would have been terrified to make any attempt to harm Steven or his property again, for fear of casting any more suspicion on our daughter."

"So rather than turn your wife in, you tweaked Bree's alibi, making sure it covered Melissa, too." The morning after the fire, Bree told me she'd been home the night before watching TV with her dad. But according to Nick, her parents told the police all three of them had been home watching TV together. I could picture it all playing out in my head. "Melissa didn't take that photo of the two of you in your living room that night. While you and Bree were home watching TV, your wife was setting the fire."

Ted shook his head. "No one else was home, just me and my daughter. She wanted a photo of us, so she put her phone on the bookshelf and set the timer."

"And you told the police Melissa took the photo, giving her an alibi," Vero said. Ted nodded. "But if you and your wife didn't hire someone to kill Steven, why did you schedule the meeting and invite Steven here?"

Ted looked confused. "I didn't schedule the meeting."

I turned to Vero. "If no one here scheduled the meeting, then who did?"

"Don't look at me," Theresa said, lifting the wine bottle to her mouth.

A crash tore through the front window as glass splintered the air.

We all hit the floor, covering our ears, cowering under the table as bullets rained into the house.

CHAPTER 40

The silence was deafening when the firing finally stopped.

"Is everyone okay?" Ted called out. Barbara cocked her shotgun.

"Who's shooting at us?" Aimee huddled beside Theresa. I looked around me at the faces under the table. Every single one of us had a connection to Feliks Zhirov.

"It has to be Feliks," I said. "You said it yourself, he doesn't like loose ends." We were all loose ends. One fell swoop and Feliks's men could eliminate us all.

Another round of bullets ravaged the house.

"We'll see about that!" Mrs. Westover rolled onto her knees and propped the barrel of her shotgun in the broken window. She fired off a few shots in the dark, interrupting their assault. When she ducked to reload, Feliks's men returned fire, forcing her to retreat back under the table with the rest of us.

Theresa cradled her wine bottle in one arm and held Aimee in the other. "I'm sorry I told my husband where we were!" Aimee cried.

"I'm sorry your husband's a dick!" Theresa sobbed.

Bullets gouged into the kitchen cabinets and pinged against the refrigerator door.

"Finlay!" Vero said, clutching my hand. "There's something I need to tell you before we die."

"I know!" I said, squeezing hers back. "I love you, too! But now is not the time!"

"No, Finn. It's about the money. I need to—"

Tires skidded in the gravel outside. Blue light flooded the window, followed by a shout. "Police! Drop your weapons and put your hands up!"

"That sounds like Nick!" Vero ducked, covering her ears as another hailstorm of gunfire erupted outside.

Vero and I crawled to the window and peered out. A blue light swirled on Nick's dashboard. His driver's side door hung open, but he was nowhere in sight. Two men dressed in solid black hid behind trees in the front yard, their semiautomatic weapons flashing as they fired into the passenger side of Nick's car.

"Where is he?" Vero asked over the pop of gunfire.

"I don't know. He must be trapped behind his car. We have to do something." The gunmen wouldn't let up, one shooting as the other reloaded, windows shattering as they fired at the swirling blue lights. I ducked under the window, dragging Vero down with me. "We have to make a distraction. Something big enough to draw their attention from Nick." It would take something brighter and louder to drag their focus away from his car. My eyes darted over the kitchen for anything we could use. Blue light shimmered off the fallen wine bottle on the table.

"I have an idea. Come on!" Ignoring the bite of broken glass, I crawled toward the table on knees and elbows with Vero shimmying behind me. Reaching blindly above me, I felt for the bottle and passed it to Vero. Theresa yelped as I plucked the other bottle from her hand and poured the contents on the floor.

"I was drinking that!"

Vero was tight on my heels as I carried the bottle on

hands and knees to the sink. "This is a very bad idea, Finlay!"

"We have to do something! They're making Swiss cheese out of Nick's car!"

I rummaged through the cabinet, shoving aside rolls of paper towels and trash bags until I found a jug of glass cleaner. I unscrewed the cap and sniffed. The fumes pinched my throat and my eyes burned. "Find me a towel."

Vero reached around me and snapped the dish towel off the handle of the fridge, tearing it into two long strips as I poured glass cleaner down the necks of both bottles. I handed one to Vero. We stuffed the ends of the cloth strips inside them and scuttled with them toward the stove. Vero reached up and switched on one of the burners. We held up the bottles, dangling the cloth over the flame. When they caught with a *whoosh,* we rushed on elbows and knees to the broken window, ducking as another round of gunfire exploded outside.

"On the count of three," I shouted over the din.

"Wait," Vero said, "on three or after three?"

"Just throw it!" Theresa shouted.

Together, Vero and I hurled the bottles toward the flashes of the men's muzzles. Glass shattered. The bottles exploded with a roar of flames. Feliks's men screamed, leaping out from behind the trees they'd been using to shield themselves.

Vero pointed at a burst of movement behind Nick's car. I spotted the back of his jacket as he darted behind a tree for cover. Nick turned, weapon drawn. He aimed toward Feliks's men and fired. One of the men cried out and dropped. Nick fired off another series of shots, and the second gunman went down.

The gunfire stopped. The night fell silent except for the low hum of Nick's engine and the snap and hiss of fire in the yard. I couldn't see anything through the thick bands of smoke and the relentless swirl of blue lights.

Glass crackled in the kitchen behind us. Ted, Barbara, Aimee, and Theresa crept out from under the table, coming up alongside Vero and me to peek out over the window frame.

A groan came from somewhere in the woods.

"Nick!" I scrambled to the door, my sneakers slipping on broken glass. I could hear Vero shuffling behind me as I burst out onto the front porch. "Nick! Where are you?"

"Finn?" His voice broke on a shout. "Get down! It's not safe."

Mrs. Westover rushed into the yard, standing over one of Feliks's men with her shotgun. She nudged him with her toe. Ted stood over the other, checking for a pulse. He shook his head.

"It's okay," I called out. "It's over."

Nick moaned. I followed the sound and found him sitting against the back of the tree. He clutched his arm, holding it close to his body. The smell of blood was thick in the air. I knelt beside him, heart still hammering as I searched him for injuries. The tree blocked the light from the house, and I couldn't see anything but the dark outline of his body. The screen of Vero's phone lit up as she dialed 911.

"I'm okay. It's just a graze." He started to get up but quickly changed his mind. He hissed, grabbing his left thigh. "Aimee and Theresa . . . where are they?"

I looked over my shoulder. Theresa stood in the middle of the yard, spraying an extinguisher at the flames. Aimee stomped on the sparks that the wind had carried. "Putting out the fire."

"Is everyone okay?"

"Everyone but you." I switched on my phone light, trying to get a better look at his wounds.

"I've been through worse." His smile was unconvincing, his voice strained.

"Hello, nine-one-one?" Vero said. "I've got an emergency. This is—"

"Please don't say it," I murmured, squeezing my eyes shut.

"This is Officer Ruiz. I need a medic! I've got an officer down. I repeat, I've got an officer—"

Nick reached to snatch the phone from her hand. "This is Detective Nicholas Anthony with Fairfax PD . . ." Nick gave the dispatch operator our address and requested an ambulance. He disconnected and handed Vero back her phone, resting his head against the tree as he held his arm. "Do you mind calling Joey for me?" he asked her. Vero dialed Joey's number as Nick rattled it off. She plugged one finger in her ear and moved a few feet away from us.

I peeled back Nick's sleeve for a better look. "How'd you figure out Aimee and Theresa were here?"

"Aimee's been texting with her husband. We traced the pings to a tower nearby and found an old address for Theresa's mother in the vicinity. Seemed like too much of a coincidence. Figured it was worth checking out. Do I even want to know what you and Vero are doing here?"

"Same thing you are. Solving mysteries. Stopping bad guys," I said, erring on the side of less is more. "Only I guess we were faster."

"Remind me never again to question the efficacy of your research skills." Sirens wailed in the distance, their whines growing closer.

"At least I brought my partner with me. What the hell are you doing out here alone, Nick? You could have been killed. Where's Joey?"

"He's spent all day looking for your ex after Steven gave us the slip this morning. I didn't want to pull him off surveillance. I was only planning to do a drive-by to see if Aimee was here, but I heard gunfire and called for backup."

Vero returned, frowning at her phone. "I tried Joey's number three times. He didn't pick up. I left him a message and told him to meet you at the hospital."

The hair on my neck bristled. The more I thought about it, the more this didn't sit right. Nick said the reason Feliks was able to get away with so much was because he had a few dirty cops in his pocket. Joey became partners with Nick right after Feliks had been arrested. Right after Feliks had developed a fascination with Nick. And Joey knew Nick and I were having dinner last Saturday night at Kvass, which would explain how Kat had known we were there. Then there was Cam . . . Cam was Joey's CI, but he'd chosen to reach out to Nick when he knew Joey was out of town. Why? And why clam up and run as soon as Joey got back?

I give you everything I have, and then Joey and I are done.

Cam said that finding *EasyClean*'s identity had cost him. He knew something about *EasyClean,* enough to give us a clue, that *EasyClean* wasn't necessarily a woman. It was as if he'd wanted us to figure out who *EasyClean* was, but he was too afraid to be the one to tell us.

Never assume you know who you're dealing with online.

What if it wasn't Feliks's men who'd roughed Cam up, but a cop? A cop who didn't want anyone to know about the forum because he'd been using it himself. A cop who'd been moonlighting because he needed money. A cop who'd been spending a lot of off-hours surveilling my ex in the name of helping his new partner. What if Joey only claimed Steven had given him the slip to deflect suspicion and clear the way for a well-timed attempt on Steven's life? What if Joey had known where Steven was all along because he'd been the one to put the app on Steven's phone?

Shit! His phone! Steven's phone was in the van. He'd used it to tell Ted he was on his way here. And we hadn't had time to remove the tracking app.

Which meant Joey could be following him right now.

Sirens blared. Red-and-blue lights flashed as cop cars and ambulances turned in to the Westovers' driveway. EMTs rushed to Nick's side, two of them hovering over him. I grabbed Vero's hand, hauling her behind me around the side of the house. "We have to find Steven."

Her breath puffed out in a cloud between us. "Why? He's on his way here. Why don't we just wait for him?"

"Because I'm worried he won't make it this far. I think Joey might be *EasyClean*."

"Joey?" I could feel her mind spinning backward in her sudden stillness, as if she was seeing the events of the last few days differently, the same way I had. "This isn't good, Finn. We have to tell Nick."

"No, Vero! We can't say a word to him about this. We don't have an ounce of proof. We thought for sure Aimee was *FedUp,* and we were wrong about all of it."

"But what if you're right this time?" Vero handed me the keys to the Aston. "Go. Find Steven. By now, he must be close. I'll stay here in case he makes it this far."

Nick shouted my name as I sprinted into the woods.

CHAPTER 41

I dialed Steven's cell phone as I raced through the dark woods behind Carl's house. The Aston glimmered in the parking lot ahead. My lungs burned as I reached for the door.

Steven answered without bothering to greet me. His voice was as chilling as the cold night air. "You have so much explaining to do."

"I know," I panted. "And I will. I swear. But you need to listen to me." I pressed random buttons on the key fob until the interior of the car lit up and the doors unlocked. Ducking inside, I studied the controls and pushed a button to start the engine.

"I'm *finished* listening to you. I've been very, very patient with you, Finlay, but my patience is shot. As soon as I get home, I'm making an appointment to meet with Guy. This bullshit is over. Do you hear me? Over!"

"Steven, listen," I said, throwing the car in gear and making a tight circle behind the country store. The parking lot was pitch-black, and I flipped on the Aston's high beams. "You have to get off the road. You have to get somewhere public. Somewhere with a lot of people. And lights. Like a store or a gas station." If he was as close as I thought he was, his options were already limited. The roads out here were all rural and unlit. There were miles between small mom-and-pop convenience stores, nothing likely to be open this late.

A dark laugh rumbled out of him. "See, that's the funny thing. I'm already off the road. Because your damn van just gave up the ghost, and now I'm stranded somewhere in bumfuck, waiting for a goddamn tow!"

No. No, no, no! I put my foot down hard on the accelerator. It felt like I'd just kicked seven hundred horses into a run. Trees rushed by. G-forces pulled me back against the seat as the Aston hugged the turns in the winding roads. "Steven, where are you? Just give me a street name or a landmark. I'm on my way. Stay in the van and lock the doors. I'm coming right now!" He'd probably followed the same route Vero and I took to get here. If I doubled back, I'd find him. He couldn't be far.

"Are you kidding me? Your nanny clocked me on the head, Finlay! I'm probably concussed! You took me hostage, gagged me, and abandoned me in some crap motel. Don't you get it? You're the last person I want to see right now!"

"Wait. I think I see you." Yellow hazard lights flashed from the shoulder of the road ahead. I released a held breath as I recognized the familiar grille of my van. Steven paced alongside it with his back to me. I let off the gas, my heart rate decelerating in time with the car.

"Thank god," Steven said under his breath, "the tow truck is here. I've got to go." I watched him step out into the road, waving his free hand at a set of oncoming headlights closing in from the opposite direction. A cold dread hit me as the other vehicle began to slow.

"That's not the tow truck, Steven. Get back in the van!"

"We'll finish this conversation tomorrow with Guy."

I shouted into the phone as he disconnected and

tucked his cell in his pocket. Shielding his eyes from the glare of the car's headlights, he flagged the other driver down. The car passed him with its turn signal on, easing to a stop about fifty yards ahead of the van. I sped up, squinting against the car's high beams as I flew past him, groping for the right button to roll my window down. Steven stumbled back as the Aston screeched to a halt beside him.

"Get in!" I shouted.

His eyes went wide. "Where the hell did you get that car?"

"Never mind that! Just get in!"

He turned his back on me, throwing up his hands. "Go home, Finlay."

"Steven!" I put the Aston in reverse, matching his pace as he walked toward the other vehicle. "The person in that car is going to try to kill you. You have to come with me. Right now!"

"You are a real piece of work, Finlay. You know that?" Steven kept walking as I reversed slowly alongside him.

"Steven, please," I begged him, reaching for his arm through the open window.

He shook me off. "I knew you were nuts when you left me in that motel room, but this? This is . . ." Steven stopped walking. I braked as he grabbed my sleeve. "What the hell is that on your hand? Is that blood?"

"I don't have time to explain." A figure stepped out of the other car. Steven followed the direction of my stare and waved to the driver, holding up a finger, asking him to wait. The man raised his hand, too. He pointed it toward us.

"Get down, Steven!" I threw my car door open hard, catching Steven in the groin as the driver's gun fired. Steven doubled over into the open window as the bullet whizzed past his head.

Steven's eyes flew open wide as another bullet hit the asphalt by his feet.

"Get in the goddamn car!" I shrieked. I threw the car in drive as Steven scurried around the hood and scrambled into the passenger seat, his face incredulous.

"Did you see that? That guy just tried to shoot me!"

"What do you think I've been trying to tell you?"

"I didn't think you were serious!"

"Seat belt!" I shouted in my mom-voice as a bullet struck the back window. I hit the gas pedal hard, leaving a trail of rubber. Taillights flashed behind me as the other driver got in his car and made a three-point turn in the road.

Steven buckled himself in. "Holy shit, Finn. This is a fucking Aston Martin!"

"I know what it is, Steven."

"Just, tell me the truth. Where'd you get the car?"

"It's not important. Give me your phone."

"Why?"

"Just do it!"

He handed it over. I powered it off and pitched it out the window. Steven opened his mouth to argue, snapping it closed when I held up a stern finger. When the speedometer climbed over a hundred, he pressed back in his seat. "You're going a little fast. Maybe you should slow down."

"Now is *not* the time to criticize my driving!"

"Right. Sorry." He twisted to look behind us. "I see his high beams. I think he's following us."

"Did you get a look at him back there when he passed you?"

"No, his brights were on. Looked like a sedan. Maybe a Chevy."

Joey drove a Chevy sedan. But so did a lot of people. "What color?"

"I don't know. It was dark. And I don't want to let

him get close enough to find out." Steven turned back to the windshield, ducking his head to check out our surroundings. "There's going to be a blind intersection on your left, about a mile ahead. If you can make the turn before he rounds the bend, shut your lights off. Maybe we can shake him."

I pressed down harder on the gas. I could feel Steven watching me. Could feel all the questions building in the tense space between us. Yellow warning signs appeared ahead. I braked into the sharp curve of the road, caught sight of the turn, and killed the lights as I jerked the wheel hard to the left. I took my foot off the brake, praying I didn't collide with anything in the dark. We both held our breaths. A moment later, *EasyClean*'s headlights rushed past the rear window.

"I think we lost him," Steven said, checking over his shoulder. "Let's get out of here before he circles back."

I put the headlights on, letting Steven navigate us through a maze of backcountry roads until we finally came to an intersection I recognized.

"Pull in there." Steven pointed to the empty parking lot of a strip mall. We turned in to an alley behind a grocery store and parked the Aston behind a dumpster. I shut off the engine, the silence in the car sudden and heavy as I rested my forehead against the steering wheel.

Steven leaned against the passenger door to look at me. "You want to start from the beginning?"

"Not really." I was too exhausted to explain. All I wanted was to get home and hug my kids. "Someone wants to kill you, Steven. I don't know who. But they were angry enough to post an ad online, offering to pay a hit man a hundred thousand dollars to get rid of you, preferably before Christmas. Any idea who it might be?"

Steven's face blanched in the dim light. "When I

recognized your voice on the security recording the night of the fire, I just assumed this was all some big scheme."

I rubbed my eyes, trying not to lose my temper. "I was there looking for clues, trying to figure out who wanted my children's father dead."

"That's why you were spying on me at the Christmas tree lot," he said, finally catching on. "Because you were afraid they would come after me while I was with the kids."

I nodded, my hands still shaking as I pushed my hair back from my face. "I think the hit man took your phone that night so he could track your movements more easily."

"The gas leak at the house . . . the tires on my truck? That was all him?"

"Everything but the fire. That," I said with a dark chuckle, "was Bree's mother, but apparently she had nothing to do with the ad or any of the attempts on your life."

Steven was quiet as he let that sink in. "So that's why you kidnapped me and took me to the motel. Because you knew this guy was after me and you thought you'd keep me safe." He shook his head. "Jesus, Finn. Why didn't you just tell me?" My mouth flew open. Steven held up a hand, closing his eyes, as if he realized his mistake the moment the words were out. "I know. You tried. And I didn't listen. I'm sorry," he said, his voice softening. "So what now?"

I leaned my head against the window. "I wish I knew."

Steven glanced at the alley around the car. "You think anyone will try to shoot me if I get out to take a piss?"

My laugh was weary. "I think it's probably safe."

Steven got out of the car and disappeared behind the dumpster.

I checked my phone and found a missed call from Vero. I tapped her number, breath held as it rang.

"Thank god, you're okay. Did you find Steven?" she asked.

"I've got him. The van died a few miles from the Westovers'. I found him just before *EasyClean* showed up. Any word from Joey?"

"No. The ambulance left with Nick a few minutes ago, and Joey still hadn't called."

"Not surprised." It only confirmed my suspicions. "It's hard to make a phone call when you're shooting at someone."

"Shooting!"

"Don't worry. Steven and I are both fine, and we got rid of his phone."

"Speaking of phones, I forwarded a copy of *FedUp*'s email to *EasyClean*. By now, he probably knows neither one of us is getting paid. Doubt he'll waste any more time chasing after Steven."

"That still doesn't answer the question of who hired him."

"A mystery for another day. How's my car, by the way?"

I glanced in my rearview mirror at the splintered hole in the glass. "I'll explain everything when I pick you up."

"Don't bother. Ramón called. He was pissed when he drove all the way to that motel and the van wasn't there. He's coming to pick me up. If he doesn't murder me when he gets here, I'll look for the van on the way back and ask him to tow it in. Meet me at the garage."

Vero disconnected.

I thumbed through the notifications I'd missed during the chaos of the last few hours.

A missed call from Sylvia, two from Julian, one

from my sister, and three from my mom. My mom rarely called this late, and a ripple of concern washed over me as I pressed her number.

She answered on the first ring. "Finlay? I talked to Georgia." Her voice was strangled and panicked, the words flying fast from her mouth. "Is Steven okay? She said someone is trying to kill him. What's going on? And why are the children with your sister?"

"Steven's fine, Ma."

"Are you sure?"

"He's with me right now. Georgia's just babysitting."

"Oh, thank god. I've been worried sick. Wait . . ." she said, her tone growing suspicious, "why are you out with Steven?"

"He had a little car trouble and I came to pick him up."

"It's not a date, is it?"

I laughed. "No."

"Good. Oh, and call your sister. She's looking for you." My mother disconnected.

I reached to set my phone down as a notification popped on my screen. An email from *EasyClean*, replying to the message Vero had forwarded to him.

> *Anonymous2, Nice try with the pics. Seems we both got duped. A little professional advice? Always insist on half up front. And next time, stay the hell out of my lane.*

Steven opened the door and dropped into the passenger seat. I closed the message and tossed the phone in my lap.

"Everything okay?" he asked.

"Fine," I said. "Turns out the impressive bounty being offered for your murder was an empty promise. Vero and I sent some very convincing photos of your corpse, but it appears the person who wanted you dead never intended to pay up."

Steven unzipped his coat, plucking at the raspberry-colored stain on his sweatshirt. He licked the tip of his finger and laughed. "Someone's not going to be happy when they realize I'm still alive."

"Probably not, but I doubt that guy with the gun is going to come after you again." I released a heavy sigh. "Nick's a good cop. He'll chase down the evidence from the gas leak and your slashed tires. Eventually, he'll get to the bottom of it. But in the meantime, maybe you could try not to piss anyone off?"

"I'm trying." He stared out the windshield, tracing the frame of his window with a finger. "So you and Nick, huh? I'm not saying I'm happy about it, but I guess I'm okay with it."

"I don't remember asking your opinion *or* your permission."

"At least he's old enough to shave."

"You said you were trying," I reminded him.

"You're right, I'm sorry." He sniffed, wrinkling his nose. "If you're sure that guy's not coming back, maybe we can get out of here. That dumpster reeks."

I sniffed, too. The sweet, putrid smell of decay wafted from somewhere behind our seats, but I was pretty sure it wasn't coming through the broken window. In all the chaos, I'd forgotten all about Carl.

"About that," I said, starting the engine. "There's something I need your help with. And I need you to trust me. Completely."

Steven looked hesitant, even as he nodded. "Name it."

My hands ached with phantom blisters as I gripped the wheel and hit the road for the farm. "I need to borrow a backhoe."

CHAPTER 42

On the way to Steven's farm, I told him all about what
had happened to Carl. Steven had already known Carl
was ill, but he took the news hard, a tinge of remorse
touching the corners of his eyes. I explained how Theresa had used the farm's business account to pay for the
storage unit to hide Carl's body, and how Vero and I
had found the records when we'd broken in the night of
the fire. He laughed in spite of himself when I told him
how we'd delivered the contents of the freezer to Theresa's door, and how Vero and I had been so terrified
for the children when we'd left Theresa's house, we'd
forgotten we'd left a piece of Carl in the trunk of Vero's Charger. Steven's smile withered, a look of horror
flashing across his face as he realized what was causing
the smell in the back of the Aston Martin.

"You want me to help you bury him. On my farm."
I thought maybe it was shock that had flattened his
voice. After all, it had been a strange night. I imagined
it might take a lot to surprise him anymore. And maybe
that was for the best.

"I can't take Carl back to his house," I reasoned.
"The place is crawling with cops. And I definitely can't
take him home with me. The farm is the safest place. For
now." Maybe one day, after the dust settled, Steven could

coordinate with Barbara and return this last piece of Carl to his final resting place behind the Westovers' house.

Steven nodded slowly, coming to terms with the fact that this was our only option.

We took the back entrance into the farm, the Aston Martin crawling over the deep ruts in the gravel road. Déjà vu hit hard as we passed the fallow field where Vero and I had buried Harris, and I had to resist the urge to turn my head and look. Steven was quiet as we passed it.

"There." He pointed behind one of his outbuildings, where the long neck of a backhoe was silhouetted against the night sky. Steven directed me across a narrow stretch of grass between the fields.

"Wait here," he said, getting out of the car.

I rolled down the passenger side window and called after him, "I can help, you know."

He turned, smiling at the lines of adhesive on his wrist. Hands braced against the side of the car, he leaned into the open window, something akin to pride in the gleam of his eyes. "I know you can. But it's better if you stay in the car." He pointed to my shoes and bare hands. "As far as the police are concerned, you were never here."

A laugh burst out of me. "If I didn't know better, I might think you'd done this before."

His shrug was a little humble. "I haven't slept much over the last few weeks. I might have read a few of your books. You know, to pass the time." He dropped his head, kicking at the ground with the toe of his boot as my jaw slackened in surprise. The overdue library book I'd found in the front desk of the trailer—the one next to the couch where Steven slept—hadn't been Bree's at all. Steven's eyes lifted to mine. "Let me do this for you,

Finn. I owe you this much." When I nodded, he patted the roof of the car and said, "Pop the trunk. Let's get this over with."

Under the glow of the Aston's headlights, Steven hauled himself up into the cab of the backhoe and fired it up, excavating a deep, clean hole. Shoulders heavy, he lowered the last of Carl into the ground. Then he climbed back into the tractor and filled the grave, parking the backhoe over the mound.

He pulled off his work gloves as he wandered back to my side of the car. I rolled down the window. "Do you have someplace to stay tonight?" The charred remains of the trailer were a shadow in the distance, and for now, his house probably wasn't safe.

He shrugged. "I'll call Guy. I'm sure he won't mind if I crash on his couch."

"Hop in. I'll give you a lift."

Steven shook his head. "I can take the farm truck. It isn't far." He rubbed a bit of dirt from the side of the Aston. "Besides, someone's probably missing this thing. Do I even want to know where you got it?"

"It's probably better if you don't." The dealership was long closed. I could picture Alan sitting in the darkened showroom, waiting for Irina to return the car. I had no idea if Irina would be inclined to cover for me, and if so, for how long. "I should probably go. Vero's waiting for me." We'd have to figure out what to do with the Aston Martin, then ask Ramón for a loaner until the van could be repaired. And who the heck knew what had become of Vero's beloved Charger? "Hey, the kids and I are having dinner at my parents' house on Saturday night. Do you want to come along? Delia and Zach have really missed you."

Steven laughed, shaking his head. "So your mom can remind me what an asshole I am while she regales me with stories about your boyfriends over ham? No, thanks. I was actually thinking maybe I'd take a little time off. With the office gone and business pretty slow, I figured now might be a good time to visit my sister. You know, get out of town and lay low for a while. But maybe I could come by your place and see the kids tomorrow before I go?"

"Sure. They'd like that."

"Finn," he said, stopping me as I rolled up my window. His face sobered as he fidgeted with his gloves. "There's something I've been meaning to talk to you about since the fire. About that safe word for the security system. It's not that I'm holding out hope that we could ever fix things. It's just . . . you and the kids . . . you've always been the one constant."

"Even when you were buying the farm?" A thick silence fell. He hung his head. If Steven signed that contract with Ted and Carl while we'd still been married, then by law, a portion of that farm probably belonged to me. "Did Guy know?"

Steven gave a noncommittal shake of his head. "Guy's a friend. He's always been good about looking in the other direction." He glanced up at me, shame naked on his face. Guy had probably known about a lot of things. "I'll make this right, Finn. The assets, the custody, all of it." There was a plea under the promise. A question he was too afraid to ask.

In some ways, Steven would always be a constant in my life, too, but he wasn't a net I could safely fall back on. I wasn't falling backward anymore. From now on, there was only falling forward. And if I had to pick a safe name of my own—someone I could count on to stick beside me, no matter how messy my life got—it'd be Vero's.

"I know you will," I said.

Steven patted the side of the car with a sad smile, waving as he watched me go.

A single light was on in the office window of Ramón's garage. Vero held open the gate in the chain-link fence, directing me through it. The bay door at the back of the building was open, and Ramón waved me inside.

I climbed out of the Aston as Vero and Ramón circled the car. He sucked a tooth as he traced a bullet hole in the rear panel. His eyes lifted to his cousin's, too many questions gleaming inside them. Questions neither of us would ever answer. He shook his head at the shattered window glass. "What the hell did you get yourself into this time, Veronica?"

"Can you fix it?" she asked him.

Ramón opened the passenger door and leaned into the car. He dug a finger into the back of the headrest and dragged out a bullet. His jaw was hard-set as he tossed it to me. "It would take me days just to get the window glass, not to mention the paint. And that headrest will cost a fortune to replace, *if* I can even find one."

"Maybe Javi knows somebody," Vero suggested, following him around the car.

Ramón turned abruptly and leveled a finger at her. "I'm not breathing a word of this to Javi, and neither are you. You're better off getting rid of it."

"We can't do that," I said. "We borrowed it from a dealership. We have to return it." Alan may have been bending rules for Irina by letting me take the keys, but this car was too valuable to go unnoticed by the dealer for long, and Irina's interest in protecting me wasn't without limits. "How long would it take you to fix it?"

He planted his hands on his hips, turning to face me. "That headrest is a problem. I've got a guy who might be willing to get his hands on one, but he's not cheap."

"We have cash," I assured him.

"No," Vero said quietly, "we don't." A cloud passed over her eyes. The same one that had flattened their shine when I'd told my mother Vero was handling my money and she would never let me grow old and broke. Vero gave a small shake of her head, silently begging me not to ask her about it here in front of Ramón.

My throat worked around a swallow. After all we'd managed to survive over the last few weeks, there was no way I was going to let us go to prison for a car.

Numb, I heard myself say, "We'll find a way to pay for it."

Ramón's eyes dipped to the bloodstains on my coat. "I can disable the tracking on the car tonight. Start the bodywork in the morning. I'll need seventy-two hours at least. But if anyone finds out about this, Vero—"

She threw her arms around him, holding back tears. "No one will find out."

"I spend way too much time cleaning up after you," he muttered into her hair. As she pulled away, he dragged a clean rag from his back pocket and tossed it to me, inclining his head toward my hands. "Vero and I found your van. I'll need a couple of days to look at it, but it probably won't be a quick fix. After parts and labor, you might do better to replace it. You want me to stick a FOR SALE sign in the window and put it out front?" he offered. "See if I can get you a few bucks for it?"

That van had been through a lot. Ramón was probably right. It was probably long past time to put it out of its misery and find a new one. But I'd test-driven the hot, flashy sports car that handled like a dream yet felt too much like a midlife crisis. And I'd driven Vero's Charger, with its growling engine and confident lines, which sometimes felt too much like a police car. In spite of the crumbled Cheerios in the carpet and the car seats in the back, there was something simple and comforting about my van, and I wasn't entirely sure I was ready to give that up yet.

"Can you give me an estimate to fix it?" I asked, rubbing the last of the dried blood from my fingers.

He nodded. "Sure thing."

"We'll need a loaner," Vero said. "Can we borrow some keys?"

"Wait here." Ramón disappeared down the hall to his office.

An uncomfortably long silence stretched out between us before Vero finally spoke. "I didn't invest the money," she confessed quietly. "I lost it. All of it."

"Thanksgiving weekend. After you left my parents' house, where did you go?" I already knew. I just needed to hear her say it.

"A casino. In Atlantic City. I . . . owe some people money. We had all that cash from Irina, but it wasn't enough to pay them back. I thought for sure I could double it and everything would be fine. And it would have been." She clasped her hands, pleading with me to believe her. "I was hot that first night, Finn. I was already up by a few grand, and some guy at my table noticed. As I was heading back to my room, he told me about a private party—big buy-in, high stakes. He said he knew someone who could hook me up with a marker if I wanted to go."

"A marker?"

"Like an advance on your book—a loan."

A loan she would have to win back. The marker Delia had overheard Vero talking about.

If she can't get two hundred, Delia had said, *she'll be in big trouble.*

"How much was the marker worth?"

Tears brimmed in her eyes. "Two hundred thousand."

She started as Ramón came back into the garage. He tossed her a set of keys. Her hands shook as she caught them against her chest. He held out a folded envelope. "This was in my mailbox at my apartment this morning. It's addressed to you."

Vero took it, glancing at the name printed in bold letters—**Veronica Ramirez**. Her face paled, and she and Ramón exchanged a long look. "Thanks," she said, tucking it in her coat pocket. "I'll bring the car around."

Ramón grabbed my sleeve as I turned to follow her out. His brow furrowed as he watched her go. "Keep an eye on my cousin. I love her, but she's reckless. She can't afford any more trouble."

I thought of the photo album I'd found in the closet of her bedroom. About the scholarship letter addressed to a last name I didn't know. About the man who'd gone to her mother's house looking for her, and how the best place to hide a dirty secret was across a state line.

True, Vero was impulsive. She took risks, but calculated ones; she'd always been careful to weigh the odds whenever it came to money. If Vero had put our savings on the line without telling me, she'd done it for a reason. "What kind of trouble is Vero in?"

Ramón rubbed at a grease stain on his thumb. "That's not my story to tell."

I watched him retreat to his office. I knew, maybe better than anyone, that some stories had a way of getting stuck inside our heads. Usually, because we were afraid of what those stories revealed about us—our fears and our inadequacies, our mistakes and our failures. Sometimes, those stories needed a little nudging to come out. I tucked the bloody rag in my pocket, along with the bullet. Whatever trouble Vero was in, we'd handle it together.

CHAPTER 43

It was nearly four in the morning by the time Vero and I made it to the hospital. Georgia had called my phone no less than a dozen times since she'd heard about the shoot-out at Carl's, and when I finally answered, she let loose with a string of swears that would have scandalized our mother. After I explained for the umpteenth time that Vero and I were both fine, she'd told me that Nick had been admitted—apparently his injuries weren't as minor as he'd let on. Vero, hearing the worry in my voice, had passed right by South Riding and drove straight to the hospital.

"I'm sorry," said the attendant at the information desk when we asked to see Nick, "but visiting hours aren't for another six hours. You'll have to come back then."

Vero thanked the woman, stealing a glance at the computer screen as she slid her hands from the counter. She pulled me aside, smirking as she revealed the visitor pass she'd palmed from the desk. "Nick's in room 402," she whispered, tucking it in my hand. "Go on. I've got this."

Vero backed away from me and started fanning herself, whining about how hot she was. She clutched her chest with a dramatic moan, then collapsed in front of the reception desk. There was a flurry of activity, and someone called out for a nurse. I clipped the visitor pass to my shirt, ducking into the elevator as the doors closed.

The fourth floor was quiet and dimly lit, the only sound the occasional beeps of a monitor and the soft chatter of conversation from the nurse's station. I peeked inside Nick's door. The sconces behind his bed were lit, but his eyes were closed, the monitors in the corner beeping a steady, slow rhythm in time with his heart.

I took a few steps into the room and froze.

Joey sat in a chair beside the bed. He turned toward me as the sliver of light from the hall stretched across the floor. His smile was weary as he stood, offering me his chair.

I stepped cautiously to the far side of the bed, forcing myself to smile, reminding myself that I could still be wrong about Nick's partner. I had no proof. Anyone could have been driving that car.

"How is he?" I asked.

"He's fine. Just resting. He took a pretty deep graze to his arm and caught one in his thigh. He'll be desk jockeying for a while, but after some physical therapy, he should be good as new."

Nick's face was peaceful, framed by a shadow of dark stubble against the stark white sheets.

Joey leaned back against the wall with his hands in his pockets. "He was worried sick about you. He said you ran off just as the ambulance showed up. He panicked when they loaded him into the bus and no one could find your van."

"I let Steven borrow it. Vero drove me to the Westovers' house. She parked down the street."

"Yeah? Where'd you run off to?" Joey had that familiar cop-bright shine in his eyes, an intensity that seemed to burn through all the smoke and mirrors. In my sister, it was annoying. In Nick, it was endearing. In Joey, it made my skin prickle.

"I was worried about Steven. I hadn't heard from him in a few hours. Nick said no one knew where he was."

In the low light, I thought I saw a little color rush to Joey's cheeks. "Steven's place had been quiet all morning. Guess at some point, I must have drifted off and your ex gave me the slip. If it's any consolation, Nick read me the riot act over it."

"It's okay. I talked to Steven a little while ago."

"Yeah?" His focus sharpened. "How is he?"

"Fine."

"Where was he?"

"Apparently, he had some engine trouble with the van. He was stranded on the side of the road for a while, but he managed to find a safe ride home." I watched Joey's face for a reaction. I sensed he was watching mine just as carefully.

"That's good. Maybe now that Steven's would-be killer is behind bars, we can all rest a little easier."

The room seemed to narrow until it was only the two of us. "What do you mean?"

"Got a call from a friend down at the station about an hour ago. Apparently, Ted Fuller and his wife were taken into custody right after the shooting. Melissa Fuller confessed to starting the fire at Steven's farm."

"And you think she was the one who posted the ad on the forum?"

"She hasn't confessed to anything other than harassing him and starting the fire, but it paints a pretty damning picture." He shrugged, sliding a toothpick into his mouth. "With the website gone and no concrete proof connecting her to the gas leak or Steven's slashed tires, the DA will have a tough time bringing additional charges, but she'll do time for arson. That'll keep her busy for a while."

"What about Steven? How can we be sure he's safe?"

Joey shrugged, rolling his toothpick between his teeth. "Melissa Fuller's arrest should make the local news tomorrow. With any luck, someone will leak the fact that she's also suspected of murder for hire. Journalists love that kind of stuff. They're sure to run with the story. The killer will see it and put two and two together. If his meal ticket is about to be carted off to prison, he'll realize the deal is off."

"You seem awfully confident." If Joey was *Easy-Clean,* that would be a very convenient resolution. He could leak the story himself, piling more suspicion on Melissa, destroy whatever evidence Cam found, convince Nick and everyone else that the killers were long gone, and let *EasyClean* disappear into the sunset.

"These guys are only in it for the money. With so much police attention on the case and no easy way to get paid, trust me, he'll abandon the job."

"So you think the killer's a man?"

"Most hired guns are."

"Both of them?" I asked. Joey's head tipped curiously. "It's my understanding that two people accepted the job, but it sounds like you're only concerned about one of them."

The only sound in the room was the soft beep of the monitor. Joey frowned, his eyes guarded as he studied me. "Nick told you that, did he? He shouldn't be leaking those kinds of details."

"I won't tell anyone."

"Like you didn't tell anyone when Steven turned up to borrow your van?" He shuffled his toothpick thoughtfully between his teeth. "You were supposed to call me, Nick, or Roddy if you saw him. I spent all afternoon canvassing three counties looking for him. You could have clued me in."

"Would you have answered if I did?"

"Is that what all this is about?" he asked, stirring the air between us. "You're upset with me because I didn't pick up when Vero called? You think I don't care that I wasn't there when my partner got shot?"

"Where were you?"

"I was at your house, relieving Roddy so he could take a piss and grab some dinner. I was actually having a chat with your neighbor, Mrs. Haggerty, when the call came over the radio about the shooting. When Vero called, I was already on the phone with dispatch, trying to get an update on Nick's condition. The hospital was closer to your house, so I came straight here."

"Oh," I said, tension and resolve slipping from my shoulders. Mrs. Haggerty, the indomitable president of the neighborhood watch, would have logged Joey's arrival and departure, taking note of their conversation in the spiral notebook she kept on the table in her foyer. Which meant Joey couldn't be *EasyClean,* and I had no idea who was.

"I promise," Joey said, "no one is more upset about what happened to Nick than I am."

I blew out a long, frustrated sigh, feeling like a fool. "I'm sorry. I didn't mean to imply that you weren't. It's just been a very long day. What happened to Aimee, Theresa, and her mom?" I asked, steering the conversation to more neutral territory.

Joey's posture eased a little. He tucked his hands in his pockets. "Theresa's in protective custody. Sounds like Aimee and Theresa's mom could both face aiding and abetting charges. But the DA's probably so glad to have Theresa back in time for the trial, maybe she'll go easy on them."

"Did the police identify the goons with the guns?"

"They work for a private security firm owned by Feliks Zhirov. Looks like he sent them to clean up a few witnesses before the trial. Speaking of which," he added, pulling his toothpick from his mouth and pointing it at me, "everyone who was in the house during the shooting was asked to give a statement. Someone will probably drop by your house in the morning to take one from you and Vero."

I nodded, having assumed this much.

"I'm curious though," Joey said, one foot propped on the wall behind him. "What were you and Vero doing there?"

"Just following a hunch."

"Is that all?"

I held his dubious gaze across the bed.

"Enough with the third degree, Joe." We both turned at the sound of Nick's voice. It was deep and groggy. His heavy eyelids blinked open, a smile creeping over his lips when he saw me. I moved closer to his side as his fingers stretched out to meet mine.

"I'm going to hit the coffee machine and let you two catch up. Don't strain anything." Joey gave Nick a pat on the shoulder, careful to avoid his bandages. He gave me a tight nod before leaving the room.

"Thought you ghosted me," Nick said once Joey was gone. "Before you ran off, I was working up to a sympathy kiss. How am I doing?"

"Not so great," I said, leaning a hip against his bed. "Your partner blew your cover. He says you're not dying and you're actually going to be fine. It seems you missed your window of opportunity."

Nick's grin widened, teasing a lethal dimple from one cheek. He laced our fingers together. "How about sympathy dinner at my place?" He raised a sleepy eyebrow. "I promise, no dumpster diving this time."

"We'll discuss it when you're back on your feet.

Meanwhile, you should get some rest. Sounds like you have a lot of paper pushing to do once you're out of here."

He groaned, his eyes drifting closed again. "Don't remind me."

I gave his hand a squeeze as the painkillers kicked in. "I've got to go rescue Vero from the ER, and my sister's burning up my phone. Call me when you're feeling up to it." Nick nodded, already half-asleep. Despite my earlier protest, I leaned down and kissed his cheek. His weak smile still managed to look triumphant. "Be safe," I whispered.

Vero sent me a text from the car, letting me know she'd made it out of the ER in one piece. I replayed my conversation with Joey all the way to the parking lot, fidgeting with the bullet in my pocket. I had been so wrong about Aimee. Wrong about Joey. *FedUp* and *EasyClean* were still out there, nameless and faceless, and while Steven was probably safe on Guy's couch tonight, none of this felt like a victory. I opened the passenger door to the loaner car, hesitating before getting inside. When I turned to glance up toward the window of Nick's room, I could have sworn I saw a shadow staring down at me.

CHAPTER 44

The police showed up at the house to take our statements early the next morning. We kept our stories simple and consistent. As far as the investigators were concerned, we'd known Theresa had family in the area, only because Steven had mentioned it before. We'd gone to the Westovers' home to try to convince Theresa to turn herself in, and shortly after we'd arrived, the shooting had started.

I thanked the investigators and showed them to the door, peeking down the street to find Officer Roddy was no longer parked along the curb. If the DA and the police were all convinced Melissa Fuller was *FedUp,* as Joey had suggested last night, they probably assumed the threat to Steven was over and there was no reason to continue surveillance. I only wished that were true.

In a few hours, Steven would be on a plane to his sister's house in Philadelphia. With any luck, we'd figure out who *FedUp* was before the new year, when he returned.

When the police left, I stared at my phone. How many hours could I stall this before Alan called Irina, searching for his missing Superleggera? Or worse, before Irina figured out what I'd done and sent Feliks's goons to come after me?

Vero gave me an encouraging nod. I dialed the number for the car dealership and asked for Alan, listening to Christmas jazz through an excruciatingly long hold before he finally picked up.

"Alan speaking." He sounded anxious, harried. I could picture him tugging at the knot in his tie.

"Hi." I cleared my throat. "You probably remember me. We spoke last night when I picked up a vehicle with Irina Borovkov? I just wanted to let you know an emergency has come up and there's going to be a little delay returning it. I'm really sorry. We had fully intended to—"

"There's no need for an apology," he said quickly.

"There's not?"

"We have everything we need. We've issued a receipt for the payment, and the title and registration were picked up by the courier thirty minutes ago. Unless you require anything else, there's no need to bring the vehicle back to us." I held the phone to my ear, stunned. "Now, if there are no other concerns about the purchase, I'll be going."

The call disconnected. I stared at my phone.

"What happened?" Vero asked, setting a mug of coffee in front of me.

"I don't know. I think Irina paid for the car." It was the only explanation.

Vero's body went boneless. She dropped into the chair beside me. "So we don't have to bring it back?"

I shook my head. "Not to the dealership." At some point, Irina would probably show up to claim her Superleggera. But hopefully by then, it would be fixed, and this entire nightmare would be behind us.

Vero let out a relieved sigh. She threw open the pantry door and reached up on her tiptoes for her hidden stash of cookies. The doorbell rang. Vero froze, her hand around the bag as our eyes caught.

"Who do you think it is?" she asked.

My sister wasn't supposed to bring the kids home for another hour. "I don't know."

Vero followed me to the door. I peered through the curtain. Cam stood on the stoop, his hoodie pulled low to cover his face and a sealed envelope under his arm. I unlocked the bolt and swung it open.

"You!" Vero lunged for him as I threw out an arm to hold her back. "You stole my car!"

"I didn't steal anything." Cam held up a fob. "You left the dealer spare in the owner's manual in your glove box. It was practically an invitation."

Vero snatched it from his hand with an angry growl. "If there's so much as a scratch on it, I will end you." She shouldered past him out the door. Cam shook his head as he watched her storm off to the driveway to inspect her car.

"What are you doing here?" I dragged him inside my foyer, checking Mrs. Haggerty's windows before shutting the door. Cam slid off his hood. His greasy bleached-blond hair had been dyed and shorn. He'd traded out his old army jacket for a leather one that smelled expensive and new. If it hadn't been for the fading purple-and-green bruises on his cheek, I wasn't sure I would have recognized him.

He handed me the envelope.

"What is this?" A blood-colored wax seal held it closed. The swirling impression of a *Z* matched the one on the signet ring Kat wore.

"Don't ask me. I'm just the errand boy."

"You're working for Feliks?"

"Mr. Zhirov offered me a job. Said his people have been watching me. He was impressed with my skills, so we made a deal. I do a few odd jobs for him now and then. In return, he keeps certain people off my back and I earn a generous paycheck."

"That's it?" I had a feeling Cam wasn't just running errands.

Cam shrugged. "He said if I stay in line and don't bring unnecessary attention to our arrangement, he'll let me work my way up from there. That's why I brought your friend back her car. You know, as a show of good faith." I raised an eyebrow. "And because Mr. Zhirov told me to," he admitted.

"You and Feliks aren't the only ones who had a deal, you know." I reached up and turned his chin, examining his cheekbone. The swelling had gone down, but bursts of hideous colors had bloomed around his eye. I wasn't sure if it looked better or worse. He swatted away my hand, but there was no real malice in it. "Nick says you haven't been at home or school. Your mother must be worried sick about you." My heart ached at the brief flash of pain in his eyes.

"She'd have to be there to notice."

"What about your grandmother?"

He rubbed the dark bristles on his scalp. "She's fine. I'm taking care of her."

"Who's taking care of you?" Cam was just a kid. A kid who'd grown up too fast and was in over his head. And while he might feel safe under Feliks's arm, that safety was an illusion; a deal with Feliks didn't make you bulletproof. "There has to be something . . . *anything* you can tell me about *EasyClean,* Cam. Who is he? Who did this to you?"

Cam winced. He dragged a roll of bills from the front pocket of his jeans and peeled off a fifty, folding it into my hand before returning the rest to his pocket. "Look, I wish I could help you. Just trust me when I tell you, you're better off not knowing. Besides, even if I knew the guy's real name, I couldn't tell you anyway."

"Why not?"

"Mr. Z made me give him that flash drive I was

going to hand over to your cop friend. That was the other part of our deal. But don't worry," he said, pitching his voice low, as if maybe the walls were listening. "I might have scrubbed a few things."

My throat worked around a hard swallow. How much had been on that drive?

Cam rubbed the bruise on his cheek. He blew out a hard, guilt-ridden sigh. "Look, the only thing I know for sure is that *EasyClean* is a cop. A real dirty one. Which means he has a lot more to lose if he gets busted, and he's got all the tools he needs to cover his tracks."

"How do you know he's a police officer?"

Cam jammed his hands in his pockets. "I've been around cops all my life. My dad was one. They have their own slang, their own language. I read all his posts and the emails in his sent files. *EasyClean* talks like a cop."

My mind raced back to my conversation with Joey. Every clue fit. Joey had means, motive, and countless opportunities to try to kill Steven. But last night, he'd also had an alibi. One I had yet to verify.

"Hey," Cam said, dragging my attention from the window. "You still want my advice? Forget about *Easy-Clean*. He isn't anybody a nice mom like you ought to be messing with. Neither is Mr. Z." Cam withdrew a flimsy-looking flip phone from his pocket. It vibrated as he passed it to me. "This is for you."

Before I could ask him who it was, he slid his hoodie over his head and slipped out the door. As he slunk across my lawn, a dark green Jaguar with tinted windows lurched to a stop at the curb in front of him. Cam opened the back door and ducked inside. Vero flipped him off from the front stoop as the Jaguar sped off.

The disposable phone continued to vibrate as Vero came inside and shut the door. *Unknown Caller* flashed across the screen. I thumbed it open, putting the call on speakerphone so both of us could hear.

"Who is this?" I asked.

"Greetings, Ms. Donovan." Ekatarina Rybakov's voice was all business. "Mr. Zhirov regrets that he could not deliver the package himself, but I believe the contents are self-explanatory."

Vero held the phone as I tore open the wax seal, thumbing through the pages inside the envelope. A title and registration from the car dealership were inside, along with a bill of sale for a *Superleggera Volante* in *Modern Minimalist (black)*. The payment was made in full. In cash. By Feliks Zhirov. Vero took the sales slip from me, her eyes wide.

"Why are you giving me this?" I asked through a thin breath. Though as I read the name on the vehicle's registration and title, I knew. *Owner: FD Independent Consulting, LLC.*

FD. Finlay Donovan.

Feliks had tied my name to a fake corporation. To a car he'd paid for.

I had become one of Feliks's shell companies. At any point, Feliks could tip off the police and Nick would jump down the rabbit hole and find me. Feliks knew exactly what Nick and I had been doing after our dinner at Kvass.

And this was a message in return: Feliks Zhirov *owned* me.

"My client has been watching you for quite some time." I could practically hear Kat's mouth twist with amusement. "You must have made quite an impression."

"What does that mean?"

"I think that means you get to keep the car," Vero whispered.

"I don't want the car," I said, yanking the papers back.

Vero's hand chased them. "Yes, you do."

"The car is yours, of course," Kat said as I took the phone from Vero. "But unless you want to risk certain information coming to light, I would strongly discourage you from driving it."

Kat was right. One minor traffic violation and a cop would pull the registration. There were too many red flags. The car would have to be scrapped. Every single piece of it would have to be destroyed. Maybe Ramón could put it in one of those giant crushers. Then we could burn the paperwork and pretend it never existed.

"What does Feliks want from me?" I asked. He knew everything about me, which meant he knew I couldn't possibly repay him the value of that car.

"For now, only your silence," Kat replied. "Good day, Ms. Donovan."

I should have felt relieved when the call disconnected. The car was handled. No need to bother Irina with the whole sordid story of how we got it. No need to make up a fake one for Alan, and no need to pay the money back. But two lingering questions weighed heavily on me as I slid the papers back inside the broken seal of the envelope: How had Feliks known about the car, and what had *for now* meant?

I tugged on my jacket and shoes and crossed the street to Mrs. Haggerty's house, part of me hoping she wouldn't answer when I knocked. That she hadn't been home to notice Cam or the dark green Jaguar that had picked him up.

The chain lock rattled and a dead bolt slid open. Mrs. Haggerty opened her door, squinting at me as she reached for her glasses on their slim gold chain. She still looked confused, even after she lifted them to her eyes.

"Hi, Mrs. Haggerty," I said quickly, hoping to avoid any uncomfortable small talk, which usually involved her criticizing the brief and humiliating moments of my life she could make out from behind her kitchen curtains. "I was wondering if you remembered seeing someone at my house yesterday evening. A police officer?"

"You mean the one that's been parked outside your house for days?"

"No, a different one."

"This street has been far too busy," she said with an aggrieved harrumph. "I'm lucky if I can even keep track."

"This would have been right around dinnertime. He's about this tall," I said, holding my hand above my head. "Blond hair, blue eyes, in his early forties. He says he spoke with you."

Mrs. Haggerty thought about that for a moment as she scratched the thinning hair at her temple. "I did go outside to take my trash out just after dinner. There was a gentleman parked right there," she said, pointing to where Roddy's car normally sat. "He got out of his car to help me roll my bin to the street. He asked if I had seen you or Steven in the last few hours. I told him about all the comings and goings. Then he got a phone call and left before I had a chance to ask his name and write it down."

"Do you remember what color car he was driving, or what he looked like?"

"It was dark and it was cold," she said a little defensively. "The man was wearing a hat. I don't know what color his hair was." And she couldn't see well enough to notice the color of his eyes, I was sure. But Joey had said he'd spoken with Mrs. Haggerty. And he'd also said he had gotten the call about Nick while he'd been here, sitting in for Officer Roddy. Everything about his alibi checked out, but I couldn't shake the feeling he'd been hiding something.

"Thanks, Mrs. Haggerty," I said, drawing my coat tighter around me as I stepped away from her door. At the last minute, I turned, catching her before she pulled it closed.

"Do you happen to remember if he was smoking?" From our few brief encounters, I suspected Joey couldn't go long without a cigarette.

"I don't recall. But now that you mention it, he did have something in his mouth while we were talking. For such a polite young man, you'd think he'd know better."

Joey's toothpicks. The ones he was always chewing on when he couldn't smoke. My parting thanks rang flat as I turned for home, no further along in my search for *FedUp* or *EasyClean* than I had been the night before.

CHAPTER 45

My feet froze at the foot of my driveway. A burgundy Jeep was parked outside my house. Julian stood at my front door, hanging something from the knob as I approached.

"Hey," I said quietly.

He whirled at the sound of my voice. The sand dollar he'd hung from a loop of satin ribbon knocked gently against the front door. He started toward me but stopped an arm's length apart, sliding his hands in and then out of his pockets as if he wasn't quite sure what to do with them. "I didn't want to bother you. It's okay if you're not ready to talk. It's just . . . I bought you something when I was in Florida. For Christmas. I wanted you to have it." He scraped off his hat, holding it in front of him as he came closer. His eyes were almost gray against the cold, damp sky. "I'm sorry. About everything. Parker had no right to get involved."

"No, she did," I said, arms folded around myself. A sigh blew from my lips in a thin, white cloud. "I asked you for help and she came to the station for me. And she's your friend. She cares about you. She had every right to say what was on her mind."

"She shouldn't have put words in my mouth." He looked hesitant as he said, "And neither should you.

I wasn't ashamed of you. Or of us. I admit, maybe I have been hiding, but it's only because you deserve someone who's ready to commit. And that's not really where I am right now. I like what we are."

"What are we?" I could see him wrestle with that, his lips parted as he waited for the right answer to come. But there was no right answer. "Maybe we both need some time to figure that out."

I leaned up on my toes and kissed him on his cheek, resisting the urge to let it linger. "Merry Christmas, Julian." With a tender smile and an ache of regret, I slipped the sand dollar from the doorknob and carried it inside.

My phone was ringing on the counter when I came into the kitchen, my fingers numb, my nose slightly frostbitten, and my heart somewhere in my throat.

"It's Sylvia. She's called three times in the last five minutes." Vero leaned against the counter, nursing a glass of wine.

"It's eleven o'clock in the morning," I said, gesturing to the open bottle beside her.

"Don't get on me. I'm having a day." She poured a second glass and pushed it in front of me.

"I don't need a drink," I said.

"Your face says otherwise. And you'd better answer that. It must be important."

I reached for my phone, catching the call before it slipped to voicemail. "Hey, Syl."

"Finlay, where the hell have you been? I left you a voicemail last night."

"I was dealing with a family emergency. What's up?"

"I talked to your editor. She loved the sample. That scene in the jail with the hot cop was top-notch. She still thinks you should consider killing off the lawyer in the third act."

Vero smirked as I reached for the wine. "I'll take it under advisement."

"And she wants the rest of the manuscript right after the holidays." I downed half my glass. Of course she did. "One more thing. I sent the pitch to a film agent. He loved it. He's got a big-name producer who might be interested, and he wants to set up a call."

Vero's eyes bugged wide.

"But Sylvia, the manuscript isn't even halfway—"

"We're talking A-list actresses, a big Hollywood studio, and lots of media exposure, Finlay. This could be very good for both of us. Don't let me down."

I sighed. I'd already seen this story play out and it had been terrifying enough the first time, but it didn't sound like Sylvia was leaving me any choice. "Fine."

Sylvia and I exchanged a few trite holiday greetings and she disconnected.

"It's a great story, Finn," Vero said, refilling my glass. "Don't undersell yourself."

"You've read my story. When do I get to hear yours?" Vero's eyes lifted to mine, the empty bottle suspended between us. Vero's and my story had begun in medias res, in the middle of an already rapidly moving plot, leaving us to discover so many things about each other as events unfolded. But every great mystery starts somewhere else, deep in the backstory. And if Vero and I were going to solve her problem, I needed to know who the real Vero was. "What are we?" It was the same question I had asked Julian a moment ago, only with Vero, I knew the answer.

"We're friends," she said.

"No, we're more than that, Vero. We're partners. Friends make mistakes. Partners face them together. No more secrets." I held out my glass.

She tapped hers tentatively to mine. "No more secrets." After a few quiet sips, she said, "I've been thinking. The car belongs to us now. But we can't use it. I could ask Ramón to strip it. Javi could sell the parts. You could keep the money. All of it." There was an apology in that offer. The promise of a down payment to repay what she'd lost. But that car wasn't Vero's or mine; it was Feliks's. And I had no interest in touching it.

I rose from the table, carried his envelope to the stove, and lit the burner. Holding the edge of the paper to the flame, I watched the bill of sale and registration burn. Smoke rippled through the kitchen as I carried the flaming mess to the sink. The smoke detector blared to life, then the garbage disposal, as I washed the remnants of Feliks's favor down the drain.

CHAPTER 46

My mother's house smelled divine, like maple, citrus, and allspice. Vero made a small noise of pleasure that bordered on indecent. Pots and pans clattered in the kitchen, and I set the children loose to assault their grandfather where he lounged on the couch in front of the TV as I hung up their coats. Vero followed them, greeting my father with an enthusiastic hug.

A kitchen cabinet slammed, and I followed my nose to the kitchen. My mother stood in front of the stove in one of her favorite Christmas sweaters, fussing over a steaming glazed ham. I kissed her on the cheek.

"Hey, Ma."

She was unusually tight-lipped, her jaw hard-set as she jerked tiny clove grenades from the skin and tossed them into the sink. "Where's Vero? I thought I told you to invite her for dinner."

"She's in the living room with Dad. Need any help?" I asked, careful to keep my distance as she dropped a lethal-looking serving fork on the platter and plucked a carving knife from the block.

"You can carry this to the table. Tell your father and your sister to turn off the TV, and bring the children in for dinner." She jammed serving spoons into the au

gratin potatoes and roasted brussels, and slapped a set
of tongs on the tray beside the rolls.

"Everything okay, Ma?"

"Everything's fine."

I rested a hand on hers, forcing her to set down the
sprig of garnish she was dismembering. She blew out a
heavy sigh. "I'm fine," she said softly as she gathered
herself. "I'm just irritated with your father. That's all."

"What'd he do?"

"He sat on the couch all day watching football, while
I wrapped and baked and cleaned and cooked. What
else?" My sympathetic laugh dragged a reluctant smile
from her.

"You and Dad okay?"

She squeezed my cheek. Her fingers smelled like rum
balls and gingerbread. "We're always okay. He may be
difficult to live with at times, but goodness knows, I'm
no peach. There comes a time in your life when it's easier to take the good with the bad, Finlay. Anything else
is too much work. No man is perfect. The best we can
do is settle for a good one. Now help me get all this out
to the table before the brussels get cold."

While my mother finished dressing the ham platter
in greens, I scooped up the serving bowls and carried
them to the dining room. Her Christmas linens were
crisply pressed and snowy white, and even though I
knew my children would inevitably spill juice cups and
smear their sticky fingers all over them before the end
of the night, my mother would find a way to get them
spotless in time for New Year's.

I set the serving bowls gingerly in the center of the
table, moving a few shimmering crystal goblets and
glistening pieces of silverware to make room for the
rest of the feast that was coming. In the next room,
the TV clicked off, and Georgia and Vero wrangled the
children. The doorbell rang.

"You expecting someone?" I asked my mother.

"Your sister invited a guest for dinner."

"Seriously?" I couldn't remember the last time Georgia had invited someone over to meet our parents. I hurried to the door, eager to beat my sister there and greet her mystery guest. As the door swung open, my tongue stuck in my throat.

Nick stood in the threshold, his left arm in a sling under his open coat and his right leaning on a crutch. He looked amazing in polished dress shoes, crisp khaki slacks, and a cashmere sweater that hugged him in all the right places. His face was freshly shaven, his hair recently cut.

A smile pinched the corners of his eyes. "It's good to see you, Finn. You look great."

"You, too." I shook my head, struggling to unscramble my thoughts. "I mean, you look a lot better than the last time I saw you. In the hospital. What are you doing here?"

"Your sister invited me. Can I come in?" One side of his mouth kicked up, teasing out a dimple. "Or, if you want, we can hang here a little longer." I followed his upward glance to a cluster of mistletoe my mother must have hung. My cheeks warmed as I stepped back from the door.

"Looking good, Detective!" Vero sprang out of nowhere, planting a kiss on his cheek.

"Merry Christmas, Vero. Do you mind?" He held out a gift bag, balancing precariously on his crutch. "I'm still getting the knack of this thing."

"Presents? For me? You shouldn't have!" Vero took the bag from him, shamelessly peeking inside.

"They're for Delia and Zach," he corrected her as she whisked them to the table. "And the wine is for your mom," he said to me as I helped him maneuver over the threshold.

"You didn't have to do all this."

"I wanted to." His crutch snagged the doorframe.

I reached up to steady him, catching him by the chest. "Careful, don't fall."

"Trying not to." His voice was a low rumble through the soft warm wool of his sweater, and a spark of mischief lit in his eyes. "Just dinner," he reminded me.

"Right." We did an awkward dance as he balanced on one leg and I moved around him to help him out of his coat. Keenly aware of the rattle of his crutch behind me, I led the way to the table.

"Nick!" Delia jumped down from her seat. My sister intercepted her, scooping her up before she could crash into Nick's leg.

"Easy there, kiddo. He's still got some healing to do, and we'd all like to see this guy back on the job."

Nick ruffled her hair. "Brought you a present." He jerked his chin toward the bag. "There's a little something for your brother, too."

My mother wiped her hands as she came out of the kitchen. She stopped dead in her tracks, her mouth falling open. "Nicholas! What happened to you? Georgia didn't tell us you were hurt!"

"It's nothing," he assured her as she fussed over him. "Just a couple of scratches. I'll be back on my feet in a few weeks. There's something in the bag for you, too, Mrs. McDonnell."

"Please, call me Susan," she insisted. I was just grateful she hadn't asked him to call her Mom.

I took my sister forcefully by the elbow, hauling Georgia out of the room. The kitchen doors swung closed behind us. I set the wine down too hard as I rounded on her. "What are you doing?"

"What? I'm not allowed to invite a friend for dinner?"

"I thought you invited a date."

"I couldn't really think of anyone special I wanted to bring. And Nick was going to spend the holidays alone. His mom's in Colorado and his sister's in California. Between the crutches and the brace, the guy couldn't even cook himself dinner. It was the least I could do." She rummaged in a drawer for a bottle opener and wrestled the cork from the wine.

"You're a horrible liar."

"Fine. I invited him because he's a nice guy and I want you to be happy."

"What is everyone's obsession with finding me a husband?" I whisper-shouted. "I don't need someone to swoop into my life and rescue me!"

"I know that!" she said, slapping the corkscrew on the counter. "I've known that ever since the day Steven walked out on you and the kids! You've been holding the three of you above water ever since. But just because you *can* survive alone doesn't mean you should have to." She took me by the shoulders with a gentle shake. "I love you, you idiot. No one's saying you have to find a husband. But sometimes it's nice to have a decent partner riding shotgun." She dragged me under her arm by my neck, kissing the top of my head. Then she grabbed the wine and carried it to the table.

When I came out of the kitchen, the children were sitting on the floor, tearing into their presents. Delia jumped up and down, holding a shiny box of checkers to her chest. Zach abandoned his gift, distracted by the sparkly red ribbon it had been wrapped in.

My father sat down at the head of the table. My mother took the chair at the opposite end, pulling out a chair beside her for Delia. I sat at my mother's left beside Vero and snapped Zach in his high chair between us. Georgia helped Nick into the chair across from me, setting his crutch against the wall and claiming the seat beside him. My sister made funny faces at Delia behind

Nick's back as my mother led us through a quick grace. She crossed herself, darting sharp looks at Georgia as she reached for the open bottle of wine. She poured herself a generous helping, grimacing as she knocked back a deep swallow while the rest of us began to pass plates and serve. Georgia and I locked eyes across the table. Our mother rarely ever drank, and when she did, it was never more than a sip or two from our father's glass.

"Go easy there, Ma," Georgia teased. "You won't last through dinner. And I already bragged to Nick about your pecan pie."

"Don't mind your mother. She's just upset," my father grumbled.

"Why's Ma upset?" Georgia asked.

"It's nothing," our mother said curtly.

Our father dropped a mountain of potatoes on his plate. "She's been in a mood for weeks. She got tangled up in some online scam, and now she's got people sending her photos and harassing her for money."

"No one's harassing me," she said, stabbing her ham. "Not anymore. It's over."

"See?" my father said. "I'm not the only one who fell for something I saw on the internet."

"They're asking for money?" Nick asked.

"It was probably one of those online pyramid schemes I've been hearing so much about. They prey on people like us."

"You mean old people," Georgia said.

"Watch it," Dad warned her.

"It wasn't a pyramid scheme," my mother argued. "It was just someone's idea of a practical joke."

Nick set down his fork and dotted his mouth with his napkin. "Online harassment is actually a crime. If someone's bothering you, I can ask the cyber guys at work to look into it."

"It's fine," my mother insisted. "It was only one picture. No one has bothered me since."

"Since when?" I heard myself ask. A sick, dark feeling was settling in my stomach as my mother tossed back another gulp of her wine.

"Two weeks ago," my father answered.

"What kind of picture?" Georgia asked.

Our father shrugged. "She won't tell me."

"Because it's nobody's business," my mother snapped, ending the discussion. Her jaw was tight as she cut into her ham.

"So, Nick," my dad said. "How'd you injure yourself?"

Nick's attention swung to my father. "Took a couple of slugs on the job."

My father's eyebrows shot up. "No kidding. I bet that's quite a story."

Nick's gaze slid to me. I shook my head in warning. "I'm surprised Finn didn't mention it, considering she was there."

My mother's head snapped up. "What? Finlay, you didn't tell us anything about this!" She looked to my sister. Georgia held up her hands, using her full mouth as an excuse not to answer.

"I'm fine," I insisted. "Nick got there just in time."

"Yeah, well, I wouldn't have made it out of there without your help." His eyes caught mine across the table and held them.

"Mommy's a hero?" Delia asked, pushing brussels around her plate.

"Yeah, she is," Nick said in a low voice that felt like it was just for me.

Vero fanned herself with her napkin. "Is it a little warm in here? It feels a little warm in here."

"What on earth were you doing in the middle of

a shoot-out?" my mother cried, dragging my attention from Nick.

"It's a long story. Not one for the table," I said, clearing a lump from my throat. "Delia, honey, if you've finished your dinner, you can be excused to play with your toys." Delia leapt from her seat and raced off to the living room, leaving Zach behind to rub au gratin in his hair.

My sister talked around a mouthful of ham. "So that whole internet-forum-hit-job thing turned out to be real after all?"

My mother's fork paused halfway to her mouth.

"As far as we can tell," Nick said. "But the investigation is deadlocked. The website disappeared before we could get anything useful out of it."

"What website is that?" my father asked, dragging his roll over the last of the sauce on his plate.

"We think a local arm of the Russian mafia was using a women's chat room as a front for organized crime."

My mother's fork dropped with a clatter.

I felt Vero go still beside me.

I set down my glass, unable to hold it as my fingers went numb. I turned to my mother.

The arsonist who'd started the fire at the trailer, the clever cover-up of Carl's murder, the identity of the person who'd hired a contract killer to murder my ex-husband . . . Up until a moment ago, they had all seemed like entirely separate mysteries, their motives completely disconnected from one another. But what if they were, at their very core, connected by one common, unbreakable bond—by the most powerful motive of all—the one I hadn't stopped to consider when Vero and I were sitting on the floor over a box of Crayola markers, struggling to sleuth it all out?

A mother's love. The irrepressible instinct to protect her child.

Holy shit! Was my own mother *FedUp*?

My mind reeled back to that first message on the forum. *A real piece of work . . . 100 Good reasons the world would be better off without him . . . FedUp* hated Steven, but she had never come out and stated she'd wanted him dead, or that she was willing to pay for it. Nor had she voiced any overtly sinister requests in any of the emails we'd exchanged. Vero and I had thought *FedUp* was speaking in code, being intentionally vague to avoid detection, but what if it was all just an innocent mistake? What if *FedUp* hadn't schemed to hire a contract killer and stiff the bill? What if she was just an angry mom, bitching about her awful ex-son-in-law, oblivious to the chain of events she was setting in motion?

I lifted my wineglass, downing the entire thing in one long swallow. Nick glanced up from his plate, his brows drawing together as I stared hard at my mother. "This website sounds like a real cesspool," I said. "A lot of awful, horrible people doing awful, horrible things. Steven could have been killed. Nick's lucky he survived." Vero pinched my elbow under the table.

My mother tossed her napkin on her plate. "Finlay, if you've finished, I could use some help in the kitchen."

"Gladly."

She pushed up from her chair and carried her dishes with her. I followed her through the swing doors.

"So," Vero said through a nervous laugh, "who's got money on the game tomorrow?"

The sounds of their conversation faded as the doors swung closed behind me. My mother's plate thunked down on the counter beside the sink. I stacked mine on top, folding my arms, watching my mother as she opened the refrigerator and searched for the whipped cream. "What on earth were you thinking?" I asked in a low voice.

"I don't know what you're talking about."

"Mother, I know you're *FedUp*."

Her hands shook as she closed the fridge door. She cast an anxious look toward the dining room. "How could you know that?"

"You're the only one who hates Steven that much."

"Does your sister know? Or Nick?" she whispered.

"Only Vero."

She crossed herself as she sagged against the counter. Her voice shook. "That picture they sent . . . the emails asking for money. I had no idea that website was run by the mob. Or that someone would think I wanted Steven to die. I mean, I'm not saying I never thought about it. Or secretly wished that a bus would come out of nowhere and—"

"Mom."

She pressed her mouth shut. "I had no idea I would be putting you or the children in danger. It was a misunderstanding. A mistake. I never should have posted on that forum."

"What were you doing on that website to begin with?"

My mother wrung her hands. "Do you remember how I told you I hired that service to help me fix our computer after your father downloaded all those nasty viruses?" I nodded, recalling the awkward conversation we'd had in my kitchen. "I was so embarrassed and upset about what your father had done, but the technician they sent to the house was so lovely and understanding. She assured me it happens to a lot of people our age. I made her lunch, and she told me all about some of her other clients who had gotten themselves into trouble like that—you know, visiting questionable websites . . . that some of them couldn't help it—and their wives had to go to lengthy measures to keep anyone else from finding out. Time got away from us, and before I knew it, she was telling me about this special privacy software. She even helped me install it. And then she showed me this women's group where she said lots of wives go to complain about their husbands. She showed me how to set up my own email account, separate from your father's, and she even helped me register a profile on the forum and pick a name. I spent hours reading messages on the group after she left, and she was right; it was so cathartic, Finlay! There were so many other women like me, whose husbands had done foolish things. And some whose partners were just downright terrible, like Steven. I know you don't like it when I speak unkindly about him, but I've been so frustrated and angry, watching the way he treats you, knowing there's nothing I can do to make it better. He's so proud of himself and that stupid farm, always rubbing his money and success in your face, and I thought people should know who he really is. That he's not a nice man. That he hurt someone I love. And I just wanted a place to get those feelings off my chest." She looked up at me, apologies brimming in her eyes.

For a moment, all I could do was stare at her, trying to make sense of how we got here. I reached for her and pulled her to me, holding her as she cried.

"I didn't mean to put anyone in danger," she sobbed against me. "When that picture came, I was sick over it. I was so afraid. When I called and you said Steven was fine, I've never felt so relieved. I thought maybe the whole thing had been a joke. A scam. Someone out for my money."

"Have either of them contacted you since?" Two weeks' worth of tension slipped from my shoulders when she shook her head. I drew back to look at her, wiping tears from her cheeks. "It's okay, Ma. I don't think anyone will try to hurt Steven again. I know you're angry with him. I am, too. He may have been a horrible husband, but he's trying to be a good father. Delia and Zach love him very much, and they would have been destroyed if anything happened to him."

My mother's lip trembled. "I'm so sorry, Finlay. Please"—she shook her head—"don't tell your father or Georgia about this."

"I won't. But you have to swear to me you're going to delete that email account. We're going to pretend this never happened. No more forums. No more chat groups."

She nodded as she dabbed her cheeks with a dish towel, taking a moment to collect herself before carrying the pie and whipped cream to the table. Vero slipped into the kitchen behind her with an armful of dirty dishes. She set them beside the sink, her eyes wide with the question I knew she was dying to ask me. I nodded, a hand pressed to my temple.

"Jesus," she whispered. "I can't believe I sent those photos of Steven to your mom. Is she okay?"

"I think so. Just a little shaken up."

"Has *EasyClean* contacted her?"

"Not since that night." I leaned a hip against the counter, exhausted. "I should probably call Steven and tell him it's safe for him to come home."

"Do we have to?"

"Vero."

"I'm just sayin'."

I sighed, looping my arm in hers as I led her back to the table. "Maybe we can let him sweat it out for a little while."

CHAPTER 47

I always looked forward to my mother's pecan pie, but this year, I hardly remembered eating it. The wine bottles were empty, the eggnog drunk down to a swirl of nutmeg-dotted dregs. The children had conked out on the floor beside the tree, and I was pretty sure my father had discreetly unbuttoned his pants under the table.

My mother got up with a heavy sigh and asked my sister to help her clear the dishes. I sat back in my chair, my lips slightly numb from the extra shot of brandy Vero had poured in my eggnog. One hand rested on my belly full of pie. I hadn't managed to eat much dinner, but by dessert I'd found my appetite. Once the shock of learning my mother was *FedUp* had worn off, I felt strangely light for the first time in a month. The nightmare really was over. Steven was safe. My children were happy. *EasyClean* was off the job. Theresa was going to testify as planned, and thanks to her mother, Carl's murder wouldn't come back to bite anyone. And Vero had made arrangements with her cousin to get rid of the Aston. With any luck, Feliks would spend the rest of his life behind bars and that would be the last we'd hear of him.

The plot of my story was finally coming together into a book I knew Sylvia would be proud of. Soon, the rest of my advance would find its way into my bank account. Overall, I had a lot to be grateful for.

Nick rose stiffly to his feet, reaching for his crutch as he thanked my mother and father for dinner. He said goodbye to Georgia and Vero, and I walked him to the door. He paused in the foyer, resting his weight on his crutch, his voice soft and his eyes heavy lidded. "Help me with my coat?"

I was pretty sure he was capable of doing it himself. Maybe it was the wine. Or the simple relief I was feeling. I reached for it anyway.

"There's something in the breast pocket. Grab it for me?" There was a strange gleam in his eyes as I plucked his leather jacket off the coatrack. Curious, I slipped my hand inside his pocket and withdrew my phone. Not my new one, but the one I'd lost weeks ago, the day we'd first found Carl.

My mouth went dry. "Where did you find this?"

"An officer recovered it from the scene at Mrs. Westover's house. He found your name on the lock screen when he powered it on and thought you must have dropped it during the shooting. I told him I'd get it back to you."

"Thank you." My throat felt tight as I tucked it away. My lock screen would have kept them out, I assured myself. If the police had suspected there was evidence on this phone, they never would have returned it to me. And Nick definitely wouldn't be looking at me the way he was looking at me now.

"Speaking of lost things, I've been wondering if your heroine ever found her missing attorney?"

The foyer seemed to shrink around us. The scrubbing sounds in the kitchen grew suddenly, suspiciously quiet.

"She did," I admitted. "But the end of their story didn't quite turn out the way I planned."

"I'm sorry." He leaned lower, letting me draw the heavy leather jacket around him. I tried to ignore the intoxicating scent of it as I maneuvered his good arm into the sleeve. "There's something I've been wanting to ask you since that night we went to dinner." He pitched his voice low, his warm breath tickling my ear as I tugged his coat around him. "See, I've been dying to know what you and Vero were doing in Steven's trailer the night of the fire." My hands froze on his collar. I opened my mouth to tell him he must be mistaken, but words failed me when his nose grazed my temple and trailed a path slowly down my cheek. "I'd love to know why your voice was on that security recording. Why a piece of your credit card was in the weeds out front and a set of high-performance sports car treads were found in the mud out back." His mouth paused beside the shell of my ear. "I'd love to know where you and Vero learned how to make those very effective Molotov cocktails, and how you knew Theresa was hiding at the Westovers' house, which I'm guessing had something to do with your missing phone. But here's the thing," he said, his lips close enough to draw a surprising shudder of desire from me. "More than all of that, I'd really like to kiss you right now. And the answers to those questions would probably ruin it. So I think, for now, I'd rather just not know."

I clutched the collar of his coat, my knees a little weak. "Who says I'd let you kiss me anyway?"

He tipped his head toward the sprig of mistletoe above us. Then he dipped his chin, brushing his lips softly over one corner of mine, his chaste kiss leaving me breathless and wanting. "Merry Christmas," he whispered. He drew back slowly as my traitorous mouth followed.

I let go of his jacket, unsteady on my feet as he turned to go. Head resting against the doorframe, I touched the tingling edge of my lips as he hobbled on his crutch to his car. My mother appeared beside me, drying her hands on a dish towel. She sighed, watching him over my shoulder. "He really does have very nice biscuits."

EPILOGUE

I set my screwdriver down beside the level and tape measure on the mantel and straightened Vero's hot pink stocking on its hook. It looked nice there, bookended between the children's and mine, filling out the empty spaces between us and returning a sense of balance.

I stole the glass of eggnog from the hearth that Vero and the children had left out for Santa, and I sipped it under the lights of the tree Steven had picked out. Feeling nostalgic, I remembered the significance of each of the ornaments I'd hung on it tonight: first steps, first birthdays, and now first lost teeth . . . There was another box of ornaments upstairs, packed away in my closet: first date, the wedding, our first anniversary. Somehow, the tree didn't look any less full or shiny without them.

Vero was upstairs in her room, wrapping the last of the presents she'd bought for Delia and Zach. The kids were fast asleep in their beds and the house was blissfully quiet.

I dragged my computer into my lap and opened my manuscript, determined to put a dent in it while the children were sleeping. A dam had broken in my writer's block, and the story was finally coming together in ways that made sense. My heroine had broken out of jail, recovered her stolen bounty, and found her missing attorney on her own. But in the end, she made the decision not to go back with him to stand trial; she hadn't been guilty of anything she wouldn't have made the choice to do again. And Sylvia was happy. The hot cop was back in the plot, determined to catch the assassin, the two of them slow dancing on a tightrope that felt dangerous and uncertain, but also inexplicably right.

My assassin just wasn't sure she was ready to be caught yet. She was content to be the hero of her own story for a while.

My phone vibrated on the coffee table, the screen glowing with a new notification: *Julian Baker wants to connect with you on Instagram.*

My thumb hovered over the *Accept* button.

Vero crept up behind me and peeked over my shoulder. She set three presents under the tree and sat down beside it, her head tipped back against the arm of the sofa. "Which one of them is your heroine going to choose in the end?"

"Who says she has to pick one?" I closed the invitation and set down my phone.

"So she's just going to ride off into the sunset with all that book money on her own?"

"And end the story there? No," I said thoughtfully, "I have to leave my heroine a few mysteries to solve. Besides, she's not keeping the money."

"She's finally getting around to buying a new car?"

"No. She's giving it to her accountant."

Vero went very still. Tree lights glistened on the sheen in her eyes. "Why would you do that?"

"Because you need it. And we're family." I swung my legs off the couch and tossed her a bag of stocking stuffers before either of us started crying. "As soon as the holidays are over, we're going to Atlantic City to deal with this lost marker. And then we're going to get the people you owe off your back. Now, grab me those stockings so we can get them filled and go to bed. I'm exhausted."

I tore open a bag of candy, stealing a few pieces for myself as Vero gathered the empty stockings from the mantel. She held mine aloft with a bemused frown. It crinkled when she squeezed the fabric.

"There's something in yours," she said, setting the others aside. She reached in, withdrawing a cream-colored envelope. My heart stopped when she turned it over, revealing a crimson wax seal.

Vero came to sit beside me on the couch, both of us too stunned to speak as she passed me the envelope.

Slowly, I tore it open, unfolding several sheets of printed images on computer paper. Vero read over my shoulder as I skimmed them.

"They're screenshots. From the women's forum," I said. The posts had been decoded in the margins in pen: drop locations for drug deals, shipment information for weapons, names of Feliks's associates and targets. Someone knew that site was a front. And they knew exactly who was behind it.

A price had been written in bold, red ink. The message had been signed.

"*EasyClean*'s blackmailing Feliks," I whispered. "He wants two million dollars to keep quiet."

I turned to the last page and found a message for me.

Someone is making a mess, Ms. Donovan.
I want EasyClean found and this business tidied up.
Don't disappoint me. —Z

ACKNOWLEDGMENTS

This novel was written during the COVID-19 pandemic. My deadlines and word count goals were bookended by lockdowns, a tumultuous election, and an endless stream of horrifying news headlines. There were many days (and most nights) when I stared at an empty screen for hours, wondering if I could dredge up an ounce of humor from a well that felt discouragingly dry. Writing comedy is hard; writing comedy when the world is on fire takes "hard" to a whole new level. Sometimes I wasn't sure I could. I have many people to thank for helping me bring this book to the finish line.

To my first agent, Sarah Davies, thank you for your steadfast belief in Finlay and me. And to Steph Rostan, for picking up the reins with such enthusiasm. I am so grateful to have found you.

To my editor, Catherine Richards, for your support and kindness, professionalism, and care. And for making this entire experience so much fun!

To Kelley Ragland, for welcoming Finlay and me into your publishing family. I count myself so lucky to be part of it.

To my team at Minotaur: Sarah Melnyk, Allison Ziegler, Nettie Finn, David Rotstein, John Morrone, Janna Dokos, Laura Dragonette, and Gabriel Guma.

Thank you for making Finlay Donovan more than just a book, but a MOOD! This character has taken on a life of her own, and I credit all of you for it.

To Hannah Whittaker at Rights People and my publishers far and wide, thank you for sharing Finlay and Vero with the world.

To the extraordinary I. Marlene King and Lauren Wagner, thank you for your excitement for these characters and their story. I'm the luckiest author alive to have the opportunity to work with you. I can't wait to bring Finlay to the screen. And to Flora Hackett and Sanjana Seelam at WME, for bringing us together and making this dream possible.

To the generous and talented authors who took the time to read *Finlay Donovan Is Killing It* and shared their endorsements with the world: Megan Miranda, Wendy Walker, Kellye Garrett, and Lisa Gardner—I'm so grateful to you.

Thank you to Jessica Sartorius for fielding my law school questions. And my husband, Tony, for putting up with all my IT-related "what ifs." Any mistakes I've made regarding the world of hacking and criminal law are entirely my own, many of them intentional, in the name of creating more entertaining fiction.

This book would not be a book without my real-life partners in crime, Ashley Elston and Megan Miranda. I will always carry two extra shovels in my heart. You remain the very best part of this crazy adventure.

For my early readers, who endured messy first drafts of this book with honesty and kindness, who brainstormed plot points, made me laugh, and reminded me why I love this job. Christina Farley, Romily Bernard, and Ashley Elston, I couldn't have pulled this one off without you.

For my family—Tony, Connor, and Nick—thank you for your patience, love, and understanding. For putting up with my grumpy mornings when I've been up all night chasing deadlines and struggling to find the right words. And thank you for always believing in me, even when I sometimes forget to believe in myself.

And finally, for Bookstagram. Thank you for embracing Finlay so passionately. Your photos, buddy reads, and reviews have brought me immeasurable joy during a very dark year. I hope this book is worthy of you.

Read on for a sneak peek at
Elle Cosimano's new novel

FINLAY DONOVAN
JUMPS THE GUN

Available now

CHAPTER 1

The man's voice cracked on the other side of the partition. "I'm going to prison for this, aren't I?"

"You're not going to prison," I assured him through the gap in the door. A small, familiar giggle issued from the other side and the man whimpered. "What's your name?" I asked him, distracting him with small talk as I rummaged in my diaper bag.

"Why do you want to know my name? Are you reporting me to the police?"

"I'm not going to report you. Trust me."

"Trust you!"

"Do you seriously think I want this to end badly?" I listened to his ragged breaths, waiting for an answer.

"Mo . . ." he said tentatively. Another giggle came from behind the partition and the man cried, "Mo! My name is Mo! Dear god, please do something!"

"I need you to stay calm, Mo. Listen to me and do exactly what I tell you."

His voice climbed. "You've done this before?"

"Yes," I assured him, "I have dealt with this before." Just never in the men's room of a Walmart. "Listen to me carefully, Mo. I'm going to bend down very slowly and reach into the stall. Whatever happens, don't move."

Mo started hyperventilating in earnest. "Wait, you're

going to *what*? I really don't think that's a good idea. There must be some other way—"

"There is no other way, Mo. Are you going to let me help you or do I need to call someone to unlock the stall door?"

"Don't call anyone!" he begged. "Do whatever it is you're going to do. But please hurry!"

I eased to the floor, cringing as I pressed my palms to the sticky tiles. I didn't want to think about what might be growing in the grout between them as I lowered my head and peeked under the partition at Mo's feet.

His slacks pooled around his ankles, and a pair of Argyle socks were drawn high over his calves. My son's light-up Buzz Lightyear sneakers flashed a few feet in front of him.

"Zach," I pleaded as he babbled and grinned at the man. "Come out of there, right this minute."

Thirty seconds. In the thirty seconds it had taken me to relieve my bladder, my toddler had managed to slither under the door of my stall and slip out of the women's restroom and into the men's, probably on the heels of some unsuspecting young person who had never been responsible for small children or zoo animals and hadn't had the forethought to stop him.

Zach laughed as I groped under the partition for him. The baggy hem of his overalls slipped from my fingers as he retreated deeper into the stall.

"He's coming closer!" Mo shrieked, his knees clamping together. "No, no! Stay back!"

"You don't have much experience with children, do you?"

"No! Why would you ask that?"

"Just a hunch." I dropped my shoulder under the partition, my arm outstretched. Forgoing two other empty stalls, Mo had chosen the larger accessible toilet, and the commode—and now my child—were in the farthest corner of it. "I can't reach him. He's too far from the door."

"I thought you said you knew how to fix this!"

"I'm working on it. Don't panic."

"Don't panic? Do you have any idea what happens to men who get caught in bathrooms with small children without their pants on? I was just in here minding my own business!"

Zach's giggles fell suddenly, ominously silent. I dug furiously in my diaper bag. Where were the damn Cheerios when you needed them?

"Something's wrong," Mo said through a strained whisper. "The child is holding very still. I think he might be up to something."

I wrinkled my nose. Zach was definitely up to something.

"He's grunting and his face is turning red. I think he's possessed."

"He's not possessed. He's having a bowel movement."

"He's *what*?! That's it! I'm coming out—"

"No! Whatever you do, do *not* stand up!" I buried my arm elbow-deep in my bag. There definitely wasn't time to run out to the cereal aisle. The poor man would probably suffer a heart attack and wind up dead on the floor before I made it back, and the last thing I needed to deal with was one more corpse. Especially one with his pants around his ankles.

New year, new me. I wasn't a criminal or a killer, at least not by my own choice. Harris Mickler, the sleazy accountant who had turned up dead in the back of my minivan three months ago, was not murdered by me, regardless of the fact that his wife, Patricia, had insisted on paying me to kill him. And yet, no matter how many times I explained to Mrs. Mickler that I was not a contract killer, disturbingly similar job offers continued to find me. The list of resolutions I'd adopted two weeks ago had included three very important bullets: no more junk food, no more men, and no more bodies in my minivan. Not necessarily in that order.

Zach finished his business with a delighted squeal, clapping his hands with exclamations of self-praise. He stomped toward Mo with an outstretched hand.

"I don't understand!" Mo screamed. "What does it want from me?!"

I dumped the contents of the diaper bag onto the floor. My police officer sister, who would rather clean up crime scenes than wipe her nephew's backside, had spent the last few weeks attempting to potty train my son despite my insistence that Zach wasn't ready. While my barely-two-year-old now grasped what he was expected to do in the bathroom, Georgia's training strategy had only managed to whet his appetite for bribes. "He wants a reward."

"A reward?! Why would it expect a reward for this?"

I grabbed a plastic baggy of Cheerios and thrust it under the door. Zach turned toward the sound as I shook the cereal inside, his chubby hands chasing the bag as I drew it closer toward me. As soon as my son was within reach, I looped an arm around his waist and dragged him out of the stall.

Mo's hands fell limp at his sides. I plopped Zach down on the floor beside me, wiping my brow as he puzzled over the seal on the snack bag.

"It's safe, Mo. You can come out now." I gathered the diaper creams, packets of wipes, and random mom-survival gear, stuffing them back into my purse. A quick glance under the stall revealed that Mo hadn't moved. "Mo?" I paused, listening for signs of life through the door. "Mo? Are you okay?" *For the love of god, let him be okay.*

"I am far from okay."

I released a held breath. "Do you need me to call for help?"

"I'd rather you just go," he said, "and take the tiny demon with you."

"Fair enough." I plucked the bag carefully from Zach's hands and scooped him up. Holding him over the sink on one raised knee, I washed both of our hands twice, rigorously and with plenty of soap, before returning the bag of snacks to him.

"It was nice meeting you, Mo," I called out.

A stoic grunt issued from the stall. I comforted myself with the fact that at least Mo had survived. It was past noon, twelve days into a brand-new year, and I hadn't broken any of my three resolutions—at least not yet.

CHAPTER 2

After a quick diaper change and several more rounds of handwashing, I hefted Zach into a shopping cart, handed him his threadbare nap blanket and a sippy cup, and pushed him up and down the aisles, searching for Vero. I found my children's nanny in the women's clothing department, scrutinizing a generic fleece hoodie, which did not jibe with the brand-name-wearing, hip fashionista I'd grown to know and love. She jumped nearly a foot when I rolled my cart up behind her and tapped her on the shoulder.

"What are you doing?" I asked as she dropped the sweatshirt into her cart. She pushed a pair of oversized sunglasses up the bridge of her nose. I could hardly make them out under the low bill of the baseball cap she'd been wearing since we left the house that morning. "You already have a black hoodie." I gestured to the designer logo on the one she was presently wearing. She looked like a cat burglar in yoga pants.

"You can never have too many hoodies." She darted cautious glances around the women's department, giving a heavy dose of side-eye to a sketchy-looking man with a greasy comb-over who was talking to himself as he browsed through a rack of padded bras. He'd either shoplifted a pair of tube socks or he was sporting a boner—I didn't want to think very hard about which. She grimaced as he gave a set of double *D*'s an inquisitive squeeze. "How much longer until the van's ready?"

I checked my phone. "At least another thirty minutes. And we still have an hour before we have to pick up Delia at preschool."

"Let's head over to the accessories department. This guy's freaking me out, and I could use a few extra pairs of shades."

"If you were so worried about being seen in public, we could have taken my minivan to your cousin's garage instead of bringing it here. Ramón probably would have changed the oil for free."

Vero gave a vehement shake of her head. "No way. We're safer here." Her last address of record had been her cousin Ramón's apartment, which, according to Vero, was too close for comfort to his auto repair shop to risk being seen there.

"I don't get it, Vero. All this paranoia doesn't make any sense. You're in debt to a couple of sorority girls in Maryland, so you drop out of school and leave the state, and the second these girls' parents show up at your cousin's door looking for you, you run off to Atlantic City and take a marker from a loan shark? Wouldn't it have been easier to just drive back to Maryland and tell your sorority sisters the truth, that you didn't take their money so you can't give it back?"

"I told them a year ago, and they didn't believe me."

"Then they're not worth the effort you're putting into avoiding them. Are you just planning to wear disguises and stay in the house indefinitely?"

"If a couple of sorority girls managed to track me all the way to my cousin's place because they think I stole their stupid treasury money, how long do you think it will take a professional loan shark to find me after I lost his two hundred grand trying to pay them back?"

"You can't hide forever. The spring semester at the community college starts in two weeks."

"Doesn't matter, because I'm not going."

My cart lurched to a stop. Zach gripped the handlebar and giggled in his seat, spilling juice down his overalls. I used his nap blanket to wipe him up. "Vero, you're only a few credits away from your accounting degree!"

"And smart enough to know that the more I leave the house, the higher the statistical probability people will find me. It's a matter of karma."

"Karma has nothing to do with it. Just because you made a few mistakes doesn't mean you deserve to be miserable. Look." I grabbed her hood as she skulked down the aisle. When her cart stopped, I turned her by the shoulders to face me. "Let's focus on solving one problem at a time. Steven's flying home from Philadelphia tomorrow. We both agreed it's probably safe for him to come back." My ex-husband had been lying low at his sister's house for weeks after several attempts had been made on his life. (Don't ask. It's a long story.) "We have no reason to believe anyone's trying to kill him anymore—"

"Because the universe is clearly punishing me," she said, as if that proved her point.

I rolled my eyes and pressed on. "Steven hasn't seen Delia and Zach in weeks. He'll probably jump at the opportunity if I ask him to take the kids for a few days. Then you and I can drive to Atlantic City and negotiate a deal with this loan shark person."

"Loan sharks don't negotiate, Finn. They break kneecaps and chop off fingers."

"He's a businessman. I'm sure he can be reasoned with."

"Like you've been reasoning with Feliks Zhirov?" I pressed a hand to her mouth, as if simply speaking Feliks's name could conjure the Russian mob boss into the women's sportswear department of a Walmart. I checked the surrounding aisles, making sure we hadn't been overheard, but the old man in the lingerie section behind us was too busy sniffing the panties in the clearance bin to care. "Feliks is a businessman," Vero insisted over my protests, "and I don't see you waltzing into *his* office and reasoning with *him*."

"Feliks doesn't have an office," I reminded her in a low voice. "He has a jail cell. And he isn't a businessman, he's a narcissistic sociopath with an army of enforcers who like to slit people's throats. Of course he can't be reasoned with."

"And he's expecting you to stay in town and do a job. So unless you want his goons following us to New Jersey and dumping our bodies in a ditch, I say we stick close to home and start looking for *EasyClean*." *EasyClean* was the screen name of the mysterious contract killer who had been cultivating hit jobs through one of Feliks Zhirov's websites, a popular women's forum that had doubled as a front for the Russian mob. When I'd learned my ex-husband was *EasyClean*'s next target, I'd coerced Feliks into shutting the entire website down. *EasyClean* had resorted to blackmailing the mob to compensate for his losses, and Feliks was holding me responsible for it all.

"If we can figure out who *EasyClean* is, maybe your very wealthy Russian friend would consider paying us a reward."

"Feliks is not my friend." I whispered. "He tried to have us both gunned down, in case you've forgotten."

"That was *before EasyClean* started blackmailing him." She stirred the air with a finger. "That whole *enemy of my enemy* thing makes you and Feliks friends by default. And your mob boss friend has rubles coming out of his piroshki."

"One, I don't want to think about Feliks's piroshki. And two, Feliks doesn't want me to turn *EasyClean* in, he wants me to *kill* him." I'd only laid eyes on *Easy-Clean* once. It had been dark when he'd climbed out of a very cop-like sedan, holding a gun. I didn't stick around to get a good look once he'd started shooting at me. Even if Vero and I could figure out who *EasyClean* was, I seriously doubted Feliks was going to pay us for half the job. I was already in debt to the man for the price of one very expensive sports car—the Aston Martin I'd "borrowed" from a dealership was now riddled with bullet holes and titled in my name. One misstep with Feliks and he'd make sure a copy of that title made its way to the police.

It wasn't hard to guess which detective Feliks would tip off first. Feliks was disconcertingly curious about the nature of my relationship with Detective Nicholas Anthony. Truth be told, so was I. But no matter how charming Nick was (or how amazing he smelled), there'd been too many skeletons in my closet (or, more literally, in my washing machine, my minivan, and Vero's trunk) to risk letting the detective get any closer to me than he already was.

"If Feliks wants *EasyClean* dead, he'll have to do it himself," I said firmly. Killing a man in cold blood was a line I wasn't willing to cross.

Vero shook her head at her reflection as she tried on a pair of dark sunglasses. "I can't believe you're playing chicken with the Russian mob."

"I'm not playing chicken. I'm putting my foot down. Feliks's trial is in less than a month. He's going to be convicted of murder and shipped off to prison, and this whole nightmare will be over."

"If Feliks goes to prison, he'll have nothing left to lose. You'll be lucky if he doesn't tip off Nick just to spite you. He called again, by the way."

"Who?"

"Detective Hottie."

I studied a rack of scarves, feigning disinterest. "What did you tell him?"

"That you were in the backyard, burying a body—Ow!" She giggled to herself, rubbing the spot where my elbow had jabbed her. "You can't keep avoiding him, Finn. He's been leaving messages on your cell phone since that dinner at your mom's, and you haven't once called him back."

I smacked my forehead. "You must be referring to the dinner Nick attended on crutches because he'd been shot by Feliks's thugs, who—incidentally—had really only been intending to murder the two of us. Yes," I deadpanned, "I can see where that would have been a promising start to a healthy and honest relationship."

"You're forgetting about the part where Nick made googly eyes at you across the ham platter while he thanked you for saving his life. Face it, Finn, he's crazy about you. And you two have great chemistry."

She wasn't wrong, but no amount of chemistry was going to change the fact that I had done some pretty terrible things that Nick could never know about. Still, I couldn't help the flutter in my stomach whenever I heard his voice in my mailbox. Or when I remembered the low purr of it against my ear the last time we'd spoken, under the mistletoe at my parents' house. "What else did he say?"

"That he still owes you dessert. I'm pretty sure that's code for: he wants to see you naked." She drew a scarf over her head, wrapping it around her face until only the dark lenses of her sunglasses were showing, waggling her eyebrows at me over the rims. "You saved his life, Finn."

"No more than he saved ours."

"Doesn't mean you can't indulge in something sweet

if he's offering." She threw up her hands at my shocked laugh. "I'm just sayin', you know he's only going to keep calling until you answer."

A ringtone started deep in my diaper bag.

We both turned to stare at it. Vero drew her sunglasses down her nose. "Holy shit. I think you just manifested dessert."

I took a step back. "I'm on a diet."

"That resolution of yours is a load of horseshit." She reached into the bag for my phone before I could stop her. "This is the age of sex positivity, body positivity, and hashtag MeToo. It's Lizzo's world, Finn; we're all just living in it. Don't let anyone tell you you can't have dessert." Her eyes dulled as she read the caller's name. "It's Sylvia," she said, holding the phone out to me.

It may have been the first time I'd ever been relieved to see my agent's name on the screen. I swiped to connect. "Hey, Syl. I'm at Walmart. Can I call you back?"

"No, you can't," she said bluntly. Her accent was always more pronounced when her patience was thin. More Jersey than New York. "We have something very important to discuss. Your editor called. She read your manuscript."

I pushed my cart farther from Vero's as she hovered in my personal space, her head tipped to hear. "What did she say?"

"She's not paying you."

"What do you mean, she's not paying me?" I slapped Vero's hand as she lunged for my phone. "I turned in a finished manuscript, Sylvia. I'm supposed to get the second half of my advance."

"Only if your editor approves it. She wants a revision."

"What kind of revision?"

"She wants more of the cop in the story."

"But I put the cop in the story. There's plenty of the

cop in the story." There was far more cop in my story than there probably should have been.

"The cop is hot, but the romance is not, and your publisher's not paying you for fifty shades of boring." I held the phone away from my ear as Sylvia shouted for a taxi. A car door slammed and she barked out an address. "You're holding back on this one, Finlay. The cop and your heroine waste too much time staring longingly at each other's assets. By the second act, they should be sampling the goods."

"She's still mourning the attorney," I argued.

"The attorney disappeared in chapter one. That relationship is over. It's time for your heroine to move on."

"Well maybe she needs a minute to figure out what she wants." I pinched the bridge of my nose. It had been almost three weeks since I'd broken things off with the younger law student/bartender I'd been dating, and while breaking up with Julian Baker had felt like the right thing to do, I still ached a little thinking about it.

"Your heroine knows what she wants. She wants the cop. She said as much on page forty-three when she was lying in bed, alone, staring at the ceiling. If you're not going to let her have the cop in the second act, at least let the woman have a sex toy."

Vero gave me an *I told you so* smirk. I turned away from her.

"It doesn't matter what my heroine wants, Syl. She's a criminal! She can't just jump into bed with a cop. She'll risk getting caught."

"That's precisely what I'm talking about. Raise the stakes. Take some risks! You've got the perfect setup for a star-crossed romance. Your assassin has escaped from jail. She's on the run from the one man she shouldn't want but can't deny her feelings for. Meanwhile, the cop is hot on her trail, determined to catch her. Only the

longer they play cat and mouse, the more he wants to
bring her to bed instead of bringing her to justice."

"Oh, that's good," someone said in the background.

"See?" Sylvia assured me. "Even the taxi driver
loves it."

"You put me on speaker?!"

"Yes," Sylvia and her driver said.

"The cop and the assassin should give in to their de-
sires," Sylvia insisted. "They should do it someplace
dangerous—"

"On a plane," the driver suggested.

Sylvia answered with a "Meh."

"As it's crashing into shark-infested waters?"

"Better."

"Fine," I snapped. "I'll rework a few scenes."

"While you're at it, rewrite the ending," Sylvia said.

I gripped the phone tighter to keep myself from
throwing it. "What's wrong with the ending?"

"Your heroine can't ride off into the sunset with
her sidekick. This is a romance novel, not *Thelma and
Louise*."

"*Thelma and Louise* won an Academy Award."

"They held hands and drove off a cliff, Finlay." I bit
my tongue through her exasperated sigh. "The assassin and the cop are good together. Give your heroine
the happy ending she deserves. And do it quickly," she
added. "I, for one, would like to get paid."

"Me, too," the driver and Vero said in unison.

"Great. I'll tell your editor you're on board with the
changes." Sylvia disconnected before I managed to respond.

I handed my phone to Vero. "Happy?"

She shook her head as she dropped it in the diaper
bag. "I don't understand your hesitation with the cop."

"Because whenever the cop and the assassin get together, somebody dies."

"Only because you make them."

"Way to rub it in." I checked the time and turned my cart toward the front of the store.

"How hard can it be to write a happy ending? Just pretend your characters are Delia's Barbie dolls. Take off all their clothes and mash their faces together."

"It's not that simple."

"You're absolutely right," she conceded. "The cop should ask for the assassin's consent first. Then, when she soberly, mutually, and enthusiastically agrees, they can jump each other like jackrabbits and you can write a bestseller."

"Any other brilliant revision advice?"

She looked at me sideways as we pushed our carts toward the register. "Maybe this time, try not to kill anybody."